THE CHRONICLES OF A
TYRANT II:
SLAYER

THE CHRONICLES OF A
TYRANT II:
SLAYER

SIERRA J. BALL

BALBOA.
PRESS
A DIVISION OF HAY HOUSE

Balboa Press books may be ordered through booksellers or by contacting:

Balboa Press
A Division of Hay House
1663 Liberty Drive
Bloomington, IN 47403
www.balboapress.com
1-(877) 407-4847

Because of the dynamic nature of the Internet, any web addresses or links contained in this book may have changed since publication and may no longer be valid. The views expressed in this work are solely those of the author and do not necessarily reflect the views of the publisher, and the publisher hereby disclaims any responsibility for them.

The author of this book does not dispense medical advice or prescribe the use of any technique as a form of treatment for physical, emotional, or medical problems without the advice of a physician, either directly or indirectly. The intent of the author is only to offer information of a general nature to help you in your quest for emotional and spiritual well-being. In the event you use any of the information in this book for yourself, which is your constitutional right, the author and the publisher assume no responsibility for your actions.

Certain stock imagery © Thinkstock.
Any people depicted in stock imagery provided by Thinkstock are models, and such images are being used for illustrative purposes only.

ISBN: 978-1-4525-4566-0 (sc)
ISBN: 978-1-4525-4565-3 (e)

Printed in the United States of America

Balboa Press rev. date: 01/25/2012

My Precious Memories

I am flooded with many memories. I think back to the time my twin brother Levetin and I were tiny tots in Mesopotamia's Fertile Crescent. Our mother Tai used to tell us how precious we were. Soon, she and my father would leave us in the care of two servants, Syrah and Uhn.

My next memory is of when Levetin and I turned six. The servants mysteriously died, and our parents became a bit more strict. Our father Alden had introduced us to five of the six Eternal Ones; Revelatianus was nowhere to be found, and I hadn't learned that there was a sixth Eternal One until my father fell on his face and thanked him for his beneficial crops.

My thoughts then jump over to when my brother and I were ten, and we got our Golgohoth tribal band tattoos; Levetin got attacked by a wild boar and wound up receiving a nasty scar on his upper left arm, breaking the band. I was then scolded, by my parents, for the mishap.

My next memory is when we were twelve. I watched helplessly as an old Mesopotamian Demon named Thanatos Aqueous, or Thanatos of the Waters, carried Levetin off. Later, a large amount of blood was found near our playing area. I didn't want to believe that Levetin was murdered, but the amount of blood I saw was a dead giveaway; no pun intended, mind you.

My parents became more distant than ever. My mother grieved over Levetin's disappearance often, and my father began to believe that my unknown condition, known today as albinism, was a curse and that it made Thanatos come and take Levetin away. Four years had passed, and my mother fell ill. I don't know what her ailment was, but I do know that I tried everything to help her get well. My treatments consisted of strong remedies, but she died not long after starting them. I think that her death was caused by grief more than by being sick.

The next day, at Mother's funeral, the Eternal One, Drakengaard Hark, took me away from my father. He killed me; I was dead, just like my twin brother who, unbeknownst to me, was sojourning the earth as Acanthus of

1

Corinth, called the Phoenix Mantrap, but would later be better known as the Deathbringer; one-third of the famous but dangerous Immortal Trio.

Because Revelatianus, master of the Eternal Ones, had mercy on me, so to speak, he revived me and I became a tyrant; a dead immortal that must feed off the blood of Humans to sustain 'life.' Much like a Vampire, only except tyrants can walk out in the sunlight; I didn't like the sunlight much, for I am an albino, and I burn easily.

I wandered around the continents of Africa and Asia for over three-thousand years, looking for clues on why Levetin was killed and where his body may have been placed. It wasn't until I traveled to Europe that I found out that Levetin was Acanthus. I was shocked and surprised to see that my twin brother was alive, but he was angry that I hadn't found him sooner, and he let me know how he felt by using physical violence.

Now and again, throughout the years, I'd see him; even though I was glad to see him, it was never hardly a pleasurable experience.

In the 21st century, I found Mordecai Weinstein in Jerusalem; I was invited by him to attend his bar mitzvah. I took him away from his parents, Sheldon and Jess, when I decided to settle in the U.S. I had left them a note stating: *Tyrant Leviathan will be taking care of your boy from now on. Thanks for everything.*

Sheldon Weinstein had to have misread the note because, not long after, I heard that he murdered his wife and then offed himself. Once hearing of this, I had decided to put Mordecai in foster care with my friend Marilyn DeFranco, a woman I had met while working at the AFL-CIO. She and her Italian husband Ned agreed to raise the thirteen-year-old. The same day I put Mordecai in the care of the DeFrancos, I discovered that my next door neighbor to the left, whose name was Levi Mollis, was someone from my past, or so it had appeared.

My thoughts skip over to the second week in March 2004 A.D. It was a Sunday, and I killed a Los Angeles police officer named Logan Terry. The very next day, I killed a wanted man from Tijuana, Mexico; it happened in San Juan Capistrano. His name was Javier Torres.

On Tuesday, I was questioned by the FBI about the two murders; I lied to the agents to make myself look innocent, although my neighbor Levi knew exactly what was going on.

On that night, I had taken the murdered officer's sister Jessica out to dinner in Pasadena. I then took her to my mansion and we got closer.

After bringing her home, I tried to think of some ways to make the authorities get off my back on the murders. By then, my neighbor revealed himself to me . . . . but he wasn't who I thought he was. I always thought that he was my twin brother, in a cheap disguise, but it turned out that Levi was actually a servant to my brother named Balcanicus, sometimes called Tarsus the Chameleon; Levetin was actually taking refuge in the greenhouse next to his home.

On Wednesday, the FBI came back to my mansion and questioned me again. Of course, once again, I lied.

Later that night, I took my plan to gain innocence and made it happen. I killed Jessica's boyfriend Caleb Hershee, and pinned Terry and Torres's murders on him . . . but not before making him write a 'suicide' note, then torturing him and hanging him. The police tried to get as much info out of me and Mordecai, after the boy was discovered dead in his bedroom by his mother, but the death was ruled out as a suicide.

On Thursday morning, the bodies of Logan Terry and Javier Torres were found due to the suicide note I had made Caleb write. I was free from all suspicions, and the case was closed. When Jessica heard the news, she was very upset and hurt.

That night, after going to bed, I had a strange vision that something would happen to me, and possibly the Eternal Ones.

On Friday, I picked up Jessica and took her and my adopted daughter Anticlea to the shopping mall. She then spent the day at my mansion and we made passionate love that night, and twice the next morning.

My thoughts then jump over to after I drop Jessica off at her house and I make it back home. My brother Levetin, known as Acanthus to most, was acting really strange and telling me to lock myself away. He stated that he was coming, and I wasn't so sure who *he* was, but I completely ignored his warning. I wasn't in my house too long before I discovered that Anticlea was missing and Draken Hark left me a note that was compatible to the warning my brother had given to me.

After reading the note, I heard knocking on my door, which soon turned to pounding. I got a surprise when I answered the door; I was captured by Inhuman servants loyal to Tyrant Arch-Peteryx Feathervault; Imhotep Feathervault to some; Peteryx to others.

I was thrown into a van and later escaped, taking refuge in the mountains, but I was followed. I took shelter in an old abandoned hut that overlooked a cliff's edge. When Peteryx's team, led by Rahm, caught up to me, they tear gassed me and threw a grenade in the hut, which I promptly returned to them; the explosion took out their van and the flames engulfed the hut.

I was at the edge of the cliff, trapped by flames, Peteryx's men, and the raging waters of the Pacific Ocean below me. I was in a tight situation, but I couldn't allow those men to get me, so I chose the waters. I fell until I blacked out and knew nothing else.

Extradition

I slowly regain consciousness. I start to stretch, but I realize that I can't; I see that I am locked up in some sort of steel cage, like a wild animal.

I look around. It looks as though I am in some kind of vehicle; a van. Looks like I'm back to square one, only except there's tighter security: I'm in a cage, and there are two armed men sitting across from me, their red eagle-like eyes are fixed on me as if it's a permanent stare; they sit as still as statues.

"He's awake." says one of them, and I recognize the voice; it's one of the five men that chased me into the mountains!! "I wonder if he's okay." He gets up and moves over to the cage.

"Be careful, Roule." the other guy says. "He might be dangerous."

"Well, look at him, Ash. He's weak; what harm can he really do?"

The one called Roule reaches into the cage and touches the crook of my left arm. I look down and notice that there is a needle in my arm and an I.V. attached to it. There's blood in the I.V. bag. Had I lost some blood in the fall?

"It's amazing that you didn't die." he tells me. "That was a long way down."

I don't say anything; I simply stare down at the I.V. in my arm.

"Can you remember your name?" Roule asks me. "Can you say your name for me?"

"You know my name." I say.

Roule is silent; he removes his hand from the cage.

"Can I get you something to drink?" he asks, opening an igloo. "Soda, juice, water, tea, Gatorade?"

"Blood." I say.

"You're already receiving a transfusion of O-negative; if you consume more, your skin may bloat." he chuckles. "Would you want some water or juice, perhaps?"

"Blood . . . perhaps?"

Roule nods. He then reaches into the igloo and gets out a 20 ounce bottle of Gatorade; he hands it to me.

"I said blood." I tell him.

"And I said no." he replies.

Not looking forward to arguing with the guy, I twist open the bottle of Gatorade and take a sip. Feeling nauseous, I set it down.

I watch as Roule adjusts the I.V. bag that's filled with blood.

"Now," he says, sitting in front of me. "Will you refresh me and my partner's memories? Please tell us your name?"

"Again," I say. "You know my name; everyone like you does."

"Everyone like us?" Ash asks.

"Slaves to Peteryx."

"Anubis servants."

"Lap dogs."

Ash and Roule chuckle. They think that this is a joke.

"Tell us your name," Roule says. "And we'll let you have a phone call."

A phone call, huh? I'll have to make a tough decision on who I can get in touch with. There's Marilyn, Mordecai, Levetin . . . . or Jessica.

"My name's Leviathan Golgohoth." I say.

"An excellent answer." Ash says. "I am Ash, and I believe you know Roule? He's the guy that butt-stroked you with the assault rifle in California."

In California, I think. *Aren't we still in California? Why would we not be?*

"Where are we?" I ask.

"We're in a van." Roule says.

"I mean, where is the van heading?"

"Nevada."

"Nevada?"

"That's right; you're being extradited."

"Extradited? I'm not in prison."

"But you are *our* prisoner."

My memories come back to what they had said when they first caught up to me: *"We're going to Las Vegas."*

"How did I get into this cage?" I ask.

"Rahm found you lying on the rocks down below." Ash says. "We helped him gather you up and we took this van from a impounded vehicle lot. We stole this cage from a kennel."

"We're in San Bernardino County right now." Roule says. "We should be there soon."

"Huh?" I ask. "What time is it?"

Roule checks his watch; he nods his head.

"It's eleven-thirty in the p.m." he says.

"Really?"

"Yes, Leviathan." He draws closer to the cage. "Where's your brother?"

"What?"

"Where's Acanthus? I don't see him coming to rescue you."

"His name is Levetin Golgohoth."

"He was born Levetin Golgohoth, in Mesopotamia; he's now Acanthus of Corinth."

"I can fight for myself."

"You need him more than you know."

Levetin did tell me that. After all, we are twin brothers, and we're both killers.

"I know where he is." Ash says. "He's got his mind set on Arachne and Dante and not his kin."

"I need to get out of this cage." I say. "My legs are cramping in this small space."

"No can do." Roule says. "Rahm and Arha said to keep you locked up."

"Where's the fifth guy? Weren't there five of you?"

"Cas was killed by the van explosion in the mountains."

"I see. Well, I won't hurt you; will you let me just stretch my legs out?"

"No." Ash says.

"I won't do anything."

"I don't believe you; we're not risking it."

Well then, I guess I'm stuck in this cage until we arrive to our destination.

I Confess

As the van travels to Nevada, or so I believe, I decide to take Ash and Roule up on their offer.

"Can I have my phone call?" I ask.

"Who are you gonna call?" Ash asks.

"I gave you my name, and now I get a phone call."

"My partner just asked you who you plan to call." Roule says.

I sigh in frustration at the personalities of these guys.

"I want to call my girlfriend, Jessica." I say. "I'm sure she's worried about me."

"You have a girlfriend?" Ash asks.

"Yes." I say.

Ash laughs. He then hands me a wireless phone. Despite my fingertips being slightly numb for some odd reason, I manage to punch in Jessica's home phone number. It rings . . . once . . . twice . . . three times . . . someone picks up.

Anonymous: Hello?

Good, it's Jessica. I know her beautiful voice.

Me: Hi, Jessica, it's me.

Jessica: Leviathan? Oh my goodness, hi!

Me: Hi. Were you asleep?

Jessica: No. I was just thinking about you. I tried to call you and talk about the next time we can make love, but I guess you were busy; your cell phone would go straight to voicemail. I'm worried about you.

I honestly thought that she would be grieving over her dead brother, I think. *Why would she be thinking about me when her brother's services are tomorrow?*

Me: I thought you might've changed your mind about the wake.

Jessica: No. I told my parents that I didn't want to go because it would be too sad, but I said that I will be there at the funeral. They understood; they always do.

Poor girl, I think. *I have put her through a lot this last week; she shouldn't be going to a funeral. I need to tell her what I have done. She needs to hear the truth from me before someone else tells her . . . like Levetin; he was bad at tattling when he was young and alive. However, my brother never gave me away to the authorities, so he may not tell Jessica anything.*

Me: Jessica, sweetie. I have to tell you something.

Jessica: What? What is it?

I don't say anything, I feel tears stinging my eyes. I can also hear Ash and Roule chuckling.

Jessica: Leviathan, are you okay?

Me: No.

Jessica: What's wrong? What happened?

Me: I—I'm not at the mansion.

Jessica: What? Where are you?

I am silent, and I feel the tears coming again.

Me: I've been captured.

Jessica: Captured? What are you talking about?

Me: Some servants of a sworn enemy have taken me and I must fight.

Jessica: Why, Leviathan?

The tears roll down my cheeks; I dash them away. This is it. I must tell her the truth.

Jessica: Leviathan, please talk to me. Tell me what's going on.

My heart aches. How I long to hold her and kiss her, but I feel that I may never do that again; I wish I could confess to her in person, and not over the phone.

Me: I have done something unforgivable.

Jessica: No, Leviathan. I'm not worried about your past. You're a good person.

Me: No, I'm not, Jessica. You know nothing about the real me. I am a tyrant; I have killed in the past, and I have killed again . . . . recently.

Jessica: What?!

Me: I speak the truth. I have killed, and I don't think you'll ever forgive me for it.

Jessica: Oh my god, Leviathan. Was it Logan?!

I begin to weep. She suspects that I killed her brother, and she couldn't be any more right. I must confess.

Me: Yes.

Jessica: Oh my god, Leviathan!!! Oh my god!!! How could you do that and not tell me?!?!

She starts to cry, too. I can't stand to hear her so upset; it's entirely *my* fault. I want to comfort her so bad, but I cannot.

Me: Jessica, please. Please, don't cry.

Jessica: Why, Leviathan?! I cannot believe this!!! What in God's name were you thinking?!

Me: I'm a killer.

Jessica: Too right you are, you psycho!!! You're a disgusting sand monkey!!! You filthy Arab!! All of you are the same—mean, heartless, and evil!!! You're no different from your brother!!!

Me: Leave Levetin out of this, Jessica.

Jessica: He's Acanthus of Corinth!!

Me: His name is Levetin Golgohoth.

Jessica: Leviathan, why didn't you just tell me that you killed Logan?! Was it an accident?

Me: No. I physically and mentally tortured him, slit his throat, and buried him in the woods.

Jessica: NOOOOO!!!

Jessica cries even more. It makes my heart hurt. I had no idea that I was capable of feeling this much grief.

Jessica: Did you kill Javier Torres?

I cannot lie to her anymore. I have to tell her.

Me: Yes.

Jessica: Oh my god, you're insane!!!

Me: You're right.

She is silent for a moment; I know exactly what she's thinking. It's almost like a voice is telling me what she's going to ask next.

Jessica: Does this mean that you killed Caleb, too?!

She knows, and I will not lie.

Me: Yes.

Jessica: NOOOOO!!!!! NO!! WHY?!?!

Me: I had to frame a culprit; I had to place the previous two murders on someone. I couldn't be thrown in prison.

Jessica: Oh god!!

Me: And, just because I could.

Jessica: OH GOD!!!! I'm gonna be sick!!

I listen as Jessica cries over the truth. I also watch as smiles form on Ash and Roule's faces.

Jessica: Leviathan, think back on all we have done together!! Didn't that mean something to you??!!

Me: Yes.

Jessica: Then why did you allow me to have a great time, all while knowing what you did?!

Me: Because I could.

Jessica: Do you really love me, Leviathan?

I think about it. I have grown quite fond of Jessica; she's my present-day love, and the closest thing I'll have to Tigris, my one true love.

Me: Yes, I do.

Jessica: If you love me, then why did you kill my brother?!

Me: I had no intentions of killing him. He was secretly recording our interview we had last Sunday, and . . . I suppose I overreacted.

Jessica: Overreacted?!

Me: I killed him, did I not?

Jessica: So, while you were sleeping with me, you knew what you had done!!

Me: Jessica . . . .

Jessica: It's true, isn't it?! Can you deny it?!

Me: No. It's true; I knew all along.

Jessica sniffs; I continue to stare out at Ash and Roule.

Jessica: Where are you?

Me: I'm going to Nevada.

Jessica: Nevada? What part?

Me: I'm not sure, but I'm not going back to Los Angeles.

Jessica: Leviathan . . . .

Me: I cannot go back.

Jessica: What about Mordecai, Anticlea, and . . . .

Me: Levetin. Levetin will find me, no matter what. As of now, I cannot return to Los Angeles; you will turn me in.

Jessica: Leviathan, I . . . .

Me: No, Jessica. Now goodbye.

Futile Escape

I end the phone call with Jessica. I then toss the wireless phone back to Ash. I begin to feel anger and hatred building up inside of me; I stare into Roule's eyes.

"Let me out of this cage." I demand. "Right now."

"We cannot." he tells me.

"NOW!!"

"He said that we cannot!" Ash cuts in. "Rahm's orders."

"Who gives a flying rat's ass about Rahm's orders?!" I shout. I grasp the bars and try to bend them. "Let me out!!!"

"We cannot!"

"LET ME OUT, YOU INFIDELS!!!"

"We can't, under any circumstances!!"

I stop trying to bend the bars.

"You weren't afraid of me before." I say. "Why are you afraid now?"

"We're not scared of you!" Roule shouts.

"Oh? Well then, you're brave enough to release me from this confinement."

"You will stay in the cage until we arrive at our destination."

I smile and nod. I then feel my pulse pounding in my head. My anger hasn't exactly died down, due to the fact that these bastards will not let me out of this cage. I now know what I must do.

I conveniently pull the needle and I.V. out of my arm; the remaining contents in the bag runs out onto the floor of the vehicle.

"What are you doing?!" Roule shouts. "You need blood to live!!"

"YOURS!!!" I shout.

I burst into rage and begin to kick the cage bars until they start to bend and snap.

"HE'S BREAKING OUT!!!" Ash shouts.

"SHOOT HIM NOW!!" Roule cries out. "HEAD SHOT!!!"

"NO!! PEPPER SPRAY!! NOW!!"

Roule grabs a can of mace. Before he can spray the contents of the can into my eyes, I break out of the cage; I charge into him and wrap my hands around his throat.

"Do you want to live?" I ask. "Or do you want to die?"

As I choke Roule, Ash is too terrified to intervene. After a few moments of partial paralysis, Ash aims a pistol at me; the barrel pressed again my temple.

"Now," he says. "Do *you* wanna live or die?"

I slowly remove one hand from around Roule's neck. Next, with lightning speed, I slap the pistol away from my head; Ash pulls the trigger, firing a bullet straight through one of the doors. I then kick him; he flies backwards and slams into the side of the van, becoming groggy shortly afterwards.

I can hear Roule trying to say something; I turn my attention back to him.

"What?" I ask, leaning in to hear him. "I can't hear you; speak a little louder."

I begin to hear something crunching. I realize that it is Roule's windpipe; black blood begins to gush from his open mouth and runs over my hands; he is dead. I then glance over at Ash, who is now riddled with fear.

"So," I say, picking up the dropped pistol. "You must be next."

Not knowing what else to do, Ash gets on his radio and calls for help.

"RAHM!!!" he shouts over the walkie-talkie. "WE HAVE A CODE RED!!!!"

I fire a round from the pistol; the bullet hits Ash in the left leg. He cries out in pain and clutches his injured limb.

"Nice try." I say.

"YOU SHOT ME!!!" he shouts. "YOU BASTARD!! THAT WAS MY KNEECAP!!"

"Quit bitching; it'll heal."

I feel the vehicle stopping; the tires make a loud skidding sound on the asphalt. Now's my chance to ditch this place.

As I dart for the doors, they swing open. I see Rahm and Arha aiming shotguns at me.

"Are those things loaded?" I ask.

Rahm and Arha both remove the safety from the guns and keep them aimed at me.

"Well," I say. "Go ahead; shoot me. I dare you."

Rahm and Arha do not fire. I do not smell gunpowder emitting from the shotguns; those firearms are not loaded.

I smile. I then fire at their feet; they drop their guns and back away.

"If you two want to live," I tell them. "You better do everything I say."

"Take it easy, Leviathan." Arha says. I aim the pistol right at him. "I'm patient."

"What do you want?" Arha puts his hands in the air.

"Release me into the wild. I insist! Now!"

As I keep the pistol pointed at Arha, I turn my attention to Rahm.

"Vegas is a mighty jungle." he says to me. "You'll never make it out alive; Arch-Peteryx will find you."

"That he will, but I will reign victorious."

"You're nothing!"

I hear chuckling from behind me; Ash thinks it's funny.

I aim the pistol behind me and fire; Ash is hit in the other leg. He cries out in pain again.

"Shut up!" I shout. I then aim the pistol back at Arha. "If you don't want to end up like your friend," I speak of Roule. "I suggest you release me."

"We cannot fail our master." Rahm says.

"You already failed; two of you are dead . . . and the rest of you will be following shortly."

"What do you think you're talking about?!" I hear Ash ask. "We're servants to Arch-Peteryx Feathervault!! We will never fail!!"

"Peteryx has been proven weak in the ancient times."

"Please, don't kill us!! I don't wanna die!!"

An evil sneer crosses my face. It is time for all of them to perish.

"And now," I say to them. "You regret having been born."

I quickly fire a round; it hits Arha in the middle of the forehead. Just as the Anubis servant is falling to the ground, I turn the gun on Rahm and fire another round. It catches him in the right eyeball. Both men are stone dead. I then turn to Ash.

"Not ready to die, huh?" I ask, approaching him. Once I step over Roule's rotting corpse, Ash begins to cry; how pathetic.

"No!" he begs. "Please, have mercy."

"Mercy?! Ha-ha!! Mercy is for lowlifes." I stoop down next to him and wipe the tears from his tan cheek. "You cry like a girl. Now, you die like a pig."

"Leviathan, please. Think of the children!!"

"Children?"

"I have a little girl; she's about eight. I adopted her from Cairo. Please, she needs me."

He has a child. I had a child, not long ago. Her name was Anticlea Georgopoulos, and she was my heart. Now, I may not see her again, unless I make it out of this whole Peteryx ordeal alive.

I chuckle and place the barrel of the pistol to Ash's temple.

"Do you have any last words to say?" I ask. "That is, before I blow your brains out, you miserable shit?!"

"I wanna live." he says. "My baby needs me."

"Oh, *now* your child is important."

"Yes."

I smile slightly.

"You know," I start. "I had a little girl, too. She meant the world to me. I rescued her from death and took her in my care. I loved her; she was my child . . . and she needed me more than ever." I cock the hammer of the pistol. "And now, she's gone . . . and I may never see her precious little face or hear her innocent little voice again. And, it's all because of you and your scumbag colleagues, you filth!!"

"No, Leviathan!! I can help you. I can get her back for you."

"Not necessary. She's in a safe place."

"Leviathan!! Please, don't kill me."

"Hmm, nope. Not good enough. Say goodbye."

"PLEASE!!!! DON'T KILL ME!!"

"Too bad."

"My baby!!"

I blow him a kiss goodbye. I then pull the trigger, sending a bullet straight through his brain. I am sprayed with black blood.

"Ugh," I say as I wipe spattered blood from my face. "Good riddance."

I am now free to go where I need to go. Los Angeles will have to wait. I must locate Peteryx in Vegas and finish him off once and for all.

Enter Las Vegas

I toss Ash and Roule's carcasses out of the van and leave them on the side of
the highway to rot, along with Rahm and Arha.

"Now," I say to myself. "To Vegas; to Peteryx."

I get behind the wheel of the vehicle and start it up. I begin to drive. As I
cruise down Highway 15, I take a look at the gas meter. It's close to empty, but
I can make it to Vegas; I can see the city's magnificent lights already.

As I drive, I think about Mordecai. I wonder what will happen if he finds
out I'm not in Los Angeles and that I am being hunted by my worst enemy?
What if he already knows?

Poor boy; I'll have to mail him my chronicle passages until I can get back
home.

I start to think about Anticlea. My precious little baby; what will she think
when she finds out that I am a cold-blooded killer and a monster? Will she still
love me? Perhaps she knows, since Acanthus of Corinth and I are brothers, that
we are just alike in violence? She would be right.

I begin to think about Jessica. She was so very upset when I told her
about me being her brother and boyfriend's murderer. All I wanted to do,
while she wept, was hold her in my arms and comfort her; to tell her that I
love her. I cannot do that now. Though I miss her very much, I cannot return
to her. I will only have to fantasize about her soft touches, her sweet kisses,
and everything.

I will miss her beautiful emerald-green eyes, her long soft dark-brown hair,
her smooth creamy skin, her luscious lips, her beautiful voice, and her smile.

A wave of sorrow passes through me; I pull the van over and fight back the
tears. I dash them away with my sleeve.

"No time to cry, Leviathan." I scold myself. "You are a monster; no tears.
You have a job to do; it involves no sorrow . . . all anger; white-hot rage."

I look out into the distance. Right up ahead are the city lights; the
multicolored jungle, and somewhere in it is a savage beast that must be
exterminated, pronto.

I start up the van and start driving again. Once I reach the city, I try to think of a good place to stay.

"Perhaps the Vegas Hilton?" I ask myself.

I drive around the city until I locate the magnificent hotel. I park and get out of the vehicle; I realize that I have been driving a state penitentiary van; those jerks stole a prison van!! They said they got it from an impound lot.

I look at myself and see that I am in a dark-blue top and bottom; prison clothing! They must've come with the van, but I can't be seen in these; I have to get a room and clean up.

I gather myself up and walk into the fabulous hotel. Surprisingly, there's no one in the lobby and no one behind the front desk.

"For a thousand dollars a night," I say, dashing over to the desk. "I'll need an extravagant place to rest." I move stealthily behind the desk and grab a room key. "But with no money on me, I guess I'll have to sleep here for free."

I head upstairs to the room I have chosen.

"Suite two sixty-eight." I say as I reach the right door. I slide the card key in the door and unlock it. Wow!! I have made an excellent choice: There's a king-sized bed, a television, a coffee maker, an elegant bathroom, etc. Oh, and it smells clean; I am totally content.

"Wow." I say to myself. "Where should I start?"

I get out of the penitentiary clothing and take a hot shower; I can feel my aching muscles relaxing as the water trickles over my pale skin. I watch as the black blood runs off of me, turning slightly brown as it runs into the drain.

I dry off and sit down on the king-sized bed. I don't care if I'm naked right now; I need to relax myself for a bit.

I then notice, on the end table next to the lamp, a stack of papers and a fountain pen. I can write my chronicles on them!! I'll buy stamps and envelopes later.

"Alright." I say as I grab the papers and the pen. I retrieve a heavy phone book and place a sheet of paper onto it. I take the pen and date the paper: 27 B.C.

"Okay, Leviathan," I say to myself. "Let's begin."

Pax Romana

I t was the year 27 B.C. The Roman emperor Augustus established a period of peace called the Pax Romana; that's Latin for *Roman Peace*.

New roads were built, buildings were constructed, and water systems were created. Large marble temples and government buildings were added to the Forum. Nearby were brand new theaters and public baths; I preferred to use my own bath though. Also, there were these waterways called aqueducts that were built to bring fresh water into the city.

The aqueducts were nothing new; they were new to the Romans, but the structure was already being used by Acanthus of Corinth; the Immortal Trio's Deathbringer . . . my twin brother. He had one constructed in his lair that brought this strange black water to a reservoir, which fed his monstrous plants. I later learned that the water was the same stuff he and his acanthus servants drank to repair themselves. It was called Unholy water; a mixture of Holy water, brimstone, and Human blood.

"This is so cool." I told Molicles.

"I can finally live in peace." she said to me.

"Yes, but it won't be for long."

"Why?"

"Look at us, my dear. We are immortals; we will be sought after for our immortality."

"Just like how the Trio took Coria's."

I flinched. That was an awful day when the Immortal Trio killed Coria. The thought of watching Dante Lord Haven hack off his limbs still runs vividly through my mind; damn Acanthus for making me watch!! I decided to shake that nightmare out of my head.

"Coria would've really loved this time of peace." I said.

During this wonderful time, I treated Molicles like a queen. I gave her gifts that were brought to Rome by foreign merchants; the gifts included Spanish silver coins, Egyptian linens, even expensive Chinese silk clothing.

"Leviathan," Molicles said. "Can you do something for me?"

"What is it, my sweet?" I asked her.

"Can you get me a pony? Please? I've been wanting one for a very long time."

"Okay. If it's a pony you want, it's a pony you'll get."

"Oh, thank you, Leviathan!!" She hugged me tight. "You're the best!! I love you."

"I love you, too, honey." I hug her back. "I love you, so much." I kiss her cheek.

Poor girl, I had thought. *She's getting older and older, but she's still trapped inside a little girl's body.*

I took her in my arms and slowly rocked her back and forth.

"Poor baby." I whispered to her. "You're so little."

"That's okay, Leviathan." Molicles told me. "I'm your little baby doll."

"I know that, but I don't look at you as if you were made of synthetic materials, like cloth and yarn; you're so much better than that. You're my little angel."

I kissed her on her little cheek again. I then held her close to me. I swore to myself that I would never let anything bad happen to her.

Trying To Sleep Here!

I stop writing. I sit my pen down and look at what I have written. It's not much, but it's part of what I've experienced in my past life.

I open the drawer of the bedside desk and sit the papers in it; I close the drawer. I then stand up and stretch; I begin to realize just how fatigued I really am. I need to lie down and try to sleep.

I need to do something about that penitentiary uniform that those jerks dressed me in; I cannot wear that in public without having a thousand eyes glued to me. People know who I am; if they see the prison clothes, they'll begin to think back on me being a suspect on the triple deaths in L.A.—they'd have the murderer in their sight.

"Time to go to bed." I say to myself.

I climb into bed and pull the sheets up to my chin. I think to myself for a moment: *How will I get around in such a wild city like Las Vegas? I got around well in Los Angeles because I had gotten familiar with it; it's what I'll need to do here. I have to get familiar with Sin City.*

I start to think about Los Angeles, my beautiful mansion, my friends . . . everything that I owned and loved.

My constant thinking begins to make me tired. As I am drifting, I can hear moaning and strange noises in the suite next to mine. I know what's going on in there; it reminds me of how Tigris and I were, back in our lovemaking days.

"Hey!!" I shout. "Trying to sleep here! Can you keep it down?!"

"You're next, pal!" a man shouts from next door.

The noise continues, and I chuckle. Apparently, I'm next, but who cares?

I allow myself to make the noises relaxing ones; I instantly drift off to sleep.

The Nicaraguan Maid

I am woken up by the sound of a vacuum cleaner. I roll over onto my back and start to stretch.

"Buenos dias, Mister." says a maid who is, no doubt, Spanish. "How are you this morning?"

"Naked." I say.

"Que?"

"Huh? What time is it?"

"It's a little after noon. I always start my cleaning shift at noon."

My former Nicaraguan maid used to always start cleaning my mansion around noon.

"You had to pick my suite first?" I ask, sitting up.

"I didn't have to." she grabs a can of lemon Pledge from her cleaning cart. "I'm on this floor, and I have to clean the rooms; we have a camera crew coming to stay here, so they'll need to . . . ."

I see that the maid is staring at me as if she has seen a ghost. I can't help but admit, I've seen her before.

I watch as the maid's gaze goes straight to my right wrist; she eyes my Golgohoth family tribal band.

"Mr. Jonathan?!" she says.

"Lupe?!" I ask in amazement.

The maid that is cleaning my suite is Lupe Guzman-Dominguez, my old Nicaraguan maid. I found out she was stealing articles from my home, and rather than killing her in cold blood, I had her deported back to her home country. I suppose Nicaragua didn't have much to offer her, so now she's in Vegas trying to make a living.

"What are you doing here, Mr. Jonathan?!" she asks.

"What are *you* doing here?" I ask her.

"I had to find more work. You?"

"I killed some people. Now, I'm being hunted?"

"By the cops?"

"No. By another killer."

Lupe doesn't comment on it; she slowly places the can of lemon Pledge back on the cart.

"So," she says. "Are you gonna be here for a while?"

"Just until I kill my stalker." I say.

"Did you say the Stalker?"

"No, I said *my* stalker."

"Oh . . . because the Immortal Trio's Stalker is impossible to kill."

Duh; I know that already. And how does she know about the Trio's immortality?

"What is there to do here?" I ask as I get out of bed; Lupe turns her head quickly to avoid seeing anything. I walk into the bathroom.

"There's lots to do here in Vegas, Mr. Jonathan." she says.

"Uh-huh." I say as I put the prison clothes back on, inside out. "Tell me."

"There are casinos, bars, restaurants, night clubs, the Luxor, Mandalay Bay. There's also places where you can go see . . . ."

"Did you say the Luxor?"

"Well, yes. It's that big black pyramid."

"I know what it is. What goes on there?"

"Well, it's a hotel and casino. Also, it holds shows in the performing arts category; lots of famous people go there, like Blue Man Group. And, the Cirque du Soleil has performed there."

And . . . a perfect place for Arch-Peteryx Feathervault to hide. As an Egyptian, he'd be comfortable inside of a pyramid.

"I'll check it out." I say. I walk out of the bathroom. "What can I do in the meantime?"

"Well," Lupe says. "There's the theaters; they're showing this new movie; it's called *The Passion of the Christ*. You should go and see it."

"Why would the viewing of a Holy movie be shown in a place like Sin City?"

"I don't know, Mr. Jonathan."

"Well, I'll go see it, and stop calling me that."

"What?"

"My name's not Jonathan, Lupe." I put on my shoes. "Stop calling me Jonathan."

"What is your name?"

I say nothing to her. I grab the card key, papers, and pen and head for the door.

"I'll go see The Passion." I tell her.

"Oh, that's great." Lupe says.
"Just to fill you in, I actually met the real Jesus."
"What did you say, Mr. Jon . . . I mean . . . ."
"Golgohoth. Leviathan Golgohoth."
Lupe gasps as I walk out the door.

The Crucifixion Film

I slip past the front desk and exit the Hilton. I head over to where I had parked the van; it isn't there anymore.

"What?" I ask myself.

Who could've taken it? Perhaps it was law enforcement . . . or perhaps it's another group of Anubis servants loyal to Peteryx? Whoever it is, if they are after me, I'll gut them like a fish.

"A theater." I say to myself.

I search the busy streets for a cab. I finally locate one and flag it down. Even though I don't know how I plan to pay for the ride to the theater, I get in the backseat anyway.

"Where's the closest theater?" I ask the cabbie.

"Well," the cabbie says. "That would be The Colosseum at Caesar's Palace."

"Sounds good. Take me there."

The cab driver takes me to Caesar's Palace in a jiffy; I am grateful for that.

"Thanks, man." I say, leaning over the back of his seat. "I appreciate your service."

I quickly wrap my hand around his throat and snap his windpipe. I do not kill him; I simply put him in a still point. He'll be awake in the next few hours wondering what exactly happened.

I see a crowd standing outside to get their movie tickets. I decide to listen to what they're going to see.

"Six tickets." a man says. "To see *The Passion of the Christ*."

That's my cue to step in. I slip in amongst the group of six.

"Seeing The Passion, huh?" I ask the man who bought the tickets.

"Yes." he says. He stares at me for a moment. "Are you . . . Jonathan Note?"

"Yes. Yes, I am."

"I knew I recognized that voice. My name is Steven Regal. Why don't you join us?"

I look over at Mr. Regal's guests. All adults, all dressed casually; all appear to be of the Christian faith.

"Okay." I agree.

"Do you have a ticket? I didn't see you get one."

"I kinda left my cash and cards at my hotel room. I didn't think I'd want to see a movie."

"Well, no worries. We'll get you one."

"Seriously?"

"Of course."

Mr. Regal buys me a ticket to see The Passion and we all walk inside Caesar's Palace. We head over to the Colosseum.

"So, Jonathan," one of the people in the group say. "Are you an albino or something."

"Yes." I say. "Thanks for pointing that out, Mister . . . ."

"Arthur Max."

"Mr. Max."

We walk inside the theater. I consider getting some kind of concession, but I feel like I would be disrespecting the Good Lord if I munched on popcorn and candy during a Jesus film.

The group and I walk inside the dark theater and take a seat; I find that the lack of light is relaxing to my weary eyes.

So, no commercials for new movies are being shown, which means the movie will start right away.

As I watch, I'm confused. Why does the movie begin with Jesus praying in the Garden of Gethsemane? Why doesn't it start with the teachings? That's the essential parts.

"The Passion is referring to the death of Jesus, Leviathan." says a voice in my head.

I begin to look around to see if anyone of the people in the group had said it, but their eyes are fixed upon the screen.

"No need to look around, Leviathan. I'm only in your mind."

The voice I hear inside my head . . . . I have heard before, and am very familiar with it. It was the voice that said they will save me, when I fell off the cliff in L.A.

I listen to the people in the movie speaking in Hebrew. There are English subtitles, but I do not read them; I understand every word they are saying.

When your best friend is an Israeli, straight out of Jerusalem, you learn Hebrew pretty quick.

In no time, the movie gets more heavy and violent. After Jesus spoke with Pilate, He was ordered by the people to be crucified. He is taken to the city and is beaten; I hear the people in the theater gasping and crying. I keep my eyes glued to the screen.

Suddenly, I have flashbacks. Flashbacks of when the real Jesus was being tortured; I was there. Such violence was shown by the Romans.

I snap back to the present. I see Jesus struggling to carry that huge cross to Calvary. I feel tears stinging my eyes.

In no time, there's the crucifixion; it actually shows the nails being hammered into Jesus' hands and feet. The tears stream down my cheeks. I think to myself: *This movie runs very close to the actual death of Jesus. How did Mel Gibson do it? I'll have to ask him when I see him again.*

The sufferings of Jesus, in this movie, are so tough to handle. However, the actual Passion, that happened in real life back in 29A.D. was a lot more worse than what I see in the movie.

Finally, The Passion ends when Jesus walks out of the tomb; you can see straight through the hole in one of His hands.

I don't know what to say or do. I look over and see a priest standing by the screen; so many people, including the group I'm with, rush over to him. They're giving up their lives of sin to follow Christ. It's definitely something I would like to do, soon.

I go to get up from my seat, but I feel something push me back down.

"Leviathan," says a familiar male's voice. *"What the hell do you think you're doing?! You are a tyrant!! You survive off of other people's bloodshed!!"*

"I'm doing the right thing." I say.

"Walk out of that theater now, Leviathan, and go hunt down Peteryx!! I will be there shortly."

"Wait a minute . . . Levetin?"

The voice stops talking to me. I look around and see no familiar faces; none that resemble my twin brother's. Listening to what the voice told me, I walk out of the theater.

Meeting Powers and Rolfe Bentley

I exit the Colosseum at Caesar's Palace. I decide to hike it on foot back to the Vegas Hilton and draw out my plans to hunt down Peteryx.

I see that the cab that I rode here to the theater is gone; he must've driven away and wondered what happened before he was knocked out.

As I wonder what happened to the cab, I feel a hand touch my right shoulder.

"Excuse me, son." says a male's voice. I turn around and see a young man with short dark-brown hair and bright hazel-blue eyes.

"Yes?" I ask.

"I don't mean to bother you, but—aren't you like—that tyrant?"

"Huh? What are you talking about, kid?"

"You *are* that tyrant! I know you are! I read about you in a book based on the Immortal Trio. Also, I read passages on you in a thirteenth-century anno Domini book based on sorcery and alchemy; you were under the references of Edward Gaudio. Your name is Leviathan!"

"Leviathan Golgohoth." says another guy with red hair and dark-brown eyes. "He's the only albino tyrant in the Tyranny Squad."

"He's also the twin brother of Acanthus the Deathbringer." the dark-haired guy says.

I stare at the both of them. How do they know that I'm Leviathan Golgohoth, and not just some albino commoner?

"Okay," I say. "How do you know that I am the tyrant you speak of?"

The red-haired guy grasps my right wrist and draws his left pointer finger around my tribal band.

"The tattoo." he says. "Acanthus of Corinth, Levetin Golgohoth, has the same one around his upper left arm."

"Which is broken because of an accident with a boar when he was ten." I tell him. "I was present when it happened."

"That's true!!" the dark-haired guy says. "You definitely *are* Leviathan Golgohoth!"

"And, who might you two be?"

The dark-haired guy extends his hand out to me.

"My name is Edward Bentley." he says. "People call me Powers."

I shake his hand.

"Powers?" I say. "Like Powers Boothe?"

"He's only my favorite actor." he says. He gestures to the red-haired guy. "This is my cousin Rolfe Bentley."

I shake the cousin's hand.

"What's with the prison uniform?" he asks.

"It's a joke." I say, not knowing why. "What's with the feminine accent and the lisp in your voice?"

"It's a joke." he says. He chuckles; I do not find any of this funny.

"Look, I have to go." I say. "I'm staying at the Hilton right now; I have to escape from Los Angeles life for a while."

"You don't have to stay at the Hilton." Powers says. "You can come stay with us."

"What? No. I'm going to the Vegas Hilton."

"Are you sure?" Rolfe asks me.

"I'm pretty sure."

"Look," Powers says. "Rolfe and I are scientists and historians of the ancient past."

"No kidding?" I ask.

"No kidding. Will you change your mind about the Hilton and come stay with us? We want to know so much about you; what made you immortal, how you managed to survive the unthinkable, how you need blood to thrive."

The cousins are curious; they have read about me, and now they want to know more.

"I guess I'll go stay with you for a little while." I give in.

"Great!" Rolfe says. "You'll like it at our place."

"No strings attached?"

"I'm not sure what that means, but yes. No strings attached."

I'll Find You, My Brother!

Yes, little people. You will hear my end of the story. I, Acanthus of Corinth, am here in this shit can state, wondering what I must do to save my twin brother, Leviathan of Mesopotamia. Of course, it doesn't take me long to figure it out. I have to go to Las Vegas.

"Tarsus and Spinosus should've been here." I say to my daughter Poppy.

"What are they doing?" she asks me.

"They're preparing to hunt down the rest of the Anubis servants loyal to Arch-Peteryx. They will not find Leviathan before I do."

"Where is Uncle Leviathan?"

"Vegas, of all places. That well-lit jungle."

"Is he in trouble?"

"You tell me; Arch-Peteryx is out there."

"Will he find Uncle Leviathan before you do?"

"Possibly so, but Leviathan's strong."

"Who's going to watch me while you're gone?"

"Oniwaka. You're familiar with him, yes?"

"Syriacus. The youngest acanthus boy."

"Good girl."

"Can I beat up that Channing kid while you're away?"

"Help yourself."

"Can I pour acid in their swimming pool and spray paint their house?"

"Yes."

"Can I pull up their azalea bushes?"

"No."

"Can I bake them a pie made out of dog food?"

"Will you shut up?"

I look over at the Note Manor. I see my brother's Jewish friend walking up to the door; he rings the doorbell.

29

"Leviathan?!" he calls out. "It's me, Mordecai!! Are you home?" He presses the button on the call monitor. "Leviathan, I have the craziest thing I have to tell you!!!"

"Stay here." I tell Poppy.

I cross the fence over to Leviathan's yard. I watch as the Jew fumbles with a padlock on the front door.

"What's this?" he asks himself. "Why is this on Leviathan's door?"

"I put that there." I say.

Mordecai turns around and when he sees me, he nearly drops the object in his hand; some sort of a weird spinning top.

"Oh boy." he says with fear in his tone. He backs against the door. "I am so dead."

I stare down at him. I watch as he swallows and looks slightly to the left.

"Expecting someone?" I ask.

"Acanthus of Corinth." he says.

"That's me; Leviathan isn't here."

"What happened here? I've been trying to call him, but he doesn't answer his cell phone."

"He lost it in the ocean."

"The ocean?"

"The Pacific Ocean. Where else . . . you can lighten up; I'm not going to kill you."

"You're not?"

"Leviathan's best friend is my best friend."

The Jewish kid moves away from the door. He stares at me as if I am some sort of magnificent marvel of the world, and that I am; me, Arachne, and Dante all are.

"I'm sorry," he says. "I'm still having this strange feeling, being around you."

"Does it have something to do with the Christmas tree?"

I held a grudge against Mordecai ever since I watched him help Leviathan carry a Christmas tree into Note Manor in December of 2000 A.D. I mean, the kid's Jewish, for one; they don't celebrate Christmas. And second . . . . it was a fresh pine tree, and it was calling out to me for help.

"No." Mordecai says. "I mean, I know you're Leviathan's brother and all, but . . . the history about the Immortal Trio, and what I've read in Leviathan's passages, you're just . . . ."

"Leviathan's passages?" I ask. "So, he's writing a book about me."

"He's writing a book about his past. Well, I'm writing it; he's giving me all of the details."

"I see. So, I suppose you read something about me that you disagree with?"

Mordecai the Jew says nothing; I know he's not comfortable around me . . . but why would he be around Leviathan? My brother and I are both cold-blooded monsters; we kill to satisfy our undying rage and terror for a bit. What makes him think that Leviathan won't turn on him in desperate times?

"Come with me." I say to him.

"You're really not gonna kill me?" he asks.

"If you come with me, I won't."

Mordecai follows me over to my yard, where we sit down on the lush green grass.

"Nice garden you have." he says. "Do you know where Leviathan is?"

"Yes." I tell him.

"Is he okay?"

"For now."

"What do you mean *for now*?"

"One of Leviathan's archenemies has turned up unexpectedly; he tracked him down, and now it's getting personal."

"Who?! Who is this archenemy?!"

I don't think this kid will understand me, even if I have to explain it in detail to him all day. If he doesn't get it after the first time I tell him . . . . I'll kill him; I'll deal with Leviathan's grieving and anger later.

"Has Leviathan ever told you about Arch-Peteryx Feathervault?" I ask.

"I read about him." Mordecai tells me. "I'm not too familiar with what he's done."

"Arch-Peteryx Feathervault, sometimes called Peteryx, is an Egyptian tyrant who had it out with Leviathan once because he claimed he had more superiority than him. The feud ended when Leviathan pushed Peteryx into a pit of scarabs. What Leviathan didn't know, back then, was that Peteryx would escape and seek revenge."

"Leviathan hadn't killed him?"

"No, and Peteryx will be seeking Leviathan to pay him back for the scarab incident."

"Leviathan is strong; he will win."

"You just don't get it." I stand up. "Anyone of us in the Immortal Trio could've killed Peteryx, but we left him to Leviathan because it's only fair. Why would my colleagues and I take a fair game away from Leviathan?"

"To protect him."

"No. This feud is personal."

"Personal?" Mordecai stands up. "Leviathan could've killed him already!!"

"And he never did because of the switch."

"Switch? What kind of switch?"

"You'll find out soon enough. Now, I have to go find Leviathan."

I start to walk toward my greenhouse to equip my torture tools, but I am stopped.

"You never told me where he is." the Jew says.

I smile.

"He's in Las Vegas." I say.

"Sin City?"

"A well-lit area, and Peteryx will see him there; I have to find Leviathan and prepare him. He's not ready for what's to come."

The Bentley Residence

On the way to the Bentleys' home, I lie down on the backseat of the car; I feel tired. Before I shut my eyes, I think: *Were Powers and Rolfe holding hands? That's just crazy; they're cousins.*

About ten minutes have passed; we arrive at a marvelous suburban house right outside the city.

"Okay," Powers says. "Here we are."

We get out of the car. I stare out at the house; it's so very neat. I think I'll actually like it here. Maybe I'll get rid of the Bentleys and live here, all by myself.

What am I thinking? My mansion is in L.A. I have to go back as soon as I find Peteryx and extinguish him.

"Come with us, Leviathan." Rolfe says.

I follow the Bentleys. Rolfe unlocks the front door; we then walk inside. I am surprised by what I see. All over the walls are paintings of ancient immortals of the past.

"Do you like our works of art?" Powers asks me. I nod my head.

"I painted that one." Rolfe says, pointing to a portrait of what appears to be the Ghoul Lord Tach Schnep and Dante Lord Haven in a dispute. After all, Ghouls eat the flesh of the dead, which means they would walk right up to the Vindicator's zombies and tear their flesh clean off their bones.

Wow, I think. *That painting looks so realistic. They look exactly like Tach and Dante. How do they know what they look like?*

"I also painted this one of you and Acanthus." Rolfe continues.

The painting is, indeed, one of me and my twin brother; I am sitting on a rock while Acanthus appears to be giving me some sort of lecture on life as a monster.

Amazing, I think.

I also view portraits of Arachne the Spider Queen, the late Vampire Lord Percival Vancroft, Demonic Lords Abbaddon Forsythe and Akem Manah, and Werewolf Lord Romulus Fierce.

"These are so neat." I say. "But, how did you know what everyone's faces looked like?"

"We saw their faces on a prehistory website." Powers says. "It was on prehistory dot com, forward slash immortals of the centuries."

I see paintings of the Eternal Ones. I see a painting of the brothers, Azrael and Drakengaard Hark, standing next to this weird prehistoric bovine thing. There's another one that depicts Murabbi Paleohenge and Colai Calsambra teaching a youth how to sing and dance. I then see one of Angeleal challenging a wise old sage with a riddle.

I look around to see if there's any more that would show Revelatianus; not a single one. I was really expecting to see him.

"Have you ever seen Revelatianus?" I ask.

"No." Powers says. "I've heard that *you* did though."

"Well, of course I have; he made me into what I am today. I can still see his face clearly, in my mind."

"Well," Rolfe says. "Perhaps later, you can help us paint a picture of him?"

"Absolutely."

"Leviathan," Powers says. "Why don't you make yourself at home while I prepare the extra room for you. It belonged to my older brother Ronny, but you can have it."

"You brother doesn't live here with you guys?" I ask.

"No. Ronny decided to leave when I told him that Rolfe was moving in."

"Why?"

"He isn't really fond of Rolfe."

"But," I turn to Rolfe. "He's your cousin."

Rolfe says nothing. He simply shrugs his shoulders.

"Anyways," Powers continues. "You can have Ronny's room, Leviathan. He left all of his belongings in there. You'll fit into his clothes; he's about your size, and tall like you. He really loved books, and he left a bunch of them behind. You're more than welcome to read them."

"He's not coming back for his possessions anytime soon?" I ask Powers.

"No. He called me, after he settled into his new place, and told me that I can have everything; I couldn't take his stuff though; I'd feel uncomfortable."

"But, he gave his stuff to you."

"And now, I'm letting you have it."

"Well, thank you, Edward . . . I mean . . . Powers."

My First Vegas Phone Call

I think: *I really need to get in touch with Mordecai. I'll bet he's wondering where I am. The bad news is I lost my cell phone.*

"Uh, Powers," I say. "Is there a phone I can use?"

"Yes." he tells me. "There's one in Ronny's room."

Powers takes me to his brother's old room. Wow, everything looks neat and trendy. I don't see why Powers wanted to prepare it for me; it's already straight.

I look over and, sure enough, there's a phone sitting on a little desk by the window. I go over to it and sit down in the rolling chair. I pick up the phone and punch in the number to the DeFranco Foster Home. It rings . . . someone picks up.

Anonymous: Hello?

It isn't Mordecai who answers the phone. I have no idea who this could be.

Me: Hi. Who am I speaking with?

Anonymous: Stuart French. Who is this?

It's just Stuart, the young boy the DeFrancos adopted from Fullerton.

Me: Stuart. This is Mordecai's friend Jonathan.

Stuart: Jonathan Note?

Me: Yes. Is Mordecai around?

Stuart: No. He said that he was going to your house.

He's going to my mansion?!?! I'm not there . . . and Acanthus is next door. Oh shit!!

Me: Well, when he gets back, can you tell him to call me from this number?

Stuart: Sure. It's on the caller I.D. as Edward Bentley. Who's Edward Bentley?

Me: Never mind that now. I have to go.

Stuart: Don't you wanna talk to your daughter?

Me: My daughter?

Stuart: Anticlea, Jonathan. She's your daughter, right? I mean, she ran right next to me when I asked if you're Jonathan Note.

Anticlea's with Marilyn and Ned. Draken Hark tells the truth; she *is* in a safe place.

Me: Put her on, please.

I strictly told myself that I would not go by Jonathan Note anymore, but I guess it's not possible, here in the United States.

I can hear Stuart talking to Anticlea.

"Your daddy's on the phone." he says to her. I hear the phone being placed against something; Anticlea's ear, no doubt. I also hear footsteps; Stuart is walking away.

Anticlea: Hello? Leviathan?

Me: Anticlea, my baby girl?

Anticlea: Where are you? When are you coming home?

Me: I'm in Las Vegas; I'll be home soon.

Anticlea: Where's Las Vegas?

Me: Nevada.

Anticlea: Are you in trouble?

Me: No, honey. I'm okay. I'll be home to get you soon. You have to be a good little girl for Marilyn and Ned, okay? Are they being nice to you?

Anticlea: Yes. Where are you staying?

Me: I'm staying with a couple of nice guys; they're cousins. Don't tell anyone where I am, okay?

Anticlea: Okay.

Me: Can you promise me that, my dear?

Anticlea: I promise.

Me: When you see Mordecai, tell him that I'll be mailing him some stuff; he'll know what it is.

Anticlea: Okay, Leviathan.

Me: I'll be using a different name to mail the stuff to him; I can't risk using Jonathan Note or Leviathan Golgohoth.

Anticlea: Why?

Me: It's a long story, honey. And besides, Chip, who's my friend at the post office, will make sure Mordecai gets them safely.

Anticlea: Okay.

Me: Don't forget to ask Mordecai, when you see him, if our house is okay.

Anticlea: I won't forget. Oh . . . what do you think Acanthus is doing?

I have not thought about what my brother is doing. I have a dark feeling that he may be in Vegas shortly.

Me: Acanthus will not let me be alone for a while.

Anticlea: Will he bring you back here?

Me: It is certain that he will find a way.

Since my brother is still in Los Angeles, as far as I know, my mansion will be guarded. However, if he comes here, to Las Vegas, trouble will be stirred up, and Peteryx will become more of a threat than ever . . . right?

Anticlea: Leviathan?

Me: Yes, honey?

Anticlea: Mordecai and that girl that he likes were making noises this morning.

Me: Noises?

Anticlea: Yeah, like they were moaning or something.

Me: Well, my sweet. We won't discuss what that was. Anyways, have you noticed Mordecai on the computer often?

Anticlea: Well, yeah. Isn't he typing some things you're giving to him?

Me: Yeah, but is he using the Internet more often?

Anticlea: I don't know; I'll look and see, when he's here.

Me: Okay. Look, Anticlea. I'll be back as soon as possible. Until the time being, don't go outside by yourself. If you want to go outside and play, make sure you have an adult with you; Marilyn, Ned, whoever. Don't go out by yourself.

Anticlea: Why not, Leviathan?

Me: It's not safe yet. Listen, honey, I will call again. When Mordecai gets back, have him call me at this number, okay? It should be on the caller I.D. Tell him to call me, okay?

Anticlea: Okay, Leviathan. Be careful; come home soon.

Me: I will, my dear.

I hang up the phone from talking with Anticlea. Maybe I'll be able to contact Mordecai later . . . and I hate to see what plans, if any, Levetin is cooking up to make my run-in with Peteryx not as difficult.

I sigh. I then grab my fountain pen and another sheet of paper; I begin to write where I leave off.

The Times Of Christ

Twenty-three years had passed since the Pax Romana began. It's the year 4 B.C. Emperor Augustus announced an order, stating that a census would be taken throughout the empire. Everyone had to return to the towns they were born in, so that they could be counted.

Well, I wasn't planning on leaving Rome and taking Molicles back to Corinth, especially with the Lair of Acanthus being there, and I wasn't going back to Mesopotamia. No way; Molicles and I were sticking together.

We headed to Israel. We settled in a little town called Nazareth; it took Molicles and I about three days to get there.

On the way there, we learned about the birth of the Christ Child, our Lord Jesus.

"I want to see the baby, Leviathan." Molicles had told me. "Let's go to Bethlehem and see Him."

"We'll have to see Him later." I said. "It's not like I don't want to see Him, it's just that . . . . we don't have the strength to travel further to Nazareth."

Molicles understood me, but I could tell that she was disappointed. Actually, the cold truth behind us not going to Nazareth was that the Immortal Trio was there; they, too, have heard about the birth of Jesus, and wanted to see Him. And, I couldn't let Molicles see them. They were, no doubt, one of her biggest fears.

Twelve years had passed since that special night. Young Jesus went to Jerusalem with His parents to celebrate the Passover, a Jewish holiday that begins on the 14th day of Nisan—the 7th month of the civil year on the Jewish calendar.

In the year 26 A.D., when Jesus was thirty years old, He started teaching to multitudes of people. He even healed the sick, removed evilness from the possessed, and performed many other miracles!!

"Did you see that, Leviathan?" Molicles asked. "Jesus just healed that blind man with mud!!"

"It's a miracle." I said to her. "He is the Son of God."

Jesus and His twelve disciples went around Galilee to spread the Word of God. The teachings became a religion; a religion known as Christianity, taken from Christ's name. The followers of Jesus were called Christians, and are still called that today in the present.

"I want to be a Christian." Molicles had said to me one year. I smiled and gave her a hug.

"You have every right to be one, my dear." I said, kissing her on her cheek.

As the time went by, people began to be afraid of Jesus. Many even began to hate Him, especially the Pharisees—members of a Jewish sect of the intertestamental period noted for strict observance of rites and ceremonies of the written law and for insistence on the validity of their own oral traditions concerning the law. By God, I hated those guys.

I heard about the Lord's Supper, or the Last Supper as we know it now. There, the New Covenant was made. Then, while Jesus prayed to God, in the Garden of Gethsemane, Judas Iscariot betrayed Him with a kiss on the cheek; Jesus knew that this incident would happen.

Jesus was arrested and taken to the city. Molicles and I were there, in the city, when the Roman soldiers arrived with Him.

"I sense trouble." I told Molicles.

"Me, too." she said to me.

"Perhaps this is all just a misunderstanding, and everything will be okay tomorrow."

I was wrong about that. It was early on the next morning; Peter, one of the 12 disciples, denied Jesus three times before the rooster crowed . . . Jesus said that it would happen.

Later on, during the day, Jesus was taken to the governor, Pontius Pilate; Pilate said that he saw no guilt in Him. The people had said that He was blaspheming God because He said that He was the Son of God; Jesus spoke the truth, but why didn't the people believe Him? It was clearly shown when He performed all of those miracles.

Pilate gave the people a choice; he gave them the choice to release either the prisoner Barabbas, or Jesus the Son of Man among them. Molicles and I were both shocked and surprised when the people shouted Barabbas's name; because of that, Pilate had Barabbas released, and I could guarantee it that he would kill again.

"So now," Pilate said. "What shall I do with the One called Jesus?"

"Crucify Him!!!" the people shouted in unison.

"NO!!" Molicles shouted. "Let Him go, too!!!"

Poor little Molicles. She tried so hard to make someone hear her pleas; it was no use, really. The people shouted 'Crucify Him' louder than ever.

"I find no guilt in this Man." Pilate said to them, but they shouted even louder, "Crucify Him!! Crucify Him!!!"

Pilate saw that he could do nothing more to stop the crowd from shouting that awful chant. He then washed his hands in front of them and said, "I am innocent of the blood of this just person. You see to it."

Then, the people said, "His blood be on us, and on our children."

Jesus was then taken to the town square. Molicles and I decided to follow from a distance.

The Roman soldiers had Him chained. Two of the soldiers each had a weapon called a cat-o'-nine-tails; they began to beat Him across His back with them.

It was so horrible!! Horrible doesn't describe just how bad the beatings were.

As I watched the torture, I felt an evil presence near me; an evil presence that I have felt before on some occasions.

"Sick." said a familiar voice. "They're just as sadistic as me."

I looked over and saw Acanthus of Corinth. The Deathbringer; my twin brother. His face was emotionless as he watched the two soldiers do what they were doing.

I couldn't let Molicles watch that madness, or be near Acanthus.

"Go!" I demanded. "Molicles, go!! Get out of here! You cannot watch this!!"

"Leviathan," she said. "I . . . ."

"GO!! NOW!! Run away! Don't look at it!!"

"Why?!"

"Because I said so." Acanthus stepped in.

Molicles said nothing else; a veil of fear covered her face when she saw the Deathbringer's presence before her. She ran away and I stayed behind with my twin; together, we watched as the soldiers tortured Jesus.

I felt so sick inside. As a tyrant, I torture people so badly, but nothing like this. Acanthus, on the other hand, did not flinch once as he watched; deep down inside, he had no feelings of sympathy for nothing or no one. Seeing this, no doubt, brought a flood of satisfaction to his cold soulless shell of a being.

After Jesus had been whipped thirty-nine consecutive times, the Roman soldiers made Him take up a heavy wooden cross. I wanted to take those soldiers and torture and kill them; I wanted to hurt them for hurting our Lord. I felt my brother's strong hand wrap around my upper arm.

"You cannot show your fury." he said in my ear. "Not here; not now. Contain your hatred, Brother."

"Aren't you and your colleagues going to go after Barabbas?" I asked. "He will kill again."

"No. We will not; we're just going to let him get caught again. Now, contain your hatred."

The soldiers made Jesus carry the heavy cross to Calvary, Golgotha in the Hebrew language. There, He was crucified.

Acanthus and I stood in the distance and kept our eyes fixed on the sight of Him on that cross.

Sweet Jesus had been beaten beyond recognition, but I still knew it was Him. It was just so bad to see Him in that condition.

The soldiers mocked Jesus and shouted, "If you're *really* the Son of God, get down from up there!"

Those evil soldiers took Jesus' clothing and cast lots. I then could see His mouth moving; I heard Him say, "Father." He was talking to God. He said, "Forgive them. They know not what they do."

I hung my head; Jesus had just asked His Father to forgive everyone for their sins.

I felt my brother's hand grasp me under my chin; he tilted my head up and made me look at Jesus and the two others as they hung on the crosses.

"Our sins may have been forgiven," he said in my ear. "But we are still monsters. We must continue with our savage natures. Nothing shall ever take our insatiable thirst for blood away from us. Do you understand me, my brother?"

"Yes." Was all I could say.

It was late, and the sky became dark. It wasn't just dark, there was no light anywhere; it was just . . . . black. It was the darkest day that I have ever seen. Even with my superhuman eyesight, I could see nothing.

"I think I'm blind, Leviathan." I heard Acanthus say. "I can't see a single thing out here."

"It's the same with me, Levetin." I told him. "We're not blind; it's just pitch black."

Not long after it got black, I heard Jesus say, "My God!! My God!! Why have You forsaken Me?"

I understood then; the sky was pitch black because God had turned His back on His Son. He couldn't look upon sin, and all the sins of the earth were on Jesus. I imagined that Acanthus and I had the blackest most deadliest sins of them all.

Well, it was later, and Jesus decided that it was time for Him to die. He called on God and gave up the ghost.

I stared out in the distance for a while. I then felt tears rolling down my cheeks; it isn't no time before I feel a cloth cover my face.

"No tears, Brother." Acanthus said. He couldn't stand to see tears; he claimed that salt water was harmful to plants. I, however, think it's because he has no sympathy.

I suddenly felt the ground shaking violently. I began to run and my brother followed; we ran until we arrived to the city.

"I have to find Molicles, Levetin." I say. "Perhaps you should find your colleagues?"

"They're not here." he says. "Be careful, Leviathan."

Once Acanthus bid me farewell and disappeared into the dark, I continued my search for Molicles. I figured she went back to our little house, so I went there.

When I arrived at our home, I discovered that Molicles was tucked into bed; she was sound asleep. A candle had been lit and cast a thin light in the dark room; someone was sitting by Molicles and gently caressing her hair.

"It's okay, little angel." said a sweet and familiar voice. "Leviathan's here."

I walked up next to the person, who turned out to be a female, and took her hand in mine.

"It's good that you're here, Colai." I said to her. "Did you watch Molicles while I was away?"

"Yes." she said. "Revelatianus sent me here to guide her home, especially since Acanthus of Corinth was in the area."

"Where's Arachne and Dante?"

"Jordan. They will find Acanthus soon enough and wreak more havoc amongst the living."

Colai reached out and touched my cheek.

"I know what happened." she said.

"Yes." I replied. "It was awful, but He did it to save all humanity."

"The Ultimate Sacrifice."

"Indeed. Levetin said that . . . ."

"Disregard all negativity that Levetin Golgohoth says."

I thought about that. Acanthus of Corinth may be one of the most evil and ruthless creatures that walks this earth, but he is my twin brother . . . ., and I can't just not listen to what he says; some of his words, I hate to admit it, were very helpful to me.

"No." I said.

"What?" Colai asked me.

"I will not disregard the words of Levetin Golgohoth."

"Leviathan, he's . . . ."

"The Immortal Trio's Deathbringer, yes, but he is my flesh and blood . . . and I still love him like he's normal Levetin."

Colai says nothing more on the subject; she looks up toward the ceiling.

"Leviathan," she said. "I have to go; Master Revelatianus calls to me."

"Is it about what I said?" I asked.

"He didn't say; he just wants me to return to the Sacred Haven."

"Yes. Thank you for helping Molicles."

Colai moved in closer and she hugged me. I hugged her back.

"Please take care of yourself and Molicles, Leviathan." she said. "Please don't let what happened to Coria happen to that little girl."

"I will not." I said. "I promise."

We parted. Colai then disappeared. I knelt down next to Molicles; I ran a finger down her cheek. I heard her moan and I shushed her.

"It's okay, Molicles." I said. "I'm right here, and I'm not leaving you."

She fell back asleep. I then walked over to the window and stared out at the night sky; I thought to myself: *That was a very caring thing Jesus did for mankind. He didn't have to die for us, but He did so that we can all have a chance to get to Heaven; that includes me . . . an evil bloodthirsty tyrant. What a huge debt He had paid.*

Rolfe's Painting Session

I stop writing. I take the passages, along with the ones I wrote about the Pax Romana, and put them together. I then look inside the desk and, lucky me, find large manila envelopes and stamps.

"Now," I say. "To address it to Mordecai."

I decide to send the passages to Mordecai by using his mother's name: Jess Weinstein.

Although I don't really want to use the name *Jonathan Note* anymore, it would be better to put that instead of Ahmed al-Khalid Hassan; anyone sees that, and they'll think that anthrax is inside the envelope.

Deciding that I'd rather remain well-hidden, I use Edward Bentley's name. I then write down the address to this house in the top left hand corner of the envelope. I put two stamps in the top right hand corner.

"Powers!!" I call out to him. Powers Bentley enters the room.

"Yes?" he asks. "What can I do for you, Leviathan?"

"You can mail this off for me."

I hand him the manila envelope; he stares at it.

"Jess Weinstein?" he asks.

"Yes." I say. "She's my best friend's mother. I'm using a different name for protection."

"Protection?"

"Do you have any idea what people will begin to think if they find a piece of mail with Leviathan Golgohoth written on it?"

"People will place it with Levetin Golgohoth; Acanthus of Corinth."

"I'm sure plenty of people who see me think I'm Leviathan Golgohoth in disguise; they'd be right."

"They would." Powers smiles. "I'll mail this off for you; I have to run to the post office anyway."

"It better get mailed off, because if it doesn't, I will find out."

"Don't worry, Leviathan. It'll get to where it has to go." Powers looks at the envelope again. "What's your best friend's first name?"

"Mordecai. He'll be eagerly awaiting my letters."

"Of course."

"And, you don't want to do anything that will delay the arrival of them, do you?"

"Absolutely not."

"Good."

Powers nods and leaves. I then grab a book from the bookshelf called *Alchemy, Sorcery, and Chemistry of the Thirteenth Century*. I begin to read some passages. A few moments after I finish reading a passage on Evan the Malevolent, Rolfe enters the room; he has with him an easel equipped with a blank canvas and some oil paints.

"Leviathan," he says. "Can you help me with something?"

"Well," I say. "It depends on what it is."

"Well, remember when you said that you'd help me paint a picture of Revelatianus?"

"Yes."

"Do you think you have the time to do it now? I have my supplies right here."

Well, I *did* promise Rolfe that I would help him paint a picture of the Eternal Ones' master, so I must.

"Sure." I say. "How about I describe what he looks like, and you paint what you hear? It'll be like a police sketch art."

"Or a courtroom artist." Rolfe says and chuckles.

"What?"

"Nothing. Let's begin, shall we?"

I follow Rolfe to the living room where he sets up the easel and canvas, along with the oil paints. He offers me a seat on the couch. As I sit down, he gets out a charcoal pencil.

"Do you remember exactly what Revelatianus looks like?" he asks.

"Yes, I do." I tell him.

"Great!! Then this painting shall be excellent."

"It shall be."

I begin to describe, in detail to Rolfe, Revelatianus's facial features; he nods and begins to draw on the canvas with the charcoal pencil. I give him every little detail from the golden crown to the violet-colored eyes.

After about a half an hour, Rolfe has completed the pencil drawing of Revelatianus. I take a look and I am amazed by what I see; it's as if a photograph of him has been snapped. In the background is a beautiful ocean and the sunset; Revelatianus stands on a chasm and looks out at the horizon.

"Splendid." I say. "It looks exactly like him."

"I am a skilled artist, you know." Rolfe says. "What I hear is what I create. Now, we need to add some color; color always accentuates things."

Rolfe begins to paint; he mixes colors and uses black and white to add dimension. Because of how skilled Rolfe is, he has it done in the matter of minutes.

"Well," he says. "There we are."

I am astonished by such skill and beauty Rolfe possesses in creating art. I want, so badly, to touch the painting, but it's still wet.

"It's amazing." I say.

"Thank you." Rolfe tells me.

"Where did you learn how to paint?"

"I took art in high school. Do you know how to paint?"

"A little bit."

I actually know how to paint realistically; even better than Rolfe. I learned how to paint in what was then Gaul; it was a long time ago.

Off the topic, I also remember this four hundred-twenty year period that was just a mystery to me; I remember this white light hitting me back in the year 1280 A.D., and I wasn't in my original body; I was in another's body. It wasn't until 1700 A.D. that I got my albino body back.

I remember exactly what happened to me. I was put under this weird spell by Edward Gaudio the First, in the Middle Ages.

"This is a wonderful painting indeed." Rolfe speaks of the magnificent portrait of Revelatianus. "I think I'll celebrate with some ginger ale and a Cosmo."

Hmm, I think. A Cosmo? That seems a little odd; I picture that as a ladies' drink.

"I'll have some orange juice." I say. "Do you have orange juice?"

"Yes, I do." Rolfe says. "I'll fetch you a glass. Do you like Minute Maid?"

"Whatever you have will work."

"Okay."

Bromine

Rolfe goes to the kitchen. I go back to my room. As I reach the door, I smell a faint scent of chemicals; it smells like freshly developed pictures.

"What in the world?" I ask myself.

I follow my nose; it leads me to a dimly lit room.

"What's this?" I ask myself, picking up a volumetric flask that contains a reddish-brown liquid. The cork is removed, so I take a tiny whiff; it stings my nostrils and I shake my head.

"Yuck!! This is bromine."

I put the cork back in the flask and slip it underneath my shirt. I walk back to my room; I pull the flask out and stare at it.

"What is it that you do?" I ask, almost expecting an answer back.

I hear footsteps, so I hide the bromine under my pillow. Rolfe walks into the room with my glass of orange juice.

"Here you go, Leviathan." he says, handing the juice to me.

"Thank you." I say, taking a sip.

Rolfe nods and leaves the room. I then take the bromine out again; I'm curious about what its purpose is.

I look for a book that talks about the elements. I find a chemistry book on the shelf.

"Section B." I say. I turn the pages of the book. "Okay. Barium, berkelium, beryllium, bismuth, boron . . . ah ha! Bromine. I found it."

I begin to read. The passage says that bromine vapors are very irritating to the eyes, the nose, and the throat; no kidding! It will cause severe burns if it comes in contact with skin. Well then, I better be careful; my skin burns easily.

The main use of bromine is in photography. Hey, I can develop pictures with it; it's no wonder the smell of it reminded me of a photo lab.

I read on. Bromine is used in medicine as sedatives. Hmm . . . .

"I wonder if . . . ." I start. I pull the cork out of the flask; I pour a small amount of bromine into my orange juice. "I must be crazy." I put the cork back into the flask; I look at my glass of orange juice, which is now an amber color. I take a sip.

"Hey," I say. "Not bad."

I drink the rest of my orange juice and wait; I don't feel any difference. I decide to read some more about bromine.

"Its compounds," I begin. "are usually found together with those of common salt."

Hmm . . . salt. Oh well. I decide that I want to write some more; I pick up my pen and begin to write some more of my chronicles.

Jesus Has Risen!!

It was morning, back in the year 29 A.D. It was Sunday morning, to be exact; the third day since the crucifixion of the Lord Jesus Christ.

Molicles and I spent our morning fishing in a lake; I built a small fire in order for us to cook the fish, if we caught any.

"Are you going to catch any fish?" I had asked Molicles.

"Why can't *you* catch them?" she asked.

"I'm old; you're quicker than me, my dear."

"No, I'm not. *You're* quicker than *me*."

"Maybe, but still. Go catch some fish; show me that you can."

Molicles got up and walked down by the water; she turned and looked at me.

"I don't have anything to catch them with." she said. I smiled and picked up a slender stick.

"Do what I do." I say, unsheathing my dagger. "Catch them."

"With what?"

"Well, if you don't have a net." I began to sharpen one end of the stick with my dagger. "Do the next obvious thing."

"Catch them with my hands? How am I supposed to do that? They're slippery."

"You don't have to do that, because I'm making it a lot easier for you." I toss the sharpened stick; it plants itself in the ground next to Molicles. "You'll spear them."

Molicles pulled the stick out of the ground and tried to spear a fish with it. As she did that, I threw more driftwood on the fire.

"Molicles," I called to her. "Any luck?"

"I can't catch any." she said to me. "They're too quick."

"It's not that they're too quick." I got up and walked over to her. "It's because you're not aiming in the right spot." I took the stick from her; I had to show her what her downfall was. "Listen, honey. The fish aren't where you think they are."

"What's that supposed to mean?"

"It's the light."

"The light?"

"Yes. Light bends objects that are submersed in water. So, the fish aren't in the spots that you see them in. Are you following me?"

"I think so."

"Okay." I point to a fish with the stick. "Do you see that fish there?"

"Yes."

"Alright. The light is bending it." I put the tip of the sharpened stick in the water. "It's the reflection you're looking at." I position the stick in the right spot. "The fish is actually right . . . . here!!"

I thrust the stick in the water. When I pulled it out, the fish was on the end, wiggling.

"Wow, Leviathan." Molicles said. "That was amazing!"

I handed Molicles the stick with the fish on the end.

"You can have that one." I said. "Now, go cook it over the fire. Don't stand too close to the flames, or *you'll* be the one on fire."

Molicles walked over to the fire and held the fish over it. After a few moments, I could smell the savory meat.

Suddenly, I heard someone shouting, "He lives!! He lives!!"

Who lives, I thought.

I walked away from the water and strained my ears so that I could hear much clearer. Still, I heard, "He lives!! He lives!!"

I wondered who they were talking about. As I walked further away from the water, my heart skipped a beat when I heard, "Lord Jesus!!"

Jesus had risen from the dead!!! What a miracle!!

"Molicles," I said. "C'mon. We have to see something."

"What?" she asked, still holding the now blackened fish over the fire.

"C'mon; follow me. I heard that Lord Jesus lives again."

"What?! He lives?!"

Molicles tossed the fish and the stick into the lake. She then ran toward me; I took her hand and we ran to the village. When we arrived, we saw someone, who looked an awful lot like Jesus, talking to the people.

I then noticed something; there were prints on His hands and on His feet; the places where the nails had been. I knew it, right then . . . . I was looking at the Lord Jesus Christ. He had risen from the dead and was alive again!!

"Look at that, Molicles." I said, showing her. "Our Savior."

"He lives." she said with tears of joy. "He lives."

Bromine Trip

I stop writing because I begin to feel sick. I thirst; I feel dehydrated. It's that bromine; I shouldn't have drank it. What the hell was I thinking?!

I get up and start to move toward the door when I suddenly feel my legs go limp; I collapse. I try to call Rolfe, but I black out.

I start to sink into darkness. I then land on a soft surface; it's as soft as cotton. It feels like a mat of some kind.

My vision clears and I see that I am in Mesopotamia; my home. I look down and notice that I'm sitting on the sand near the banks of one of the two rivers that flows through the land.

I begin to walk down the shore. I suddenly see something rising up from underneath the river's surface. I see that it's a beautiful young woman; I'd have to say, she is the most beautiful woman I have ever laid my eyes on; her dark wavy hair and bright-green eyes sparkle in the soft sunlight. I can feel my heart beating faster when she steps onto dry land.

"Leviathan," she says. "There you are, after so many years."

I see who this gorgeous woman is. Tears well up in my eyes and my bottom lip quivers.

"Leviathan," the woman says. "Do you remember me, my love?"

I walk up to her and take her hands in mine. My sight has become blurry with tears.

"Tigris." I say. "My precious Tigris."

She smiles at me.

"I've been waiting all of these years for you, Leviathan." She tells me. "And now, you're finally here."

I can't say anything; my tears spill over and roll down my cheeks. I close my eyes and embrace Tigris.

"It's you." I whisper. "It's really you." I lean my head on Tigris's shoulder and begin to weep. "My precious jewel."

Tigris begins to cry, too. She strokes my pale white hair gently.

"I thought that I've lost you forever." I say to her.

51

"I knew you'd be coming back to me." she whispers to me and kisses my brow. "You are finally here, my darling."

I pick my head up and stare into Tigris's beautiful bright-green eyes.

"Are you really alive?" I ask.

Tigris runs her finger delicately down my cheek.

"Yes." she replies. "And, as you can see, I have my youth back."

"Yes."

"I'm only alive in this world though."

"Then I shall remain here with you." I say. "It's been too long of an absence."

"That's wonderful, Leviathan, but you cannot stay here forever."

"What?"

"Imhotep Feathervault is out there, and you must defeat him before you can return here for good."

I sit down on a patch of green grass next to the banks of the river; I realize now that this is the Tigris River because that is where I buried my love when she died; it's the river she was named for.

"How long have you been waiting for me, Tigris?" I ask. It's a stupid question, but I want to hear an answer from her.

She sits down next to me and takes my hand in hers.

"You should know the answer, Leviathan." she says. "Ever since I passed away; my spirit has been waiting for you, but you kept on living. I've seen all that has happened to you."

"So . . . you've seen all of the other lovers?"

"Yes. There was nothing I could do about it, Leviathan. I was dead and gone."

"I thought about you while I was with them."

"I know you did."

We hug each other. I kiss Tigris lightly on her ear.

"I missed you so much, Tigris." I say. "I really have."

She kisses me on my cheek.

"I missed you, too, Leviathan." she says to me.

We part and stare into each other's eyes. Tigris smiles; I think she can read my mind. She must know that I want to kiss her. She must also know that I want to do much more than just kiss her.

"Tigris," I say. "Can I . . . ."

"Of course you can." she says. "It's what I want."

We begin to kiss, and at this moment, it feels as if I'm no longer capable of doing anything evil; it feels like I'm in a world of paradise. And, the thought of me being with my one true love again, after thousands of years, excites me.

After a long time, Tigris and I part from our lip lock. We then lie down on a soft patch of grass.

"I'll take care of you, Leviathan." Tigris says, cuddling up next to me. "Don't you worry." She produces a silver ring from her robes; *my* silver wedding band! She slips it onto my left ring finger.

"My ring." I say.

"We're still married, Leviathan." Tigris tells me; she shows me her elegant ring I had given to her on our wedding day.

"Indeed, we are . . . but Tigris, besides this, it is *I* that should be taking care of *you*." I stroke her dark sandy-black curls. "You are so precious to me; so delicate." A thought runs through my head. "Do you want to . . . do something?"

"Do what?" Tigris asks.

"Make love. Do you want to make love?"

"Yes, I want to."

"Then, let's do it."

We start kissing. I begin to remove her robe, but she stops me. I am puzzled; Tigris had never refused to have sex with me before.

"What's wrong?" I ask.

"It'll have to wait." she tells me.

This is so strange; usually Tigris would be the one jumping on me! Every opportunity she got, she'd do it, and she enjoyed it . . . every single bit of it.

"Why does it have to wait?" I ask. "I'm cocked; I'm ready to start."

Tigris smiles; such a wonderful smile. My vision suddenly gets blurry.

"What's wrong with me?" I ask. "I can't see."

I begin to rub my eyes, but Tigris stops me.

"They'll bleed if you do that." she says.

"I can't see." I tell her. "My vision's blurry."

Suddenly, the crook of my right arm begins to hurt; I start to feel lightheaded.

"Leviathan." I hear Tigris say. "Everything will be okay."

"What?" I ask.

"You're waking up; I'll see you again. I promise."

I don't understand what she just said. Just then, I black out.

Who Stole My Blood?!

I wake up to see that I'm lying on my bed, in my room. I look around and see that nothing is out of place. I then look down and see a needle stuck in the crook of my right arm; there's a tube attached to it. It appears that blood has been drawn.

I remove the needle and rub the spot with my left hand. Suddenly, something catches my eye; there's a silver ring on my left ring finger. I bring my hand closer to my face to study it. I then get a shock; it's my silver wedding band!!!!

"Oh my god!!!" I shout. "She was here!!! She was here!!!"

I cover my face and begin to weep. My Tigris was here with me, and she gave me my wedding band back!!!

I sense a presence nearby, so I quickly recover myself.

"Leviathan," I hear a voice say. It's Powers; I know it because there's no lisp in his voice, like Rolfe. "Can I come in?"

"Yes." I say.

Powers enters my room.

"How are you feeling?" he asks.

"Uh—fine." I say. "Why?"

"Well, I got home from the post office and I saw you lying on the floor; you were unconscious. I tried to wake you up, but it wasn't working. Rolfe helped me put you in the bed. Oh, and after a while, I came to check on you, and I saw a needle and tube stuck in your arm."

"Why was there a needle in my arm?"

"I don't know, but I can guarantee you that blood was drawn."

"Rolfe. He must've drawn the blood from my arm."

Powers shakes his head; he disagrees with what I say.

"It couldn't have been Rolfe." he says. "He told me he didn't know you were out cold. He said that you were awfully quiet and figured that you were reading or taking a nap."

"Oh." I say. "So, how did that needle get in my arm?"

"You must've stuck it there."

"Excuse me?"

"Rolfe and I don't perform phlebotomy or bloodletting. A ghost may have done it." He chuckles; I'm not impressed.

"Are you trying to be smart with me? Because, if you are . . . ."

"I'm joking, Leviathan."

"I do bad things when I'm crossed, and you know this."

Powers says nothing more on the topic. And, on top of it all . . . I am a little thirsty. I won't attack Powers though; he hasn't given me a real good reason to do it.

Rolfe, on the other hand, seems a little suspicious. Despite being nice to me as I helped him paint, I think he's the one who drew blood from me.

"May I have a glass of orange juice, please?" I ask Powers.

"Sure." he agrees. "I'll be right back."

Powers leaves and I stare at my ring again. I think: *I drank that bromine, and I dreamed that Tigris came back to me. She has to be alive because she gave me my ring back!!*

Powers returns to my room with a glass of orange juice.

"Here you go, Leviathan." he says.

I take the glass from him and begin to drink the orange juice quickly; my craving for blood lessens, but it's still there. It's not so bad though.

I finish drinking the juice and I sit the glass on the desk.

"Thank you." I say to Powers. "I needed that; I was feeling parched."

"You're welcome." Powers tells me. "Can I get you anything else?"

"No, but do you have the time?"

Powers takes a look at his wristwatch.

"It's ten o' clock." he says. "I guess it's time for bed. Goodnight, Leviathan."

"Goodnight, Powers." I say.

The Golgohoth Plot

Powers exits the room and closes the door behind him. I then hear fumbling with the door; I hear something click.

I jump out of bed and walk over to the door; I turn the knob, but it won't budge.

"Powers!!" I shout. "Edward!! You locked the door!!"

I become angry; he doesn't trust me. Oh well, I don't blame him; who would?

"Great." I say and sit back down on the bed. "Just great. I should kill him next time I see him."

I am startled when I hear loud knocking on my bedroom window. I grab my dagger and slowly go over to check things out.

I unlock the window and look outside. Seeing nothing, I pull my head back inside.

"That's strange." I say. "I could've sworn something was out there."

I decide to leave the window open to let some of the cool night air come in.

Just as I turn to the bedroom door again, I hear rustling outside. I am then shocked when I see someone climbing through the window and into my bedroom.

"Leviathan," says a familiar male. "It's me."

I see that this male subject is tall, like me; he has a head of spiky dark-brown hair and a pair of emerald-green eyes that seem to burn straight through the things they stare at.

He is clad in black pants; no top. He has a utility belt around his waist that contains torture devices: Scalpels, spikes, shears, nails, a hammer, pliers, etc.

I see that there are long vines that snake up his forearms. Now, I know who I'm looking at.

"Levetin?!" I shout in surprise. "What are you doing here?! How did you find me?!"

"I have my ways, Leviathan." he says. He moves in closer to me. "I had to find you; I can't let you face Peteryx and his servants alone. You know this, right?"

"Yeah. Uh, Levetin, how did you get here from Los Angeles?"

"I traveled on foot; best way to do it."

I nod. I then walk over to the window and look out it again.

"What do you see?" Acanthus asks.

"A suburban neighborhood." I say. I pull my head back in. "Do you think Peteryx will find me here?"

"Yes."

I sigh. I then sit back down on my bed. Acanthus takes a seat in the rolling desk chair.

"Powers locked me in." I tell my brother.

"Edward Bentley." he says. "The historian."

"Yes. How do you know?"

"It doesn't matter. Your best friend was looking for you today."

"Mordecai?"

"Yeah. He said that he had something to tell you."

"I see. I guess I'll try to contact him when I think he's home."

"He's taken to chat rooms more often."

"He has, huh?"

"He'll learn the consequences of them soon enough."

I lie back on my bed. I hear the creak of the chair as Acanthus stands up; he walks over to the bed and sits down next to me.

I grasp his right forearm and allow my pointer finger to travel up the strong vines.

"My dear brother." I say, turning my gaze to him. "This was not supposed to be your fate."

"I'm pretty sure it was." Acanthus says, pulling his arm back. "We're the way we are because of things we did."

"You mean *didn't do*. We were innocent kids."

"Don't fool yourself, Leviathan."

I sigh and turn my gaze toward the ceiling again.

"I wonder if my passages made it to the post office safely." I say.

"They did." Acanthus says, patting my knee.

"How do you know?"

"I have my ways, Leviathan."

"Powers doesn't trust me."

"Well, of course he doesn't trust you; you're a tyrant. If I were you, I wouldn't trust myself."

"Really?"

"You tell me. Besides, Powers also knows that we're brothers."

"If he doesn't trust me, then why did he take me in?"

"They want to study your body chemistry. If they had the opportunity to become immortal, like the both of us, they'd be glad to . . . especially Powers."

"Why?"

"You'll know why soon."

I sit up.

"I think that one of them stole my blood." I say. "I think they *are* trying to become like us."

"You'd love to kill them both." Acanthus says. "Right?"

"I guess so."

"The answer's yes, Leviathan; you're a killer. You should have no hesitation in killing someone who would take from you. Remember the Nicaraguan maid?"

"Yes."

"I would've killed her."

"Well, of course *you* would've; you're the Deathbringer."

"What's that supposed to mean?"

"Nothing."

"Bullshit."

I allow myself to fall back onto the bed again. My brother mimics me and does it, too.

"Does the police know?" I ask.

"About what?" Acanthus asks.

"Do the police know that I killed that officer, and the Mexican, and the racist pushover?"

"No, but they have a hunch."

I turn my head toward my twin; he does the same.

"Why did you not kill Peteryx, Levetin?" I ask.

"Peteryx lives for revenge, Leviathan." he replies. "But I believe that you'll overthrow him. Those who live for vengeance will not prevail."

"So, you and your partners didn't kill him because you want to see the final fight?"

"Not exactly, but good enough."

I smile and nod. I then stare up at the ceiling.

"Will you at least tell me how you managed to snatch up the Chicanos?" I ask.

"I credit Balcanicus and Spinosus for most of it." Acanthus says. "I knew about the stolen limousine and the fake license plate."

"I figured it was a fake."

"The police ran the plates, after the gang was rounded up; they were registered to a two-thousand-one Toyota Camry; owner's name was Lisa Colón, age twenty-four. She was reported missing a year earlier."

"Where is Miss Colón now?"

"She's dead."

"No surprise."

"And they threw her body in a wood chipper; tossed her remains in the ocean. She became fish food . . . fast."

"I see. So, what was it like killing Juan Jimenez?"

"Refreshing." he grabs the pair of pliers from his utility belt. "I used this to grasp his tongue while I slowly cut it out with a pair of dull rusty scissors."

"I heard that you cut his ears off, too."

"Yes, I did; I even tried talking into them, just to see if he could hear me."

"Levetin, that's sick."

"I finished him off when I shoved my thumbs into his eyes. I think I felt his brain."

"Okay, I've heard enough." I sit back up. "Your methods of torture are twisted."

"Are you sure you're not getting soft on me, Leviathan?" he asks as he sits up. "I want you to be able to defeat your worst enemy."

"I will."

"I will be here in Vegas until you get the job done." He looks down at my left hand; he stares at my wedding band. "Leviathan, did you get married?"

"No." I say.

"Then, what are you doing wearing that?"

"It's from Tigris."

"I'm sorry?"

"It's my old wedding band. I know it is; the vow is on the inside."

"Never to leave, never to part. My darling Tigris, I love you with all my heart."

I stare at my brother confusingly. How does he know what my wedding band's vow says?

"How did you know?" I ask.

"I have my ways, Leviathan." he says.

"You have your ways, yes. I realize this, my brother, but tell me now . . . do you have a plan for me to slay Peteryx?"

SIERRA J. BALL

"That's for *you* to figure out, Leviathan. Peteryx is not my fight; he's yours."

"But . . . what about that thing you said that you and Dante made him do in Galilee?"

"Never mind that; I'll tell you later. Now," Acanthus gets up and walks to the door. "How do you plan to escape this place for the night?"

"Oh, Levetin, I'm not going out tonight."

"Yes, you are. Peteryx isn't sitting back and waiting for you; he's out and about, causing a stir. Balcanicus and Spinosus are seeking out his Anubis members and destroying them."

"I can take them on."

"Peteryx is your fight, not the wild dogs." he twists the door knob. "You can break this door down, you know. If you can break through a solid brick wall and a steel cage, you can definitely get through this flimsy thing."

"I don't cause disturbances; I'm more of a silent predator."

"Now, that's the Leviathan I know." He walks over to the open window and looks out it. He seems to be looking around for any signs of danger; like I can't sense it? "It's not really that late; why don't you go out and explore your new surroundings?"

"Do you think I should explore Vegas?"

"If you want to get familiar with the city, and you want to get a feel of where Peteryx may be, I would explore it. And, don't forget your dagger."

I stand up from my bed and stretch a bit. I grab my dagger from the desk and stuff it in my back pocket. I then go over to the window and stand next to my brother.

"I'll check out Sin City." I agree. "Do you think anyone other than Peteryx or the Anubis people will recognize me?"

"That's a stupid question. Yes; they'll recognize you as Jonathan Note."

"But, I am Leviathan Golgohoth."

"Yes, you are."

"What if I am ambushed or caught?"

Acanthus turns and looks at me as if I'm really serious.

"Really?" he asks. "So, now you need advice? C'mon, Leviathan. You're a coldhearted bastard; get it together. The Golgohoth plot is to kill those who are contemplating killing you."

"Kill, or be killed."

"Now you get it. Oh, and by the way, don't call that bitch whose brother you killed; she doesn't need to know anything about what's going on here."

I look over at Acanthus.

"What did you say?" I ask.

"Oh," he starts. "About not calling her . . . or that she's a bitch?"

"Don't you say that!!"

"Leave her be; she's not to be trusted!!"

"I SAID SHUT UP!!"

With a great lunge, I shove my arms and hands into my brother's chest. As he falls out the window, he pulls me out with him; I hear a sickening crack as we hit the ground.

"Leviathan!!!!" Acanthus shouts. "How could you?!"

"What?" I ask. "What's wrong?!"

As we roll over onto the grass, I see that I have pushed Acanthus right out the window onto a hollow clay garden gnome; its head somehow found its way under his right armpit.

"Levetin!" I say. "I didn't mean it, I . . . ."

"Chill, Leviathan." he says as he pulls a piece of clay out of his arm. "I'll heal. Sadly, the garden gnome won't make it." He gets up and dusts himself off. "Why'd you push me?"

"You called Jessica a bitch." I say as I get up.

"She *is* a bitch, Leviathan. You have to believe me; I've never lied to you."

"Enough, okay? What do I do now?"

"Seriously, Leviathan? Hunt for Peteryx. Try to stay well-hidden though."

"And what about you?"

"I have to find my acanthus boys; I heard that there's something suspicious about the dealers over at the Monte Carlo."

"Hardcore Vegas types."

"More than that, Brother. I may have to adjust to heavy artillery with them."

"And, I still say the worst thing that has happened in the history of the Immortal Trio is you being introduced to firearms."

"Either that, or when Arachne started using Sadist and Masochist techniques to lure rapists to their demise."

Acanthus chuckles. He then pats me on my shoulder.

"Good luck out there." he says. "If you need assistance, I'm just a foliage away."

"I follow you." I tell him.

We part and go our separate ways, like we have done plenty of times in the ancient past.

Showdown At The Monte Carlo

Leviathan may do the exact opposite to what I just said; if I tell him to look for a certain someone of something, he'll disregard my advice and do something else. It's no wonder our parents were always yelling at him and not me.

I, Acanthus of Corinth, must do my own thing now; I have to find my servants, Balcanicus and Spinosus. I will meet them at the Monte Carlo and help them eliminate those Anubis pests that are waiting to foil my brother's plans of stomping Peteryx in the ground.

Leviathan was right: The worst thing that could've happened to me was being introduced to firearms. I love them!! They explode, and the person you want dead falls down!! I let Balcanicus and Spinosus full-well know that firearms will be a part of our plan to rid my twin of these stepping stones.

11:23pm—I race through the streets and locate the magnificent Monte Carlo on Las Vegas Boulevard; I make my way over to it, ready for action.

"Tarsus," I call out to Balcanicus by his other name.

"Master," says a familiar voice. I see Balcanicus standing off to the right side of me; his built figure gives off an intimidating appearance (not to me, but to others), and his dirty-blond hair is brighter than usual in the extreme lights of the hotel/casino.

Spinosus is on the left side of where I am; his dark-brown hair and scruffy beard are the perfect camouflage for someone who is a monster trying to hide.

"We located at least fifty in there." Balcanicus asks me. "Are we ready?"

"You tell me." I say. "Do you have what I asked for?"

"Oh, yes, Master. We got the best stuff available."

Balcanicus produces a massive shotgun, two magnums, and two assault rifles with scopes attached to them.

"Silver chased." Spinosus says.

"Silver." I say as I take the magnums. "Splendid."

"They hate silver." Balcanicus says, passing one of the rifles to Spinosus. "They're just like Werewolves."

"And Vampires." Spinosus replies.

I smile as I get ready to attack.

"On my cue." I say.

"Yes, Master." Balcanicus and Spinosus say in unison.

"They'll be disguised as normal Humans, but we will know who's Human and who's not. Their scent is so different."

"And we're doing this at Leviathan's leisure?" Balcanicus asks me.

"Yes." I say.

"But, Master, look at all the stuff he's done in the past to . . . ."

"To what? Harm me? He would never."

"He doesn't care about you; he thought that my cheesy disguise was really you."

"Yes, he does care. And besides, you are a chameleon, are you not? You could disguise yourself as anyone."

"So," Spinosus says. "What's the main point in doing this?"

"To help Leviathan's run-in with Peteryx to be a lot easier." I tell him. "Enough said; we attack."

Balcanicus, Spinosus and I are ready to take on the Anubis servants, loyal to Peteryx, that hide within the walls of the Monte Carlo.

I cock back the hammers of the two magnums simultaneously. My servants and I head inside in a horizontal line.

"Reservation, please." says the doorman.

"Sure." I say. "Here it is."

I aim one of the magnums to his forehead; I pull the trigger. Almost instantaneous, a blood spatter pattern stains the door.

As the doorman falls to the floor, we push the doors open and head inside.

We see people gathered around the craps and blackjack tables; once we aim our weapons at them, they scream and begin to scatter like cockroaches.

We scope out who's Human and walk by. However, we do see the Anubis servants (those who have fierce eagle-like eyes) mingled in with them, and we open fire.

As my followers go after a group of hesitant Peteryx-mongers, I go after what appears to be the ringleader of the bunch; I follow him up a flight of stairs, shooting at him as I go.

"You'll never take me alive, Deathbringer!!" I hear him shout.

I fire another shot; it hits him in the ankle. He cries out and staggers up the stairs onto the overhead balcony. Once I make it to him, I snatch him up by his garments and hold him over the edge.

I read the fear in his red embers for eyes; I can smell it as well. I stare into his eyes a few more seconds before I release him over the railing; I watch as he falls to his death at about 70 feet above; he smacks the floor and spatters like a watermelon.

The gunfire below begins to minimize; Balcanicus and Spinosus must've finished their job as well.

I take the easy way down the flight of stairs; I ride the railing sideways as I hold the magnums out in front of me. Once I reach the bottom floor, I skid across it on my knees. I slow to a stop and look back and forth. I then hear a shotgun blast from the left side of me; I'm sprayed in a fine mist of gunpowder-scented blood and there's a thud behind me. I turn and see that a member of the Anubis group had been blasted, and Balcanicus was responsible.

"Whoa," I say as I gather myself up.

"He was about to take your head off, Master." Balcanicus tells me. I see that my servant is right; the Anubis guy had a huge double-bladed axe in his hands.

"Close call," Spinosus says.

"Come, my boys." I say. "We leave this trash to the law."

My servants and I rush out of the Monte Carlo and into the hot Vegas night.

Bellagio For A Bit

As I walk down the sidewalk on the Vegas strip, I can't help but wonder how Levetin's plan to kill the Anubis servants at the Monte Carlo will work out.

I see my brother's alleged destination in the distance, but I decide to not go there; I think I'll go somewhere else to search for clues on Peteryx's whereabouts.

I pass people walking down the sidewalks; they look like they're having a peaceful time. I then walk over to a middle-aged man who is counting coins.

"Excuse me, sir." I say. "I'm new here, and I don't know my way around."

"Well," he says. "Look no further; you're in the right spot to have a good time."

"Well, can you tell me where a good place to gamble is?"

"A good place to gamble?! Everything here is Vegas certified, otherwise, it would be somewhere else."

"Oh. Well, what would you recommend?"

The man points to the Monte Carlo.

"That is one of the best hotel/casinos here in Vegas." he tells me.

"Oh, yeah." I say, remembering that Acanthus and his boys are most likely heading there to wreak havoc. "I've heard of that place. I think I'll go there; thank you, sir."

I dash across the street, avoiding on-coming traffic and getting a few insults. When I'm near the Monte Carlo, I look around for my brother and his followers; not present.

"Maybe later." I say and walk down the Vegas strip.

As I go a little further, I notice a beautiful and magnificent fountain display out front by a place called the Bellagio; I decide to visit this place for a while.

11:23 pm—I enter the splendid hotel/casino. I see a bar section, so I head over to it and sit down.

"Bartender," I say, waving to her. She approaches me.

"Yes, sir?" she asks. "What can I get for you?"

"Can I get a scotch on the rocks, please?"

"Would you like a bowl of pretzels to go with it?"

"Okay."

The bartender nods. She then gets out a glass and fills it with some ice cubes; she pours some Jack Daniels over them. She then sits the drink next to me and fetches a bowl and fills it with pretzels; she gives them to me.

"I'll be working on getting the money to pay for this." I tell her.

"Don't worry." she says. It's on the house . . . Jonathan Note."

She knows who I am. Perhaps she's pretending to be someone that she really isn't?

I reach into my back pocket and grip the handle of my dagger. Will I really cause a stir in this here grand casino by killing her? Not tonight; I sense no threat emitting from her. She's a Human; I smell the familiar essence that tells me.

I remove my grip from my dagger and bring my arm forward; I grasp my drink and bring it to my lips; I take a sip.

Just then, a young and attractive redhead sits down next to me.

"Hi there." she says, batting her eyelashes at me. "You remind me of someone I know."

Anger begins to build inside my chest; I'm not very attracted to redheads. Or, better yet, I despise them. I had a little fling with one in the past in Sparta, and it was no good for me. Sure, it was a good screw, while it lasted, but it wasn't what I was hoping for, and I had to end it, with bloodshed. Rolfe Bentley's lucky that he isn't a woman, but he sure carries himself like one.

"Do you know me?" I ask the redhead.

"I know I have seen you before." she tells me. "You look so very familiar."

"Yeah, I get that a lot. Look, if you don't mind, I'd like to be left alone; move away."

"Oh, I'll leave, but I just wanted to make chit-chat." she scoots close to me, and I am sickened by the smell of her perfume; too strong. "You look like an albino."

I *am* an albino, you dumb broad!! Can't you see that? Are you sure you're not a blonde in disguise??

"Sorry, honey," I say. "I'm not interested. Can you move along now?"

"Well," she says. "Although your offer is a good one, I just can't accept."

"Are you telling me no?"

"Guilty."

My god, what a bossy little chick she is. What does she want with me? I don't see any evil intentions in her, so what could she possibly be after?

A thought pops into my head; I can get rid of her if I kill her. Acanthus wonders if I'm turning into a cream puff, so I'll show him that I can still get my hands bloody.

"Hey," I say, smiling. "I'm sorry, but I didn't ask you who you are."

"The name's Cherry." she says. "Cherry Davidson. And, I think I know who you are . . . aren't you Jonathan Note?"

I stare at her for a few moments.

"No." I say. I'm actually telling her the truth.

"Oh, but of course you are." Cherry says. "I heard the barkeeper say so."

"She's wrong."

"Well, you didn't correct her."

I didn't; I wanted to stab her, but I didn't do that, either. Plus, I'm beginning to think that this woman isn't really a blonde in disguise.

"You're right." I say. "I'm just trying to hide, but it's hard to conceal your identity when you're an albino."

"And a celebrity." Cherry says. She then reaches into her purse and pulls out a slip of paper; she hands it to me.

"What's this?" I say as I unfold the paper. On it is written: Cherry—702-555-2365.

"Call me sometime." she says.

"No can do. I'm married." I flash her my ancient wedding band. "I'm a faithful husband."

"Well, perhaps so, but maybe you can stray once. Think back to when you were a bachelor."

Just as I am about to shred the paper in front of her, I begin to hear screaming from a distance; it's coming from outside the Bellagio.

"COME QUICK!!!!" a guy shouts. "SOME PSYCHOPATHIC GUNMEN ARE SHOOTING UP THE MONTE CARLO!!!!"

A bunch of people head outside to see what's going on. I have a big feeling I know who's responsible for the attack on the casino.

I rush outside, and Cherry follows me. I see a large crowd of people rushing toward our way; they're screaming and crying in fear.

Levetin, I think. *I just missed you; what are you doing to benefit me?*

I feel someone grasp my hand.

"Why don't we get out of here?" Cherry suggests.

"I'm going home to sleep." I tell her.

"Honey, this is the city that never sleeps. C'mon; I like walks. Let's go."

We walk, hand in hand, away from the Bellagio.

Well, Levetin, I think. *While you're doing what you're doing, I'll be getting my hands dirty as well. I'll show you that I am not weak.*

Hoe Down

s Cherry and I walk, I think: *What a demanding little bitch. She's so pushy; I hate that in women. I have to get away from her . . . or else. Hmm . . . well, I am kind of thirsty, and . . . what would twin brother Levetin do???? I did agree to get my hands dirty.*

"So, Cherry," I say. "Shall I call you when I get home?"

"Of course, Jonathan." she says. "You can call me anytime you want to."

"Perhaps, but what would my darling wife think about that?"

"Log me in your cell phone as your mom or a sibling. Do you have any brothers or sisters?"

"I have a twin brother, but he's . . . ."

"Good. Use his name for me."

If she knows who Acanthus of Corinth is, perhaps she wouldn't want that name as her secret identity. He'd find her himself and flay her alive.

"So, Cherry," I say. "Where are we going?"

"I love the desert." she says. "The temperature is perfect at night."

"What are we going to do in the desert?"

"I can think of something."

I chuckle. We are then silent. I look over at Cherry as we walk; she's got this stupid smile on her face. I think I'll carve it off with my dagger shortly.

I then notice something shining from an opening of her purse; I see that it's the barrel of a gun . . . a stainless steel .45 caliber revolver. I can faintly smell gunpowder, so I know it's loaded, or it has been fired recently. I wonder if she carries that thing for protection. If so, wouldn't it be attached somewhere to her body, and not in her purse?

Without her noticing, I discreetly grasp the barrel of the firearm and pull it from her purse. I then stealthily attach it to one of my belt loops.

"Cherry," I say.

"Yes, Jonathan?" she asks, looking up at me; I'm a little taller than she is, obviously.

"Do you like Las Vegas?"

"Like it? I love it!! You make excellent money out here. What about you? It's a lot different from Hollywood, right?"

"I live in Los Angeles, not Hollywood."

"Same place."

What an idiot, I think. I wonder how many men had to avoid bursting out laughing at her, or smacking her around like a punching bag?

We make it to the desert. I start to think: *She's going to find out who I am eventually, and I'm going to kill her; I'm going to prove to Levetin that I'm not a wimp. Plus, my thirst for blood is painful right now. I may as well have a midnight snack.*

Just as we arrive, Cherry stops walking; she puts her arms around my neck and begins to kiss me.

As we kiss, I reach around my waist and place my right hand around the handle of the revolver. I then give Cherry a surprise; I bite her bottom lip.

"Ow!!" she says, pulling back; she touches her lip. I have drawn blood. "Jonathan, why did you . . . ."

I aim the revolver right at Cherry's head and cock the hammer back.

"Oh my god . . . ." she stammers. She goes to look into her purse, but I stop her.

"No need to search." I say. "This is yours. Now, walk."

"But, Jonathan, I can't just . . . ."

"No Jonathan. I said walk."

"But I . . . ."

"WALK, DAMN IT!!!"

She begins to walk further into the desert. I keep the revolver pointed to the back of her head this time.

We continue to walk until I decide that we are far enough from civilization.

"Stop." I say. "This is far enough; turn around."

Cherry slowly turns around and faces me; she looks very frightened.

"What are you doing?" she asks, coming close to tears. "Please, Jonathan, what is this?!"

"That's not my name." I tell her.

"What? Yes, it is. You're Jonathan Note."

"That person no longer exists." I move closer toward Cherry; I keep the revolver pointed at her. "My real name describes me perfectly."

"But . . . you're Jonathan Note."

"Jonathan Note is a lie!! My name is Leviathan Golgohoth!! I am a six-thousand year old tyrant."

"No, you're not!! No one can live tha . . . ." she stops for a moment; I can tell she's thinking. And, I think I know exactly what she's thinking; she's putting two and two together. "You told me that you have a twin brother."

"Levetin Golgohoth." I say and smile. "Acanthus of Corinth. Now, sit down before I do away with you."

Cherry does what she is told. I aim the gun at her heart.

"The Immortal Trio's Deathbringer." she says. "It's just a myth."

"So," I say. "I suppose I'm a myth as well? I stand here, a tangible being."

"But . . . ."

"Acanthus of Corinth is very real . . . and he's the one who fired shots in the Monte Carlo; he did it to protect me, his twin brother; his flesh and blood!!"

"No! It's not true!!"

"Yes, it is. Now, don't try anything stupid."

"Are you going to kill me?"

"Maybe, maybe not; it all depends how you play your cards. No puns."

"So, there's a chance that I'll get to live?"

"There's a slim one; I'm not the Deathbringer."

I'm not the Deathbringer . . . but I *am* a murderer.

"Actually," I continue. "The chances you'll live are slim and none."

"Huh?!" she asks.

"Or better yet . . . make that no chance."

"OH GOD!!"

I kneel down next to Cherry and place the gun barrel in between her eyes; a smile grows on my face.

"You know," I say. "Like my brother, I have to kill in order to gain something that I need. And, if I let you go, you won't get too far anyway."

"Why?" Cherry asks.

"Really? You have no idea why? REALLY?!"

I whack her in the head with the revolver; she screams and covers her face.

"Please, don't!!!" She cries. "NO!!!"

"Shut up, bitch!!" I shout. "You wouldn't be in this predicament, if only you had walked away when I told you to, but instead, you needed a piece of ass and couldn't take no for an answer. Now, you're on the brink of destruction." I step away from her, but keep the gun aimed at her. "Isn't this lovely?"

"Are you a serial killer?" Cherry voice shakes uncontrollably.

"Well . . . it's kind of obvious." I reach into my back pocket and pull out my dagger. Even though I plan to use the firearm in this death, I have to have my precious knife present to witness it.

"What are you going to do with that?" Cherry asks. My eyes burn with hate.

"We're going to play a little game." I say. "It's called the Quiet Game; it requires a sharp blade . . . and the removal of the tongue."

Cherry shuts her eyes and begins to whimper like a baby. Now that, I like; she's really exciting me.

"Shall we begin?" I ask.

"Please," she says. "Please, don't cut me."

I kneel down next to her again. Cherry continues to keep her eyes closed and whimper.

"Hey!" I shout at her. "Open your eyes; you need to see the blood."

She opens her eyes; she gasps when she sees that I am close to her again.

"Please, don't!!" she cries. Tears pour down her face.

"Shhhh . . . ." I say, grabbing my shirttail. "Stick your tongue out."

"Nooooo!"

"Stick it out. C'mon. You can do it; c'mon. You won't feel a thing; trust me."

Cherry slowly sticks her tongue out; I grasp it with my shirttail.

"It'll only be a second." I say as I position my dagger over her tongue. "It'll all be over soon. Shhhh, it'll all be over soon."

She whimpers some more and grasps my shoulders tightly. Her screams are loud as I carve into her tongue with my dagger; I can feel her trembling heavily; her nails digging into my flesh. My shirt is being spattered with blood. Within seconds, her tongue is free from her mouth.

Cherry lets go of my shoulders and begins to drag herself across the sand. Her hands cover her mouth; blood gushes from between her fingers along with muffled cries of pain.

"Oh, wait." I say as I follow her across the hot sand. "I wasn't supposed to do that."

She stops moving; she spits out a mouthful of blood onto the sand. She tries to speak, but her words are jumbled.

"I was supposed to pull your teeth out first." I say. "Aw, I should've asked my brother to lend me his pliers. Oh well, a severed tongue isn't too bad; you got off lucky."

Her cries for help are gurgled. She spits out more blood, which covers her chin and cheeks in a brilliant vermillion red; if I were Acanthus, the sight of it would make my eyes go coal-black with excitement.

"Do you want to live?" I ask.

Cherry nods her head yes.

"Why? I wouldn't want to live life as a mute." I yank her up and press my dagger to her throat. "Perhaps not hearing you will be better for me? Your muffled cries irritate me just as much as your voice did."

She begins to cry; a shower of blood covers my face.

"Can you tell me why you deserve to live?" I ask.

Cherry tries to tell me, but her words are way too jumbled up; it's like she's talking with a mouth full of cotton.

"I can't hear you." I say, leaning in closer. I can feel her hot breath on my right ear; flecks of blood sprinkle it. I stare into her eyes again.

"Shall I remove your ears?" I ask.

Cherry tries to scream, but more muffled sounds and blood gush out.

"Or perhaps I shall make a meal out of you?" I suggest. "I'll bet you're delicious."

Cherry tries to pull away from me, but I add pressure to her throat with the dagger.

"Now, now." I say. "It's not good to struggle with a killer." I smile and bring my lips closer to her left ear. "Perhaps I let you go?"

She nods quickly. Had she completely forgotten what I had said? If I let her go, Acanthus will find her and finish her off.

"No can do." I tell her. I take the dagger away from her throat and place the barrel of the gun against her temple. "It won't work. It's just not good enough."

Cherry reaches out to try and touch my cheek, but I slap her hand away.

"You're not good for me." I tell her. "I'm a married man."

It is true. Tigris and I never divorced; I was widowed. Now, she's alive, and I'm wearing my wedding band.

Cherry begins to make more muffled sounds; I believe I hear the phrase: *Please, don't kill me.*

"Hush," I say. "Be quiet before you lose more than just your tongue." I smile. "I must kill you because I am so very hungry."

She screams loudly and yanks herself out of my grasp; she begins to run for the highway, screaming for help in the best way she can.

Before she can reach the highway and flag down a vehicle for help, I point the revolver in the air and pull the trigger; the sound is so loud that tongue-less Cherry falls, facedown, onto the sand and covers her head.

"Stay!" I say, cocking the hammer again. "Good." I walk over to her and plop down on my knees. "Face me." I grip her upper arm and turn her over; she lies on her back and stares up at me. The blood on her face is coated in a thick layer of sand, giving her the appearance of having a beard. "I want your blood, and you *will* give it to me freely. I am hungry, and I need blood to live."

Cherry is shaking her head no. I cover her mouth to avoid having to hear her muffled screams.

"Shut—up." I demand, pointing the gun barrel right between her eyes. "Or, I will pull this trigger." I slowly remove my hand from her mouth. "Now . . . how do you want me to take your blood? Do you want it quick and clean, or do you want it slow and painful?"

Cherry starts to muffle something that sounds like neither option.

"Did you say slow and painful?" I ask.

She muffles no.

"Okay." I say. "I'll take my time."

I present my dagger again; I grasp Cherry's right wrist.

"You know," I say as I cut into her skin. "The sight of blood makes me excited; it gives me intense pleasure. When I drink it," I bring her wrist to my mouth and begin to draw blood from her. Once slightly satisfied, I take her arm away. "Mmm . . . it gives me a rush." I can feel myself getting aroused; my pants get tighter. I feel the impulse to just whip it out and work it.

Instead of satisfying my burning urges, I conveniently slip my hand up Cherry's dress; I sigh when I touch her between her legs.

"I need more blood." I say, slipping a finger inside her; she tenses up and begins to sob. I remove my hand and go to cut her throat, but she begins to mumble more stuff; I clearly hear the words: *I don't want to die.*

Ah, she says the phrase I want to hear. She's decided to end the game, so I must kill her now; I must take what she has.

"And now," I say as I yank her up from the sand. "You regret having been born."

I place the gun to her forehead and pull the trigger; I am sprayed in the face with blood and brain goop. Cherry falls back onto the sand and I smile brightly.

"Good deal." I say. "The deed is done."

I take my dagger and cut into Cherry's flat chest. I rip her heart out; it's still beating slightly. I take a huge bite out of it as if it's a fresh ripe peach.

"Yum." I say. "It's warm. I love it."

I devour the rest of Cherry's heart and I drink her blood. It has a slightly sour taste to it; she has used drugs in her past.

"Sour blood won't last long." I say.

"And," says a familiar voice. "She was a prostitute."

I see that it's Draken Hark; he kneels down next to Cherry's dead body.

"She had a controlling way with men." he says. "Cherry Davidson; lovely on the outside, but sinful on the inside."

"Oh well." I reply. "She deserved what she got; it's not like anyone's going to notice her absence from the planet."

"Only if you bury her."

"I'm not burying that hooker; that would be doing her a favor. I'll let the buzzards have their way with her."

Draken Hark chuckles. He stands up and stares at me.

"You know," he says. "I think you have made your brother proud by using his methods of torture."

"Yes." I say.

Draken Hark pats me on my shoulder.

"That's my boy." he says. "You've done beautifully this evening, but now, it's time to go back to the Bentleys'."

"I think I should stay out here; Peteryx expects me."

"Peteryx is laying low and allowing the Anubis dogs to hunt you down. However, it appears that Levetin loves to clean house."

"He was the one who opened fire on the Monte Carlo, isn't he?"

"You were right when you said it to Cherry." Draken Hark touches my shoulder. "It is time; you must get some rest. You've seen enough of Vegas for tonight."

We are engulfed in a bluish-white light; the same light I saw thousands of years ago when Draken Hark took me away from Mesopotamia for the first time. A few seconds later, I'm back in my bedroom at the Bentley residence.

"Well, Leviathan," Draken Hark says. "How's Vegas treating you so far?"

"You can see how it's treating me." I tell the Death Dealer. "It's a jungle."

"Indeed, it is. Well, I do have to depart now."

"Will I see you again?"

"Of course; and, remember to confide in your brother. He said that when you need him, he's just a foliage away." Draken Hark bows. "Goodnight, Leviathan."

"Goodnight, Draken Hark."

Draken Hark vanishes. I then sit down on my bed.

"What a night." I say and lie back.

I look over at the door. It might be unlocked by now; maybe it isn't. I'm not bothered by it; I'm so tired.

"I'll worry about it in the morning." I say to myself.

I close my eyes and allow myself to drift to sleep.

Monte Carlo Aftermath

Balcanicus, Spinosus, and I watch as the local coroner orders a team of forensics workers to carry out the dead carcasses of the Anubis servants from the Monte Carlo, one after the other. There are a handful of curious bystanders watching and talking amongst each other.

"There has to be at least fifty or more, sir!" one of the team members says to the coroner. "Somebody massacred the place!!"

"I don't think it was just one person." another member on the forensics team says. "As you can see," he points to a bullet wound in the forehead of one of the bodies. "This guy was shot with an assault rifle; look closely. It looks like one shot, but when you get closer, it's actually two shots; that rifle had to have had a scope attached to it. And look here," He points to another wound. "This is a blast from a shotgun."

"Wow." I say. "They're good."

"Did we get them all, Master?" Spinosus asks me.

"I think we got all the ones here; there's more out there though. You have to consider places like Mandalay Bay, Caesar's Palace, and of course, the Luxor."

"What about Bellagio?" Balcanicus asks.

I think about it; Leviathan was just there, not long ago. I saw him walk out of the place with an attractive redhead. And, he killed her; I'm so proud of my twin brother.

"If there were any Anubis servants at the Bellagio, Tarsus," I start. "Leviathan would've sensed it; there was no commotion there."

"But, I saw a bunch of people rushing out of there when we exited the Monte Carlo."

"Probably because they heard the gunshots and the screaming; Bellagio isn't that far away from Monte Carlo."

We watch in secrecy as the forensics team zip the dead bodies in large heavy duty black bags and load them up in several coroner's vehicles.

"Do you think we'll have to deny this?" Spinosus asks. "Like Leviathan did with those guys he killed in Los Angeles?"

"People saw us." I tell my servant. "They will give tips to the police, and we will openly admit that we caused this problem. They won't stop us; we're too strong."

"Where is Leviathan now?" Balcanicus asks.

"He killed a hooker and went home." I say.

With Drakengaard Hark, I think. Those Eternal Ones were so involved with his past life that I could hardly get time to express my true self to him. I think I'll have to fix that real soon.

"Where do we go now, Master?" Spinosus asks me. "What do we do?"

"Nothing." I say. "We wait."

As my servants watch the forensics team work, I place my hand against the palm tree we're standing by and listen to what it has to say.

You were spotted, Master Acanthus, the tree says.

"Spotted, you say?" I ask it.

One of the Anubis dogs managed to slip away.

"Slip away?"

He will tell Peteryx what went on at the Monte Carlo; more enforcements will move out in an attempt to destroy your brother.

"They will not kill Leviathan; they only want to take him to Peteryx. Peteryx wants revenge, but he's not going to get it."

Master Acanthus, sir. Peteryx knows now that you're involved in this.

"What's he going to do? He's afraid of me."

Indeed, he is. He may send the Anubis servants out to kill you, while he deals with Leviathan.

"Then so be it; that's the way it will be. I'll take out every single one of those mutts, and Leviathan will have Peteryx's head."

But Master . . . .

"Enough, Palm Tree. You're such a Doubting Thomas." I pat the tree's trunk. "I am Acanthus of Corinth; I cannot die just yet. Everything will be fine."

Everything will be . . . fine.

"Imhotep Feathervault will fall."

Imhotep Feathervault . . . will . . . no, Master!! He's far more sinister than he used to be!! He has the power of the scarabs.

"As he had for thousands of years. He's no different from what he used to be."

I take my hand away from the doubting palm tree and look over at Balcanicus and Spinosus; they are looking around and watching out for anything suspicious.

"Come, boys." I say. "We must make haste; Peteryx hasn't given up yet."

"Yes, Master." they say simultaneously.

We take off down the Vegas strip, ready for anything that may ambush us.

First Morning With The Bentleys

I wake up. Today is Monday . . . March 15th, 2004.

I get up and stretch. I then go over to the door and turn the knob; it's unlocked, that's good. They have decided to release me from my temporary prison.

I find the bathroom and see that my face is spattered with blood; that hooker's blood.

"I can't let them see me like this." I say to myself. "Not just yet. Even though they know about my past killings in the ancient world, I can't let them see blood on me." I turn on the lavatory faucet. "They'll wonder where and who it came from."

I wash the blood from my face. I then dry off and rush back to my room, where I change into some fresh clothes; the ones I slept in were soaked in blood.

I walk down the hall and I enter the kitchen. I see Powers and Rolfe; they're sitting at the table and eating breakfast.

"Leviathan." Powers says. "Good morning."

"Good morning, Powers." I say. "Good morning, Rolfe."

"Good morning, Leviathan." Rolfe says. "Would you like some breakfast?"

I chuckle; that lisp in his voice is rather funny. I've heard that same voice in many of the male fashion designers out in L.A.

"No, thanks." I say, getting a glass. "I'll just have some orange juice, if that's okay."

"Sure. Help yourself to as much as you want."

I pick up the pitcher of orange juice and pour myself some; I take a sip.

"Tell me, Powers," I say. "Why did you lock my bedroom door last night?"

"I want to keep you safe." Powers tells me. "You know, you *are* Leviathan Golgohoth."

"Keep me safe from what?"

I take another sip of orange juice. I then notice that Rolfe is just staring at me; he looks confused.

"Leviathan," he says. "Is that . . . blood?"

"Blood?" I ask. "Where?"

"Your right ear."

Dammit!! I forgot to wash it off!! I got the blood that was on my face, but I was totally oblivious to the blood on my ear . . . and Rolfe spotted it!

"Oh." I say, wiping my ear, trying to play it off. "That's not blood."

"It sure looks like blood." Rolfe says.

"No. It's . . . red ink."

"Red ink?" Powers asks.

"Yeah." I tell him. "It's from a red pen I found in the desk."

"Ronny never kept red pens; only blue and black ink pens."

I am caught in a lie. So what? What are they going to do? I am Leviathan of Mesopotamia; I am the deadliest of the six tyrants who walked the earth . . . . and they're Humans.

"Look," I say. "I'm just going to be in my room, if you guys need anything from me."

"Sure, Leviathan." Powers says.

I go back to my room and close the door behind me. I sit down at the desk; I decide to write some more of my chronicles. I get out a pen and some paper and I begin to write where I left off.

Arch-Peteryx? Alive?

An entire week had passed since Jesus ascended into Heaven to be with His Father. It was an early morning, and I decided to take a little walk around the town of Nazareth.

I decided to just let Molicles sleep while I ventured. I checked on her before I left, to make sure she was okay and all.

"I love you, Molicles." I had said to her before walking out the door.

I walked around the little town in Nazareth, saying hi to the people as I passed.

"Good morning, Lavan." a woman said to me. The word *Lavan* means "white" in Hebrew, and that's what the people here referred to me as; it sounds almost like they cut some stuff out from my first name.

After a while, I began to hear screaming in the distance; it was screams that you'd hear from someone who was frightened to death.

I decided to go and check out what was going on. As I continued onto a dirt path, I began to smell smoke; there had to have been a fire somewhere.

Suddenly, I saw this young man running up to me. It looked as if he had been crying; his face was all red and puffy. He approached me and gripped my shoulders.

"Lavan!! Lavan!!" he shouted. "It was awful!!!"

"What's going on?" I asked him.

"He just . . . went inside the house and it . . . it caught on fire!!"

"What? You're not making any sense. What house?"

"Your house!! It was this mysterious-looking man!! He went in, and then . . . the screams!!"

"Screams?!"

"Yes!! It was a child screaming!! My two sisters and I heard it!!"

My house was on fire!! And there was screaming coming from it; a child screaming . . . Molicles!!!

I ran past the young man and hurried back to my house as quick as I could. As I traveled, I could see a huge cloud of smoke billowing up to the sky; my eyes began to sting.

"No!!" I said to myself. "Why?! Why would someone set my house on fire?!"

When I arrived, I saw that my house was charred and black; it was obvious that fire had claimed it. However, when I walked inside, everything was how I last saw it; it was all okay. I became confused.

"What in the . . . ." I said to myself.

I begin to look around; I called out Molicles's name, but she wouldn't answer.

I searched the house some more, and what I saw next just horrified me. Lying in a corner was Molicles . . . or what was left of her, rather. She still had her shape, but her body was completely made up of ash; a look of fright was on her face. I touched her little cheek, and she disintegrated into a pile of dust.

"MOLICLES!!!!" I shouted. I knelt down next to the heap of ashes and began to weep.

Who could've done this? I thought.

My first hunch was the Immortal Trio, but it then occurred to me that they were all somewhere in Rome, and that none of them knew how to turn their victims into ash.

"Well, well, well." I heard a voice say. "If it isn't Leviathan Golgohoth. What a surprise."

I've heard that voice before; it was one of the most evil and cruelest voices I've ever heard; so dark and cunning. It had a low mellow tone to it, but I could still hear the sinister chill in it.

I stood up straight and turned around; I could hardly believe who I was looking at.

"Imhotep Feathervault?!" I said. "I thought that I . . . ."

"Though that you killed me?" he asked. "Wrong, tyrant."

"What are you doing here in Nazareth?!"

"That's funny; I was going to ask you the same thing." He moved in a little closer. "I've come to pay you back."

"Pay me back? What for?"

"Have you forgotten that quickly what you've done to me?! A tyrant never forgets!!"

I know now why Peteryx was looking for revenge. Back in the year 1900 B.C., I fought Imhotep Feathervault, better known as Arch-Peteryx, the Egyptian tyrant from Thebes. I beat him senseless and trapped him in a pit of scarabs; I had a feeling that he was stuck with those beetles until just recently. He smelled of salt and sand.

I stared at Peteryx; he looked the same, after nearly 2,000 years; that spiky coal-black hair with the red tips, that tan skin, and those bronze-yellow eyes.

Despite having the same features from many years ago, I notice that there were long black scars all over his face, hands, and legs; it had to have been the scarabs that made them, no doubt.

"Look at you." Peteryx said. "You haven't changed a bit, Leviathan; you look no different than you did two-thousand years ago."

"Indeed." I said to him. "And, I see that the scarabs have did a number on you."

"THE SCARABS?!?! No, tyrant. *I* made the gashes in my skin; I have allowed my body to become their dwelling. They bow to me!!"

So, I was wrong; it was Peteryx, and not the scarabs, who made the gashes. And, from what I understood, the scarabs had set up shop in Peteryx's body. Gross.

I noticed that he was holding something bundled up.

"Is that . . . ." I started. "A baby?"

"Why, yes it is." Peteryx said, staring down at it. "That little Greek girl you took care of somehow managed to acquire it."

"Whose baby is it for?"

"It's *my* baby. I'm its biological father, and I am going to take care of him."

"Over my dead body!"

"Precisely!!"

I am silent. Seeing another opportunity to speak, Peteryx continues on.

"When you left this place," he said. "The little girl woke up from sleeping; she left to look for you. I have acquired some news about your whereabouts, and I knew that you were traveling with a girl child, so I disguised myself as a commoner; I handed her this baby, and you know . . . no little girl can resist the charms a baby naturally has. When she asked me what the infant's name was, I ran away."

"Where did you go?" I ask.

"I came here, of course, of course. I knew that the little girl would eventually come back here after looking for you; she'd wait until you'd get back, yes. Well, what do you know . . . she came back, and I was here!! I then revealed myself to her."

"My poor little angel; she must've been afraid."

"Not exactly; she was a little tougher than I thought. I did inform her that I only wanted to talk to her, but she was still hesitant."

"She didn't believe you, did she?"

"No, no, no. She didn't. She wanted me to leave. I agreed to, but before I would leave, I wanted something from her."

"The baby."

"And her life; I wasn't leaving without either one, yes."

"So . . . you killed her."

"Yes; my scarabs came in handy."

"The scarabs."

"Yes; they live within the recesses of my body. They devoured my Egyptian viscera, they love my Egyptian blood, and they have decided that they shall stay with me."

I was absolutely right with my prediction; the scarabs had made a home out of Peteryx.

"What did they do?!" I shouted.

"I sent them out to drain her." he said.

"They drank her blood?!"

"Yes. They took her blood and left her skin and bones behind; she immediately turned into ash."

"What about the . . . ."

"The flames? Ah yes. Perhaps you thought that the flames did that to her; no. The flames were magic; they distracted the townspeople. I knew that you'd be drawn here by the screaming."

The child's screams were heard during the fire, I thought. *How could they have been Molicles's? According to Peteryx, she was dead before he set the flames to the house.*

"Whose screams did I hear?" I asked Peteryx.

"The girl's." he told me.

"Molicles?!"

"If that's her name, yes."

"How? You killed her before you set the house on fire!!"

"Ah, good thinking, Leviathan. You see," He moves in closer. "Once my scarabs devoured the girl's blood, a piece of her became a part of me; I can now . . . ."

He said, in Molicles's tiny voice, "Speak just like her."

"You monster!!"

"And, my magic worked!!" It was now his voice. "You're here!! And now, I finally get the payback I want!!"

I should've taken Molicles with me when I left the house. I messed up bad, and because I did, Molicles paid with her life. I had promised her that I would never let anything bad happen to her, and now, she was as dead as Coria.

I felt tears stream down my face.

"You really are pathetic, Leviathan." Peteryx said. "You weep over the most senseless things!! Why can't you be callous and cold . . . like your brother?"

"How do you know about my brother?"

"Well, who doesn't know about Levetin Golgohoth . . . Acanthus of Corinth?"

Many multitudes of people, good and bad, know about the Immortal Trio. Perhaps Peteryx did some extensive research after he found his way out of that pit?

"You really are weak." Peteryx told me.

"NO, PETERYX!!!" I shouted. *"You're* the one who's weak!! I loved that little girl, and you took her away from me!!"

The baby started to cry. The poor thing; I'd cry too if I had to be stuck with a worthless nothing like Arch-Peteryx Feathervault.

"Hush!!" he shouted at the infant. "Hush, now!! Shut up!!"

I hated to see him yelling in that baby's ear. I dashed my tears away and cleared my throat.

"Peteryx," I said. "Perhaps if you let me take care of the baby, I'll raise it right."

"No!!" he yelled at me. "He's *my* child, and I will raise him how I want!! He says with me!!"

"Well, can I at least hold him for a moment?"

Before Peteryx could say something else, I went over and took the baby from him; I stared into his eyes, and he immediately stopped crying. He even gave me a little smile.

The tears came to my eyes again. I thought: *My little Molicles held this precious child. I wonder if he cried, or if he was good . . . because he was away from Peteryx.*

"You precious little baby." I said to him. "What's your name?"

"His name is Jonathan." Peteryx told me. I looked over at him.

"How do you know that's his name?" I asked. "Tell me the truth . . . whose baby is this, really?"

"It is mine, and I named him." Peteryx reaches for it. "Now, it's time for you to hand him over, yes."

I began to back away.

"Yeah, sure." I said, chuckling. "You'll get him back . . . only when you pry him from my cold white tyrant grip."

Peteryx wasn't too happy about that.

"Leviathan," he said. "Give me my baby!!" A strange sharp pair of ivory-white teeth slid down from his top gums. "Now."

"No." I simply said.

"Yes!! Give—him—to—me!!"

"I said no!"

"NOW!!!"

"NEVER!!!"

"YOU'RE JUST JEALOUS!! You lost a child you loved, and now you want mine!!"

"Indeed, you're right, Peteryx. And, you are far from being father material." I smiled at the Egyptian tyrant. "It's payback, Peteryx."

Peteryx leaned his head back and began to moan. I didn't know what he was doing at first, then I saw it; big black beetles began to crawl out from the scars on his skin. He used the scarabs to kill Molicles, and I realized that he was going to do the same thing to me; the baby would most likely be killed in the process as well. Just to get rid of me, he'd put a child's life at stake; he already did it shortly before this.

"Peteryx!!" I shouted. "You're crazy!!"

I began to stomp on the scarabs as they approached me; Peteryx began to shake violently.

"NO!!" he shouted. "DON'T!! Scarabs, retreat!! Come back!!"

The scarabs turned around and went back to Peteryx. As they did, I climbed out of the window, with the baby in my arms, and ran away. I had to get away from that tyrant and his new family of disgusting beetles, so I ran as fast as I could, far away from there.

I collapsed underneath a tree and wept. I wept for Molicles; that poor sweet innocent little angel; how could Peteryx have done something as savage as kill her?!

I heard the baby moaning, and then it smiled.

"You sweet little thing." I said to him. "Why did Peteryx have you in his possession? Who are your real parents?"

Peteryx had told me that he was the biological father of the infant, but I didn't believe him. From what I heard, Imhotep Feathervault hated everyone and everything, especially women and children.

What was Draken Hark thinking when he chose that man to be his personal immortal?!

I shook the thoughts out of my head. I then turned my attention back to the baby.

"You're so cute." I said, kissing him on his cheek. "Why were you with Peteryx, really?" I pulled the swaddling cloth away from him and blew a raspberry on his tiny tummy; he started to laugh.

"Okay, okay." I said, laughing. "I'll stop."

The baby grabbed a lock of my white hair and tugged it.

"Hey, hey," I said. "Don't do that, little Jonathan." I wrapped the baby back up in the swaddling cloth and kissed his forehead. "Don't worry, little John. I won't let that monster take you away from me."

I got up and started to walk away; I stared up into the sky.

"I'll never forget you, Molicles Naustausis." I replied. "You were truly a brave little girl."

Mordecai Makes Contact

I stop writing when I hear the phone ringing; I pick it up.

Me: Hello?

Anonymous: Leviathan, it's me.

Me: Mordecai?!

Mordecai: Yep.

Me: The caller I.D. says you're calling from Los Angeles High.

Mordecai: Yes. I had to call you; Stu said that you tried calling yesterday, and I wasn't home.

Me: Yeah. You were at my mansion.

Mordecai: I was looking for you; I had to show you something. I saw Acanthus.

Me: He didn't try to harm you or anything, did he? You remember the Christmas tree incident, right?

Mordecai: Yes, but he said that any friend to you is a friend to him.

Me: Well, that's somewhat true . . . somewhat not.

Mordecai: Really?

Me: Yeah.

Mordecai: Well, he looks really cool and intimidating up close.

Me: I guess. Anyways . . . how's Anticlea?

Mordecai: She misses you.

Me: And I miss her. I'll be home soon though.

Mordecai: Of course. Look, Leviathan, Acanthus said that you are in Vegas and that he was going to find you.

Me: He has.

Mordecai: Wow. I hope he's not causing any trouble.

Me: Not on my end; he's helping me.

Mordecai: I see.

Me: Have you heard from Jessica?

Mordecai: I saw her today.

Me: At the school?

Mordecai: Yeah; the day after her brother's funeral, she's at school, laughing and talking with her friends.

Me: Huh?

Mordecai: She's also hanging around with Anson Vickers.

Me: Really? At the school?

Mordecai: No. Anson graduated from L.A. High a while ago. I saw him and Jessica at a local park. It looked like they were holding hands.

Me: That can't be right.

Mordecai: I know what I saw, Leviathan.

Perhaps Levetin is right about Jessica, I think.

Me: I had an interesting night last night; I went to the Bellagio.

Mordecai: That sounds nice. I've never been to Vegas; I hope to go soon.

Me: When all is good, so to speak. Anyways, what did you want to show me?

Mordecai: I wanted to show you this weird beetle I found outside the DeFranco house.

Me: A beetle?

Mordecai: Yeah; it almost looks like one of those scarab beetles you see in Egypt.

This is serious, I think. *Was Peteryx in L.A. before he went to Vegas, or did he have the Anubis guys patrol the place?*

Me: That's what you wanted to show me?

Mordecai: Yes, but there's more to it.

Me: What is it?

Mordecai: Acanthus said that an Egyptian guy called Arch-Peteryx is looking for you; he mentioned a pit of scarabs. I read about that in your earlier passages.

Me: Yes.

Mordecai: I . . . I didn't tell Acanthus about what I had found.

Me: I'm sure he knows about it anyway.

Mordecai: Perhaps. Well, I did give this some thought: What if it was Peteryx that left the beetle?

Me: It is certain. He's in Vegas now, and is looking for me.

Mordecai: Are you afraid?

Me: I fear no one.

Mordecai: I know. I got your passages in the mail.

Me: That's great; I knew you would. The next set should be coming soon.

Mordecai: Okay, great! I finished the ones you sent to me.

Me: Good boy. Listen, Mordecai . . . thanks for calling me. I have to go though; I have something that I need to do. Can I call you later, or you can call me?

Mordecai: Sure, Leviathan.

Me: I'll call you.

Mordecai: Thanks. Uh, Leviathan . . . .

Me: Yes?

Mordecai: Are you going to be okay? I mean, with the Egyptian looking for you?

Me: I'll be fine.

Mordecai: Okay. I'll talk to you later, then.

Me: Sounds good. And, Mordecai . . . whatever you do, do not come here to Vegas, even if you're just wanting to visit; I have a feeling Peteryx may know that you're associated with me.

Mordecai: Leviathan, I have to . . .

Me: No, Mordecai. Stay in L.A.

Mordecai: But I . . .

Me: Don't argue with me, Mordecai. I'll talk to you later.

Mordecai is silent for a few moments. He then sighs in agreement.

Mordecai: Okay.

Me: I'll talk to you later.

Mordecai: Okay. Goodbye, Leviathan.

Another Visit With My Wife

I hang up the phone after speaking with Mordecai. I then take the passages I have written so far and stuff them in a drawer of the desk.

"I need to pay my wife another visit." I say. "And maybe do stuff to her this time." I grab the volumetric flask of bromine and remove the cork. "Cheers."

I take a swig of the halogenous element and place the cork back into the flask; I hide it. I then lay back on my bed.

"Any time now." I say.

I suddenly begin to feel the effects; I thirst and my limbs twitch. I close my eyes, and in no time, I'm drifting; it feels like I'm falling.

I finally land on something soft; it feels like a bed. I start to moan. I then feel something running gently through my hair; it feels like fingers.

"Leviathan," I hear a voice say. It's Tigris. I open my eyes and see my first and only real love staring down at me and smiling.

"Tigris." I say, bringing my hand to her cheek. "My love."

"How are you feeling, Leviathan?"

"Great." I sit up and take her hands. "How are you, my beautiful wife?"

"I'm fine."

I look around; I see that I am in a beautifully furnished bedroom. Everything is colored gold, silver, and red.

"What a lovely place." I say. "Is this our bedroom?"

"It's whatever you want it to be, Leviathan." Tigris says to me. She kisses my temple. I place my arms around her and hold her close.

"I want to love you." I say. "Like a husband should love his wife." I slip my hand into her silk robe; I cup one of her magnificent breasts in my hand, feeling a sensation of life flowing into me. "I love you so much."

"Then make love to me, right now."

Now, *that's* what I've been wanting to hear; it has been over 5,600 years since I was inside her.

"Of course, my dear." I say to her.

We begin to kiss; I place gentle kisses on Tigris's neck and breasts.

"Do you remember our first time?" she asks as she gently caresses my head.

"Yes." I say. "Yes, I do; I think about it often."

"I still remember how you held me close and whispered to me that you love me."

"It was a very precious thing, and still is."

Tigris and I lay down on the soft bed.

"Oh, Leviathan," she says. "I've missed you so much."

"I have missed you, too." I tell her as I feel myself growing. "My goddess; you just don't know."

After a few moments of touching and kissing, Tigris and I make love; we whisper to each other; I'm noticing that Tigris is really excited about it all. I can't blame my wife; she has missed me so much.

Just then, Tigris begins to howl with excitement, and to hear it in her sweet voice . . . it just makes the sex so much more passionate.

After a long time of touching, kissing, and grinding, Tigris and I finish; we continue to breath fast.

"Leviathan," she says, putting her hands on my shoulders. "I . . . I never though that this would happen."

"What do you mean?" I ask.

"I never thought . . . that we . . . would ever make love . . . again." She calms down a bit. She then leans her head forward against mine; she exhales deeply. "Your body feels so different."

"You've noticed." I say.

"Yes. You're much stronger, more built, and more rigid."

"Rigid, huh?" I chuckle.

"Yes. You've always been, but you've improved."

"Thanks."

"Mm-hmm. You've gained more muscle . . . and you have more scars." Tigris runs her finger down the scar on my chest. "I remember this one; Father must've *really* hated you."

I remember, so clearly, how Tigris's father Dalgine tried to kill me because I had fallen in love with his daughter. He plunged a dagger, dipped in snake venom, straight into my chest; I was very lucky that it didn't pierce my heart; I would've drowned in my own blood.

Tigris also places her hand on the scar that runs across the right side of my abdomen. Dalgine had thrust a spear through my side.

"You know," I say. "Levetin has one on the same side as me."

"Yes." Tigris says. "You are twins, aren't you?"

I was the one who put it there, when we fought at the amphitheatre in Athens, Greece.

"Also," I start as I feel Tigris's finger touching my scar. "A feud with Dalgine wasn't necessary."

"But Leviathan," Tigris says. "He wanted to kill you because you loved me."

"I still love you; I always will."

Tigris shakes her head no.

"Father didn't want you and I to be together." she tells me. "He wanted to kill you the moment he saw us together."

"I killed Zosimos." I say.

"It angered Father more. But, he failed to kill you . . . and now, you're here with me."

"And happily married."

"Yes, we are."

We lie down on the bed. I run my fingers through Tigris's dark-tawny ringlets; she kisses me lightly on my ear. We hold each other for a while as we breathe in the sweet aroma of the rose-scented sheets.

"I'm worried about you, Leviathan." Tigris says.

"You don't have to do that, my wife." I say. "I'm stronger than Imhotep Feathervault."

"But, I must. I love you."

"I love you, too . . . but you must trust in me."

"And, do you really think that Levetin will make your run-in with Peteryx a lot easier by taking out those servants?"

"I trust my brother, despite his crazy past; he is my twin, you know."

"Levetin cannot help that he is Acanthus of Corinth; it was his undesirable destiny. However, he does grasp the fact that he is Levetin Golgohoth and that he's your brother . . . and he will do anything to help you, even if he does tend to criticize your methods of torture and killing. He did tell you that he has always loved you, remember?"

Yes, I do. I think. *Right after he knocked me halfway unconscious in his lair.*

"I remember." I say. "Thanks, Tigris. He still does have the mind of a child sometimes."

Tigris smiles. She kisses my forehead.

"I know that you can take Peteryx out, Leviathan." she says. "He has tried so many times, throughout the last two-thousand years, to kill you."

"But," I say. "He has failed every time."

"But you do remember Gaudio's spell, don't you?"

All too well, I think. *Gaudio's spell caused Peteryx and I to switch bodies; it was pure hell, and the only people that knew who I was were my tyrant colleagues, the Eternal Ones, and . . . the Immortal Trio.*

"You don't have to worry about me, Tigris." I say. "I'll be okay."

"Do you trust Levetin?" she asks me.

"Well, of course; he's my brother. Like you said, my dear, despite his evil past and his current reputation, he has always loved me and will never allow me to go out in vain."

"No, he won't."

We sit up in bed. I then begin to feel a sharp pain in the crook of my right arm; it's the same pain that I felt before, when I visited Tigris on the shores of the Tigris River.

I get dizzy and lean my head on Tigris's shoulder.

"You're waking up again, my love." she says. "Good luck, Leviathan. I love you."

"I love you, too, wife." I say before I black out.

Black

I have Balcanicus and Spinosus scavenge some clothing at a fancy department store while I draw out plans to rid this place of the remaining Anubis servants.

"I never understood why Leviathan said to wear modern-day clothes." I say to myself as I scope out various places that may be harboring those pathetic reinforcements. "Now, I get it. In a time like this, if I wear my regular attire, enemies will know that it's me." I scoff. "Oh, how stupid!!! I don't need to be in a disguise, look at me!! I'm Acanthus of Corinth; people fear me . . . especially the wicked ones . . . like Peteryx."

Just as I am finishing up my job, my servants return with the clothing.

"Easy as pie." Balcanicus says as he hands me an extra large black pullover and some black jeans. "They didn't even see us take this." He hands me a pair of black boots and a black beanie.

"What is this?" I ask.

"It's your camouflage."

"No, no, no, I mean . . . what are these? They're . . . black."

"Yes."

"So, I'm back in the Middle Ages? I'm reliving the Goth era?"

"Master, black is a stealthy color."

"Actually," Spinosus chimes in. "Black isn't a color; it's the combination of all colors . . . or the absence of colors."

Now, it hits me. Black is the absence of colors. No one will know it's me, even if Las Vegas is about 99% lights.

"So," I say. "Wearing black is the next step to becoming invisible."

"You can call it that." Spinosus says.

"Oh. Well, I'm not making this black thing a habit; I'll leave it all to Arachne and Dante after this whole thing blows over. They look a whole lot better in it than I do."

Mordecai Talks Peteryx

I wake up from my bromine stupor. Everything looks normal in my room.

"What a visit." I say, smiling.

I sit up and look at my right arm; a needle is stuck in the crook of it again, and, like the last time, there's a tube attached to it.

I yank the needle out of my arm in disgust and start to think: *Rolfe is doing this; he's stealing my blood. But why?* Another thought pops into my head: *What if it's not Rolfe? What if it's Peteryx? Then again, it can't be him; he wouldn't only take my blood . . . he'd slit my throat in my sleep.*

I look over at the clock and see that it's 3:15pm. How long have I been knocked out?! I remember getting orange juice for breakfast, which was around 8:30am-9am.

I jump slightly when I hear the phone ring. I go over to the desk and pick it up.

Me: Hello?

Anonymous: Leviathan, it's Mordecai.

Me: Mordecai? Are you home from school?

Mordecai: Yes; Marilyn picked me up and brought me home.

Me: Got any news?

Mordecai: Leviathan, I have to confess something to you.

Me: Mordecai, please don't tell me that you're gay. If you are, that's cool, but I don't think that I can . . .

Mordecai: What? No! I'm not gay!! It's much worse.

Me: The pre-leukemia didn't return, did it?

Mordecai: No.

Me: Then what is it?

Mordecai: I saw him.

Me: Saw who?

Mordecai: The guy that wants to get his revenge on you; Arch-Peteryx Feathervault. I saw him.

Me: What?! When?

Mordecai: On the day I talked to Acanthus. I went back home and he was there.

Me: Mordecai, how do you know that it was Peteryx?

Mordecai: He had an Arabic accent; could've been Egyptian.

Me: Can you remember his appearance?

Mordecai: Yes. He had olive skin, spiky black hair with blood-red tips, yellow eyes, and he . . . he had lots of dark marks all over him.

Me: Like scars?

Mordecai: Yes. Oh, and he also carried this huge sword with him.

Me: Mordecai . . . what . . . what did he say or do?

Mordecai: Well, I had left your house after Acanthus said he was going to find you. Then, when I got home, I decided to spin my dreidel for a bit, out on the sidewalk. Well, a few moments later, I saw a shadow cast over me; I looked up and I saw that it was him; Peteryx.

Me: What then?

Mordecai: Well, he didn't say anything to me; he was just staring down at me, menacingly. I said hi, then he said hello. Then, he asked me if my name was Mordecai Weinstein. I said yes.

Me: Did he ask about me?

Mordecai: Well, of course; he must know that you and I are associated somehow.

Me: Did you tell him that you know me?

Mordecai: I had to, Leviathan; what if he would've killed me if I lied?

Me: Mordecai . . .

Mordecai: Please, don't be mad at me, Leviathan. Please.

Me: I'm not mad at you; Peteryx doesn't scare me.

Mordecai: But . . . he seemed very intimidating.

I begin to think: *Mordecai said that Peteryx confronted him after Acanthus left to go find me. To my understanding . . . Peteryx has been in Las Vegas, and his Anubis boys found me and were going to take me to him. Is it possible that Peteryx was in Los Angeles on the day of my capture? Was it possible that he arrived in Vegas after I did?*

Mordecai: Leviathan, are you still there?

Me: Yes, go ahead.

Mordecai: He told me that he was a friend of yours. I knew that he was lying, but I didn't call him out on it.

Me: Yeah, good call.

Mordecai: Well, I didn't tell him where you were, but he said he knew exactly where you are and what you're doing.

Me: But, I don't think he knows who's wiping out his servants.

Mordecai: Acanthus of Corinth.

Me: Yes. Peteryx is scared of Acanthus.

Mordecai: I see. Well, on top of Peteryx saying that he was a friend, he also said that he's gonna find you, and when he would, he is gonna kill you. Then he added that it was gonna be for real this time.

Me: Then what did you do?

Mordecai: I told him that he doesn't stand a chance against you. He didn't comment on that.

Me: Figures.

Mordecai: Anyways, before he left, he told me that I hoped I enjoyed my times with you because I'd never see you again. Then, he purposely stepped on my dreidel and crushed it.

Me: That son of a bitch; he's just as bad off as he was way back then.

Mordecai: I'm very lucky that he didn't kill me.

Me: Yes, you are. It's rare that Peteryx will let someone go.

Mordecai: Leviathan, the weirdest thing happened before Peteryx departed.

Me: What?

Mordecai: He pulled a big black beetle out of his mouth and sat it down next to me; it looks exactly like the previous one I had found by the house. Do you think he was at the foster home while I was at your mansion?

Me: It is certain. Do you still have both beetles?

Mordecai: Yes; they're in separate jars.

Me: Okay, good. Listen carefully to me, Mordi, do not . . . and I mean, do NOT cause any harm to those beetles.

Mordecai: Why?

Me: Peteryx will know if something rash is done; those scarabs are his life; they are a part of his body. Don't make it worse on Peteryx, or worse . . . you, by killing them.

Mordecai: I tried feeding them smaller bugs.

Me: No good; you're encouraging cannibalism. They're only attracted to blood.

Mordecai: What kind?

Me: Human is the most satisfying to them, but they will feast on any kind, I imagine. Try feeding them raw meat for now, okay?

Mordecai: Beef? Pork? Chicken?

Me: Take your pick.

Mordecai: We don't keep pork in the house, Leviathan. I'm Jewish.

Me: Beef, then.

Mordecai: Good choice.

Me: And Mordecai, please . . . I have said it before, do not come to Vegas for anything.

Mordecai: Leviathan . . . .

Me: Do not debate on it, nor argue with me.

Mordecai: Okay, Leviathan. Please, be careful, okay?

Me: I will. I'm sending the next set of papers soon.

Mordecai: Okay, good. I'll talk to you later.

Me: Sounds good.

Mordecai: Trust your brother, Leviathan. He's the only blood family you have left.

Those last words are hard to accept, but I have to do it; the Deathbringer is my twin brother, and I have to believe that he will not betray me on this matter.

Me: I will. I'll be careful; talk to you soon.

I hang up the phone. I then decide to continue where I left off in my chronicles.

"Next chapter in life." I say as I pick up my pen and grab some paper. "Let's go."

Releasing Jonathan

Taking care of little Jonathan was so much more difficult than taking care of Molicles; Molicles was seven and knew how to behave when told to; John, on the other hand, was only an infant . . . maybe about a couple of days old, when I got him. He would cry when he was hungry, he would cry when he needed to be changed, and he would cry when I tried to get some much-needed rest. I didn't care though; babies cry. John was very special to me; I raised him as my own. It would give me experience when I'd have children of my own someday.

It was the year 40 A.D. and Jonathan was celebrating his 11th birthday. I wasn't sure that it was his birthday, but it was the day I took him from Peteryx the Monster; I considered that to be his birthday . . . the day of true freedom.

I decided to take John sailing out on the Mediterranean Sea. We had a great time out there; it was a really great moment when John finally grasped the concept of fishing. Previously, when I'd try to teach him how to fish, it was a bit frustrating. When a fish would get away, John would whine. It was so hard not to laugh; I would just tell him to keep trying.

John tossed his fishing net into the water. I started to think as I watched him: *He looks an awful lot like Peteryx; no doubt now who his biological father is.*

I snapped back to reality when I heard John laughing.

"Hey, John," I said. "What's so funny?"

"I caught some!!" he shouted. "I can't believe I caught some!!"

"Splendid. Let's pull the net up."

"Okay."

I helped John pulled his net back into the boat. I then chuckled.

"Well," I said. "This should last us for the rest of the month."

"Yay!!" John cheered. "Fish!!" He began to count them. "One . . . two . . . three . . . four."

Such a good boy, I thought. *Such a smart boy; he knows how to count so well.*

"I think you can stop counting, John." I said. "There's too many."

"I bet there's over a hundred in here!!" he said.

I smiled and laid down on the deck; I looked up at the clear blue sky. The sun wasn't out, so it wasn't killing my eyes.

I began to think about the Eternal Ones and what they may have been doing at their sacred temple.

I shut my eyes and tried to relax a bit as the boat swayed back and forth in the waters of the Mediterranean.

"Father," John said. "Can you help me count all of my fish?"

John called me Father; he had called me Father ever since he learned how to form words. I didn't mind though; he was my son, so to speak.

I began to realize that Jonathan was getting older, and he needed to know the truth about who his real father was. But, how was I supposed to tell him? What was I supposed to say . . . . *"John, I'm not your father, but I'll love you like one."*

I sit up.

"John," I say.

"Yes, Father?" the boy asks.

"How about we go back to the shore?"

"Okay."

As we rowed the boat back to the shore, I couldn't help but wonder: *Who would want to sleep with Imhotep Feathervault? Someone desperate, I imagine.*

"John's mother was raped." said a familiar voice. I turned to see who spoke.

"Oh," I said. "Hello, Colai. Come to criticize me about me not having children of my own yet?"

"Why would I do that?" Colai had asked me. "I came to talk to you about Imhotep Feathervault."

"No need; I'm trying to spend some time with my son on his birthday."

"He isn't yours."

"Oh, thanks for reminding me. Who cares if he's not? I raised him as my own."

"Father?" I heard John say. "Who is she? Where did she come from? How did she get on the boat?"

John stared at Colai like a bug that needed to be squished; a bug like Peteryx's scarabs. I see now, the dark resemblance; Peteryx's hateful stare.

"Remember how I told you about my magic friends?" I asked.

"Yes, Father." John said.

"Well, this is one of them. Now, why don't you cast that net back out and catch some more fish?"

"But don't we have enough for the whole month?"

"Who says we can't use a little extra?"

"Okay, Father."

While John tended to the fishing duties he was given, I continued to speak with Colai.

"So," I said. "What do you have to tell me?"

"About how Peteryx acquired John," Colai stated. "And how his mother lost him."

"Too depressing."

"Nothing's too depressing for you, Leviathan Golgohoth."

She was wrong; I had three events that I had found depressing, up to this point: #1—the death of my beloved Tigris. #2—the discovery of Levetin Golgohoth (I was happy that I found him, but depressed at who and what he had become). #3—the Crucifixion of Christ; I was forced to watch.

"Speak to me." I said.

"Peteryx had been trapped in that pit of scarabs for fourteen-hundred years."

"I thought it was until just recently."

"He managed to escape in five-hundred B.C.; it was while you were living in Rome with Coria for the first time. Peteryx had spent fourteen-hundred years in a deep dark pit, experiencing nothing but pain and misery from those scarabs."

"Good."

"Well, when he finally decided to give in and allow the scarabs to possess his body, only then was he able to get out. Although those black beetles have eaten much of Peteryx's internal organs, they left his brain behind; the only thought that he dwells on is destroying you."

"What a pitiful sob story."

"Now, Leviathan, you're beginning to sound as cold as your brother."

"I am a tyrant."

"Uh-huh, and he's Acanthus of Corinth; he has no mercy. Well, after Peteryx escaped from Egypt, he traveled to Mesopotamia and killed several hundred people in an attempt to scope you out. Well, he later learned that you were in Nazareth; this was the year before Christ's crucifixion. He decided to go there and spy on you for a bit, seeing when the right time to strike would be. Well, while waiting, he got weak from the lack of blood. A young Nazarene girl saw him and took him in. Despite being kind to him, Peteryx was evil; he had beaten the girl senseless and proceeded to rape her. He then fled."

"That swine."

"Well, Peteryx had unknowingly impregnated her; obviously, the scarabs had not consumed his reproductive organs."

"Who would?"

"Leviathan. The girl was afraid to tell anyone what happened; after all, any kind of intercourse was looked down upon unless the people who did it were married . . . to each other, of course. Now, the girl began to feel sick and later found out that she had conceived. And, it was on the day that Jesus was crucified that she gave birth."

"I see."

"Well, it was a bittersweet time for the girl; she had her baby . . . under bad circumstances; she would be reminded that her child was a product of abuse and rape."

"What a pity."

"Leviathan, that's a no-no. Anyway, she only got to care for her baby for three days; three. It was on the day that Jesus rose from the dead, Peteryx had returned to her home and saw the child; he took it from her, by force, and was gone."

"Disgusting."

"Yes. Well, as you know, Jesus ascended into Heaven forty days after rising from the dead."

"Yes."

"Well, it was a week later, and Peteryx decided to hunt you down."

"So, John's actually a little older than just eleven."

"Yes. He celebrated his eleventh birthday about a month and a half ago; he was almost two months old when you took him from Peteryx."

"I see. So, is that it?"

"Basically."

I sigh and look out at the blue waters of the Mediterranean.

"I'm not telling him who his father is." I said.

"Then why not take him back to his mother?" Colai suggested. "She still lives in Nazareth."

I stared at John for a bit. He seemed at peace as he fumbled with the nets and counted more fish.

"Colai," I said. "I . . . ."

Colai had disappeared; she had to have gone back to the Eternal's Ones' sacred temple in Babylon.

"Let's go to the shores, John." I said.

"Yes, Father." the boy replies.

Shortly after, John and I made it back to dry land. We then walked back to Nazareth. As we walked, unbeknownst to John, I asked a few people if they knew about a Nazarene girl who was raped by an Egyptian about 12 years ago.

"No." said one elderly woman. "But I do remember seeing a young man of obvious Egyptian nationality around here about twelve or thirteen years ago."

"Do you remember what he looked like?" I asked.

"Oh, well, he had dark hair; red streaks in it. He also appeared to have dark marks on his skin."

She did, indeed, see Peteryx, but it didn't answer my question about the raped Nazarene girl . . . Jonathan's mother.

"Well," I said. "Do you know of any Nazarene girls who gave birth around the time of Christ's crucifixion?"

"There were many women who were expectant around that time." the elderly woman told me. "But there was one who actually tried to keep her pregnancy a secret. Her name is Mara, and she now lives on the outskirts of the town."

"How did you learn of her pregnancy?"

"A tall, muscled man told me about it; he said to keep an eye on her."

A tall, muscled man, huh?

"Tell me, my dear lady," I said. "Did he happen to have dark-green eyes, a slightly light-green tinge to his skin, and vines wrapping around his forearms?"

"Why, yes." she told me. "How did you know that?"

A wild guess, my dear.

"I know him from my past." I said. "So, you said that her name's Mara?"

"Yes." the old woman told me. "You'll find her easily; she lives in a little stone hut in a quiet and secluded area. You won't miss it."

Well, after excusing myself, I took John to the outskirts of Nazareth to find Mara. We searched until we found the right place.

"Father," John said. "What's this place?"

"This is your mother's house." I said to him.

"I never met my mother before."

"I know, and now you'll get to."

I took a deep breath and exhaled. I then knocked on the wooden door; a very beautiful woman answered it.

"Hello, dear." I said. "Are you Mara?"

The woman doesn't say anything right away; she just stares at me for a while.

"Yes." she finally speaks. "Who are you?"

"My name is Leviathan Golgohoth." I told her. "I think I have something that belongs to you."

Mara stared down at John for a few moments, then looked back at me.

"Did the plant man send you?" she asked me.

"I take it, you're speaking of Acanthus of Corinth?" I asked her.

"Yes."

"No. I learned of your whereabouts from someone else; I know about your past with Arch-Peteryx Feathervault."

I could sense Mara tensing up. She looked down at John again.

"He's my son!" she says. "Isn't he?!"

"Yes." I said to her.

Mara couldn't believe it; she immediately took John in her arms and hugged him tight.

"My Jonathan!!" she exclaimed. "You're okay!! Oh, I thought that bad man had killed you!!"

"What bad man?" John asked.

"Oh, it's not important; you're home with me!!" Mara stood up straight and looked over at me. "Thank you so much, for returning my baby to me." Tears rolled down her face. "I thought that he was dead."

"I would've brought him sooner." I said. I reached out and dashed Mara's tears away. "I raised John to be a survivor; he can take care of himself, and you."

"Bless you, good sir. Bless you."

I knelt down next to John and ruffled his dark hair. I kissed his cheek.

"John," I said. "I must be going now."

"But Father," he said. "I don't want you to go."

"I must; I have a long journey ahead of me. Please, promise me you'll take care of your mother."

"I promise."

"Don't let anything bad happen to her, okay?"

"I won't. Goodbye, Father."

I buried my face in my sleeve; I tried not to let Jonathan see my tears. I then stood back up and faced Mara.

"No need to worry about Arch-Peteryx Feathervault." I said. "I will handle him."

"Please do." Mara replied. "For me and my son."

I nodded. After bidding farewell to her, I began to walk away. As I walked, I heard the pitter-patter of tiny footsteps behind me.

"Father!!" it was John. "Where are you going?"

"To places I don't even know." I told him.

He grabbed my hand and wouldn't let go.

"Please," he said. "Don't go, Father."

"I must; you have to stay with your mother."

The little boy looked as if he wanted to cry.

"Why can't we go with you?" he asked, close to tears.

"The journey is dangerous." I said to him. "You're too little to come along. You must stay with your mother and take care of her. Remember what you promised me?"

John hung his head.

"Yes, Father." he said.

"Now," I said, turning him in the direction of Mara's stone hut. "Do what you promised me you'd do; protect your mother. Run along, John."

As John walked away, I could hear sniffling. I then heard a sob escape from him. I shut my eyes tight and clenched my teeth; I began to choke back my own sobs and tears.

It was so very hard to let him go, but I had to. Peteryx would kill him if he remained with me.

As I walked back towards the town, I thought about the place I would travel to next; some place that I would get used to quickly. I had my mind made up; I was going to travel to Saudi Arabia.

Angeleal Returns

I stop writing. I put my papers together and place them in the desk drawer and decide to take a shower.

I open the dresser drawers and pull out a long-sleeved bluish-green shirt and a pair of peanut butter-colored khakis.

I think twice about the boxers that are in the drawers; how do I know that they are safe? Deciding differently on them, I walk to the bathroom.

"Peteryx," I say as I pull off my dirty shirt. "You can't kill me. And, I'm sure you know, by now, that your reinforcements are falling to the Deathbringer." I pull off my bottoms and hop into the shower; I adjust the water's temperature. "I'm a lot older than you, and a lot wiser. I'm also a lot tougher than you are."

I soap, rinse, and hop out.

"I will kill you, Arch-Peteryx Feathervault." I say as I stare into the mirror. I reach up and tug at a lock of my hair. "I'm thinking . . . ."

I open the medicine chest; I see a pair of scissors sitting near a bottle of pills.

"Yes." I say as I grab them. I close the medicine chest and look into the mirror again; I notice that there's someone standing behind me. I quickly turn around and hold the scissors to their throat; they gasp in fear.

"Leviathan!!" says a woman. "It's me!!"

I see now who I almost sliced up.

"Angeleal!" I say, quickly taking the scissors away. "What . . . what are you doing here?!"

"I'm here to speak with you, Leviathan." she says.

"But, I thought you weren't coming back."

"What do you mean?" She leans in and kisses me on the lips. "I could never abandon you."

"I thought that after we were together last Monday night, you were going to let me go."

"I thought that, too, but Revelatianus said that you need me."

"Yes, I *do* need you; I need all of you, and especially Revelatianus. I haven't seen him in nearly six-thousand years; I thought that the Eternal Ones were supposed to be there when their tyrants need them."

"Actually, any of the Eternal Ones can assist any tyrant."

"Did Draken Hark ever want to get Peteryx out of that pit?"

"He did, once, but he decided differently."

"He thought well."

I see that Angeleal is holding out a pair of boxers to me.

"Are those . . . ." I start.

"Clean?" she asks. "All of the clothes in that room you're staying in are clean; Powers is a neat freak, and wanted to keep his brother's things like new."

"So, they're clean."

"Why wouldn't they be?"

I take the boxers from Angeleal and put them on. I then stare into the mirror.

"I think I'll need to cut my hair." I say.

"But, Leviathan," Angeleal says. "I love your hair the way it is; it's so . . . you."

"I know. I thought about doing it like Levetin's."

"The way it sort of kicks out?"

"Yes; his hair is neat."

"Twigs and leaves are credited for that, Leviathan. Speaking of Levetin Golgohoth, do you know that he's whacking those Anubis servants and paving an easier path for you to get to Peteryx?"

"Yes, I know. He told me to leave those guys to him and his servants."

I take a lock of my hair and stretch it out; I position the scissors in my hand and place the lock of hair in between the blades. I then shut my eyes and squeeze the handle together, hearing the somewhat unfamiliar snipping of strands. I open my eyes. Seeing that this will actually turn out good, I begin to pull more locks of hair out and cut them; once I am done, I reveal myself to Angeleal.

"Wonderful." she says and smiles. "I can get used to that. And, you might want to get rid of the peach fuzz, too."

"Levetin's got it, and I want to be just like him."

"Perhaps not?"

"Haven't fully decided."

I grab a razor from the medicine chest. I then shave the stubble from my chin. After shaving, I pull on my khakis; before I put on my long-sleeved blue-green shirt, I grasp my amber and jade pendant.

"It's just like new." I say to Angeleal. "It's hard to believe that you gave this to me almost six-thousand years ago."

"It's hard to believe that you still have it." Angeleal replies. "I'm pleased that you've taken such good care of it."

I chuckle and pull on my shirt. I then embrace Angeleal.

"That Arch-Peteryx is so hell-bent on killing me." I say.

"Well, Leviathan," Angeleal says. "He has been seeking revenge from you ever since he got out of that pit of scarabs over in Giza." She pats me on my back. "Wouldn't you want to get revenge on someone who has crossed you?"

"Yes. Besides, he's lucky that it was a pit of scarabs and not a pit of vipers."

"Indeed." Angeleal parts from me. "Did you know that Draken Hark experienced something closely related to Peteryx's entrapment?"

"What?"

"Yeah. Draken Hark got stuck in a pit of scorpions one time; I don't know the whole story behind it, but if you ask Murabbi or Azrael, I'm sure they could tell you."

Angeleal and I walk out of the bathroom and go back to my bedroom; we sit down on my bed. I take her in my arms.

"Arch-Peteryx Feathervault is a coward." I tell her. "A scared and fearful chicken heart."

"I don't think he is." Angeleal says. "I think he's very callous and dangerous."

"According to Levetin, he fears him and his colleagues."

"Yes; Peteryx does fear the Immortal Trio, but who doesn't?"

"Innocent people."

"You're right. The only people who should fear the Trio are those who do wrong."

"But they're not good people."

"They're not people at all, Leviathan."

She is right; the Immortal Trio were once Human, but now they are vicious monsters that prey on blood . . . they're just like me.

"Why does Peteryx fear the Trio?" I ask.

"Long story." Angeleal tells me. "I know why, but it's too revolting. It's best that you don't know."

"I can handle it."

"No. Anyways, do you remember what happened to you and Peteryx back in twelve-eighty?"

I hated that year; it was the year that the evil wizard Edward Gaudio the First cast a spell that caused me to enter Peteryx's body, and Peteryx to enter mine. I then spent the next 420 years wandering around as Peteryx and enduring the creepy-crawly feeling of the bugs, while Peteryx spent those years relaxed and murdering innocent people, as me.

Among the people Peteryx killed were two of my colleagues in the Tyranny Squad. Finally, in 1700 A.D., the spell was broken; Peteryx had tried to fool Acanthus into thinking he was me . . . my brother already knew what had happened, but Peteryx was stupid to think that he didn't. He was captured and an old warlock named Gilford Byrne, who was a slave to the Trio's wrath, broke the spell. He was then extinguished.

Three years later, Dante Haven, the Trio's Vindicator, cast a spell on me to try and take vengeance on me for a personal reason, even though it was a matter that was settled in 389 B.C., in Ancient Rome. Angeleal swooped in and saved me.

"I remember everything." I say. "That was a tough time, living as Peteryx. It was like being trapped in a howling hole with the sensation of bugs crawling over me."

"It's exactly how Peteryx felt when he was trapped in that pit." Angeleal says. "Now, you know what he went though."

I shudder. I hardly ever do, beings I'm a tyrant and that I rarely experience fear, but the thought of being confined to Arch-Peteryx Feathervault's disgusting shell of a body would make any monster like me tremble with detest.

"I'm so sorry that we couldn't break the spell right away." Angeleal tells me. "Draken Hark knew what ancient magic would break the spell, but he said that you needed to experience what Peteryx felt."

"Really?" I ask.

"Yes. He also knew that Dante Haven was a master at spell-casting, hexes, and jinxes. So, there was also a possibility that the spell would be reversed; with Acanthus of Corinth being Levetin, your twin brother, he could've convinced Dante to end it."

"Which he did, right?"

"Yes; he did. Well, in a sense; he asked Dante to find that warlock, in order for the spell to be erased. Levetin has some kind of good in him."

Gaudio cast the hex so quick and clean that I had no idea I had been sent to Peteryx's body, until I saw my reflection in a pond not long after.

"How did Gaudio learn such dark magic?" I ask.

"He was taught by many dark wizards." Angeleal says. "He started his practice at a very young age, and quickly became a master in the arts; he was the first and only sorcerer to manipulate and trap Thanatos Aqueous."

"Which, in turn, caused him to capture the Trio and use them to advance in his own forces."

"But he did fail, you know."

"Yes, he did . . . but, not before he . . . ."

"Trapped you."

I am silent. Yes, I remember Edward Gaudio too well; I met him in 1215 A.D., when I was on my way to England to see Arachne and Acanthus's twins; they were turning 100 that year.

The moment he placed his hand in mine, I could sense something disagreeable. As the boy talked to me, all I could see radiating from his eyes was pure evil; at the tender age of ten, he could strike fear into a seasoned killer's heart.

"The spell was called the Encasement Incantation." Angeleal says. "It was a spell that was popular amongst witches and wizards of the Middle Ages, but died out once the people who were doing it were burned at the stake."

"I remember; wasn't Arachne accused of being a witch back then?"

"Yes. She was to be burned at the stake, along with the other witches who were condemned, but Acanthus swooped in and saved her before the flames could claim her."

"But . . . he could have . . . ."

"Been burned in the process, yes. The minister in charge with the condemning of the witches wasn't too pleased about it; he witnessed the Deathbringer cut the Stalker free and get her out of there. Oh, and to make matters worse, the Vindicator discreetly turned all of the dead witches and wizards into zombies and were sent forth to attack the living."

"What I can't see is this: The Crusades began around the end of the eleventh century; Edward Gaudio rose to power around twelve twenty-five and became a bigger threat when he killed his two daughters the moment his son was born."

"What's your point?"

"My point is . . . why didn't the Roman Catholics try to overthrow Gaudio due to his tremendous power in wizardry?"

"Edward Gaudio came to power during the Sixth Crusade, in twelve twenty-eight; the focus was more on the Middle East than in Europe at the time. Edward saw this to be an advantage."

"But he fell from power in twelve-eighty."

"The same year the spell was cast."

I scoff. It *was* the same year that it happened; I knew exactly how it happened . . . and I was too slow to stop him; better yet . . . I was unaware of what he was doing.

"My friends were killed." I said.

"Leviathan," Angeleal says. "Phaize was the first to go, in thirteen forty-nine, during the Black Plague."

"Yes, and it wasn't the Black Plague that killed him."

"No, it wasn't; you saw who did it."

Yes, I did.

"Enough with my friends' deaths." I say. "The spell was broken."

"Yes." Angeleal agrees. "In seventeen-hundred."

"After you rescued me from Dante Haven a few years later, remember what we did?"

"Well, of course I do. We went to Versailles and we got closer."

I nod. I then start to think about something I need to do.

"I have to go back into the city soon." I say.

"But, Leviathan," Angeleal says. "That wouldn't be wise right now; with Peteryx knowing what's happening to his servants, he could . . . ."

"I'll be okay; I have weapons and my brother is just a foliage away."

"Can you really trust what Levetin is doing?"

"Why not?"

Angeleal nods; she gives in to the fact that I do trust my brother, even if he has done some stupid things to me in the past to advance himself and his colleagues.

"Okay, Leviathan." she states. "I'll need to go now." She gets up from the bed. "I'll be watching you; please make the choices that seem right to you, okay?"

"Okay, Angeleal." I say. "I will. I suppose I'll talk to you later."

"Yes, you will."

"Good." I hug and kiss her. "I love you."

Angeleal smiles and vanishes.

Interrogating Rolfe

Just as I am preparing myself to go out for another night out in Vegas, I hear knocking on the door.

"Come in." I say.

The door opens and in walks Rolfe Bentley. Ah, just the person I need to see . . . and, he's alone.

"Hello, Leviathan." he says. "Just checking up on you."

"That's nice." I tell him. "Come in . . . and close the door behind you."

Rolfe seems a bit confused by the remark, but he does what he is told. Without any warnings, I rush over to him with the speed of a cheetah on crack and slam him against the door.

"You may think you're innocent." I say. "But you don't fool me."

"What the hell are you talking about, Leviathan?!" Rolfe asks.

He's trying to make me look stupid, but I don't fall for it. I pull him towards me and slam him into the door again.

"I know what you've been doing!!" I shout, lifting him up off the floor; his feet dangle helplessly. "Don't act like you don't know!"

"I don't know what you're talking about!!" he says.

"Admit it, Bentley!! You stole my blood!! I want it back!!"

"I didn't steal your blood!! Don't call me a thief!!!"

"You took something that belongs to me without asking!! You *are* a thief!!"

"DON'T YOU DARE CALL ME A THIEF!!!" he pushes my face away, causing me to let go of him; he drops back down to the floor. "I don't take things without permission!! And again, I did *not* steal your blood!! Why would I want your blood?"

"For experiments; I am Leviathan Golgohoth; I am an immortal. What kind of discoveries would you find with just one drop of my ancient blood?"

"I didn't take any!"

I move in a little closer.

"Now," I grab Rolfe's shoulders. "I want what once was mine . . . or I will have to take yours to replace it."

"Leviathan, you have to believe me! I don't have any of your blood! Not an ounce, a pint, or even a tiny drop."

I stare down at the floor, then back at Rolfe; my grip on him remains strong.

"Are you being honest with me?" I ask. Rolfe nods his head quickly.

"Yes, Leviathan." he says. "I am being honest."

"Are you sure?"

"Yes."

I don't believe him; I can read a hint of deception in his voice. I'm going to give him one last chance to redeem himself.

"Are you sure you don't have anything to confess?" I ask.

"I'm positive." he says.

He's a liar; I can smell it on him and read it in his aura. However, I decided to just drop the subject for now; finding and destroying Peteryx matters more.

"I believe you." I say, even though I don't. "However, you do remain suspicious to me; if I see anything of mine in your possession that is restricted, so to speak, or if I catch you in the act of stealing from me . . . I will hastily have your penis removed, and present it to Powers on a bronze plate." I release my grip on him. "Do you understand me?"

"Yes, Leviathan, sir." Rolfe says as he catches his breath from fear. "I won't take anything from you; I promise."

"Okay." I head over to the wastepaper basket near the desk and pull out one of the tubes from it. "Would you like to explain this?"

"What is that?" he asks.

"Proof!!" I throw the tube at him. "Proof that my blood was drawn!!!!"

Rolfe gasps in fear and rushes out of the room. I yell in anger and slam the door. A few seconds later, I see his car pulling out of the driveway; I have a strong feeling that he won't be coming back for a while.

I hear another knock on the door.

"Who is it?" I ask.

"It's Powers." I hear.

"Oh. Come in."

Powers enters the room; he seems a bit concerned.

"I heard screaming." he says.

"Screaming?" I ask.

"Yeah; it sounded urgent."

"It was probably a show on the television."

"But, it sounded like it came from this room."

"No; nothing here."

Powers seems skeptical. He then nods.

"Okay." he tells me. "Well, it could've been the side effects of those pills I took earlier. Anyway, do you know where Rolfe's heading?"

"No." I say. "Why?"

"He left in a hurry; he left his cell phone here, so I can't call him."

"I guess he'll be back soon."

Powers looks at me as if he knows that I have more knowledge of this topic.

"Is there something you wish to tell me?" he asks.

"Yes." I say. I grab the last passages I wrote and put them in a manila envelope; I address it to Mordecai and put a stamp on it. "I need for you to mail these off for me."

Powers nods as he slowly takes the envelope from me.

"Okay." he says. "I'll see if I can find out where Rolfe's going."

He leaves the room. I then sit down at the desk.

"I think I need to write some more." I say to myself. I glance out the window and see that the nearby bushes are quivering in the wind . . . or perhaps it's a sign from Acanthus?

I get out some more paper and my fountain pen; I begin to scribble down some more of my chronicles.

Tieran Fang-Shah

It took me 3 hours to travel from Nazareth to the Arabian Peninsula. What was I going to do, now that I made it?

I walked around for a little while. I then noticed some merchants with their camels, so I walked over to survey.

"Salam." I said. It's *hello* in Arabic.

"Salam." one of the merchants said.

"Sho Ismak?" *What is your name?*

"Faheed. Inta?" *Faheed. You?*

"Ismi Leviathan." *My name is Leviathan.* "Keef halak?" *How are you?*

"Lateef." *Nice.*

The remaining two merchants smiled. They gestured to some crafts made from glass.

"Amazing." I said to myself in English as I picked up a small elephant figurine furnished from green glass. "Addesh?" *How much?*

"Ghali." *Expensive*, the merchant told me. "And, we do speak English, Leviathan."

I was surprised by it; they spoke English.

"How do you know who I am?" I asked.

"Your story travels all around." Faheed told me.

"I see. Are these figurines from Mesopotamia?"

The merchants nodded their heads.

"Yes." Faheed said. "They are called Golgohoth Crafts."

Golgohoth Crafts? I wondered why they were called that, but then I didn't have to think too long. My father was a skilled craft worker, and the sculptors after him must've named the art after him. Perhaps those crafts were made by another living Golgohoth besides me?

"Listen," I said. "Can you tell me where I can find some shade? My skin is starting to prickle."

"There are oases here in Arabia." one of the merchants said. "We bring our camels to them to be watered."

"Ah, yes. Shukran." Shukran means *thank you* in Arabic.

Faheed picked up a small bronze statue of an ox; he handed it to me.

"Trade?" he asked.

What was I supposed to give him in exchange for it? I couldn't give him my amber and jade pendant; it was a gift from Angeleal. I wouldn't give him my dagger; that was from Revelatianus.

I did think about one thing; I had some gold coins that I had collected back in Nazareth. I pulled them out of a pocket of the robe I was wearing and handed them to Faheed.

"Shukran." he said.

"Ahlan Wa Sahlan." *You are welcome.* I told him.

I nodded to the three merchants and walked away; I studied the bronze ox as I walked.

"This is lovely." I said to myself.

My surroundings suddenly got darker and cooler. I looked up and saw that I was standing underneath a date palm tree.

"Oh." I said.

I sat down and leaned my head against the trunk of the tree; I shut my eyes and enjoyed the shade. After a few moments, I felt a presence drawing near. I opened my eyes and saw a man of obvious Asian ancestry, definitely Chinese, walking toward me. He had a close haircut and was wearing Chinese-style clothing; a dark-green long sleeved top, dark-green bottoms, and leather sandals.

"Stop where you are." I said.

"Leviathan," he said. "Leviathan, it's me . . . Tieran."

I allowed the Chinaman to come closer. Once he was about five feet away, I could sense a strong power radiating through him; I could see it in his dark-brown eyes.

"Tyrant Tieran Fang-Shah." I said. "What are you doing here in Arabia?"

"I was going to ask *you* that, Leviathan." he said.

"I'm just traveling; just wondering when I'll meet up with Peteryx again."

"Peteryx?! Imhotep Feathervault?! I didn't know that he was still alive!! I mean . . . you pushed him into that pit of beetles a long time ago. How did he . . . ."

"He gave in to the scarabs and they spared him. He was in Nazareth about twelve years ago and confronted me for the first time since the entrapment."

"And I see that you're here, so you must've slipped past him."

"Yes, I did."

"Did you come here from Nazareth?"

"Yes. Where did you come from?"

"Corinth."

"Corinth?"

"Yes. I wanted to see the Lair of Acanthus. Plus, I was looking for Phaize Pierterch."

"I see. So, did you get to see Acanthus of Corinth?"

"No. I guess I'm glad that I didn't; I heard he's a bit violent."

"I guess. So, Tieran, the clothing; what dynasty does that come from?"

"I'm a descendant of the Xia Dynasty; the legendary one."

"The Xia Dynasty? Really?"

That word *Xia* is pronounced *Shah*, just like the last part of Tieran's name. Perhaps Tieran was born Tian Fang-Xia? It is a known fact that Tieran's real first name is Tian. Perhaps he changed his name for privacy?

"I am a descendant of Yu The Great." Tieran said, sitting down next to me.

"Yu the Great?" I asked in disbelief. "The man who established the Xia Dynasty? The guy who created flood control?"

"Yes and yes."

"So, it's safe to say that you have an upright moral character."

"I am a tyrant."

I smiled and patted Tieran on the back.

"Good answer." I said. "So, Tieran, tell me a little about yourself."

"Well," he said. "I was born Tian Fang-Xia; that's X-I-A. I was born in the year two-thousand B.C. and I became a tyrant in nineteen-hundred sixty-five B.C."

I was right about the whole Xia name. However, I didn't know that Tieran was 35 when he was changed over; he looked a lot younger than that.

"Really?" I asked. "You were thirty-five?"

"Well, yes." Tieran told me. "Murabbi Paleohenge thought that I was old enough, and wise enough, to become one."

"Splendid. Well, I was only sixteen when I became the very first tyrant, but I guess that's a good enough age to be a bloodthirsty predator."

"You were sixteen?!"

"I thought you, of all people, would know; aren't Chinese people psychic or something?"

"To a certain point. It's all in the oracle bones."

I scoffed.

Dynasty Talk

I watched Tieran as he calmly wiped the sweat from his brow with a silk cloth.

"Can I tell you about the dynasties?" he asked.

Before I could answer him, Tieran began to talk about them.

"Well, you see." he started. "The Shang Dynasty was the first historic dynasty. It began in seventeen sixty-six B.C. I was there for the entire six hundred forty-four years it existed. Then, there was the Zhou Dynasty; it began in eleven twenty-two B.C., right after the Shang Dynasty ended."

Oh, and as a reminder, the Chinese have their ways of pronouncing words; the word Zhou is pronounced *Joe*.

I knew nothing of the Chinese dynasties, but I did want to learn about them, so even if it would result in bleeding from the ears, I listened to Tieran talk about them.

"Okay," he continued. "The Zhou Dynasty lasted for nine-hundred years, from the eleven-hundreds B.C. to the two-hundreds B.C. That was the most enduring dynasty. Next up was the Qin Dynasty; it lasted only fifteen years, from two twenty-one B.C. to two oh-six B.C. That dynasty was created by China's first emperor."

Qin, pronounced *Chin*. I began to grow a bit irritated from having to decipher some of Tieran's words, but I kept on listening willfully.

"The Qin Dynasty," Tieran said. "It began to get ridiculous, so . . . . in two oh-six B.C., a revolt broke out against them. That's when the dynasty was put to an end. Then, a general named Liu Bang founded the Han Dynasty in two oh-two B.C., and it is still in existence to this day. Now, enough about me and the dynasties. Tell me a little bit about yourself."

I was surprised that it ended that quickly; I stretched my legs out to get comfortable.

"Well," I said. "I was born Leviathan Golgohoth over in Ancient Mesopotamia's Fertile Crescent. I was a farmer for a while, and my twin brother Levetin and I would help our parents and servants with the harvests.

Levetin was killed when he was only twelve. I became a tyrant about four years later and have walked the earth as one since."

"I see." Tieran said. "Growing up, I had a younger sister, so I was always helping her make clothes from silk. I guess that's why I like fashion. Maybe I should . . . ."

He stopped talking for a second; it seemed as if he was thinking of something.

"Are you okay?" I asked.

"Did you say you had a twin brother called Levetin?" he asked.

"Yes, I did."

"Levetin Golgohoth."

"Yes, Tieran. I know who he has become."

"Leviathan," he got up. "You think he'll kill us?"

"Acanthus of Corinth has reasons to kill people; he doesn't just kill for fun."

"Uh . . . I think you might be wrong there, my friend."

I got up from the sand and dusted myself off.

"I don't want to talk about Acanthus, Tieran." I said to him. Just then, I realized that I had said that while standing underneath a date palm tree; my brother has the power to communicate with plants and can listen to everything that is said around them. "Why don't we take a walk?"

"Okay." Tieran agreed.

We began to walk through the desert plains.

"I can't believe your brother's the Immortal Trio's Deathbringer." Tieran said. "That really is something."

"He's evil, Tieran." I told him. "He tortured me in his lair on the day I discovered him in Corinth after over three-thousand years. He fought me in an amphitheatre with an attempt to kill me."

"Does he grasp the reality that he's your brother?"

"Yes, but I don't think he realizes that he was born Levetin Golgohoth."

"Have you tried to tell him that he was?"

"I don't want to discuss Levetin, Tieran, okay?"

"But, Leviathan, I'm interested. Do you know that I want to meet Arachne the Spider Queen? I heard that she has some of the finest quality of silk in the world."

Tieran's voice was beginning to feel like a drill being pushed through my ear. I pulled the bronze ox out of my robe and handed it to him.

"What's this?" he asked.

"It's a Golgohoth Craft." I say. "An ox. You can have it if you can keep quiet."

"Oh, thank you! I love Golgohoth Crafts; they traveled as far as the Sea of Japan." He studied the sculpture as we walked. He then slipped it in his pocket. "Where are we headed?"

"Somewhere to rest." I said.

"There's a temple right over there; let's stay in it."

Tieran pointed over to a large temple that was carved out of stone; he and I headed toward it. In front of the temple sat a camel.

"That's a camel, Leviathan." he said. "Arab traders use them, and they usually travel in groups called caravans."

I breathed a sigh.

"Very good, Tieran." I said, trying not to sound too aggravated. "Now, c'mon, let's head inside this here temple."

The Temple Beauty

Tieran and I entered the temple. Inside, it reminded me of the Eternal Ones' sacred shrine, only except for the size; this Arabian temple was a lot bigger.

We looked over at a fountain that was in the temple and saw a beautiful young woman sitting by it; we headed over to her.

"Hello." she said in English.

"Hello." Tieran said. "I'm Tieran Fang-Shah, and this is my friend Leviathan."

The woman looked over at me with a look of surprise.

"Leviathan Golgohoth." she said. She then embraced me and kissed my cheek.

"Hey," Tieran said. "That's not fair!! How come you are always so popular with the women, Leviathan?"

"It's a mystery." I said. I turned to the woman. "Do you have a name?"

"Yes." she said. "My name is Nasada."

"Do you live here?"

"Yes."

"Oh, well, we didn't mean to intrude; Tieran and I needed some shade."

"And some fresh water." Tieran said as he dipped his hand in the water and brought some of it up to his lips; he sipped loudly.

"It's okay." Nasada said. "You can stay here as long as you want to. I had to take refuge here when . . . ."

I saw tears coming to her eyes.

"When what?" I asked.

"When a . . . a trio of bandits attacked my father's caravan; they stole the plunder that he had collected from Egypt."

"A trio?" Tieran asked. "Did you get a good look at their faces? Did they kill your father?"

Nasada buried her face in my chest; I could hear her sobbing.

"Nasada?" Tieran called to her.

"I saw their faces." she told Tieran. "It was a woman and two men; it was horrible."

"A woman . . . and two men?"

I could practically hear what Tieran may have been thinking.

"Yes." Nasada said. "And, I didn't want to believe it, but . . . it looked like the woman had two extra arms."

Yeah, I thought. *I know exactly who attacked her father's caravan. Those bastards!!*

"What did you do when the caravan was attacked?" I asked.

"I called out to my father." Nasada said. "My father shouted for me to run. So, I did. I turned and saw the woman grab my father, and that's when I saw what looked like extra arms. The taller of the two men started slaying the camels and the shorter man began to grab the treasures."

"But, you didn't see them kill your father?"

"No."

"So," Tieran started. "He could've escaped; the bandits probably only wanted the plunder."

"No." Nasada told him. "I went back and saw that the bandits had left; I saw my father walking around the dead camels. I called out to him and ran over to him. I wanted to show him that I was still alive. But . . . ."

"But?"

"Father wasn't the man I knew growing up; he was . . . dead; he was still alive, but he was dead!! He tried to grab me, and I escaped. I ran here to hide."

"Did he try to bite you?" Tieran asked.

"No." Nasada told him. "He didn't; it seemed like he was wanting me to help him, or something, but I was too afraid."

Nasada's father had been killed, drained, and reanimated into a zombie. The bandits that had attacked the caravan were Arachne the Spider Queen, Acanthus of Corinth, and Dante Lord Haven . . . the Immortal Trio.

"Leviathan," Tieran said to me. "You don't think that it was . . . ."

"It was." I told him.

"What's going on?" Nasada asked. I turned to the temple beauty.

"Nasada," I said. "Have you ever heard of a group of monsters that call themselves the Immortal Trio?"

"Yes, I have." she said. "When my father and I went to Mesopotamia to collect glass figurines and Golgohoth Crafts, he heard a couple of scribes talking about them, but they're only a myth."

They're no myth; they are very real, and they are dwelling amongst the living, just like the tyrants and their Eternal Ones.

"Yeah." I said. "They're just a myth."

"But," Nasada said. "The way the scribes talked about them seemed like they are real."

"Even *you* said that they're a myth." I walked over to the fountain and sat down by it; I splash some water on my face. "It's getting dark outside." I turned to Tieran. "Maybe we should stay here for the night."

Tieran yawned and stretched; he sleepily rubbed his eyes.

"Yes." he said. "We should. I'm going to be traveling tomorrow."

"Oh," I wiped my face with my sleeve. "Where are you heading?"

"Wherever my feet decide to take me." Tieran yawned again. "I'm going to gaze at the stars. Goodnight, Leviathan."

"Goodnight, Tieran."

When Tieran left outside to go stargazing, I went to look for a room in the temple to stay in; Nasada followed me.

"I know that it was the Immortal Trio who attacked the caravan." she said. "I know that they killed my father and turned him into a zombie." she embraced me. "I also know that Acanthus of Corinth is your twin brother."

"Yes." I said. "It doesn't mean that I don't claim him."

Nasada stared into my eyes. I had to admit, her stare was powerful; it was like I was being pulled into some kind of deep dimension. Those kind of people carry a crisp, fresh supply of blood; I thought about having Nasada for a snack.

"Are you an immortal?" she asked.

"Yes." I told her.

"You seem like the type of man who could charm women."

She brought her hands up to my cheeks; I smiled.

"Is that what you really think?" I asked.

Nasada nodded. She drew her face closer to mine; I could practically smell her blood as she came closer to me.

I gently pushed her away from me.

"What's wrong?" she asked.

"Nothing's the matter." I told her. I smiled again. "Although you see me as being this man who can charm women, my friend's a lot better at it."

Nasada seemed surprised by my words.

"The Chinaman?" she asked.

"Yes." I replied. "He's practically a prince."

Nasada thought about what I had told her. Truthfully, I believed that Tieran wouldn't know the first thing about being with a woman; he was too interested in telling stories about China's dynasties to worry about what a woman feels like.

Nasada smiled.

"Send him to me." she said.

"Absolutely." I said.

You Want To Get Me Laid?

Nasada left to find a room in the temple to slumber in. I exited the temple and found Tieran; he was sitting next to a camel and petting it on its head.

"Tieran," I said. He turned his gaze toward me.

"Hi, Leviathan." he said. "Just talking to the camel and gazing at the stars. Look at the sky." He pointed to it. "It's purple."

I sat down next to Tieran and looked up at the sky.

"I've seen too many purple skies in my days." I told him.

"Well, me, too." he said. He looked at me again. "Do you think that the temple girl is pretty?"

"Her name's Nasada, and I think she's attractive."

"I think she's beautiful. But, I think that Asian women are more beautiful."

I had an Asian lover once. Her name was Ching-Fei Lee; I met her in Anyang, and I do miss her a great deal . . . but not as much as I miss my precious Tigris.

"Hey, Leviathan," Tieran said, breaking my thoughts. "I remember when you were in Anyang; it was the year eleven-hundred B.C."

"You remember?" I asked.

"Yes. Those two priests you were living with for five years were two of the last surviving members of the Shang Dynasty; you met them during the Zhou Dynasty, and beings that they were oracles, they predicted that we'd meet."

"Yes, they did. Did you actually see me in Anyang?"

"Yes. I wanted to meet you then, since the priests predicted that we would see each other, but I was a little timid to confront you."

"Why?"

"Because you were intimidating back then."

"And I'm not now?"

"Well, yes, you still are . . . to Humans." Tieran put his hand on my shoulder. "Do you remember Ching-Fei Lee?"

125

"How did you know Ching?"

"She was the daughter of a strong general, who was a member of the Zhou Dynasty. He was General Lee Chang-Zhen, a very good friend of mine. He was killed though; I think it had something to do with Arachne the Spider Queen."

That's not surprising, I thought. Leave it to the members of the Trio to knock off figures with high power.

"You know, Tieran," I said. "I remember General Lee. Ching introduced me to him about two years before she died. He really seemed to like me; he would look beyond my weird condition."

"Yeah; he really was an understanding man. Why did he have to get thrown in the Huang He?"

Ching was claimed by that river, too. I tried so hard to save her, but when I finally caught up to her, she had drowned; her body got washed up on the banks."

I hung my head and thought for a moment: *The Huang He, the Chinese name for the Yellow River. All of that yellow soil that gets washed into it makes it that color. And, on top of that, it is known as the world's most muddiest river; I couldn't see anything when I searched for Ching, after she had fallen in. My eyes failed me for the first time, ever.*

"That river has killed many." Tieran said, breaking my thoughts again. "That's why the Chinese nicknamed it *China's Sorrow.*" He poked me in the arm. "Are you ready for bed?"

"Nasada wants to sleep with you." I said, not thinking about what Tieran might say.

"Huh?" he asked.

"I said Nasada wants you to have sex with her."

Tieran seemed surprised.

"You . . . ." He started. "You . . . you want me to have sex with her?"

"I didn't say that." I told him. "I said that *she* wants to have sex with *you.*"

It didn't take long for Tieran to decide what he wanted to do. After all, he was a man . . . just like me, and men all have those urges, whether they're normal Humans or deadly tyrants.

"Cool!!" he said, getting up. "I'm going to make this a night she'll never forget. Watch me work, Leviathan!!"

I was amazed. It never occurred to me that Tieran would want to be watched while he slept with Nasada.

I wouldn't act as a coach; just a statue in the room.

"I'll be there shortly." I said.

Acanthus's Exposures

I stop writing when I hear someone knocking on the door.

"Who is it?" I call out as I slowly reach for my dagger.

"It's Powers." the person calls out. "Can I come in?"

I release the handle of my dagger.

"Sure." I say.

Powers walks inside the room with a look of concern on his face.

"Have you heard anything from Rolfe?" he asked.

"No, sorry." I say.

"Oh, well, I mailed off your letter."

"Thanks."

"You're welcome. Well, I was just checking up on you, to see if you needed anything."

Blood.

"No, I'm fine." I reply. "Thank you."

"Okay." Powers says. "I'm going outside to water the cactuses; it's time for their semi-annual watering. If you need anything, just call me."

"Certainly. I'll let you know if I hear from Rolfe."

Powers nods and leaves the room. A few minutes later, he's out in the garden with a watering can.

I walk out of the bedroom and go to a closet in the living room. I open the door and grab a huge piece of canvas, many tubes of paint, a sketch pencil, and a paintbrush, along with a can of paint thinner.

I go back to the bedroom with the collected items. I then take some nails from a drawer and pull my chair over to a blank wall. I stand on the chair, being careful not to fall.

"Okay," I say. "Here I go."

I take one corner of the canvas and a nail; like a thumbtack, I push the nail into the thick canvas and through the wall; I do the same thing with the remaining three corners.

"Okay." I say. "I'm all set. Now, to draw the picture."

SIERRA J. BALL

I begin to sketch the outline of a giant monster; one that looks like a giant octopus. I sketch it with long tentacles. I then start to draw collapsing buildings and a long highway.

"Arch-Peteryx Feathervault." I say as I put details on the face of the monster. "He's a savage octopus; an octopus on Highway Fifteen."

I chuckle. I then hear the phone ring; I jump down from the chair and pick it up.

Me: Hello?

Anonymous: Leviathan.

I recognize the voice right away.

Me: Levetin?! How are you . . . .

Acanthus: I know how to use a phone, Leviathan; my colleagues and I owned one of the very first ones made.

Me: Why are you calling?

Acanthus: So, I guess you don't want to know what you're in store for?

Me: Levetin, please. I'm listening. Tell me what's up.

He is silent for a moment. I then hear him talking to a couple of people in the background; most likely Spinosus and Balcanicus; Spinner and Tarsus, as they are also called sometimes.

Acanthus: Leviathan, there are a bunch of them, still.

Me: Anubis servants?

Acanthus: What else? One of those bastards managed to escape the Monte Carlo massacre and ratted us out. We're looking at a lot of them now.

Me: Well . . . how many, roughly?

Acanthus: About six-hundred.

Me: Six-hundred?!

Acanthus: Don't panic, Leviathan. When have I ever left you to do hard work?

Me: Plenty of times.

Acanthus: Enough. I'll handle them; you just worry about Peteryx, okay?

Me: Yeah, I'll do that.

Acanthus: Finish your painting first; you have time.

How did my brother know that I was painting a picture? I stop wondering when I see a few branches from a tree sticking through the open bedroom window.

Me: What's your plan?

Acanthus: You know my plan, Brother. I take out the reinforcements, you take out the Egyptian.

Me: I'm sure it's hard work, having to get rid of all of them.

Acanthus: Nothing's too hard for Acanthus of Corinth . . . except for a few things, if you get me.

I bother not to walk into that; I know exactly what he's going to do: He going to laugh and say, "Ha! I knew you'd fall for it!"

Me: Where are most of the Anubis guys, Levetin?

Acanthus: The Luxor.

Me: I had a hunch.

Acanthus: You may also want to get in touch with your best friend.

Me: Mordecai?

Acanthus: So, you have more than one best friend?

Me: No; I have lots of friends, but not more than one best friend.

Acanthus: Well, yes. Talk to Mordecai.

Me: What's up?

Acanthus: Your friend's new girlfriend is going away for a while; she and her father are going to Tijuana to visit the parents of that guy you decapitated.

Me: And why's that so bad?

Acanthus: Wow, California really has turned you into a clueless celebrity; pull your head out of your ass, Leviathan. Mordecai talks on chat rooms.

Me: Yes. He told me that he talks to a person with the screen name Bunny twelve.

Acanthus: Who happens to be a German chick who wants to get next to him, sleep with him, and extort him for the story he's writing about you. She is a fanatic over immortals.

Me: I don't think that's going to happen, Levetin.

Acanthus: When have I ever lied to you, Leviathan? And stop calling me Levetin; Levetin Golgohoth's dead.

Me: No. Not to me, he isn't.

My brother is quiet . . . for a bit.

Acanthus: Worry about Arch-Peteryx first, then go back to Los Angeles and kill that girl; if you won't do it, I will.

Me: If she's going to extort Mordecai for my chronicles, she's got it coming.

Acanthus: I didn't mean her, Leviathan. I meant the knocked up bitch who's sleeping with her dead boyfriend's cousin . . . . and other people.

Me: What? I'm not killing Jessica!!

Acanthus: You will when you find out who the baby's for.

I grunt in disgust. I say goodbye to Acanthus and hang up, but not before he wishes me luck on killing Peteryx.

You Will Call Me "Master"

I go back over to the canvas to finish sketching my picture of Peteryx the Octopus.

"Good job on the sketch." I hear a voice say. I chuckle.

"Why, thank you, Murabbi." I say, turning around to face him. "It's Peteryx."

"An octopus is Peteryx?" the Eternal One asks. "I would've pictured him as one of those Anubis things."

"Like the ones Levetin and his followers are taking out?"

"Yeah, sort of. Also, like the Egyptian god Anubis; the man with the dog's head."

"And the Anubis army in *The Mummy*."

"What?"

"Nothing."

"Yeah, well, anyways . . . Peteryx reminds me of how Draken Hark used to be."

"He's worse than Draken Hark. Revelatianus himself would tell you that."

"It is Revelatianus that led Draken Hark to lead a wicked life."

I think about it. I only saw Revelatianus once in my life, and I get angry regularly for him not wanting to visit me in person.

"Angeleal said that you and Azrael know a story about Draken Hark." I say. "She said that he experienced something similar to Peteryx's entrapment."

"Yes; I know that story very well. Come over here by me."

I walk over to Murabbi, who ushers me over to the bed. I sit down.

"Tell me about it." I say. "Every single detail."

"Certainly." Murabbi says as he takes a seat in the chair, after he drags it close to the bed. "This happened over eight-thousand five-hundred years ago, in Catel Huyuk, Turkey."

"What happened out there?"

"Well, you see . . . Azrael and Drakengaard Hark lived in Catel Huyuk. Revelatianus made them Eternal Ones about thirty-thousand years ago."

"Did they always live in Catel Huyuk?"

"No. They were born in Avignon, France; they're French. So, anyways, Revelatianus made Azrael and Draken Hark into Eternal Ones about thirty-thousand years ago; they would have to obey him from then on."

"Thirty-thousand years ago, from now?"

"Yes."

"If Azrael and Draken Hark are that old . . . how old does that make Revelatianus?"

"Revelatianus? Now, that's a mystery. All I can say is this: He told us, once, that he remembers the Old Stone Age like it was yesterday."

"The Paleolithic Period?! No way!! That began about a million years before the birth of Christ!!"

"Leviathan, I'm telling you the truth." Murabbi pulls the strings on his lyre. "He's from the Old Stone Age. And, I bet you're wondering why he wears that crown."

"Well, I wasn't too curious about the crown, but since you brought it up, tell me."

"Well, Revelatianus is kind of like . . . a Neanderthal person; the top of his skull is shaped like a cone."

"Oh my god. So, he's like . . . a Cro-Magnon thing? Some sort of . . . ape?"

"Yeah, I suppose so. It would make sense that he would be apelike; his ears are pretty large, too . . . if you've noticed them. He claims that he was raised by Cro-Magnons."

"Really? Well, how did he become immortal?"

"Well, Revelatianus told us about a group of apelike men called the Primateship; he said that there were four of them. He believes that they made him an immortal."

"Okay. Tell me why Revelatianus made Draken Hark evil."

"Right." Murabbi pulls the strings on his lyre again. "Well, anyway, over eight-thousand five-hundred years ago, Draken Hark, the younger of the Hark brothers, began to grow jealous of Revelatianus; he wanted to be the leader of the Eternal Ones and for Revelatianus to take a hike."

"He was envying Revelatianus's power since . . . ."

"Since Revelatianus announced that he shall be called Master by his followers. Azrael, being older and wiser than Draken Hark, understood it well . . . but Draken Hark didn't like it."

"And, I still cannot believe that Azrael is older than Draken Hark."

"Three years his senior."

"Anyways, Draken Hark became jealous of Revelatianus in what year?"

"Well, it was thirty-thousand years from now; you'll have to calculate it."

"You should know."

Murabbi sighs and smiles.

"Almost twenty-eight thousand years before Christ." he tells me. "You have to subtract the two-thousand years anno Domini."

"I knew you'd know." I say.

"Don't be a smartass, Leviathan; you *are* Levetin's twin brother. Anyways, Draken Hark really started to hate Revelatianus, right after I became an Eternal One, which was about eight-thousand five-hundred years ago, in Catel Huyuk, Turkey. Are you following me?"

"Yes, go on."

"Okay, Draken Hark confronted Revelatianus and told him how much he hated following his word."

"Kissing ass, in today's terms."

"Perhaps. Well, he said, '*I want to challenge you to a music contest.*' Revelatianus said that he would accept the challenge. So, we all went into the city and summoned the people; they were to act as judges. The Primateship had come to back up Revelatianus; they started hooting and howling, and the leader of the bunch had to translate."

"Could he speak English?"

"No, it wasn't English that we spoke back then, but I'm translating this story into English."

"I see."

"Well, the leader of the Primateship said that the winner will be called the Master; the loser will have to face the dreaded pit of black scorpions. Our attention was directed to a huge, deep dark pit, and I imagined that it was full of scorpions."

"Yeah, hence the term *the pit of black scorpions.*"

"I said don't be a smartass. So, the people in the town of Catel Huyuk were ready to judge the contest. The leader of the Primateship handed Revelatianus a stringed instrument, just like mine." Murabbi pulls on the strings again. "And then he handed a woodwind to Draken Hark; a flute, to be exact. Okay, so everyone listened as Revelatianus went first; he sang and played music on the—uh?"

"The lyre?"

"Yes, thank you. Anyways, Revelatianus sang a song and played music that was so beautiful, so breathtaking, that it brought the townspeople to tears; it even brought the Primateship to tears, which is considered a high honor, since they were considered stone-hearted. I was crying, and so was Colai, Angeleal, an even Azrael."

"Wow, so Revelatianus is a talented musician, like Orpheus."

"I suppose. Anyways, everyone talked amongst each other and said that Revelatianus should win the contest and stay in charge of the Eternal Ones. Well, Azrael, Angeleal, Colai, and I said that it wouldn't be fair if Draken Hark didn't get to play a tune on the flute; he shouldn't have to face the pit of scorpions for nothing. So, everyone agreed to listen to what Draken Hark had to offer."

"So, how did he do?"

"He was just as good as Revelatianus; I considered picking him to be the winner. Azrael did, too; of course he'd favor his little brother's talents before Revelatianus's. However, it was the townspeople's vote that kept Revelatianus in power."

"So, Draken Hark had to get into the pit of scorpions?"

"Yes. He really didn't want to."

"Who would; they're scorpions."

"Leviathan. Anyway, he pleaded with the Primateship to change their minds. He even tried to play some more music to charm them, but it didn't work."

"So, did the Primateship push Draken Hark into the pit?"

"No. Revelatianus did; he was forced to."

"Huh?!"

"There was a catch to the contest; the winner must push the loser into the pit. Revelatianus won; Draken Hark lost. 'Push him into the pit, Revelation.' The leader had said."

"Revelation?"

"That was Revelatianus's name to the Primateship. He's destined to be the last Eternal One to live, and he is going to deliver an enlightening and astonishing secret. I don't know how it'll all play out, or who he'll reveal it all to. Anyways, the Primateship wanted Revelatianus to push Draken Hark into the pit of scorpions. I could see tears in the Master's eyes; he didn't want to do that to Draken Hark, but he had to; it was the rules of the contest. 'Yes, Master.' Revelatianus said. He handed me the golden lyre, the same lyre I have here." He holds it up and smiles. "Revelatianus walked over to Draken Hark. 'I'm sorry,' I heard him say to him. Revelatianus put his hands on Draken Hark's shoulders to push him in, but Draken Hark wouldn't go down without a fight."

"I figured that."

"Yes. He threw the flute off to the side and began to wrestle with Revelatianus; the Primateship began to yell and howl; they fled like a bunch of cowards. The townspeople got scared and ran off, too. Angeleal and Colai fled, screaming; Azrael and I stayed behind. '*Run, boys!!*' Revelatianus shouted to us, but we wouldn't. Azrael shouted to Draken Hark to stop fighting, that he was only making it worse. He was right. Just then, Draken Hark lost his footing and fell backwards; as he did, he grabbed a hold of Revelatianus's crown; he fell into the scorpion pit with it."

"Then what happened?"

"We could hear Draken Hark shouting for help down below; Azrael ran over to the pit to try and help; he was going to jump in and get his brother out of there, but Revelatianus grabbed him. '*I gotta help him!!*' he shouted. '*Let me go!*' I decided to try and help Draken Hark after a while; I leaned into the pit and extended the lyre out to him; he wouldn't grab it so that I could pull him out."

"So . . . he just stayed down there?"

"It's not that he wanted to; he was too weak to get out because of the stings from the scorpions. However, after a while, he threw Revelatianus his crown back. Azrael called out to his little brother, but he never answered him back. He and I both thought that the worse happened, but Revelatianus said that he wasn't dead; he just needed to adjust to the scorpion venom."

"So, did Draken Hark managed to pull himself out of the pit of scorpions, or did he need some help?"

"He got out himself, three days later. And, do you know what Revelatianus made him do?"

"What?"

"Well, when Draken Hark got out of the pit, he found all of us in Catel Huyuk. He was a total wreck; his hair was haywire, the whites of his eyes were red, he had sting marks all over his skin, he was just . . . a hot mess. The only thing that still looked decent on him was the red lightning bolt scar underneath his left eye."

"What did Revelatianus make him do?"

"Revelatianus hadn't put his crown back on, since he had it pulled off his head three days earlier, so . . . he made Draken Hark place it back on his head; he then had to call him *Master*. And, that's how it was to be. Revelatianus was, and still is, the leader of the Eternal Ones. Back then, Draken Hark still felt a little envious, but he didn't want what happened to him to occur again, so he asked if he could be the Master's right hand man; Revelatianus accepted, because Draken Hark resisted getting killed in the pit of deadly black scorpions."

"Right hand man, huh? Well, Draken Hark's kissing more ass now than ever before."

"Leviathan . . . mouth, young man."

"Is that the story?"

"That's all of it."

"Awesome story. And, you did say that the lyre Revelatianus handed to you is . . . ."

"The same one that I have here." He pulls on the strings. "Such a beautiful instrument."

I get up from the bed and open the window.

"I'm going to explore Sin City now." I tell Murabbi.

"Okay." He says. "Well then, I should go."

"You don't have to, if you don't want to."

"I would like to follow you around and help you out, but this isn't my battle; it's yours. Besides, you need to track down Levetin; I'm sure he has some well-thought-out plans for you to do."

"Is Peteryx here in Vegas?"

"Yes, he is. His main hideout is the Luxor, but his whereabouts are continuously changing."

"Well, he better be ready because when I see him, I'm going to kill him."

"How are you so sure that you'll get him this time? You failed to kill him so many times before."

"No; he has failed to kill *me* so many times before. Besides, I have my twin brother; I trust Levetin."

"It's because of the Trio that Peteryx never came close to killing you. They made sure that your spirit, that possessed his body, wouldn't be ruined. Also, with Peteryx in your body, they couldn't risk losing your vessel. By the way, I have to compliment you on your new haircut; Angeleal told us about it. It's really neat."

"Thank you."

"Yes, and good luck." Murabbi takes a bow. "You will win this." he vanishes.

Acanthus's Bar Story

I sit in the bar and restaurant area of a place called Mandalay Bay; Balcanicus and Spinosus watch an event called UFC 46: Supernatural, a rerun, on the TV.

"I totally think St. Pierre's gonna kick Parisyan's ass." Spinosus says.

"He did." Balcanicus tells him. "You saw this already, in January. Remember?"

As they debate about the Ultimate Fighting Championship event, I wave the bartender over to me.

"What can I get for you, sir?" she asks.

"Water." I say.

"Water?"

"Yes, water; give it to me."

The bartender nods. She then gets me a glass of Fiji sparkling water.

"Anything else?" she asks as she sits the glass down.

"No, thanks." I tell her.

She leaves to go tend to other patrons. I then take a sip of the water; I can feel it running through my veins and perking up my foliages.

"Where's Leviathan?" Balcanicus asks.

"He'll be in town shortly." I tell him. "Until then, would you guys like to hear a story from my past?"

"Okay." Spinosus says.

"Yes, Master." Balcanicus agrees. "I'll listen."

I decide to tell them about how Arch-Peteryx grew to be so afraid of me and my colleagues, Arachne and Dante.

"This is about Imhotep Feathervault." I tell my servants. "He was so determined to take Leviathan out that he was totally oblivious to life around him. Well, around the year sixty anno Domini, he stayed in Galilee, in the Israel and Jordanian provinces of the place, and searched for clues on where Leviathan might be. During his search, he met a young man who was in his early thirties. His name was Thomas, and he claimed that he knew Leviathan in the past, so Peteryx decided to build a friendship with him."

"Is that the worst part of it all?" Spinosus asks.

"Hush, and Acanthus shall tell you the rest. The friendship between Peteryx and Thomas got a little more serious. Now, when I say that homosexuality is a no-no in the eyes of the Israelite and Jordanian people, I mean exactly that; it's strictly forbidden."

"Master . . . ."

"Thomas willingly allowed Peteryx to sodomize him on a regular basis. After all, Thomas was different; he didn't like women in that kind of way. Anyways, Arachne confronted me and Dante; she told us that Peteryx was doing something that he would never forgive himself for. She then told us that she would have to mark Thomas. We were okay with it. After all, I was a little rusty on the torturing and killing, and Dante could've used some more Human essence; he was starting to sprout gray hairs. So, it was clear: Arachne was going to mark Thomas, I would kill him, and Dante would vindicate him, drain him, and make him a cold lifeless walking corpse. So, while Arachne went to retrieve Thomas, Dante and I found Peteryx in a tiny city just outside of Galilee. He tried to act tough and intimidate us; he knew that Leviathan is my brother, and he wanted me to tell him his exact whereabouts."

"Where was Leviathan at the time?"

"India, I believe. Well, I said that I would tell him, only on the condition that he'd listen to some clues that we had to give him; they were regarding Thomas. Peteryx uneasily accepted the offer and listened to what we had to say. Dante then handed Peteryx a clay bowl that was full of water; images began to reflect in it. The first few images were showing Peteryx holding his son Jonathan as a baby. It then showed Jonathan growing up and talking to Leviathan; after it showed Leviathan leaving Jonathan behind, there was an image of the boy talking to his mother. Finally, when it got to the last few images, it showed Jonathan as a young man . . . the young man that called himself Thomas . . . the young man who fell into a homoerotic relationship with Peteryx . . . his biological father."

"No way!! Incest?!"

"Yes way, and we totally caught him on it. Peteryx, in shock and surprise, dropped the bowl of water onto the ground and shattered it; you could see his legs turning into wet noodles as he tried to catch his breath. He looked like he was going to pass out, but then . . . a burst of anger seized him and he began to yell at us; he practically blamed us for making that happen."

"It wasn't your fault, Master." Balcanicus says. "Peteryx didn't do enough research."

"No, he didn't. Plus, it was never a good idea for him to get into the homo stuff." I take another sip of water. "Anyways, we informed Peteryx that Arachne found Thomas, and that she was about to mark him. He went from disbelief, to anger, to freaking out within a minute. He pled with me. '*Acanthaceae, you cannot!! You cannot have her mark Thomas!! He has no knowledge as to what has happened!! He's innocent in this!!*' I told him that Thomas made the decision to start the forbidden relationship, and that he'd have to pay."

"He called you Acanthaceae? Isn't that what the servants and other immortals call you?"

"Yes. After all, it describes me as all acanthus plants, and not just the mollis. Anyways, Peteryx, not wanting his son to pay for his mistakes, crawled on his hands and knees and practically clung to my leg like a leech; I thought he'd tear the fabric of my garments clean from my skin. He leaned his head on my hip and cried; his face was so close to my property that I thought he'd blow me off!"

"Huh?"

"Yes. The whole time Peteryx's muffled cries were vibrating into my hip, I tried hard not to laugh from being tickled, and somewhat aroused. Dante, however, couldn't stop laughing; it looked like, at first, he was crying, but closer observations showed that he was being humored. He was trying his best to stifle his amusement by covering his mouth with his hands, but it was so obvious what he was doing."

"If I would've saw Peteryx go from a tough guy to a crybaby, I would've laughed myself to death."

"Yes, well, that's you, my dear Tarsus. So, with no other options left to make us hear him, Peteryx snatched my bloodletting dagger from my belt and made Dante and I watch as he cut deep into his own throat; he was literally trying to hack his own head off."

"Get out of here!!"

"It is true. Peteryx only managed to cut halfway through his neck before he realized what he had done; begging to live, he crawled, or rather dragged himself, across the dirt and back over to us. He lost a large amount of blood, and if he didn't bind his wound, he was going to bleed out right there. Also, the scarabs were escaping from the gash. Even though I was getting hungry, seeing all of that blood, I wrapped my hands around Peteryx's neck to avoid further damage while Dante summoned Arachne; he told her to not reveal the contents of the clay bowl she had with Thomas; it would reveal his past and present. Afterwards, we managed to mend Peteryx's wound and send him on his way."

"That's it?" Spinosus asks.

"Ah, but the plot thickens. Unbeknownst to Peteryx, my dear sweet Arachne had marked Thomas for his dirty deeds; he had no idea what it meant, I'm sure. Maybe, perhaps, he wasn't even aware that he had been marked. Either way, it meant that I had to take him out."

"Do all people who Arachne has marked have to be killed?"

"Yes; they all get owned, eventually. Well, the way this all ends . . . with Peteryx long gone, off to look for Leviathan, I found Thomas, or Jonathan rather, and told him what had to be done. He realized that the maroon mark on his skin was the mark of the Stalker, which meant he was condemned to die; he gladly accepted. He asked to not look at me as I'd kill him; I obliged. So, he turned his back to me . . . and with one whack from a huge wooden club, he was no more."

"And, does Leviathan or Peteryx know?"

"Peteryx knows now, but Leviathan doesn't. I know that he'll be sorrowful if he ever found out about Jonathan, or this story."

"Do you think he got his fake name from the kid he raised?"

"Most likely."

"I see. And, where do you think the name Note came from?"

"The note he left Sheldon and Jess Weinstein after taking their son from Jerusalem four years ago."

"Oh. So, Master Acanthus, do you think Arachne could mark Peteryx and you could kill him instead of Leviathan?"

"Yes and no. A lot of people realize what Arachne's mark looks like, and when they see it, they go into hiding; Peteryx would be the perfect candidate for this, but since he's Leviathan's target, she has to pass him up. If Peteryx wants revenge on Leviathan, we'll let him have that wish."

"But he won't kill Leviathan, will he?"

"No, I don't think he will. You are familiar with the Georgopoulos family from Athens, right?"

"Yes, Master." Balcanicus says.

"Whether or not they were marked, I had to kill the both of them; Mommy was a thief and a junkie, Daddy was a sadist and a rapist, and Baby was a helpless victim who received salvation from the Golgohoth twins."

"She screamed when she saw me."

"She remembered you from when you tried to snag her from her parents on a bus ride. Do you remember that, Tarsus?"

"Yes."

"Although you weren't in disguise, she still remembered you when you donned that wig; I believe she remembered your eyes."

"Perhaps."

"So," Spinosus says. "What's the moral of this story?"

"The moral," I smile. "A wise old man once said: *He who makes mischief for all the wrong reasons, soon will find an unexplainable tattoo on him.*"

"Sure, he did. And the rest, of course, is the worst part."

"Indeed."

I drain my glass of the water and turn my attention to the UFC event.

Cop Out 2: Second Strike

I make it into the city and stand under a palm tree on the Vegas strip; I look out at a tiny bar adjacent from the magnificent Mandalay Bay hotel and casino.

"Tiny bar?" I ask myself. "Or Mandalay Bay?"

I sense that there's a strong but familiar power radiating from the Mandalay Bay; it seems that Levetin and his acanthus boys are out working as well. I won't be a bother to them.

"Tiny bar." I say.

I cross the busy street and make it to the little bar called *Archipelago*; I walk in and sit down on a barstool.

"What can I get for you, sir?" the bartender asks me.

I have no money on me right now; too bad I didn't ask Powers to loan me any.

"May I have a glass of water, please?" I ask. "It's hot and dry outside."

"Yes, sir." the bartender says. "Hot and dry, it is. One sparkling water, coming up." He pours me a glass of Fiji artesian water; he then brings it over to me. "Happy drinking."

"Thanks." I take a sip. "Delicious." Water never really agreed with me too much, but it's still refreshing and good.

"Are you from around here?"

"No. I'm from Los Angeles."

"Ah, the City of Angels. I've never been to Los Angeles; is it nice out there?"

"Yes, it's nice there, but it's a very dangerous city."

"Yeah; I heard that there's a lot of gangs, like the Grande Pacific Chicanos."

"They've been taken care of."

"Yeah, I saw it on TV; unbelievable. So, what brings you here, sir?"

"I lost somebody. She was a very sweet person, and I let her slip through my fingers."

"Oh, I hear you. We've all been there, haven't we?" the bartender looks over at someone; he nods at them. "Excuse me."

The bartender leaves and I think to myself: *When I meet up with Peteryx, what will I do? Will I put up a great fight . . . or will I just kill him in no time??*

I see that the bartender returns; he pours me some more Fiji water in my glass. He then takes another glass and pours some Jack Daniels into it.

"What's this?" I ask. "I didn't buy a drink."

"They paid for it." he says, looking over at a couple of people. "Why don't you thank them?"

I nod at the couple; they wave. I wonder who they are. Do they know who I am?

I gulp down the Jack Daniels. I then take my Fiji water and sit down at a little round vacant table; I see the young couple get up and walk over to meet me.

"Hi, there." the young man says. "Can we join you?"

"Okay, sure." I agree.

They sit down. The young man seems friendly; he has sandy-brown hair and kind brown eyes; too kind, actually.

The woman . . . I'm not so sure; she has long red hair and bright-green eyes. She reminds me a lot of that skank Cherry. Not to mention, that bigger skank, Carissia.

"Thank you for the drink." I say politely.

"You're welcome." the woman says. "You look like someone who could use a little surprise."

What's that suppose to mean, I think. Although they seem like a nice couple, I still need to watch these two like a hawk. I feel like something doesn't sit right with them.

The woman extends her hand out to me.

"My name is Rachel." she says, "Rachel Davidson."

Davidson, I think as I shake the woman's hand; I secretly wipe my hand off on my pants leg. *Why does that sound familiar?*

"This is my best friend, Foxy." Rachel continues. I shake the young man's hand.

"Foxy?" I ask. "I'm sure that's a nickname?"

"Is Foxy a nickname?" he asks. He then chuckles. "Yes, it is; my real name's John; John Everton." He concentrates on me, and I can sense something strange in his stare.

"You look like someone I know. What's your name?"

What should I tell him? My pen name . . . or my real name? I refuse to use the name Jonathan Note; it's my celebrity name in Los Angeles. However, Leviathan Golgohoth is the murderous albino tyrant who strikes fear into the hearts of many. Do they know about Leviathan? Perhaps not . . . but I don't think I'm going to take any chances.

"Jonathan." I say.

"I knew it!!" Foxy says. "You're Jonathan Note!!"

"Oh wow!" Rachel says with excitement. "The Jonathan Note!!"

"How do you know me?" I ask.

"We're detectives." Rachel says. "We heard about your story with the double murder suicide in Los Angeles."

"Detectives, huh?"

"We're with the Las Vegas Police Department." Foxy says. "We're off duty right now."

I take a sip of my Fiji water. I then notice that there's a leaf in the glass. How did a leaf end up in the glass? It wasn't there before, and there are no plants in the bar. This has to be something serious.

Leviathan, I hear a familiar male's voice say to me; it's coming from the glass. *It's your brother.*

"Levetin," I say. "How did . . . ."

Hush. They cannot hear me; only you can. Listen to me, and don't talk back, okay? Do NOT trust those two people. They are not who they say they are. They're deceptions; they are loyal to Arch-Peteryx Feathervault.

"But how did . . . ."

I said be quiet and listen. They are Anubis servants; they are loyal to Arch-Peteryx Feathervault. They are in disguise. You, of all people, should've been able to see that the moment you laid eyes on them. Can you not sense the presence of evil anymore? Is it because you don't want to? This is a dangerous world, Leviathan. There are other predators besides us that run rampant in it. Get your mind back into reality; stop acting like a clueless celebrity, because that's the last thing you are. Man up and get rid of those two before they do you in!! NOW!!

I watch as the leaf disintegrates into the water; not a trace of it is left behind.

"So, Jonathan," Foxy says. "What brings you here to Vegas?"

"I'll tell you," I say. "If you come with me."

I drain my glass of water. I then stand up from the round table and head toward the exit; Rachel and Foxy follow me. Once we get outside, I stand and face them.

"So now," I say to them. "You want to know what brought me here to Vegas?"

"Yes." Foxy says.

"Tell us." Rachel says anxiously.

I smile and pop all of my knuckles in one swift move; my hands need to be good and loose for what I plan to do next.

"Arch-Peteryx Feathervault." I say. I watch as Rachel and Foxy's mouths drop open. "I also know that you're not cops; you're servants; Anubis dogs. And, you know that I am Leviathan Golgohoth. So . . . what do we do?"

Rachel and Foxy do not give me a suggestion of what we should do. Instead, they pull out their guns; both of them being automatic pistols, .45 caliber, just like my revolver. They aim them at me.

"Well then, Leviathan." Foxy says. "Would you like to tell us how you managed to find out who we really are?"

"I have my ways." I say, borrowing one of my brother's favorite quotes.

"Tell us, or we'll shoot you!!!"

"Well, it looks like you're going to have to shoot me."

Rachel cocks the hammer on her pistol back.

"I'll nail you with one shot!!" she says.

I laugh. It cannot be done. Although I'm not invincible, like the Immortal Trio, it's going to take more than one bullet from a .45 pistol to destroy me.

"That won't happen." I reply. "I'm pretty good at dodging bullets."

"We'll shoot you through the heart!" Foxy shouts.

"Apparently," I begin. "You didn't hear me; I can dodge bullets, especially those kind."

"It's gonna hurt when we shoot you!!"

"What purpose do you serve anyway?? Anubis dogs? HA!! You make Peteryx look like more of a coward than he already is!!"

I hear the springs in Rachel's gun give way; she has fired a round. I go to dodge it, but it catches me in the left arm; I fall, face forward, onto the sand.

"I thought he said he could dodge bullets." Foxy says, laughing.

"Make sure he's dead." Rachel says to Foxy.

I sense someone approaching me; Foxy, no doubt. As he stoops over me to see what's what, I roll over quickly and stabbed him in the chest; he fires at me, but I dodge the bullet. I scramble to my feet and begin to run; Rachel and Foxy, the Anubis servants, race after me.

As I run, I begin to feel as if the trees are whispering to me; no doubt, it's the effects of the leaf that was in my water . . . the leaf that revealed Rachel and Foxy's true identities.

This feeling must be what Levetin feels all the time as the father of the plant kingdom, I think as I feel myself being drawn to the whispers of the desert palms.

I try my hardest not to collapse while I run. Rachel and Foxy are firing at me, but they do not hit me. What kind of firearm training did Peteryx teach them? They couldn't hit a barn if they were standing right next to it!!

They waste their bullets. When I hear the clicking of their guns, signaling that the rounds are spent, I stop running; I turn around, and as Rachel and Foxy get closer, I aim my revolver at them. I think that I should've used it earlier than at this time.

"Hold it, you dogs!!" I shout.

They stop running; I realize now that I might have full control of them.

"What are you doing, Leviathan?!" Foxy shouts. "Have you gone mad?!"

"Oh, so now the tables have turned. Not so big and scary without your guns, are you?" I walk up to the two servants and keep the revolver aimed at them. "On your knees, both of you."

"No way." Rachel says.

Almost instantly, the trees begin to blow in a strong gust of wind; it's almost as if they're in this game with me . . . and truthfully, I believe that they are.

Seeing that there's another force that they have angered, Rachel and Foxy get on their knees in the rough sand. I smile.

"Start talking." I say. "Why did you decide to disguise yourselves as cops to take me on? Did you think I wouldn't find out?"

I see that Foxy is clutching at the wound in his chest; it appears that I got him right above his heart. I walk around him; I keep the revolver pointed at Rachel, to make sure she doesn't do anything stupid.

"How's the wound . . . John," I said. "If that's your real name."

"How's the arm?" he asks me.

"I've experienced worse pain than this."

"You don't know what pain is."

"Really? I don't?" I face him; I place my free hand against his left pectoral. "Perhaps you believe I can't experience extreme pain . . . but maybe you believe that I can cause it." I start to squeeze his pectoral muscle, near the stab wound. "Indescribable pain." I dig my nails into the wound. Foxy clenches his teeth and tries not to scream.

"Cry out, and I'll kill you." I place the gun to his head. "Mark my words."

Rachel begins to run. Before she can get too far, one of the palms swoops its massive leaves and catches her, causing her to fly backwards.

4535678343456789034567893

I turn my attention from Foxy and over to Rachel.

"Trying to skip out on the fun?" I ask her. "You're the perfect subject for fun."

I shoot Foxy in both legs, making sure he doesn't run; he cries out as he clutches his limbs.

"Don't hurt him!!" Rachel shouts.

"Why do you care?!" I ask. I aim the revolver at her. "You know . . . I really hate redheads. I hate them all, but I do have one exception . . . one of my best friends; her hair is orange."

"Colai. She's still a redhead."

Rachel begins to laugh; I whack her in the face with the revolver. She falls to the ground.

"Red and orange are two different colors, bitch." I say as I watch black blood gush out of her nose and sink into the sand. I touch my left shoulder. "You thought that a gunshot wound to the arm would kill me?"

Rachel has a look of fright on her face as she looks at the wound on my arm; I look at it and see that there's no trace of a wound there; nothing at all.

You possess the power to ricochet bullets, Leviathan. I hear my brother's voice tell me. *A gift from me to you, for a while.*

"I . . . I shot you!!" Rachel shouts.

"No." I say. "I have the power to repel them."

"What are you gonna do to us?" Foxy calls out.

"Well," I say. "If I let you two go, you'll summon more of your Anubis buddies to take action and hunt me down. But, if I get rid of you two . . . I'll be one step closer to finding Peteryx and eliminating him for good." I wipe the blood from Rachel's face with my bare hand. "And, that's priority number one." I smear the blood on Foxy's face. "And I *will* succeed."

I pull Rachel to her feet, and as I do, I keep the revolver pointed at Foxy.

"I don't like redheads." I say to her. "They leave painful reminders of what happened to me in Ancient Sparta."

"Ancient Sparta?!" Foxy asks in surprise.

"Oh, that's right; an Anubis servant isn't old enough to know how long ago my roots date back. You and your gang are one of the newer mistakes Peteryx has made." I cock the hammer of the revolver back. "Stand up."

"You shot me in both legs, you psycho!!"

"I SAID STAND UP!!!"

I aim the gun to Rachel's temple. Immediately, Foxy tries to stand up without falling back down.

"You have a choice." I say. The palms seem to move in closer to listen. "You either snuff out this broad, or I'll do it. And, if I have to do it . . . I'll ice you as well. So, decide now, pal. What will it be? Her . . . or the both of you? Either way, the redhead is going to die."

Rachel begins to struggle. I keep the barrel of the revolver pointed at her temple.

"I cannot kill my partner." Foxy says. "We are loyal to Arch-Peteryx Feathervault; we do not betray one another!!"

"So," I say. "That's your answer? I kill her, then I kill you?"

Foxy says nothing.

"John . . ." I say.

"Rhen." he says. "My name is Rhen; her name is Rhon; that's our new names."

"Charmed." I offer the revolver to the Anubis servant. "Take it and shoot your partner."

As Rhen approaches, I see a big wet spot growing on the front of his pants; it's running down his leg and into the sand.

This sissy has just pissed his pants!! How pathetic!! I thought that Peteryx's followers were supposed to be ruthless and cruel; they are giving Peteryx a bad image!!

"Now, what is this?" I ask, holding back laughter. The palms quiver as if they are tickled. "Why did you just piss your pants? That's disgusting."

Foxy, John, Rhen . . . whoever the hell he is, doesn't answer me; he is trembling from a combination of pain and fear. I aim the revolver back at Rachel's temple.

"Well then," I say. "I guess you leave me no choice; you're too scared to follow orders. Peteryx is too soft on you. I'll have to take out the garbage myself."

"YOU CAN'T!!" Rachel screams.

"Why not?!" I ask in anger. "Your partner couldn't help you; he pissed himself. You can see that he wants to cry. He's no different from a small child! Now, if you're loyal to Peteryx . . . ." I push Rachel, or Rhon, away from me. "Why don't you try and stop me?!"

As I wait for them to attack me, I can finally sense the evil pouring from them. A rare fury seems to emit from Rhen; he forgets all about the gunshot wounds in his legs and rushes toward me.

Now!! Acanthus shouts via the palm trees.

I take aim at the renewed Anubis servant; my finger squeezes the trigger and the revolver goes off. The bullet hits Rhen, right in the forehead. He stands there, for a moment, as if he sees an unbelievable sight. He then collapses onto the sand; he is dead.

Rhon begins to scream.

"OH MY GOD!!!!" she shouts. "OH MY GOD!!!!!! YOU KILLED HIM!!! YOU BASTARD!! YOU KILLED HIM!!!!"

I head toward Rhon. She starts to back away, and the palms shield her escape path.

Ha!! I hear my brother's laughs through the leaves of the palms. *That was awesome, Leviathan!! That bullet was a magical one; it spun around inside his skull. It turned his brain into mush!! Kick-ass!!*

"Indeed, my brother." I say. "He refused to kill her, so he got what was coming to him."

"Who are you talking to?" Rhon asks.

"Someone who's taking each and every one of you out." I say to her. "Someone I trust to pave the way to Peteryx. Now, he leaves you to me. Do you have anything else to say?"

"Yes."

I nod for her to proceed. I begin to get a bit woozy from the powers of Acanthus.

"Speak, quick." I say. "Now."

Rhon wipes more black blood from her nose.

"Do you remember the hooker you murdered not long ago?" she asks me.

"The redhead, yes." I say. "Her name was Cherry Davidson . . . hold up. You're an Anubis servant. How did you . . . ."

"She was my first cousin. She moved here from Henderson to make a living, and when I heard about her death, I swore to get revenge on the person who killed her."

"So . . . you've been an Anubis servant for about a day. And, what about him?" I gesture to Rhen's dead carcass.

"We were friends for many years; he agreed to join me in the fight."

"How did you find out that I killed that whore?"

"Peteryx found me and told me himself; he said that he could help me get revenge if I decided to join forces with him."

"Which is now leading you to *your* demise." I cock the hammer of the revolver back again. "You've earned it."

"No!! Please, don't shoot me!"

"You won't feel a thing, my dear. I'll shoot you in the head, just like him; you'll die instantly and pain-free."

"No. Just let me go, please."

"If I let you go, Acanthus will track you down."

"I won't tell Peteryx about this."

"I'm sure he'll find out anyway." I aim the revolver at her. "And besides, if I release you, you'll send a hoard of dogs after me. I cannot risk letting you go."

Rhon shuts her eyes and clenches her teeth tightly; she is prepared for me to remove her existence from the planet.

I fire a round from the revolver . . . but it does not come in contact with Rhon's body. She opens her eyes to see that I have the gun pointed at the sand.

"Did you actually think I was going to shoot you?" I ask her.

"Yes." she squeaks.

I shake my head. I then move in closer and grab the back of her neck.

"You do know . . . " I say as I get my dagger out. "Human flesh makes an excellent fertilizer for growing plants. However, since you're no longer a Human," I make a slit in her throat. "Your flesh will make an excellent meal for Acanthus of Corinth's palms."

"WHAT?!" she screams.

I push her forward. The instant her blood begins to gush out of her neck, the trees bend low and are on her; she screams as she disappears within the large leaves of the palms.

Once the palms rise again, Rhon is gone; all that is left is a large black stain on the sand. The trees quiver in satisfaction.

"That was worth it." I say.

It sure was, Brother. Acanthus tells me.

That Cannot Be What I Saw!

I decide not to bury Foxy in the hot Vegas sand. Like Cherry, I'll leave him for the buzzards.

"I think it's time for me to go back home." I tell myself. "It's been a wild night."

As I walk home, down the Vegas strip, I look over at Mandalay Bay and wonder what went on with Levetin and his followers.

"I wonder how many more Anubis servants are out there still." I say as I stare at the bright lights of the magnificent hotel and casino.

Two less than the number I gave to you earlier. Levetin's voice echoes through my mind.

"Nice."

After about a half hour, I make it to the Bentley residence in the small quiet suburban neighborhood. I see that the curtains are pulled back from one of the windows. I sneak over and take a look inside, and what I see next shocks me; Powers and Rolfe are together . . .and when I mean together, I mean . . . they are naked and doing it!! They are literally lying together, like a man and a woman would!!

Realizing that I am very light-skinned, they could probably see me; I quickly duck down and hide in the nearby bushes.

"What the hell?!" I ask myself. "What are they doing?!"

I look back through the window. I see that Powers is behind Rolfe and has a huge smile on his face; Rolfe has his face buried in a pillow, but I can still hear muffled moans.

As I look in on them with disbelief, I feel a familiar presence approach me.

"Well," they say. It's Acanthus. "You don't see that every day."

"But . . ." I start. "They're . . . they're cousins."

"Do some more research, Brother."

"It's incest."

"Believe what you want, Leviathan. I'll be working all night to take care of Peteryx's rabid dogs." He stares at me for a moment. "You cut your hair?"

"Yes, Levetin."

"Oh, okay. Looks good. Well, see you later."

Acanthus departs. I then rush over to my bedroom window; I see that it's still unlocked, so I open it and climb through. I then sit down on my bed.

"Oh, Jeez." I say to myself as I take my shirt off. "That cannot be what I saw. It has to be the dark playing jokes with me."

I stare at the canvas on the wall. I then notice that there's a note attached to it.

"What's that?" I ask as I get up and head over to the canvas. I detach the note, turn on the desk lamp, and begin to read the fine print.

Leviathan,

You're really beginning to creep us out. We know about Acanthus of Corinth being your twin brother, which is cool, but we also know that you're still hooked on your murderous ways. You are one of the most provocative tyrants that ever roamed the earth, but you're also the most dangerous one. Although we did enjoy your stay, we think it's best that you leave this place; this is Rolfe's idea.

He seems really uptight about something and I think it has something to do with you . . . or the Deathbringer. We're giving you until tomorrow night to leave, or we will go to the police.

Thank You.
Edward Bentley

"I'm creeping you out?" I ask as I crumple up the note and toss it in the wastepaper basket. "What I saw you two doing freaked me out, and I am a hardened monster. Talk about calling the kettle black."

I sit back down on my bed. I then take off my shoes and leave on my khakis; I lay down and stare up at the ceiling for a few moments. I then feel myself drift off into a deep sleep.

I wake up early. Today is Tuesday, March 16th, 2004; it's 8:00am. I get out of bed and put back on my bluish-green shirt and shoes. I feel like writing, so I sit down at the desk and get out some more paper; I grab my pen.

"After I left the Arabian Peninsula," I start. "Tieran and I went to India."

I cringe at that thought. It was a good time there . . . but it was also a bad one. I decide that I will write about it anyway.

I begin to scribble down some more of my chronicles.

Meeting Rox And Phaize

On that night in the Arabian Peninsula in 40 A.D., Tieran went and slept with Nasada, and I watched, like he wanted me to do.

After they were done, I excused myself quietly and left to go find a place to sleep. When I woke up the next morning, Tieran met up with me; he didn't tell me if it was any good or not, but he did say that he got very hungry while they were together. I believed him because he had a spot of blood near the corner of his mouth.

"We did it again." he said. "After you left."

"Seriously?" I asked.

"Yes, and before she could climax, I drained her."

"Huh?"

"That's right. I drank all of her blood while I was inside her. And the euphoria of it all blew me away; I'm leaving her blackened body in the temple to rot."

I was amazed; I always took Tieran to be the disciplined type, and not vulgar like me.

280 years had passed since Tieran and I met in Arabia. We then traveled to India; it was the year 320 A.D., and the Gupta Empire, ruled by the Guptas, emerged in the Ganges Valley.

One day, while we were sitting in a temple that was used to worship the god Ganesh, Tieran approached me and handed me a bone; an oracle bone.

"Ah," I said as I studied the marks on the bone. "What does it say?"

"Well, look here." Tieran said as he pointed to a couple of squiggles. "It says here that Rox Rothbane and Phaize Pierterch are here in India."

"Is that true?"

"When has an oracle bone lied? They brought you to me, didn't they?"

They did. So, it was possible that they could lead us to two more tyrants. Wow, if oracle bones were that accurate, they could tell me where Peteryx was and what he was planning. Still, I was a bit skeptical about their prophecies.

Tieran and I walked through the busy streets of a little town that is today New Delhi. People were buying, selling, and trading goods. Tieran put a hand on my shoulder.

"Why is there a cow in the streets?" he asked, pointing to the white bovine sitting in the middle of an old dusty road.

"Well, Tieran," I said. "The Hindu people don't eat beef. Look, there goes another one." I pointed to a black bull. "They let cows run around freely."

"But why?"

"Well, here in India, the Hindu consider cows to be sacred."

"Oh, I see now."

We continued to walk, and as we did, I thought about China's dynasties. Even though Tieran would start talking up a storm, I decided to ask Tieran about them. What the hell?

"What dynasty is China going through now?" I asked him, hoping that I would get one quick answer.

"Well," Tieran said. "It's three hundred-twenty A.D.—I believe that China's still in the Han Dynasty."

"And, you told me that you're from the legendary Xia Dynasty."

"I am; I am a descendant of Yu the Great."

"Okay."

"Yes. Now, let's follow the oracle bone and find Phaize and Rox."

"If they're even here."

Tieran turned and looked at me; his Asian eyes glinted with a hidden evil.

"You, Leviathan," he said. "You underestimate the power of the oracle bones greatly. Have more faith in the oracles, my friend."

"Will do, Tian Fang-Xia." I replied.

We began to search some more when someone put their hands on our shoulders; Tieran and I turned around. It was who we were both looking for.

"Rox?" Tieran said. "Rox Rothbane."

"You *are* here?" I asked.

"Of course I am, peeps." he said in his boyish Celtic British accent. "And so is Phaize."

Phaize Pierterch was standing behind Rox, smiling at us. He didn't say one word; he was the shy and quiet tyrant. That didn't mean he couldn't kill. A silent and deadly predator, he was.

"I knew the oracle bones were accurate, Leviathan." Tieran said to me. All I did was nod; I already looked stupid by not fully believing in their powers.

I saw that Phaize was staring at me. I knew that he remembered me from the old Spartan days.

"Leviathan Golgohoth." the Corinthian tyrant said.

"Yes." I said.

"It was hard to believe, but I see it clearly."

"See what?" Tieran asked him. Phaize turned to him and Rox.

"You do realize that Leviathan has a twin brother, right?" Phaize asked. "A twin brother who killed my brother before I competed in the Corinthian warrior games?"

"Leviathan," Rox said. "There's another one of you running around here?"

"Of course not." Phaize said. "My brother, Prometheus Pierterch, was killed by his brother, Levetin Golgohoth . . . Acanthus of Corinth."

"And?" I asked. "What's your sad sorry self going to do about it? What Levetin does is not my issue."

"Whoa, no way!!" Rox said. "Acanthus of Corinth is your brother?!"

"You know that." Tieran told him. "All of us know that."

"I know; the sick bastard ripped out one of my lip rings when I said that I didn't know the whereabouts of Leviathan."

"Were you lying?"

"No, I wasn't. He knew this, and he still ripped it out!"

"And he actually let you go?"

"Yeah. He said that I wasn't marked and that it wasn't his duty to kill me; I was lucky, considering it's a known fact that one out of every hundred or so of his victims manages to escape alive. Speaking of which, where's Gogough Celdeklause? (pronounced Go Guh Kell Da Clues) I thought that he'd be with you and Leviathan."

"I'll ask the oracle bones later."

"Huh?"

"The oracle bones; they led me and Leviathan to you and Phaize."

"My bet is that he's in Mesopotamia, pretending to be Leviathan."

"Excuse me?" I asked.

"You're Gogough's idol." Rox said to me. "His hair is cut like yours and he wears clothing that resembles your style. You know, it almost got him killed."

"It did?"

"Oh yeah. I heard that it was the Trio."

"Why am I not surprised by that?"

"You know, it would make perfect sense; you are Acanthus's brother, and he'd hate for anyone to try and mock you."

"I suppose. Maybe we should try and find Gogough; we'd complete our group."

"We'll call it the Tyranny Squad; we're all tyrants."

"What about Arch-Peteryx Feathervault?" Phaize asked. "He's a tyrant, too, right?"

"Yes," I said. "But he's an outcast; he hates us."

"Why?"

"Because he hates me; I'll explain later."

"No need; I heard all about the scarab pit in Giza."

"You did, didn't you?" I stare at the pathologically shy tyrant. "Tell me a bit about yourself."

"You know about me; I met you in Sparta in the eight-hundreds B.C."

"I only met you; I don't know much about you except that you are a Corinthian."

"Yes. I am a Corinthian. I also won the Corinthian warrior games one year; I have a feeling that it was rigged for me to win."

"Really?"

"It was no surprise that Acanthus, who killed my brother because he married Arachne, would allow me to win the games; it was no coincidence. He knew who I was. But . . . why would Arachne try to kill me? She married my brother."

"They were married?" Rox asked.

"Prometheus was married to the Spider Queen for a little less than a day. Acanthus, with his jealousy and hatred, killed him in cold blood; I won the Corinthian warrior games, and then . . . I magically get attacked by my brother's black widow; no pun intended. I think Acanthus convinced her that I was the cause of Prometheus dying."

"I see." I replied. "So, you hate me because you hate Acanthus?"

"I never said that I hated you, Leviathan." Phaize told me. "I am just stunned that your twin brother is the Immortal Trio's Deathbringer."

"I know Levetin Golgohoth; the man that calls himself Acanthus of Corinth is just a shell. Levetin is alive in there, and I can feel it."

Phaize stared at me for a few moments, and I could tell that he was confused about my statement on my brother being alive. I'm sure Phaize knows that Levetin Golgohoth was claimed by Thanatos Aqueous.

"Let's walk." Phaize said.

As we walked through the dusty streets of India, Phaize began to try and break out of his shyness by telling us a little about Carissia, the redheaded Spartan whore that I killed.

"Carissia slept with everything that had a penis." he said. "She had a crazy wild affair with a guy named Arris. She slept with Coria's friends, and she slept with me a few times."

"Wow," Rox said. "That girl really loved penis, I'd say."

"Yeah. She also had a threesome with my twin cousins Odax and Ajax; they were on vacation in Sparta when she met them. They're deceased now, of course."

"That's funny!" Rox laughed. "I'm hungry; let's go find something to eat."

"Blood." I said. "Indian blood."

"Good choice. Indian blood is a very exotic delicacy, I hear."

Tieran grabbed me by my hand.

"No blood right now." he said. "We don't need it right now. We want—rice. How does rice sound?"

"Mmm . . . Mmm . . . Mmm." Rox said. "Rice." He scratched his head in wonder. "What is rice?"

"It's a delicacy, for Humans. You can find rice in many countries here in Asia."

"We'll have to pay for it though." Phaize said. "I don't have any money on me. Do you?"

Tieran and I checked to see if we had any kind of currency on us; we were also broke. Rox, however, was the only one who had plenty of money on him.

"Don't sweat it, tyrants." he said. "I have some money right here; I'll be glad to treat you all."

"Where'd you get that?" I asked.

"It was easy; I stole it from some rich old geezer who came from Rome."

"Rome?"

"Yes; Rome. It's not like there's anything wrong with that; he was in my native Wales, and he was taking over the villages . . . so I filched this right off of him."

"How long ago was this?"

"About a hundred years ago. I converted them into rupees. C'mon, let's eat."

The Accident

Rox, Phaize, Tieran, and I went to a little Indian marketplace and got ourselves each a bowl of wild rice with a lavish lamb curry. Rox handed the marketer eight rupees; we sat down and began to eat.

"How do you expect me to eat this?" Tieran asked.

"Use this thing." Rox said, handing Tieran a beautifully carved wooden spoon. The Asian tyrant stared at it for a few moments.

"I don't eat with these." he said. "I eat with chopsticks. I'm Chinese, you know."

"Look, bro. You have to make compromises; tyrants don't drink blood with chopsticks because it's not right. Try the spoon."

Tieran scooped up a spoonful of lamb curry and put it in his mouth; he continued to eat with the spoon, but he stopped when he saw that I hadn't eaten any of my food.

"Hey, Leviathan," he said to me. "Are you gonna eat your rice and curry?"

I hadn't heard what he had asked me. I had been eyeing a suspicious-looking woman; she was doing an artistic dance with two people who wore Ganesh masks. I wondered who she was. Suddenly, it dawned on me that one of the tyrants was talking to me.

"I'm sorry," I said. "What did you say?"

"Are you hungry?" Tieran asked. "I asked if you were gonna eat your rice and curry; I'll eat it if you don't want it."

"Oh, okay. You're welcome to take it; I'm not hungry."

Tieran thanked me and took my bowl of lamb curry. Rox looked over at me.

"Leviathan," he said. "You really should eat, or your veins will collapse."

"I'm fine." I told him. "I can go at least a month without any blood. Don't worry about me."

He looked over at the woman dancing with the Ganesh people.

"What do you see?" he asked.

"I'm not sure if that's her . . ." I said, getting up. "But, that woman dancing with the Ganesh dancers looks a lot like Arachne."

"The Spider Queen? Here? Now?"

I saw Phaize look up from eating and began to survey the area.

"If she's here . . ." he said. "Then . . . that means Acanthus and Dante are with her."

"Are you sure?" Rox asked. He turned to Tieran. "You, Chinaman, you can see the future; are they here with her?"

"It is certain." Tieran calmly said. "But I cannot be absolutely sure; perhaps if I had some bones on me, I could see."

"Oh, forget it."

"I'm going over there." I said.

"Leviathan, wait." Tieran said, sitting his bowl of lamb curry down and getting up. "If you're going over there, I'm going with you."

"Me, too." Rox chimed in.

"I refuse." Phaize said.

"You're a tyrant." I told him. "You have to fight."

"She was the subject of Prometheus dying, and it was *your* brother that did it."

"I know, but that's the past. Your brother would want you to avenge him, would he not?"

"Yes. However, you would not allow it; I know that you will not allow me to kill Acanthus of Corinth."

"The Trio cannot die."

"What?"

"They cannot die unless their master is destroyed; he has no internal Hellfire core, so it's nearly impossible to kill him."

"I don't believe you; you're just saying that because you don't want me to kill your brother!!"

"It's true, Phaize." Rox stepped in. "You cannot kill the Immortal Trio unless Thanatos of the Waters is manipulated and destroyed. Did you not hear about how Acanthus lost his head in Rome?"

"What?!" I asked.

"Yeah; Acanthus was decapitated by accident. About a few seconds later, his headless body picked his head up and put it back on its shoulders; he then healed the wound cleanly, permanently attaching his head back to his body."

"That's a myth." Phaize said.

"No, it's true. I heard about it."

"From who?"

Before Rox could answer the question, we heard a faint rumbling in the distance; it sounded a little bit like thunder, but it was getting closer.

"What is that?" I asked.

"It sounds like some bad weather's headed this way." Phaize said.

"But the sky isn't getting darker."

"No." Rox said. "Look at that."

We saw a cloud of dust rising up from the streets. It began to get thicker as the noise began to get louder.

"Oh no." I heard Tieran say to himself. "It's a . . . a herd of cows!"

"Huh?" Rox asked.

"Stampede!!! RUN!!!"

The four of us began to run. As we did, we heard the angry cries of charging cattle coming near. They were knocking over market stands and tossing people into the air!!

"Take cover!!" Tieran shouted. "We'll be crushed!!"

We began to climb up a nearby rocky formation to wait for the stampede to pass. Phaize, Rox, and Tieran managed to climb all the way up; I struggled a bit with a loose area. The next thing I know, I black out. When I came to, I saw that I was getting up and standing in the middle of the path where the cattle had been.

I could hear my colleagues shouting my name. Before I could answer them, I heard the familiar sound: The cows were back. I looked toward the left, but it was too late; I was pulled under the hooves of the angry beasts.

I felt myself being thrown about and kicked around; I thought that it would never end. Finally, when the stampede passed, I was left lying on the ground in excruciating pain; I have never felt no pain worse than this.

"LEVIATHAN!!!!" I heard Tieran shouting. "OH NO!! I think he's dead!!!"

I watched, in blurred vision, as Tieran, Phaize, and Rox pulled me up from the road.

Insults To Injuries

We sat in a small hut; a Hindu medicine man examined me to see how bad off I was. When he finished, he told me what was going on.

"Young weary traveler," he said. "I see no brain or spinal cord injuries, seeing as how you can still walk and talk perfectly. However, you have broken six ribs, and ruptured your left testicle. You are very lucky to have made it out of that alive."

"Wait a minute." I said, leaning forward a tiny bit. "I . . . ruptured a testicle?"

"Yes, traveler."

"Will I still be able to have kids one day?"

The doctor was silent for a bit. He then rolled up his manuscripts and silently left the hut.

"Tell me what's going on!" I demanded as he walked out.

"Leviathan," Tieran said. "While you were out, the doctor said that on top of the broken ribs and ruptured testicle . . . the accident managed to tear up your entire reproductive system."

"No. Does this mean that . . . ."

"You're inflicted with sterility."

"No."

I hung my head in sadness; I could taste blood as I felt sorry for myself.

I really wanted to have children one day. I wanted to find the perfect person and have at least 2 or 3 of my own. Now, I'd never have that dream.

For the first time, since I left Jonathan behind in Nazareth, I felt tears stinging my eyes. They then rolled down my bloody cheeks and dropped onto the dusty flood, turning into mud. Never would I have my dream of being a father to children of my own.

About fifteen minutes of awkward silence had passed before the next tyrant decided to speak.

"Okay, Leviathan," Phaize said. "Elephant in the room . . . do you miss your penis?"

"Phaize!!" Rox said in a half talk half whisper tone. "It's his testicle, not his penis!"

I tried to breath in deep, but my broken ribs were too much to bear, so I stuck with the shallow breaths.

As I struggled to breathe, in walked three familiar people; a woman and two men.

"No," Rox whispered.

"The Trio." Tieran said.

"And Dante's with them." Phaize said.

"What's that supposed to mean!?" Dante asked in anger.

"Leviathan and I have to talk." Acanthus said. "Out."

No one attempted to move out of the hut. I could sense Acanthus's anger rising.

"OUT!!" he shouted.

Spooked by the Deathbringer's tone, my colleagues rushed out of the hut; I remained right where I was.

"Leviathan," Arachne said. "Are you hurting?"

"No." I said through gritted teeth. "I'm just doubled over in pain and fighting back tears because it's a new dance craze."

"What are you saying? Are you pinning this all on me?"

"Somebody has a guilty conscience."

Acanthus stepped in to stop the escalating argument.

"That was a nasty fall." he said. He knelt down by me. "Also, the stampede didn't look too lenient." he held out an item to me. "Here's your tooth, Leviathan."

I hadn't realized that I had lost a tooth in the accident. I could feel my tongue beginning to poke at the rest of them; it stopped at a gap at the top. So, now I knew where the taste of blood was coming from.

"Oh," I said. "I don't need it."

"Oh, but you do." Acanthus replied. "I would've scooped up your testicle as well, but it's beyond repair; those cows stomped it to a pudding."

I heard snickers coming from Dante; he obviously thought that this was funny stuff.

I felt my temper spark.

"Shut that bastard's mouth!!" I shouted. "Shut his mouth before I go over there and rip his tongue out at the seam!"

"I'd like to see you hobble over here and try." Dante said. Acanthus approached the Vindicator.

"Go watch the others." he said and pushed him out of the hut. He then returned to me and offered me my tooth again.

"This is your tooth, Leviathan." he said. "I'm just returning it to you."

"Why would I need it?" I asked. "A new one's going to grow in its place."

"Teeth don't grow back!"

"Well, mine do."

"How? My teeth don't grow back!! How are your teeth growing back when . . ." My brother stared at my tooth for a little bit. He then placed it in a pocket on his dark-brown pants. "I think I'll hang on to it." He stood up. "Well, get better, Brother."

"Levetin," I said. I watch Arachne's face become angry.

"His name's Acanthus." she said. "You filthy tyrant!!"

"Arachne, dear." Acanthus said to her. "Why don't you join Dante outside; make sure the other tyrants don't do anything stupid."

"Who put *you* in charge?"

"The cows did . . . when they sterilized my brother. And the mushrooms are saying that I'm top dog."

"Mushrooms?"

"Leave."

Arachne scoffed and stormed out of the hut to meet up with Dante. Acanthus turned back to me.

"What is it you wish to tell me, Leviathan?" he asked.

"I . . ." I started. "I . . . I can't have children . . . ever."

"Well, no bull. You ripped your insides up."

"This is a nightmare!!"

"Well, Leviathan. I'd give you one of my testicles, but then I'd have only two."

"Excuse me?!"

"Well, isn't everyone supposed to have three testicles?"

"NO, LEVETIN!!" I shouted. I then grasped at my ribs; I shouldn't have exerted so much energy. "Male subjects usually have two. It would be normal if you donated one of them to your brother, right?"

"I suppose so, but I've been shooting the wrong kind of seed for centuries. You wouldn't like it. Besides, your insides are torn up; even if I did agree on donating one to you, it wouldn't fix the sterility problem."

"So, I'm . . . ."

"Yeah, you're pretty much screwed in that department. But hey, lots of men here are sterile; you should feel adequate."

I nod.

"You just can't seem to stop insulting me," I said. "Can you, Levetin?"

"I'm really sorry." he said. I could see a smile growing on his face; not a sympathetic one, but one that was of comical proportions.

"When you heal up," he said. "Come after me."

"Where will you be?" I asked.

"Here and there; I never settle in one place too long. There's this nice little delicacy called mushrooms that grow in many places now; I like to eat them."

"I see. I would be careful though; a lot of them are poisonous."

He went to leave the hut, but turned around.

"For what it's worth," he said. "I think you would've been a great father."

I felt a twinge of happiness flood though me; I could feel my pain diminishing. Despite his cruel and evil ways, my brother still had some kind of heart.

"Thank you, Levetin." I said. "That means a lot."

My brother started laughing.

"I'm just kidding, Leviathan!" he said. "You're a bloodthirsty predator; you don't do well around children. You should've seen the look on your face though." he smiled. "Thanks, Levetin." he mocked me. "What a sucker. Oh, and I don't really have three testicles; just the normal two. Sorry."

Instantly, I felt my pain return and my spirits sink. I picked up a bowl of water from a nearby table and washed the blood off of my face and out of my mouth.

I can't let Acanthus of Corinth make me out to be a softhearted tyrant, I thought.

I got up from the cot and walked outside the hut. What I saw next was confusing: All three of my colleagues were sitting back-to-back; Phaize and Tieran were wearing Ganesh masks; Rox had a weird-looking gourd in his hand.

"What are you guys doing?" I asked.

"The Trio told us to mellow out." Rox said.

"Where did they go?"

"They did this to us and ran off. We don't know where they're heading."

"You didn't act like tyrants and attack them?! Get up, now!!! We're leaving India."

"But, I want to stay here." Phaize said as he removed the Ganesh mask he was wearing.

"No!! Up, now!! We're going to find Gogough."

"Jeez, Leviathan," Rox said, getting up and dropping the gourd. "Who put you in charge?"

"The cows did." I said. "When they sterilized me."

Tieran, Phaize, and Rox collected themselves. I then hobbled with them as they walked down a dusty road. I could feel a new tooth growing in the spot where I had my old one knocked out; I wished that my reproductive system would repair itself as well.

I Need My Tigris

I stop writing and look over at the canvas. I decide that it's lacking color, so I get the tubes of oil paint and squeeze some onto the paint palette; I get out the paint thinner and open it. I also have the window open; I'll need good ventilation while doing this.

I grab my paintbrush and I start to paint. As I apply color to the canvas with light feathery strokes, anger begins to build up inside my chest. I think of Peteryx A.K.A. Imhotep Feathervault and how he caused me so much pain in the past; he is so very determined to kill me.

I also think about Powers and Rolfe Bentley, and how they were having sex last night . . . or so I saw. I also think that it *is* Rolfe who's been stealing my blood. Oh, I hope he's not drinking it or injecting it into his body; that can cause some serious damage, if taken in large quantities.

I continue to paint until the image is complete; the clock says 11:15am.

"I need my Tigris." I say as I stare down at my wedding band that gently caresses my left ring finger. "But, I need to stall Powers and Rolfe for a while."

I put away the painting equipment and exit the bedroom. I walk into the living room where I see Powers sitting on the couch; he's sipping coffee and watching the news.

"I read your note." I say. "Why did you and Rolfe decide to write it? Do you guys think I'll hurt you or something?"

Powers cuts off the TV and shakes his head.

"No." he says. "But Acanthus of Corinth will."

"Acanthus has bigger things to worry about."

"We know that he's here in Vegas, Leviathan. Rolfe and I noticed that the plants outside your bedroom window have grown quite a bit these past few days; it's kinda obvious how they got that way."

"Where's Rolfe now?"

"He's still asleep; I thought that he'd be up already. I guess he's worn out."

166

Oh, I believe Powers; I saw what wore Rolfe out last night.

"Did he say where he had gone off to?" I asked.

"Yes." Powers said. "He went to the Luxor."

The Luxor, I think. That sounds awfully farfetched, beings my blood has gone missing, and the hotel may be Peteryx's current lodging; I can almost guarantee that Peteryx would love some samples of my blood.

"He needs to get up." Powers says. "We have lab work to do. Rolfe has to help me with an experiment."

"An experiment?" I ask.

"Yes. I took some pictures of ancient stones, and I need to develop them . . . but I can't seem to find my flask of bromine. Have *you* seen it?"

"I didn't know you had bromine."

"Yeah."

"Is it missing from the chemical room?"

"Yes, but how did you know I have a chemical room?"

"I have an excellent sense of smell; I can smell the chemicals from out here."

I can't tell him that I have his bromine; what would he say if I told him that I drink it to see my wife?

Send him to the one-hour photo shop, Leviathan. I hear my brother's voice say to me.

"Why don't you just go to the one-hour photo shop?" I suggest. "I hear they develop pictures with great quality."

"Yeah," Powers says. "I guess I'll have to do that. Can you tell Rolfe I'll be back soon, if he wakes up?"

"I'd prefer not to, but I guess I will."

"Do you have anything to mail off?"

"Not at the moment, no." I go to walk away, but decide to make things clear. "I'm not leaving here."

Powers nods and leaves to go to the one-hour photo shop. I find it so amazing how, with only one suggestion, I got Powers to listen and obey. I had the power of demanding in the past, but usually, it went with procrastination from others. I think my brother's new gift to me is a wonderful possession.

I go to Rolfe's room and look in at him; he's still asleep. I wonder what he's dreaming about.

Our boy Peteryx. I hear Acanthus's voice.

"Strange." I say. "He's guilty of something."

That, he is.

While he sleeps, I decide to browse through his belongings. I'm mainly looking for devices that are used to draw blood: Needles, syringes, tubes, test tubes, etc.

You're looking in all the wrong areas, Leviathan.

"Stay out of this, Levetin." I whisper.

I will not!

Acanthus's tone tells me that I need to extend my search. I leave Rolfe's room and go to the chemical lab. I search there, and I still find nothing.

Wrong again, Leviathan.

"Levetin," I say. "Shut it; I don't need your two cents."

So, I guess you won't need me when the time comes. You're right, Leviathan. You're a strong tyrant . . . so is Peteryx.

I sigh. I have to at least listen to what my twin says.

"Where should I look?" I ask.

You already suggested it yourself, my brother. You need your Tigris. Appreciate what your wife has to offer. In due time, you'll find out what you need to know.

"Good deal." I agree.

I go back to my room and I quickly grab the flask of bromine. I stare at it.

"Should I really visit Tigris again?" I ask.

Why question it? You do miss her.

"Can she really tell me who's taking my blood?"

Trust your wife, Leviathan.

I decide to try something out. I shut the bedroom door and lock it; I lock the bedroom window. Perhaps whoever's taking my blood won't be able to get it this time.

Leviathan, what are you trying to accomplish, a longer journey down the rabbit hole?

"Whoever tries to break in," I start as I uncork the bottle. "I will hear it and wake up; I'll catch them in the act."

You're in more denial than a drag queen having to accept that she's really a man.

"Knock it off. It'll work."

Suit yourself, Leviathan.

I take a swig of the disgusting brown fluid. I then put the cork back into the flask.

I'm slowly killing myself. I think as I lay down on the bed. *Then, Peteryx will not have to try and kill me; I'm accomplishing it for him.*

"Any minute now." I say.

I feel myself sinking, so I shut my eyes; I black out soon after.

After feeling the experience of sinking and traveling, I wake up; I find myself sitting in a beautiful flower garden. There's a water fountain and a little pool with different colored fish swimming in it.

I look over and see Tigris; she's kneeling down next to a bed of roses. She touches a rosebud and the flower blooms.

I get up and walk over to her.

"You know," I say as I place my hand on her shoulder. "The only other person that can accomplish that is my twin brother."

"Leviathan," she says and smiles.

We hug and kiss each other.

"I missed you so much, my dear." I tell her.

"I think about you so often." she says. "You cut your hair!"

"Yes, I did."

We passionately kiss and hold each other for a long while.

"I wondered when you would return to me, my love." Tigris says. "I got worried that you wouldn't."

"Why wouldn't I?" I ask. I kiss her neck. "I love you; I could never forget you."

We sit down next to the bed of roses; we continue to touch and kiss.

"You know, Leviathan," Tigris says. "Roses say *I love you*."

"I thought they said *Get Well Soon*." I say.

She laughs. I love when she does; it makes me smile.

"You're so funny, Leviathan." she says, giggling.

"Just entertaining." I say.

"I love to see you in a good mood."

"It's fun."

I lay down on the green grass and look up at the baby-blue sky.

"The sun's shining." I say. "Why isn't it hurting my eyes?"

"In this place," Tigris starts. "Nothing can hurt you; it's an absolute goodness."

Nothing can hurt me, I think. *Not even Peteryx. What about the Anubis servants?*

I sit up and stare into Tigris's beautiful green eyes.

"I want to ask you something important, my wife." I say. "Do you know who's stealing my blood? I wake up with tubes in my arm; I know it's being drawn."

"I know who's taking it, my love." Tigris says.

"You do!? Who is it?"

"It's the exact person you had suspected the first time."

I knew it!!!! That bastard!! He flat out lied to me and said he didn't take any of my blood!!!

"Rolfe!!" I shout. "I knew it!! I suspected him, and I was right!! Why didn't I kill him when I had the chance?!?!"

"Leviathan, please don't hurt him; he's not the person you want."

"He stole my blood."

"I know, but he's less of a threat to you than Peteryx is."

"For all I know, he could be bringing the blood to Peteryx; Powers said that he was at the Luxor."

"But it doesn't mean that he was bringing the blood to Peteryx. Listen, Leviathan. Leave Rolfe to another power, and you focus on Peteryx."

"Tigris, I . . . ."

"Shhhh," she puts a finger to my lips. "Leviathan, I said that you should leave Rolfe to another power; do you catch my drift?"

As punishment for Rolfe stealing from me, I should leave him to . . . .

"Levetin." I say.

"Very good." Tigris says. "Brother knows the best way to fight back."

I kiss my gorgeous wife on her temple.

"You're so smart, my dear." I say. I run my fingers through her brownish-black ringlets.

"Just helping out my wonderful husband." she says. "Listen, I can only imagine how angry you must be about it right now."

"Steamed. But hey, isn't he going to get his Acanthus-based comeuppances?"

"If that is what you wish. Unless you want to do it yourself, and miss the chance of nailing Peteryx."

"But, I have to get revenge."

"Ah, but it's the other way around; Peteryx is seeking revenge on *you*!"

"I meant Rolfe."

"Focus on Peteryx."

"But, I can't let Rolfe get away with stealing my blood!"

"Levetin will handle it."

"But, it's personal!"

"Then you have to stop visiting me."

"What? No!! Never!!"

"Leviathan, that is how Rolfe is taking your blood . . . when you black out and visit me."

"That part is worth it."

"Leviathan, please."

"I can't stop visiting you, Tigris. I love you."

"If you really love me, my husband, you'll do something for me."

"Anything, my love."

"Let Levetin have Rolfe, and you get Peteryx."

"Yes. And, we need to make love again."

"We will, as soon as possible. For now, let's enjoy the flower garden and the Koi pond."

I love the different scents of the flowers; they remind me of my days back in Egypt, when perfume was popular. I remember the Beauty of the Nile fragrance that King Menes gave to me. I gave it to Colai, and I heard that, to this day, the sacred temple of the Eternal Ones smells like it; Colai had poured it into an everlasting incense burner.

I look over at Tigris. I lean forward and give her a kiss on her cheek.

"I love you, Tigris." I say to her. She smiles.

"I love you, too, Leviathan." she says. "You mean so much to me."

"You mean *everything* to me. I'd lose it all before I ever lose you."

We lay down on the grass and hold hands. We enjoy the sun and the lovely flowers, and the Japanese Koi fish. I suddenly feel that familiar pain in my arm again.

"Oh no." I say. "It's happening again."

"Leviathan," Tigris says. "What is it?"

"My arm hurts again. My blood's being taken."

"It's time. Good luck, Leviathan. I love you."

"I love you, too, Tigris. I won't fail you!"

Tigris kisses me goodbye. I then shut my eyes and sink back into the present.

I Got You Now!!

My eyes pop open; I'm back in my room. I look over and see Rolfe; he can hardly believe that I am awake.

Before he can run, I grab his wrist; I jump up and unsheathe my knife. I keep a tight grip on him as I press the tip of the blade firmly against his throat.

"I knew it was you!!" I shout. "I got you now, you piece of shit!!"

"Leviathan, wait!!" Rolfe says. "I can explain!!"

I hurl him to the floor. I put my dagger back into its sheathe and yank the needle and tube out of my arm; I produce my revolver.

"Start talking." I say, aiming the gun at him; I cock the hammer back.

"Please," he says. "Don't shoot me; I'm only doing what I was told to do."

"Are you lying to me?"

"No. Not this time."

"So, you were lying to me the previous time I caught you?"

"Yes, I'm sorry."

"Now, boy . . . you will have your penis removed."

"No, please!! I'm sorry!!"

Well, now that I have a loaded gun pointed at him, perhaps he can tell me the truth.

"Who told you to steal my blood?" I ask.

"I can't tell you that." Rolfe says.

"Tell me, or I'll blast you!!"

"ARCH-PETERYX FEATHERVAULT!!"

I knew it. Rolfe is stealing my blood, and taking it to Peteryx.

"Where is Peteryx?" I ask.

"No, Leviathan." Rolfe says. "Please."

I move in a little closer, keeping the revolver pointed at Rolfe's head.

"Now!" I demand.

"It's a secret." he says.

I aim the gun at his crotch.

172

"The Luxor!" Rolfe shouts.

"And," I start. "You're not telling me this just because I'm pointing a loaded revolver at you?"

"I swear."

I smile and nod. Now, I know where Peteryx's hideout is, and when the time is right, I'm going to attack it and take him out.

No, Leviathan. Acanthus's voice says. *The Luxor is infested with Anubis dogs; you wouldn't make it past the first floor. Let Peteryx send them out to you . . . or me, rather.*

I sigh. I then point the revolver away from Rolfe.

"Get out of here." I say in a voice that means business. "Now!"

"Yes, Leviathan." Rolfe says.

Mordecai's Plague

Rolfe storms out of the room; he leaves the vial of blood he collected behind. After a few moments, I hear the front door shut. I look out the window and see Rolfe running down the street.

"Run." I say, retrieving the vial of blood from the floor. "Just like last time." I open it and drink it all up. "I hope Levetin finds you."

I take a look at the clock. I see that it's already 3pm. Time soars.

I decide to take a shower. I grab a fresh pair of clothes and head to the bathroom; I get in the shower, shampoo my hair, and rinse it. I then soap up and rinse off.

I get out and dry off, I then shave and pull on a pair of boxers. I then put on a long-sleeved dark-blue shirt and a pair of blue jeans.

"It's three-fifteen." I say to myself. "What do I plan to do now?"

The phone rings; I'm slightly startled by it. I see that the call is coming from the DeFranco residence.

"Maybe it's Anticlea." I say. I pick up the phone.

Me: Hello?

Anonymous: Hey, Leviathan. It's me, Mordecai.

Me: Mordi. Hey, buddy. How was school today?

Mordecai: Okay, I guess.

Me: Splendid. How's my little Anticlea?

Mordecai: She's fine. Marilyn enrolled her into a daycare until, if that's okay.

Me: That's wonderful; she did want to go to a place to learn. It's kind of like school.

Mordecai: Yeah; she likes it. She's only going to be there until August, when school starts up, then she'll be enrolled in the 4th grade; she'll be nine by then, I'm sure.

Me: Great. So, why are you calling?

Mordecai: Well, I was just calling to tell you about my online friend, Bunny.

Me: Oh, you mean Bunny twelve?

Mordecai: Yeah, her. She's amazing; I got to meet her in person.

Me: You did, huh? Was Candice okay with it?

Mordecai: She and her dad went to Tijuana for a while.

It's what Acanthus said.

Me: What was this Bunny girl like?

Mordecai: She's really beautiful. She has strawberry-blonde hair; it's so much better than I could have imagined it to be. She's got cerulean-blue eyes; they sparkle all the time. She has pretty, smooth, cream-colored skin that's lightly freckled. And she smells great, too. She smells like fresh sun-kissed peaches. She reminds me of that popular doll here in the United States.

Me: Barbie?

Mordecai: Yeah, Barbie!

Me: A lot of chicks that look like Barbie turn out to be the Wicked Witch of the West.

Mordecai: Oh, come on. That's not Bunny.

Me: Is that her real name?

Mordecai: She said it is. Anyways, we were chatting and she gave me her phone number.

Me: Huh?

Mordecai: Yeah, so I called her once and talked to her.

Me: Does she have a foreign accent? German, perhaps?

Mordecai: I don't think she's German, Leviathan, but she does have a different accent. It could be Russian.

It isn't Russian, I think. Levetin said that the girl who calls herself Bunny12 is actually a German girl who wants to get next to Mordecai to cash in on my story. I think it may be true; Levetin has never steered me from the truth and has never lied to me, as far as I know.

Me: Perhaps she's Russian.

Mordecai: How did you know she's not American, Leviathan?

Me: Most of the people we've associated with in the past four years here aren't American-born. Abdullah, Anticlea, Acanthus, et cetera.

Mordecai: True. But anyways, me and Bunny agreed to meet at the Hard Rock Café.

Me: Really?

Mordecai: Yeah, so I took Ned's car; he, Marilyn, Anticlea, and Stuart are going out to San Francisco to an Eco-Friendly convention; boring. They won't be back for at least a week.

Me: So . . . the meeting?

Mordecai: Yes. I went to the Hard Rock Café, and I saw her sitting at a booth and waving at me; she had a huge smile on her face. And the cool thing was . . . she had ordered lunch for me before I got there!!

Me: And?

Mordecai: She thought it was really fascinating that I am Jewish.

I wonder why, Mordi.

Me: So, what did you guys do there?

Mordecai: After lunch, we had dessert and coffee, then she wanted me to show her the DeFranco home.

Me: And you showed it to her?

Mordecai: Yes, I did. She thought it was really lovely. I even showed her my room.

Me: I hope you only showed her the room, and nothing else.

Mordecai: Huh?

Me: You didn't show her anything . . . private, did you?

Mordecai: Private? Oh . . . yeah.

Me: Mordecai, you didn't sleep with her, did you?

Mordecai: Leviathan, I couldn't take no for an answer; she was so . . . beautiful.

Me: Oh hell, Mordi. Well, what Candice doesn't know won't kill her.

Mordecai: I used a condom, Leviathan.

Me: Where'd you get condoms?

Mordecai: Abdullah's Palms.

Me: He'd actually sell condoms to a seventeen-year-old?

Mordecai: Hosni sold them to me.

Me: I see. Still, don't tell Candice what you did.

Mordecai: I'm sorry, Leviathan. I should've said no.

Me: What man around here's going to say 'No, *I don't want to have sex with you*.' to a sexy blonde woman?

Mordecai: A homosexual.

Me: That's about it. Have you heard anymore about Jessica?

Mordecai: She still hangs around Anson Vickers enough. I saw her puking underneath a tree today at school.

Me: Was she sick?

Mordecai: I guess it was something she ate.

I'm still leaning on Levetin's statement that she is pregnant. I guess I'll see, one day.

Me: I see. Probably still sad about her brother.

Mordecai: Thanks to the tyrant who killed him.

Me: What the hell's that supposed to mean?

Mordecai: Well, you *did* kill him. Oh, hey, there's someone calling on the other line. Hang on one second.

Me: Sure.

Mordecai is silent for a few moments. He then starts talking again.

Mordecai: Bunny is calling right now, Leviathan; it's on the caller I.D.

Me: What's the name say?

Mordecai: Elsa Behrendt; I'm guessing that's her mom.

I don't think that's it, Mordecai.

Me: I guess so.

Mordecai: Can you hold on for a few moments?

Me: Sure, I'll hold.

I notice that Mordecai presses the Flash button; he also presses the three-way button; now, I'll be able to hear their conversation. I decide to stay quiet.

Mordecai: Hello?

Bunny: Mordecai, it's me.

Mordecai: Hey. Hi, Bunny.

Bunny: Bunny?

Mordecai: Yes; your name's Bunny, isn't it? That's what you told me in the Yahoo dot com chat room.

Bunny: No, idiot. My name's Elsa; Elsie, for short. Who in their right mind would have a name like Bunny?

Mordecai: Okay, so your name's Elsa?

Bunny: Call me Elsie. Oh, and I hate Jews.

Mordecai: Excuse me?

Bunny: I don't think I have to repeat myself, Jew.

This doesn't sound good, I think.

Mordecai: Okay, I'm confused.

Bunny: I am German; I come from a long line of Nazis. My father and brothers belong to the Aryan Brotherhood.

Mordecai: So, they're convict Skinheads?

Bunny: Doesn't matter. I am a descendant of Germans who killed off Jews in Odessa.

Levetin's theories are starting to come into play, I think to myself as I listen to what sounds like a blackmail plot waiting to happen.

Mordecai: Why hate me though? I'm a nice Jew.

Bunny: All Jews are exactly the same!! Vile and disgusting creatures!!

Mordecai: I'm not vile.

Bunny: They were guinea pigs, back in the Holocaust, and they still are today!

Mordecai: What's your point, Bunny?

Bunny: My name is Elsie Behrendt.

Mordecai: Elsie . . . what's your point, exactly?

Bunny: One of those dirty kikes raped me.

Mordecai: Oh my goodness!! How'd that happen?!

Oh no, Mordecai. She's going to say *you* did it, and then she's going to extort my story out of you . . . or she'll go to the police.

Bunny: I met him at the Hard Rock Café; he took me to his house and forced me to have sex with him. I didn't want to, so he took matters into his own hands; he beat me and proceeded to rape me.

Mordecai: *I* met you at the Hard Rock café; *I* took you to see my home . . . but I did not take advantage of you and sexually assault you!! I didn't beat you up, either!!

Bunny: Well, Mordecai, I went to the hospital after it happened and got checked; I have bruises and scratches on my face.

Mordecai: What?!

Bunny: The medical team located a hairline fracture on my left cheekbone when they took X-rays, and in further investigations, they found a really bad friction mark on my vagina, proving that I had been raped. So, yes, Mordecai. *You* did it!

Mordecai: BULLSHIT LIAR!!

Bunny: Can you deny it?

Mordecai: I'M DOING IT NOW, YOU PSYCHO!!

I am surprised by Mordecai's sudden burst of anger. He is being accused of rape, and he deserves to be angry. I don't say anything; I keep listening.

Bunny: The doctors used a rape kit to examine me; they found something else.

Mordecai: Oh, what? More friction marks?

Bunny: I tested positive for semen, and lots of it.

Mordecai: That's not possible!! I used a condom; it didn't brake!! You went and slept with someone else!!

Bunny: No. Perhaps you should've discarded that condom somewhere else other than your wastepaper basket.

They are both silent for a few moments.

Mordecai: Oh my god!! You inseminated yourself?!

Bunny: Sure did; it was quite easy to do.

Mordecai: But how?! I don't understand!

Bunny: A turkey baster works as the perfect tool for insemination; it's just as good as the real thing. And, I could easily conceive from it.

Mordecai: Bullshit! Semen can only last for so long in regular room temperatures.

Bunny: I can work miracles. And besides, my father and brothers will kill you for raping me.

Mordecai: *They're* probably the ones who beat your ass just for sleeping with me.

Bunny says nothing. I can practically hear her thoughts. Mordecai has struck a nerve she wished he hadn't.

Mordecai: Am I right?

Bunny: Here's the plan: Remember how you told me that you're writing a story about Leviathan of Mesopotamia?

Mordecai: Yes.

Bunny: Well, I did some research, and I compared the albino tyrant to that of your best friend, who is the famous Jonathan Note. I wouldn't be surprised if they were the same person.

Mordecai: Don't you dare!!

Bunny: No way!!! They *are* the same person, aren't they!?!

Mordecai: It'll be wise if you don't do anymore research.

Bunny: It would be a treasure to many if they could get their hands on a biography of Leviathan Golgohoth. I think I'll make it happen.

Mordecai: It's *my* story!!

Bunny: No. When you get completely done with it, it will have *my* name and picture on it.

Mordecai: You cannot do that!! Leviathan will not like that!!

Bunny: Leviathan Golgohoth!! What a joke!! I'll feel more scared if I come face to face with Levetin Golgohoth!!

Mordecai: Any friend of Leviathan's is a friend to Levetin. He will help me.

Bunny: Acanthus of Corinth helps no one. Besides, I'm still gonna put my name on the book.

Mordecai: Well then, your fate is sealed.

Me: I'm so sure. Besides, if you don't cooperate with my wants, I *will* make my brothers do something about it.

I hear Mordecai sigh on the other end; clearly, without my help, or my brother's wrath, he has to comply . . . for now.

Mordecai: What must I do?

Bunny: I need for you to meet me at The Sports Club/ L.A. You know where it is, right?

Mordecai: Yes.

Bunny: Meet me there in thirty minutes; we need to discuss business.

Mordecai: Why can't we just do it here, over the phone?

Bunny: No. Face to face; meet me in thirty minutes. The Sports Club/ L.A. Don't be late.

Mordecai: I can never be too late for you.

Bunny hangs up the phone and Mordecai begins to cry.

Me: Mordecai, nut up, pal.

Mordecai: I didn't rape her, Leviathan!! Oh my god!! I'm screwed!!

Me: No. She'll be taken care of; either me or Acanthus will see to it.

Mordecai: You have to come back to L.A. now!!

Me: I'm going to try my damnedest to get back to L.A. as soon as possible. Just hold on for me, okay? You can do that, right?

Mordecai: I don't think I can, Leviathan.

Me: Look, she knows who I am, so she may procrastinate whether or not she'll have her brothers do anything to you, okay? Do you think she'll take a chance at harming you when she knows who my brother is?

Mordecai: Germans are crazy.

Me: But they're also cowards. You can hold on, Mordecai; I believe in you.

Mordecai: Okay, Leviathan.

Me: Look, I have to go now, but don't worry; it'll be okay when I make it back.

Mordecai: Yes. Good luck.

Me: Thanks. I'll be back in no time to help you.

Mordecai: Do you think Acanthus can help?

Me: If you'd rather him settle this, he's just a foliage away.

Mordecai: But I trust you, Leviathan.

Me: Either one of us is capable of shredding that girl into ribbons. Just hold on, okay?

Mordecai: Okay.

Me: Peteryx will get what he deserves, then all will be well, and I will come back to Los Angeles. Stay strong.

Mordecai: Yes, Leviathan.

I hang the phone up and slam my fist on the desk.

"That two-timing bitch!!" I shout. "She thinks she can just take my story and do what she wants with it??" I clench my teeth and fists tightly. "No!! No one steals from me!! I will have my time with her!!"

I calm down a bit. I then get out some more paper and my pen.

"I will finish this story," I say as I scribble down the heading for my next chapter in my journey. "But no Nazi bitch is going to put her name and picture on it."

The Hunt For Gogough Celdeklause

Tieran, Rox, Phaize, and I crossed over into the lands that are present-day Pakistan and Afghanistan. We made it to Mesopotamia in just 3 hours; it would've taken less time to get there if I wasn't in such pain from being trampled earlier in the day.

"Home sweet home." I said as I sat down on a large rock to rest.

"Mesopotamia." Tieran said. "Such a pretty place; so green and fertile."

I flinched at hearing the word *fertile*. Never again would that word play a role in my life.

"What river is this?" Phaize asked.

"I believe it's the Euphrates River." Rox said. He turned to me. "Right, Leviathan?"

I realized what river it was; it wasn't the Euphrates. No. This river was the one that my beautiful wife was named for.

"It's the Tigris River." I said. My heart began to hurt more than my entire body did; I could feel tears stinging my eyes; I fought to hold them back.

"Still in pain, Leviathan?" Rox asked.

"Yeah; a good bit. I'll heal up though."

"That looked like a nasty ride, getting trampled and all; it didn't look good from where I was."

"Didn't feel that great, either."

"Wow," Tieran said. "The Tigris River; I heard that a beautiful maiden with the same name was buried along the banks."

I wanted to cry; *I* was the one who buried my precious Tigris on the banks of the river in 2517 B.C. She was 83 when she passed away.

The tears came again; they rolled down my cheeks and I quickly wiped them away before any of the other tyrants could see them.

"We have to find Gogough." Rox said. "I just hope that Peteryx doesn't find him before we do."

"Or the Trio." Phaize said.

"Especially the Trio." Tieran agreed.

181

We searched high and low for Gogough, but there was no sign of the Irish tyrant.

"Maybe he's at the old Golgohoth terrace." Rox suggested.

"It's been gone for many centuries now." I said. "All that's left, I'm sure, are just ruins."

"Come to think of it . . . have to noticed how Gogough's name is pronounced like the first two syllables in your last name?"

"No, I guess I haven't. Let's search."

As we searched for Gogough, we tried calling out to him, but we still didn't get any response.

"Gogough!!" Tieran shouted to the top of his lungs. "Here, boy!!"

"Tieran," Rox said. "It's not a dog we're looking for, you know."

"He might be in Babylon." Phaize told us.

"I heard of this Gogough."

We watched as an elderly scribe walked up to us; he had, in his hands, a stone tablet.

"You've heard of Gogough Celdeklause?" I asked.

"Oh, yes." the scribe said. "He's in Egypt, at the Valley of the Kings."

"Oh, nice." Rox said. "Egypt."

"Where exactly in Egypt is the Valley of the Kings located?" Phaize asked.

"It's near Thebes." I said to him. "It's just south of Memphis. I guess we'll have to go there and get Gogough." I turned to the scribe. "Are you sure that's where he is?"

"Yes." he said. "He told me that's where he was going, and to make a note of it . . . so, I did."

The scribe showed us his stone tablet. It read: *Gogough of Eire. Valley of the Kings. 320 A.D.*

It was written in the cuneiform language, but I could still read it.

"Thank you." I said.

"What's it say?" Tieran asked.

"It says we're going to the Valley of the Kings, in Egypt."

"Oh, great." Rox announced. "Peteryx awaits."

"Very likely, but we have to risk it. C'mon, tyrants. To the Valley of the Kings."

The Valley Of The Kings

It took us three hours to reach our destination. By the time we arrived, it was nightfall. We could see the pyramids, not the temples, because of the torches lit around them.

This area looks awfully familiar, I thought.

We each grabbed a torch from around one of the pyramids.

"Gogough!!" Rox called out. "Gogough, are you here?"

We suddenly heard soft footsteps in the sand.

"Rox?" someone said. "Rox Rothbane? Is that you?"

We saw an orange ball of light coming toward us.

"Halt!" I demanded, holding out my lit torch. "Who goes there?"

"I know that voice!" the person said, walking up. "Leviathan Golgohoth!! I'm your biggest fan!! I'm Gogough Celdeklause!! You're my idol!! Can I join you?"

"We've been looking all over for you." Phaize said. "Please, join us."

It suddenly hit me. We weren't in the Valley of the Kings; not there at all.

"Tyrants," I said, feeling a bit of pain building up in my lower abdomen. "This is not the Valley of the Kings. These are the Great Pyramids of Egypt. This is Giza, near Memphis; this isn't Thebes. We must've taken a wrong turn, or something. We're in Lower Egypt, not Upper Egypt."

"But we still found Gogough." Rox said. "Maybe we were headed to the Valley of the Kings, and we met up halfway there."

I could see that Gogough really wanted to look like me; his hairstyle was the same as mine, and he wore the same black top and bottoms that I had on.

He, however, was not an albino, like me; his hair was crimson-red, but I noticed that there were some white highlights in it. His skin was a light-peach color; he had freckles on his face, just below his eyes, and there were slight rosy-pink spots on both cheeks. His eyes were a peridot-green.

"Wow, Leviathan!!" he said in excitement. "I can't believe it's really you!!"

He moved in closer to me; I kept my torch shining on him.

"What do you want?" I asked.

"I saw you in Greece a long time ago." he said. "You fought Acanthus of Corinth, and won!! That was so cool!!"

"You were around that long ago?"

"Well, yeah; I'm a lot older than you think I am."

"I see. You can lower your torch."

Gogough took his torch away. He then turned to Phaize.

"The shy type?" he asked.

"I don't say much." Phaize says.

Gogough nodded; he turned to Tieran.

"I went to China during the Zhou Dynasty." he said. "I'm pretty sure I saw you there."

"It is certain." Tieran told him. "But a lot of us looked alike back then."

"Tyrants know other tyrants when they see them." Gogough turned to Rox. "Piercings?"

"My left ear, my right eyebrow, and my bottom lip." Rox told him. "My tongue's also pierced." He shows his tongue piercing to Gogough. "Pretty cool."

"Do the piercings state anything?"

"Well, they're popular in Gothic Wales; they're a brand, so to speak. Each piercing says something about you."

"What do yours say?"

"I'm a warrior."

"Clearly." Gogough looked over at me. "I know that Acanthus of Corinth is your brother."

"How do you know?" I asked.

"I overheard the conversation you were having in the Greek amphitheatre with Arachne the Spider Queen when you wounded Acanthus."

"So . . . ."

"If he ever tries to do something serious to us, you can tell him not to do it because we're your friends."

"It's not that easy."

"I see. So, where's Arch-Peteryx? I thought he'd be with you guys."

I had to laugh. Gogough actually thought that Peteryx would be rolling with us.

"Yeah right." I said. "Like *he'd* be with us. He wants to destroy all of us . . . including you, Gogough."

"Really?" he asked, astonished. "Why?"

"He holds a grudge against me, and he wants to kill me for it. And, he knows that you guys are my companions, and he has no problem taking you out, too."

"Oh."

Tieran looked over at the pyramids.

"Hey," he said. "Let's go explore one of these magnificent pyramids."

"Let's see if we can find any treasure." Rox replied.

"Are you nuts?!" Phaize spoke up. "We could be cursed. I'm not ready to die yet."

"We're already dead. A curse won't do any good."

"Hey," Gogough said. "I have an idea. Let's visit the Temple of Hatshepsut; it's near Thebes."

"Good deal." I agreed.

"See? Leviathan likes that idea. Let's go."

We left the pyramids behind to go find the Temple of Hatshepsut.

The Run-In

Gogough and the rest of us sped southwest of Giza, to the Temple of Hatshepsut, in the Valley of the Kings; it took us a half hour to arrive.

When we arrived there, we entered the temple. On the walls of the temple were paintings of the Egyptian gods and pharaohs.

"Look," I said as I ran my hand across a bas relief. "It's the god Osiris, and there's Isis. Here's Thoth, their protector."

"He has the head of a bird." Rox replied.

"Yes. And there are the pharaohs." I pointed to each one. "Menes; I met him once. And there's Hatshepsut. Here's Amenhotep the Fourth, Tutankhamen, Ramses the Second, and Ramses the Third."

"I don't see Cleopatra in here. Is she in here?"

"I don't know; she might be. C'mon, let's go further."

We walked further into the temple; we shined our torches on the walls. We then entered this weird chamber; there was an alter in the middle of it. It looked as if there was someone sitting on it.

"What's this?" I asked as I drew closer.

"Ah, Leviathan," said a voice. There was definitely a person sitting there . . . . and they knew who I was. Whoever it was, they were calmly smoking a pipe; I could see the soft orange glow of embers and a hint of smoke billowing toward the ceiling. "It's been over two hundred-ninety years since our last little run-in."

I knew exactly who this person was.

"How nice." he continued. "You even brought the Freak, the Lady Boy, the Wannabe, and the Dynasty Hog with you."

"They have real names, Imhotep." I said. "Just like the two of us."

"What did you just call me?" Peteryx asked, taking another puff from his pipe.

"I called you Imhotep."

"How dare you!"

"It's your birth name, Imhotep. I shall address you by it."

Peteryx got up from the alter and blew a huge cloud of acrid smoke from his nose and mouth. He then walked over to a corner of the chamber and grabbed a torch.

"Now that you're here . . ." he started as his weird Vampire-like fangs grew from his top gums. "along with the rest of them . . . I can kill you all!! And this time, I'm going to make sure . . . ." He pulled the torch back. "I DO IT RIGHT!!!!!!"

Peteryx swung the torch at me. I backed away, just in time. Phaize, Tieran, Gogough, and Rox screamed in fright and ran out of the chamber.

"Cowards!!!" I called after them. "You cowards!!!! Is *this* how you assist me?!"

Peteryx laughed at me.

"They're your friends, Leviathan," he said. "Not your battle companions. They chose not to help you because I am strong, and you are not!!"

"They're not afraid of you." I told him.

"Then why did they run away?? They're more of a disappointment to you than finding out who your brother really is."

"You leave Levetin out of this! This is between you and me now."

With a loud cry, Peteryx swung the torch at me again; he missed again.

I threw my torch at him, and he dodged it. I then drew my dagger.

"You ruined me!!!" Peteryx shouted.

As he swung the torch at me constantly, I backed away, attempting to reach the entrance of the temple.

"Don't you realize . . . ." I started, jumping out of the way of Peteryx's torch. "You cannot extinguish me!!! I'm the deadliest tyrant on Earth!! You'll always be second best!!"

Pyramid Scheme

Peteryx screamed to the top of his lungs and threw his torch at me; I ducked down before it could hit me in the head, but I got a surprise when I stood back up: Peteryx charged into me and we flew out of the entrance of the temple and onto the hard earth; I could feel my insides going haywire from this, and the damage I sustained in India.

Peteryx pulled me up, and threw me down a steep walkway. As he ran after me, the other tyrants were outside, shouting for us to stop fighting, but their words weren't enough; this fight was personal.

I came to a stop at the bottom of the walkway; Peteryx leapt onto me and we continued to scrap; we wrestled and fought in the hot Egyptian sand. He managed to wrap his hands around my throat.

As he tried to choke me to death, I gripped my dagger; I plunged it into his chest, right where his heart was supposed to be. He yelled in pain and ran from me.

"Get back here, you bastard!!" I shouted and chased after him.

Peteryx began to sprint faster across the desert sand. Phaize, Gogough, Rox, Tieran, and I chased the Egyptian tyrant all the way back to Giza, to the Great Pyramids!!

Peteryx began to climb the largest pyramid that was, unknown to us, the tomb of King Khufu.

"No!!!" I shouted as I climbed after him. "Peteryx, you scum!!! Get back here!!"

"Scarabs!!!" he yelled. "Come forth, scarabs!! Take him out!!!"

As I climbed up the side of the pyramid, a line of scarabs ran down to meet me; Peteryx had tried this stupid attack before.

"No!!!" I shouted. I climbed quicker up the pyramid, and as I did, I stepped on the large black beetles, crushing them, one by one.

"FOOLS!!!" Peteryx screamed as he reached the top of the pyramid. "RETREAT!!!"

As the scarabs returned to his body, Peteryx lost his footing and began to fall backwards.

"No!!" I shouted as I reached the top.

Peteryx clung to the pyramid for dear life; once I make it to the top, I yank him up . . . . and that's when I lost my balance.

We both began to tumble down the side of the rough pyramid at tremendous speed. As I rolled down, I tried grasping one of the large bricks, but it was no good; I couldn't stop falling.

I could feel my bones snapping every time I bounced off the wall of the pyramid; I was already in enough pain with my broken ribs and tears in my reproductive system . . . . now, I was receiving more of it.

I finally landed onto the sand after a long rough fall. As I struggled to sit up, Peteryx crashed into me like a raging bull; more of my bones snapped like twigs from the blow.

We couldn't move; we were both in excruciating pain and misery.

Tieran, Phaize, Gogough, and Rox ran over to check on us.

"You guys?" Tieran called to us.

We both couldn't talk. I sure as hell couldn't speak; my windpipe was crushed. I was in so much pain that I was coming close to tears.

Peteryx was moaning in agony, however, some of it seemed a little exaggerated.

I could hardly breathe; more of my ribs were broken, and both of my legs had been snapped right at the kneecaps. I could feel my stomach churning; it took a mighty lurch, and I leaned over and threw up blood, all over Peteryx's face.

"Ohhhhhhh!!!" Phaize, Rox, Gogough, and Tieran said in unison. Peteryx began to groan and cough. He pulled my dagger out of his chest and planted it right into my stomach, just a few millimeters above my navel. I cried out.

"What's going on here?" we heard someone ask.

At first, it sounded like the Spider Queen's voice, but then I looked over and saw Angeleal; she and Arachne's voices had similar notes to them, but Angeleal's was much more calm.

Along with Angeleal was Murabbi, Colai, Azrael, and Drakengaard; why wasn't Revelatianus with them? I needed him so much.

"What happened?" Murabbi asked.

"Peteryx started it." Gogough said. "We went to visit the Temple of Hatshepsut near Thebes, and we found him inside. He tried to kill Leviathan!!"

Draken Hark started down at Peteryx; a smiled formed on his face.

"You've done well, my tyrant." he said. "I shall heal you now."

"Brother!!" Azrael shouted and grasped Draken Hark's hand. "Peteryx isn't the one who should be healed."

"But Leviathan is?" Draken Hark asked his big brother. "Nothing that carries the blood of the Golgohoths should be healed!!"

Azrael sighed.

"The Golgohoths were good people, at a time." he said. "The two servants, Syrah and Uhn, raised the twin brothers well."

"Until the unthinkable happened." Draken Hark said. "And Syrah and Uhn died. Now, does Leviathan Golgohoth deserve praise??"

"I wouldn't praise Peteryx." Murabbi said to his colleague.

"Me, either." Angeleal agreed.

"Same here." Rox said.

"Yeah." Gogough said.

"You couldn't pay me enough." Tieran said.

"You can't make me praise Arch-Peteryx Feathervault." Phaize replied.

"And you know . . . ." Colai said, walking up next to me. "Leviathan does deserve some kind of clarity." She helped me sit up; she pulled the dagger out of my stomach. "This poor tyrant has lost one of his most precious resources; his fertility. What could he possibly gain from that? The one thing he deserves . . . is to be praised."

Colai embraced me, and I could feel my pain melting away. I could also feel my bones popping back into their right places; my ribs were completely mended, and my abdominal region felt much better.

After a few moments, I was completely healed; my dagger wound was closed up as well, but there would always be a tiny little scar there.

"There you go, Leviathan." Colai said, helping me get to my feet. She gave me a kiss on my cheek. "You're back to perfect help."

"Thank you, Colai." I said. I brought my hands to my lower abdominal area. "Am I fertile again?"

Colai's face became a bit sad; I knew, right then, that she didn't have the power to give me my fertility back; I would be sterile for the rest of my days. If I ever wanted children, I would have to raise someone else's.

"It's not fair." we heard Peteryx say. "What about me?"

"Yes, Colai," Draken Hark said. "What about Peteryx? Can you heal him?"

"No." she told him.

"Can I heal him?"

"No. Revelatianus won't allow it."

"Forget what Revelatianus says."

There was a streak of lightning in the distance, and faint thunder followed it; Draken Hark looked up into the sky; he frowned and shook his head.

"I can't believe this!" he shouted. "That's not fair!! It isn't right!!"

"What?" Angeleal asked.

"Revelatianus won't allow me or Colai to restore Peteryx back to perfect health!"

"What?!" Peteryx asked in anger and disbelief. "I've been trying to lead the best life since escaping from that pit!!"

"And you've been doing it by seeking revenge on Leviathan?!" Azrael asked. "That's a no-no."

"But he's evil!!!"

"And you're not?" Azrael turned to the other Eternal Ones. "The Master wants us back at the temple. We must obey him and do what he says."

The Eternal Ones regrouped. They said their farewells and they vanished; I walked over next to Peteryx and knelt down.

"Imhotep," I said, slapping his cheek. "You can never defeat me; you're second best."

"Curse you, Leviathan!" he said. "I'll get you back; mark my words."

"Keep dreaming."

"You're just as sorry as your brother is."

Peteryx hawked a bloody loogie, right in my face; I didn't bother to wipe it away at that moment. I slowly shook my head.

"Okay." I said. "If that's what you believe, you'll be sorry." I wiped the blood-laced phlegm from my face. "Don't ever do something like that again."

I stood up, leaving Peteryx lying on the sand. I then walk over to Phaize, Tieran, Rox, and Gogough.

"Let's get out of here." I said to them.

"Where are we gonna go?" Gogough asked.

"We'll decide along the way."

"What about Mohenjo-Daro and Harappa?"

"I'd like to visit them." Phaize said.

"Maybe later." I said.

"We could go to China." Tieran suggested. "The Han Dynasty ended exactly one-hundred years ago."

"What dynasty are they in now?"

"I don't know; that's why we need to go to China and find out."

"We'll decide as we travel." I said. "We cannot let Peteryx know where we're going."

SIERRA J. BALL

Tieran, Rox, Phaize, Gogough, and I left Peteryx behind and began to run. We eventually had to stop and rest for the night, but when morning came, we decided to just go wherever our feet would take us; it's what I had done many times for many years. Soon, we would find a nice place to check out.

"I wonder where Peteryx is going to go." Gogough said.

"He'll follow us." I said. "And, he'll be sure to stay a good distance away."

"Will he ask the Trio to help him?"

"No. I doubt it. Besides, with Acanthus of Corinth being the Deathbringer, and my twin brother, he wouldn't dare."

History Of The Immortal Trio

I stop writing. I decide to read a book instead.

I go to the bookshelf and find a chiefly Muslim book; it's called *The Arabian Nights*. To pass the time, I read the tales of *Aladdin* and *Ali Baba and the Forty Thieves*.

These tales make me happy; they make me think of my home—the Middle East. As of right now, they're at war with the U.S. I wonder how it's going over there with the Eternal Ones.

After I finish reading some of the tales in *The Arabian Nights*, I grab another book called *Facts and Truths on the Immortal Trio*. I turn to a chapter on Acanthus of Corinth and begin to read.

"Born Levetin Golgohoth in Ancient Mesopotamia." I say. "Circa four-thousand years before Christ. Known as Acanthus of Corinth by millions; called the Deathbringer by most rulers of the undead. It is said that Acanthus is the deadliest member of the Trio, most likely credited to his heinous torture methods, the worst ones being slicing off body parts, and pulling teeth with unsanitary tools and no anesthetics. Also known for neck-breaking and whacking victims' heads clean off with his bare hands."

After skimming through a passage or two about my twin, I turn to the Vindicator's chapters; I read about the deaths of his six brothers.

"It is a known fact," I read. "that Dante Haven, known as the Vindicator to many, bribed Leviathan Golgohoth, the albino tyrant and twin brother to Levetin Golgohoth (I.e. Acanthus of Corinth—Deathbringer) to kill his brothers Zeus, Knighton, Pericles (twin brother), Axle, Cornelius, and Ronan. Leviathan managed to kill them all, except the two eldest brothers, Zeus and Knighton. Later during the day, they committed suicide by swallowing hot coals. Now, Dante feels like he can do whatever he wishes with his brothers out of the way." I sigh. "Well, it *is* true." I continue on. "Dante Lord Haven is known as a Binding Youth hybrid; every victim he has made into a zombie, their youth becomes his. His hair is no longer gray or white, and his skin becomes healthy and youthful. The more victims he drains, the longer his youth sticks." I look up from the book. "I knew that about him; I never mentioned it before."

I turn to a passage regarding the Stalker.

"Arachne the Spider Queen was born Ariadne Tousoutopolous in Athens, Greece." I read. "She became Arachne at age ten. She possesses the traits of a spider; extra arms and pupils. She began to call herself the Spider Queen when she saw that she could communicate with spiders; later called the Stalker, once the Immortal Trio was complete."

I turn to the introduction and read an important passage.

"The Immortal Trio was created by one of the Four Corner Demons, Demons who possess the powers of Earth, Fire, Wind, and Water. Their master is the ancient Water Demon, Thanatos Aqueous; it has been said that Thanatos created the Trio based off of their biggest fears and were forced to prey on those who prey on the innocent."

I gasp, close the book on the Immortal Trio, and think: *Modeled off the one thing they fear the most? Who wrote this and how do they know all about the traits of the Trio from A to Z?*

I look at the cover of the book; I study the drawing of the deadly trio. I then see the author's name on the cover: Oceanus Aqueous.

"It's pretty obvious who wrote this book." I say.

LUXOR-ious Discovery

I sit with Balcanicus and Spinosus at the Luxor hotel and casino. Mandalay Bay was interesting, but it isn't where Peteryx and his reinforcements are; no. They are here, and they call out to Leviathan like he's a lost puppy or kitten.

"The Cirque du Soleil is due to perform tonight, Master." Spinosus says.

"Are you sure it's them?" I ask as I allow vines to trail up the side of the wall so stealthily. "I heard it's Cirque du Freak. We'll get to see the Bearded Lady and Madam Octa, the giant spider!!"

"Peteryx's Anubis army will strike again," Balcanicus announces. "In the most ass way possible."

"And that is?" Spinosus asks.

"Disguising themselves as pigs."

"Pigs?"

"You bet."

I know what Balcanicus speaks of. His talk of pigs is referring to the police. The odds of that plan working are slim and none; what is Peteryx thinking? Does he actually think that Leviathan is ignorant when it comes to these botched plans? These Anubis attacks are something that my eight-year-old daughter could elude. Besides, as long as I am around, Peteryx will never get the exact revenge he wants on my brother.

"Oh, look." Spinosus says, looking over at the performance stage. "Showgirls."

As my servants watch the Las Vegas showgirls spin batons, dance on the stage, and show off their asses, I come across a familiar face that I have seen quite a few times in my life; the face of a man bent on revenge and destruction. Hatred radiates in his yellow eyes; his dark scars shine in the neon lights.

"Oh, there you are." I say.

Rolfe Is Missing

Shortly after I finish reading a third book, I hear knocking on the door.

"Come in." I say.

The door opens and in walks Powers; he looks really worried.

"Leviathan," he says. "I got my pictures developed."

He hands a brown envelope to me. I'm careful as I remove them; I don't want to smudge them.

Say, these pictures are nice. It seems that Powers has taken close-ups on granite and graphite rocks; he must be studying different types of carbon.

"Uh, Leviathan," Powers says.

"Yes?" I ask, keeping my eyes on the photos; I'm starting to take a great interest in them.

"Have you seen Rolfe? He isn't here."

I look up from the pictures and stare into Powers' eyes.

"Yeah, I noticed that." I say. I smile afterwards.

"Really?" Powers asks. "Do you know where he is?"

I start to look at the pictures again.

"No." I reply. "I saw Rolfe around three-fifteen this afternoon, but then I guess he left; he didn't say where he was going, so I don't know."

"Oh?" Powers asks.

"Yes."

"Okay. Well, maybe he went out to go see a movie; he does that sometimes."

"I watch movies, too." I hand him the envelope back. "It passes the time."

"It does. Listen, Leviathan, I'm gonna go study these photos in the chemical lab. Are you gonna be okay in here?"

"When was I never okay in here? I'll find a way to entertain myself."

"I see that Ronny's belongings have amused you."

"Yes, but . . . where did he get this?" I hold up the book *Facts and Truths on the Immortal Trio*. "This, I hear, is a rare find."

"I'm not sure, Leviathan. I'll try to get in touch with him and see. Do you need anything?"

"No, thanks."

"Okay, then."

Before he leaves, Powers turns back around; he seems really nervous.

"Leviathan," he says. "Did you notice anything last night?"

"Notice what?" I ask.

"Me and Rolfe were experimenting on some important things; did you see any of it?"

"I don't know what you're talking about, Powers."

"Oh."

Powers leaves the room.

I know exactly what he meant by experimenting, I think. I saw him and Rolfe probing in places that should never be explored.

I want to write some more of my chronicles, so I pick up my pen and get out some more paper.

"Don't worry, Mordecai," I say as I write down the title for the next chapter. "That stupid Nazi bitch won't take my story away from you; just hang on for a little while longer. I'll be back in Los Angeles soon."

The Middle Ages

Our feet took us to some crazy places after leaving Peteryx, battered, broken, and humiliated, in Egypt.

In the year 330 A.D., the city of Constantinople, established by the Roman emperor Constantine the Great, became the new capital of the Roman Empire.

In Africa, back in 350 A.D., the Kushite civilization at Meroe ended after it was defeated by Aksum—a powerful African kingdom and trading center that is today, the country of Ethiopia.

According to Tieran, in the year 400 A.D., the Chinese manufactured steel. Forty-nine years later, Attila the Hun attacked Western Europe. In earlier years, northern invaders called Barbarians attacked the Roman Empire. Even though they were Germanic people, Rox, who was Welsh-born, wanted to be just like them; he used their skills to feast.

I have to admit, it was a very rough time during the decline of the Roman Empire; the raiders destroyed cities, they held up travelers, and hijacked ships so that trades couldn't be made. Also, with us, it was hard to find food; it was all around us, but in heaps of flesh and bone. A dead body's blood wasn't all that fresh, especially if it's been dead for a while.

In other news, the dead bodies were Dante Haven's wet dream; he managed to turn roughly ¾ of the fallen victims into zombies and harvested their youth. I predicted that he wouldn't have a gray hair on his head or a wrinkle on his skin for the next hundred years, if possible.

To stir up bad news, the Roman Empire fell to Germanic invaders in 476 A.D. I had a big feeling it was going to happen sooner or later; Emperor Romulus Augustulus was only a child, and there's no responsibility from children when it's about mighty cities.

Well, it was now 500 A.D., and some said that the Middle Ages began around that time.

"So, Leviathan," Tieran said. "What exactly *are* the Middle Ages?"

"Well," I said. "I guess, since the Fall of Rome, Europe has decided to try something new."

"Something greater?"

"You know, Tieran, I'm not so sure what the Middle Ages are, but I guess I'll find out soon, so that I can let you know. Or, perhaps you may find out before I do."

"Hey," Rox said. "The Roman Empire has left behind many legacies."

"Don't give us this hogwash, Rox." Phaize spoke up. "What could they have possibly left behind besides a playground of death for the Vindicator?"

"Well, uh—the Latin language, and many roads."

"Say something in Latin."

"I'm Welsh."

"Yes, Rox." I said. "Say something in Latin; it is a legacy."

"I don't know Latin. As for you, Leviathan, you lived in Rome before; *you* say something in Latin."

"Okay. Aut vincere aut mori."

"What does that mean?"

"Either conquer or die." Phaize replied. "I know Latin, too. The burning of the buildings in Rome; animadvertistine, ubicumque stes, fumum recta in faciem ferri?"

"Ever notice how, wherever you stand," I started. "the smoke goes right into your face?"

"That's what it means."

"So," Rox said. "All this time, you and Phaize knew how to speak Latin . . . and you never took the time to teach me?"

"Well," I said. "He's a Corinthian, so the language came as a normal thing to him. Besides, you didn't ask us to teach you."

"Because I didn't know you could speak it."

"You assumed it, beings I spent a lot of time in Rome."

"But I . . . oh, forget it."

We continued to walk down a dirt path toward a village.

"Do you think Peteryx is still alive?" Gogough asked.

"Well," I said. "It's only been about a hundred-eighty years since we last saw him in Egypt; there's a very good possibility that he still is."

"A hundred-eighty years? You mean, it's been that long? It only seemed like yesterday that you two were rolling down that pyramid."

And only yesterday since I had my bones broken and my insides ripped up by a herd of angry cows. Not to mention, I had a testicle stomped into a pudding, so said Acanthus.

"I wonder why it takes so long for Peteryx to find you." Rox said. "And when he does . . . ."

"He never succeeds to extinguish me." I finished his sentence. "He's an idiot, Rox. He has no motive to defeat me."

"It'll get him killed one day."

"Yes, it will."

"I think it's the Immortal Trio that's keeping him from finding you." Gogough said to me. "You know that Acanthus would do anything to make sure Peteryx doesn't get revenge on you."

"Perhaps." I said to him.

"He does love you, I think."

Yes, he does. I thought.

All I really could remember from that year, 500 A.D., was our conversation regarding the Latin language and Arch-Peteryx Feathervault. And then, we ran down the dirt road toward the little village where we decided to live and, in the blink of an eye, 300 years had passed.

It was now 800 A.D., and Charlemagne—the king of the Frankish people—became the emperor of Rome. Also, a system called feudalism developed in Europe.

"Leviathan," Tieran asked. "What is feudalism?"

"Do I have to know everything?" I asked him.

"You're the smart one."

"So, you don't rely on your oracle bones to give you answers anymore?"

"Oracle bones don't give definitions, Leviathan; they only see what's coming in the near future. As I have said before, Leviathan, you underestimate the power of the oracle bones greatly."

Tieran seized the reigns of his blond-colored horse and rode a little ways ahead of us; Phaize, Rox, Gogough, and I had to catch up with him.

"If I tell you what feudalism is," I said to him. "Will you tell us some more about China's dynasties?"

I couldn't believe I had asked him that; he'd never shut up about them.

A wide smile grew on Tieran's face; he really *did* love it whenever he talked about China's dynasties.

"Yes." Tieran said. "I'll tell you all about them."

"Splendid." I said. "Well, okay. Tieran, feudalism is a way of organizing and governing society, based on land and service."

"Oh, *that's* what feudalism is?"

"Yes." I pet my white horse on its head. "That's what it is."

"Well, I knew that."

"HUH?!" Rox, Gogough, and Phaize asked simultaneously.

"I knew that." Tieran repeated. "Just wanted to see if Leviathan knew; I still have to talk about China's dynasties. Thanks, Leviathan."

Tieran sped off past us; I breathed a sigh of disgust.

"Why did I fall for that?" I asked myself.

"Because you underestimate the power of the oracle bones." Rox said.

"Can you go be sarcastic somewhere else?"

"Not if I can help it."

The Histories Of The Dynasties

After a few moments of being perturbed, we arrived at the manor—a large estate owned by a wealthy noble; we rode our horses to a churchyard.

"I like the dynasties," Tieran said as he jumped off his blond horse.

"I heard a little bit about them." I said as I got down from my white horse. "Over in the Arabian Peninsula, where we first met in person. It was the year forty anno Domini."

"I remember."

"Of course you do."

"I wanna hear about the dynasties, too." Gogough said, petting his chestnut red horse.

"Me, too, Tieran." Rox said, getting off of his jet-black horse. "You've got me interested."

"I like Chinese things." Phaize said, jumping off of his brown horse and leading it to a patch of grass. "Let's all hear about the dynasties."

Tieran had asked me to build a small little fire, so I took some small pieces of wood and straw and made a small pile. I then took two rods of steel and knocked them together, creating sparks; they flew into the pile, causing it to smoke.

A small wind blew through and the smoke soon became flames.

"Perfect." Tieran said. "Thanks, Leviathan."

"Sure," I said as I sat down.

As we sat in a circle, around the fire, Tieran looked very excited; I have never known anyone who took pride in their country as much as he did. Yes, I loved Mesopotamia, but I wasn't obsessed with it.

"Okay," Tieran said. "The Xia Dynasty is considered to be legendary, and it was; I am a descendant of Yu the Great. I was born Tian Fang-Xia; it became Tieran later, for reasons unknown to me. I was thirty-five when I became a tyrant. How old were all of you?"

"Thirty." Rox said.

"Twenty-one." Phaize said.

"Eighteen." Gogough said.

"Sixteen." I said.

"Getting younger." Tieran said. "And . . . does anyone have a clue as to how old Peteryx was?"

"Not sure." Gogough said.

"He was twenty-five." I replied.

"I see."

"Some of us aged a little more; some of us didn't. I suppose it depends on who our Eternal Ones are."

"Perhaps." Tieran said. "Anyways, The Shang Dynasty began in seventeen sixty-six B.C. During that six hundred forty-four year period, writing on oracle bones told the Shang priests of events and customs during the Dynasty's reign. Wheeled chariots were introduced in warfare. Also, silk weaving was invented, and Chinese writing developed."

"Calligraphy." I said. Tieran smiled.

"Very good, Leviathan." he said. "Calligraphy is such a beautiful form of writing."

"What dynasty was next?" Gogough asked, lying back on the grass.

"The Zhou Dynasty." Tieran told him.

Gogough sat back up.

"I remember that dynasty." he said. "I was there in China during that time, after I had left Corinth."

"I remember that; I saw you there. Okay, the Zhou Dynasty lasted about nine-hundred years. It began in eleven twenty-two B.C. During its reign, iron casting was invented, and so were the multiplication tables. Irrigation was introduced, and the magnificent philosopher Confucius taught a code of behavior that began to spread widely."

"Confucius say . . ." Rox said. "Have wicked heart, lose wicked head."

"That's interesting." I said.

"Did Confucius really say that?" Phaize asked while he made a necklace out of clovers.

"No." Rox said. "It's just something I thought of."

"Well, it may prove to be true, one day."

"Perhaps," Tieran said, which was beginning to become one of his favorite words. "Okay, so after the Zhou Dynasty ended in two twenty-one B.C., the Qin Dynasty began. During that dynasty, a warrior king named Shihuangdi united most of China into one empire. He also declared himself China's first emperor; that's what his name meant . . . First Grand Emperor. He boasted that his Qin dynasty would last for ten-thousand generations."

"Did it?" Rox asked.

"Hardly. Anyways, a strict law code and tax system was designed. Writing, and weights and measurements were standardized in the Qin Dynasty. Oh, and the building of the Great Wall of China began."

"Wow." Rox said. "You're talking about that huge thing that stretches from the east coast of China to the far regions of the country?"

"Indeed, I am." Tieran nodded. "It stands like a huge dragon of stone stretched across the many hills of China."

"What about silk?" Gogough asked. "When did that come to be?"

"Silk." Tieran said. "Well, ancient Chinese farmers discovered how to make silk around twenty seven-hundred B.C. This was before the dynasties began."

"Do you wear silk?"

"I've worn it in the past before. Also, when silk was introduced to the Chinese emperors, they decided to keep it a secret from other civilizations; they threatened people with death if they told the secret."

"Really?"

"Yes, Rox. This threat worked for over three-thousand years!! It ended around the year three-hundred anno Domini."

"I see. So, how did the Qin Dynasty end?"

"Well, in the year two oh-six B.C., Shihuangdi's dynasty was overthrown by rebel armies led by a general called Liu Bang; some say he was called Han Gaozu. His family went on to create the Han Dynasty. And, during that dynasty, I heard that Buddhism was brought to China from the country of India."

I cringed at the thought of India. I would never forget that fateful day when I lost my perfect balance and rolled into the path of the cows. I will never forget the physical and mental pain of it all.

"Many trade routes to India and Persia were established." Tieran continued. "Paper was invented, and for the next three hundred-seventy years, some warring kingdoms kept China in disorder."

Gogough, Phaize, and Rox were so into Tieran's tales of the dynasties that they were sitting very close to him. Tieran had to advise them that he needed a bit of breathing space, and to avoid the flames of the fire.

"Keep your distance, tyrants." he said to them. "You must never crowd one's thinking space."

"So," Phaize said, sitting back. "What dynasty comes after the Han Dynasty?"

"I should know," he said. "But, please forgive me, Phaize . . . I do not know."

"That's okay. I still learned a great bit about the first four dynasties."

"Five." Rox said. "Xia, Shang, Zhou, Qin, and Han."

"I didn't hear anything on the Xia Dynasty, except that Tieran's a descendant of Yu the Great . . . and, out of context, the ages we were when we became tyrants."

Draken Hark's Punishment

We heard clapping. We looked over and saw what it was.

"Great story, Tian Fang-Xia." said a person with a very familiar voice. It was Murabbi Paleohenge; accompanying him was Angeleal, Azrael, and Colai. Draken Hark hadn't come, and I knew that Revelatianus wouldn't be with them; he would never be. I wondered if his constant absence had something to do with me.

"Master Paleohenge." Tieran said. He approached Murabbi and bowed to him. "It is so good to see you again."

"Good to see you again, too, Tian Fang-Xia." Murabbi said. "You're a well-disciplined tyrant. You make me proud to be your master."

Tieran grinned.

"Greetings, Madam DeLasceaux." Phaize said to Angeleal, taking her hand and kissing it. She smiled.

"Greetings, Phaize Pierterch." she said. "It's so good to see that you're still alive and strong; your brother would be so proud."

Strong, I thought. *Throughout all these years, I've yet to see Phaize take down anyone or kill them; maybe he did it when I wasn't noticing. I'll bet he'll surprise us soon. Or perhaps, he's wanting to seek revenge on the Deathbringer for murdering his brother? That could prove to be fatal . . . on Phaize's end.*

"You're still so very beautiful, Madam Calsambra." Gogough said, kissing Colai's hand.

"You're too kind, Celdeklause." she said, slightly blushing.

Azrael Hark walked slowly around Rox, examining him closely.

"No need to greet me, tyrant." he told Rox. "I don't need it." He stood in front of Rox and stared into his light-brown eyes; not once did Azrael attempt to blink. "Have you been fighting, like I told you to do? It's not about fighting with the Gothic style." He surveyed Rox's spiky black hair with the slight blue streaks; he eyed the piercings as well. "It's about the fury."

"I understand, Master Hark." Rox said to Azrael, keeping his eyes forward. "I fought in the fifth century A.D., during the Fall of Rome."

"Is that so? And, did you satisfy your hunger for blood?"

"My thirst is never satisfied."

"Perhaps not, but you didn't fill your blood quota back then because Dante managed to snag the youth from the fallen, did he not?"

"Yes, he did, Master."

"Blood's no good once it's defiled. Zombies carry no blood worth drinking."

"No, they don't, Master."

Azrael continued to stare into Rox's eyes. He slightly smiled.

"Despite having to deal with the Trio's shenanigans," he said. "You're doing very well."

"Thank you, Master." Rox said.

"Where is your brother?" Tieran asked Azrael. The Eternal One turned and faced the curious tyrant.

"He's facing punishment, Chinaman." he said. "He disobeyed the Master and healed Peteryx shortly after you all fled from Egypt back in three hundred-twenty anno Domini."

"And, he's been punished ever since?"

"Yes, exactly. He is to not have any communications with Peteryx for the next three hundred years."

"But, that was four hundred-eighty years ago."

"That's right; Drakengaard's punishment is to last for eight-hundred years. It was going to be a thousand years, but Revelatianus cut him some slack if he promised to tend to the plants and fountains in the haven on a daily basis."

"That's it?"

"Yes, and for his punishment, he has to carve a statue of each tyrant, in strict realistic detail."

"That's not too bad."

"Ah, that's what you think. Drakengaard wasn't given a hammer and chisel to create the art; he has to use his own fingernails."

"What?!" I asked in disbelief.

"Yes, Leviathan." Azrael said, turning his attention toward me. "Drakengaard is not a very good sculptor, and Revelatianus knows this. So, he made him do it as punishment for going against his wishing to not heal Peteryx. It has taken him nearly three-hundred years to carve only two of the statues with his fingernails."

"Huh."

"Drakengaard's fingernails get worn down so quickly, and he has to wait for them to grow back, just to continue working. The facial details on the

statues he carved are very good; I don't see how he did it. He probably had some help from someone. Usually, it takes a few hours for one of us to carve a statue, with a hammer and a chisel; it doesn't apply to my little brother."

"Which tyrants did he carve?" Gogough asked.

"Phaize and Tieran." Azrael replied. "He claimed they have no details."

"No details?" Phaize asked. "So, he's calling Tieran and me blank?!"

"Yes."

"So, what about the other tyrants?"

"He had completed a statue of Leviathan, but he broke it out of anger. I really don't see how Drakengaard manage to make the statues look so real. Right now, he's working on a statue of you, Gogough."

"I see." Gogough said.

"But, I know that it's going to take him past his punishment to sculpt ones of Rox, Leviathan, and Peteryx."

"He's actually going to carve another one of me?" I asked. "Is he going to break that one, too?"

"Not if he wants to be punished further." Azrael said. "Speaking of which, the first statue he carved of you was breathtaking. It was as if he took the actual you and cast it into marble. Once he finished it, he pushed it over, shattering it into tiny little pieces; he announced that either him or Peteryx will do the same thing to you, the real Leviathan Golgohoth."

"I'm not afraid of them. I can take them both on with my hands tied behind my back."

"Too bad the same thing cannot be said about Acanthus."

"Excuse me?"

"You refuse to fight your brother after you wounded him in Corinth; I think you still love him."

I said nothing. It was true that I could not cause harm to Acanthus of Corinth because I still saw him as Levetin Golgohoth, my beloved twin brother. Is that what made me weak? No. Not at all!

"Why are you guys here?" Tieran asked the Eternal Ones.

"We're here because of you." Murabbi said.

"What? Me? Did I do something wrong?"

"No. Not at all, son."

"There is one thing." Azrael said.

"Oh no," Tieran said. "I've offended Revelatianus."

"All of you offend Revelatianus on a regular basis. But, it's not that; you, Tian Fang-Xia, do not know the details to the rest of the dynasties."

"Oh? Is that it?"

"You see, Tian," Colai said. "Revelatianus listened to you telling the tales of the Chinese dynasties."

"Did he like them?"

"Of course, he did. Storytelling is one of the many traits he loves about you. He wanted to hear more, but he saw that you got stuck, so he sent us down here to help you out."

"Oh."

Wrap Up The Dynasties

ngeleal sat down next to the smoldering fire.

"Okay," she said. "I was in China recently, and the dynasty that followed the Han dynasty was called the Sui Dynasty."

"The Sui Dynasty?" Tieran asked.

"That's right. The Sui Dynasty began in the year five hundred eighty-nine anno Domini and ended in the year six hundred-eighteen anno Domini."

"Angeleal," I said. "How come that dynasty began three hundred ninety-six years after the Han Dynasty ended?"

"I wish I knew, Leviathan." she told me. "But even a wise Eternal One, such as myself, never has the answers to everything. Anyways, during the Sui Dynasty, some powerful and strong emperors reunited China."

"That's a relief." Tieran said.

"Yes, and a fast transportation network was made. That's including the Grand Canal; it links the Huang He and the Chang Jiang together. Also, gunpowder was invented."

"What's gunpowder?"

"You use it when you shoot a gun."

"Okay, I see. Well, what's a gun?"

"It's a weapon, Tieran. Hopefully, you'll find out its purposes soon."

"Okay. Well, what dynasty came after the Sui Dynasty? Do you know?"

"Yes, Fang-Xia. It's the Tang Dynasty; it started in six hundred-eighteen A.D., and it's still going on today."

"Do you know anything about the Tang Dynasty, Madam?"

"A little bit. I know that the Tang Dynasty emperors extended China's control to its neighboring areas. Also, the Silk Road trade grew. As of now, a golden age of art and learning is developing."

"There's no disorder in China, right?"

"Not that I know of, no. So, Tieran, that's it. Make sure you gather information on China's next dynasty, whatever year that may be."

"If there's another one, I'll be sure to. Thanks for your help, Madam."

Angeleal nodded. I looked over and saw some guy running towards us; I recognized him as a serf—a person who is bound to work on a lord's manor.

"He cannot see us!" Azrael said. "We cannot allow him to lay eyes on us! Not right now! We'd be risking it!!"

"Then" Murabbi said. "We better go. Good to see you all, tyrants. Good luck."

Murabbi, Colai, Azrael, and Angeleal vanished before the serf could reach us. He arrived a few moments later.

"Excuse me, sirs." he said. "Do one of you go by the name Leviathan?"

We didn't say anything. I wondered why this serf wanted me; did I do something harsh?

"I'm Leviathan Golgohoth." Rox said. "What do you want with me, serf?"

The serf approached Rox and took a good look at him; he shook his head.

"You're not Leviathan." he said. "You're from the Welsh part of Britain, just as I am. I was told by the lord that Leviathan hails from Mesopotamia."

I got up from off the grass and walked over next to Rox and the serf.

"You'll have to excuse my friend." I said. "He's only looking out for me. And, I'm sure he's also trying to find out what's going on."

"*You're* Leviathan." the serf said.

"Yes, I am. What do you want from me, serf?"

"The lord of the manor sent me to find you; my name is Gryphon." (pronounced *Griffin*.)

"What does he want?"

"He wants you to meet him at his castle; he has a job for you."

"First off, how did he find out that I am here, and second . . . does he have a job for my friends, too?"

"One of his knights recognized you from a war tapestry. And, I do believe that the lord has a job for your friends."

I wonder what this job could possibly be, I thought. I looked over at Tieran, Phaize, Gogough, and Rox; they all shrugged their shoulders. I then looked over at the lord's castle.

"I'll meet with him." I said.

"Great." the serf said. "I'll inform him right away."

Gryphon ran down a little dusty road back toward the lord's castle. We tyrants then got on our horses and started out.

"Why do you think the lord wants to see *you*, Leviathan?" Phaize asked me.

"That serf said that he has a job for me." I said to him. "I'd rather work for Emperor Charlemagne."

"I like Charlemagne." Rox said. "I heard that he can command his troops to conquer with a nod. I'd sure love to be in his army."

"Conquer with a nod, you say?" Gogough asked. "Hey, do you think Revelatianus could do that with the Eternal Ones?"

"He can command the Eternal Ones with the sound of thunder." Tieran said.

"He wouldn't command the Eternal Ones with a nod." I said.

"What?" Tieran asked.

"Have any of you seen Revelatianus before?"

"No." Rox said. "Only you have."

"Are you sure you haven't seen him?"

"No." Gogough said. "I've never seen him before."

"So," Phaize said. "What makes you think Revelatianus won't command the Eternal Ones with a nod?"

"He just won't." I simply stated.

Working For Lord Chapelle

We arrived at the lord's castle. He met us out front and he explained what needed to be done.

"Leviathan Golgohoth and company." he said. "Thank you for coming. I am Lord Chapelle." He gestured to his castle. "I have had quite a problem here for the past month; my castle walls are tightly wound in vines; my knights had to use large axes to cut us out of there, and not long before that, one of my servants was strangled to death by them. Also, I've noticed an infestation of spiders; they're destroying my serfs' crops and food rations. And finally, the townspeople are being plagued at night by what appears to be the walking dead."

I knew what was going on. Lord Chapelle had crossed the Immortal Trio in some kind of way, so they're giving him a little payback by destroying his household, and his village, in the city of Aix-la-Chapelle.

"Lord Chapelle," I said. "Are you familiar with the Immortal Trio?"

"Never heard of them." he said.

"You never heard of Arachne the Spider Queen?"

"No."

"Acanthus of Corinth?"

"No."

"Dante Haven?"

"Again, no."

He's lying to me, I thought. *Why would the Trio just attack a random castle if they weren't provoked? He's actually very lucky that his castle took the punishment and not him.*

"Okay, Lord Chapelle," I said. "What do you want me to do?"

"I want you to come have supper with me and my wife." he said. "Your friends will take the job of removing these . . . nuisances, from my estate."

"We have to clean up the vines and spiders?!" Gogough asked.

"And scare off the walking dead at night?" Phaize asked.

"It's not worth it." Rox said. "They're all just gonna come back."

"I'll pay you." Lord Chapelle replied.

"That'll work." Tieran said.

Anyways, Lord Chapelle wanted me to serve him as a vassal, which was a noble who was given a fief, a property, by his lord in exchange for loyalty. I told him that I had a hard time being loyal, but he didn't seem to care; he made me a vassal and gave me a fief anyway. I knew I didn't own it, but I had complete authority over its serfs, who just happened to be Phaize, Tieran, Gogough, and Rox.

Of course, I never treated them with scorn; they were my friends and they would always be.

One day, when I went to visit them and bring them buckets of water to drink and wash with, I took the liberty of helping them with their work, which was to remove some of the thick vines from Lord Chapelle's castle walls and put out poison for the spiders.

"These things just won't go away." Rox said as he hacked off one of the vines with a dull blade. I watched as the severed vine grew into two more. "Look at that, Leviathan!!"

"And for every spider that dies," Gogough said. "Three more takes its place."

"And the zombies?" I asked.

"They just won't die." Phaize said.

"Well, of course they won't die; they're already dead."

"No," Tieran said. "When we stab them, they don't stay down; this is so not worth the pay." He tossed a bag of powdered poison off to the side. "I give up."

"Tyrants don't give up." I told them. "Listen, have you ever thought of asking the Trio why they're doing this? Maybe they'd stop this."

"What makes you think that'll work?" Phaize asked.

I picked up the severed vine that Rox hacked from the castle wall, along with a dead spider.

"No severed zombie parts around here?" I asked.

"I found a tooth and a finger last night." Tieran said. "If that helps."

"Give them to me."

I was given the tooth and finger. I then spoke to the scavenged Trio bits.

"Look," I said to them. "It's not our fault that Lord Chapelle crossed you. My friends shouldn't have to do his dirty work. Can you give him another chance, for whatever he did to anger you, and give my friends a rest? We're pretty sure he's sorry; he gets your message."

After a few moments, the articles of the Trio turned to dust. Slowly, the spiders retreated from the crops and the vines untangled themselves from around the castle walls; I was almost certain that we wouldn't be hearing any screaming from the townspeople at night, due to zombie attacks, either.

"That's how it's done, tyrants." I said and walked off.

I served Lord Chapelle as a vassal for 14 years. He then decided to banish me after finding out that Acanthus of Corinth was my twin brother, and Arachne had turned all of his knights into giant spider servants; his two favorite knights, Harmon Thorn and Fritz L'Orange, became Human spiders like her ... not to mention, Lord Chapelle found his wife in their bed, frogging Dante Lord Haven.

Once exiled from Aix-la-Chapelle, it wasn't long before Lord Chapelle's castle was destroyed by a raging fire; we watched the black smoke rise in the sky.

"I thought he said that he didn't know the Immortal Trio." Rox said as we walked down a dirt path.

"He lied." I said.

"What happened to Lady Chapelle?" Gogough asked. "I heard her screaming after Lord Chapelle found her boning Dante."

"She jumped out of a window of her tower and fell to her death." I told him.

"Wow." Phaize said. "So, how do you think the Trio managed to get us banished?"

"I think it had a lot to do with the Deathbringer and I being twin brothers." I said.

The same year we were banished from Aix-la-Chapelle, 814 A.D., Emperor Charlemagne died.

"Where will we go now?" Rox asked me.

"I've decided," I said. "We're going to the Khmer kingdom. I received word from Murabbi that the king there is Jayavarman the Second. He's an elder, but he's a powerful ruler. C'mon, let's go."

So, Tieran, Phaize, Rox, Gogough, and I took off from Aix-la-Chapelle to travel to the Khmer kingdom that occupied the land that is today Cambodia.

Mordecai's Bunny Moments

I stop writing and take a look at the clock; it is after 8pm and it's getting dark, so I gathered up my passages and put them in a brown envelope. As I write down the addresses, I hear the phone ring; I pick it up.

Me: Hello?

Anonymous: Hey, Leviathan. It's Mordecai.

Me: Hey. How are you holding up? Stressed, I'm sure.

Mordecai: You can say that again.

Me: Tell me about what your chat room buddy's been up to? Why did she want you to meet her at The Sports Club/ L.A.?

Mordecai: She had to discuss business. She showed me a huge bruise on her left cheekbone, near her eye. I didn't make that, Leviathan. You have to believe me.

Me: I believe you, Mordecai. I'll bet her father or one of her brothers did it; they might know that she was with you, a Jew, and they throttled her.

Mordecai: She was silent when I mentioned that to her.

Me: I know; I heard.

Mordecai: I didn't know what to think when I saw it. She also showed me the scratches. Of course, I didn't make them, you know that. I bet she did that herself.

Me: So, what kind of business did she discuss with you?

Mordecai: Well, Leviathan, she discussed some things about your chronicles; she wants you to send the next passages.

Me: I will, and you will type them, but once you're finished, she won't get her grimy little hands on what you've typed. Once the story is complete, *your* name will be on the cover, and whatever else you want to put on it, pertaining to you.

Mordecai: But, Leviathan, her brothers will . . . .

Me: Just do as I say, and everything will be okay. Trust me on this.

Mordecai: Okay.

Me: Does Bunny have some kind of plan to like . . . become a celebrity or something?

Mordecai: I don't know what her main want is, Leviathan.

Me: Then why the hell is she so gung-ho on taking my chronicles and calling them her own? Wait, I think I know.

Mordecai: What?

Me: She's going to expose Jonathan Note as Leviathan Golgohoth. There's only a handful of people that know the real me.

Mordecai: That could be it. Then, she'll have you confess to important people, and she'll be rich.

Me: Not happening. Anyways, she talked to you about my chronicles. Then what?

Mordecai: She made me drive her back to the DeFranco foster home.

Me: Keep going.

Mordecai: She said since I'm typing the story, and giving it to her after I'm done with it, I would need a reward.

Me: Okay . . . .

Mordecai: She said that I could have sex with her, whenever I felt like it. She said she owes me that much for helping her.

Me: Hey, sweet reward.

Mordecai: This is not cool, Leviathan. It may be to you, but it's not to me.

Me: I've slept with some crazy bitches before, Mordecai. I know how they function. So, did you accept the offer, or did you decline?

Mordecai: No. I said okay.

Me: So, you said that you'd be okay with sleeping with her?

Mordecai: Leviathan, I had to say yes. I don't like the thought, but I'll do anything to not get killed.

Me: They're not going to kill you, but alright. I understand. Just pretend it's Candice, and *that's* no joke.

Mordecai: I can't do that.

Me: Why not?

Mordecai: I hate to admit, Leviathan . . . she's a lot more attractive than Candy.

Me: What?

Mordecai: But I love Candy; she's my girlfriend. I'll just cooperate with Elsa.

Me: Okay, so after you made it home, what happened?

Mordecai: She made me sit in only my underwear to type some more of the story while she lay, topless, on my bed, eating a box of éclairs and drinking a carton of cinnamon-hazelnut crème.

Me: I guess she calls that her idea of fun.

Mordecai: Fun? No, no, no, Leviathan. Her idea of fun was for us to screw for an hour or more, and then watch me type.

Me: You, a Jew, are a Nazi's sex slave; who would've thought it?

Mordecai: This is not funny, Leviathan! I'm too young to be playing these kind of games!

Me: Mordi. You're seventeen; feel lucky. I was a virgin until I was about four-hundred; I just never met the right woman until I met Tigris. Then, I realized that it was all worth the wait.

Mordecai: So, what if you were four-hundred? That's you. This is me; I'm only seventeen.

Me: There's kids who are younger than you who are sexually active. Get a grip.

Mordecai: I can't; I'm not like you, Leviathan. If you feel threatened in any kind of way, you kill to end the threats and satisfy yourself.

Me: So, why don't you do the same?

Mordecai: Because I've never killed anyone before; it's wrong.

Me: The Torah taught you that.

Mordecai: Yes, and I must abide by its words.

Me: Alright, but don't be afraid; either me or Acanthus will take care of your problem for you. Is Bunny there now?

Mordecai: If she was, do you think I'd be talking to you right now?

Me: Maybe, maybe not.

Mordecai: Is Peteryx still in town over there?

Me: As far as I know, he's still at the Luxor hotel and casino.

Mordecai: What about those Anubis things you've mentioned?

Me: They're nothing.

Mordecai: Good. Listen, Leviathan, I have to go now. I've gotta think of a way to get myself out of all this mess.

Me: If you feel like you can't, just rely on the Golgohoth twins. Have you heard anything from Jessica after today at school?

Mordecai: No; not after that. I'll try to talk to you tomorrow.

Me: Okay. Just whenever you can, Mordi. Goodbye, and good luck. When you speak to Marilyn and Ned again, tell them to tell Anticlea that I love her and miss her. Will you do that?

Mordecai: Yes, Leviathan.

Me: Good. Talk to you soon.

Peteryx Has Trained

I hang up the phone and finish writing on the envelope; I seal it and put a stamp on it.

"You're really making a great success, Leviathan." a voice says. "I'm so proud."

"Me, too, Leviathan." says another voice.

I know who the voices belong to; I don't have to turn around and face them.

"I'm sure you're proud of me." I say, turning around in my rolling chair. "Azrael Hark and Colai Calsambra." I smile at them. "Thank you for telling me though."

"We heard about your Jewish friend Mordecai's problem." Colai says. "Don't worry; he'll be okay. I promise."

"Mordecai's strong." I tell her. "With a friend like me, you know he is."

"But," Azrael says. "He's going to need some encouraging words."

"I have given some to him." I say.

"I'm not talking about *be strong* or *I'll be back soon*. He needs to hear words like *do what I would do* or *wipe her out*."

"I can't encourage Mordecai to kill; he doesn't want to."

"Which is why you're saying that you or Acanthus will handle it. It may be too late by the time you two get back to L.A. Right now, you need to be extremely cautious, especially with Peteryx out there."

"Peteryx doesn't scare me."

"Maybe not; you don't scare him, either." Azrael sits down on my bed. "The last time you saw Peteryx was in seventeen oh-three anno Domini, three years after Rox Rothbane was killed."

"I remember; he wouldn't touch me though."

"Because Dante Haven was present."

"Is he afraid of Dante?"

"It's not just Dante; it's Arachne and Acanthus as well. Besides, Angeleal swooped in and saved you from Dante's necromancy spell. Peteryx had just about enough of not being able to get rid of you. So, he went to Nagasaki, and he was trained to fight in a deadly assassin's way of martial arts. It took him three-hundred years."

"From seventeen oh-three to two thousand four; three hundred-one."

"Thanks for being precise, Leviathan."

"It took him about a month to get from Japan to the U.S." Colai says.

"Well," I start. "What took him so long? What did he do? Swim?"

"No. He traveled the entire Asian continent, and Europe."

"Really?"

"To look for more strategies in destroying you. Then, he rowed a boat across the Atlantic Ocean, and traveled, coast to coast, swooping up people, from New York to California, making them members of his Anubis army."

"He could've just taken a plane from Nagasaki to Las Vegas."

"Peteryx knew what he was doing when he traveled that far distance." Azrael says.

"I'm ready for him." I reply. "While the Anubis servants have Levetin to worry about, Peteryx will have to deal with me."

"He's much stronger than ever before, Leviathan."

"I know he's as tall as I am, but he can't be as strong as me."

"He has gained a lot of muscle."

"So, we're the same height, and he has more muscles. What big deal is that?"

"He has trained his scarabs to eat."

"Eat what?"

Azrael and Colai are silent for a moment. I think about what Peteryx's scarabs usually eat, and it comes to me: The internal organs of his victims; I knew about this.

"The scarabs eviscerate." Colai says. "But Peteryx may want to eat your heart himself."

"That won't happen." I say. "I'll be careful; no one's going to take my heart away."

"You know that we love you, Leviathan." Colai leans in and kisses my cheek. "You can do this."

I smile. The Eternal Ones are really neat friends, and I'm glad that they all care, even Draken Hark. I know that Revelatianus must care, but he has a funny way of showing it . . . by not coming down to see me.

"We gotta get going, Leviathan." Azrael says. "We just came to tell you about Peteryx."

"Thanks." I say to him. "Now that I know, I'll be cautious."

Azrael and I shake hands. I then hug and kiss Colai.
"I guess it's goodbye." Colai says. "For right now."
"I'll be okay." I tell her.
"Sure, Leviathan. We believe in you."
"We're counting on you." Azrael says. "Good luck."

Rolfe Still Hasn't Returned

Azrael and Colai vanish. I then sit down on my bed.

"I'll do well." I say. "With my brother's reinforcements, I'll be able to reach Peteryx easier."

I think about my master, Revelatianus. I don't think that he'll be coming down to see me anytime soon, but how can that be? He told me, in my sleep, that I'll get to see him again.

I suddenly hear a knock on my door.

"Come in." I say. In walks Powers Bentley.

"Rolfe never came back." he says to me.

"That's not my problem."

"I know, but where do you think he could be?"

The Luxor, cutting ties with Arch-Peteryx Feathervault.

"A hotel?" I suggest.

"Why would he be at a hotel?" Powers asks. "Rolfe hates hotels."

Well, he lied to you about that.

"I hope he didn't get into some kind of trouble." Powers continues.

"Maybe he's angry about something." I say. "Did you guys get into a fight?"

"No. Rolfe and I hardly ever fight."

"Well, why don't you try to call him?"

"I tried, but his phone goes straight to voicemail."

"Then go out and look for him."

"I did, around six, but I couldn't find him. And you know, Las Vegas is a big city."

"Yes, it is. I'm sure he'll turn up though."

Powers stares at me as if I had committed a murder.

"You didn't tell Rolfe anything to make him disappear like this," he says. "Did you?"

I shake my head no.

"Not me." I say, holding up my right hand. "I'm being honest." I place my hand over my heart. "I was here all day."

"Okay." he says. "I'll just be in the living room; I'm gonna wait for him to come back while I watch a movie."

"Okay, that's cool; I'm just going to sleep, or write, or something."

"You're not gonna explore the city, like you do at night?"

"Excuse me?"

"I'm sure no tyrant of your caliber would wanna be cooped up in a bedroom all day and night; I'm sure you like to get out, right?"

"Yeah, I suppose."

"Well, goodnight, Leviathan."

"Yeah, goodnight."

Revelatianus Predicts Death

P owers leaves the room and I get dressed for bed.

"Peteryx has prepared hard for me." I say. "But his Anubis servants are a joke."

A thought pops into my head: *What if he knows my exact location?*

"Just in case he does," I say. "And he decides to visit me." I open up the desk drawer and get out the revolver; I stare at it for a moment. "I have only a few bullets left. Two, three. Maybe four. It'll only take one to knock Peteryx on his ass."

Unless you hit him in the right spot, Leviathan, I hear Acanthus's voice. *It won't work. You're going to need something a little stronger than a gun to kill Arch-Peteryx Feathervault.*

"Get out of my head, Levetin, and continue to do what you're doing."

Which is paving a way for you. You need to get out here and find Peteryx, and get the job done. Stop dicking around!

I scoff. I then climb into bed and pull the covers over me. In no time, I begin to doze off.

I start to dream; I dream that I am falling. I'm falling fast, and the ocean is right below me; there's jagged rocks sticking out of the water, and I know that I'm going to fall on them.

Suddenly, I feel something catch me. I am then dropped safely into the water.

I fight to stay afloat, to keep my head above the surface, but I am beginning to feel faint and fatigued.

"Leviathan," said a familiar but lost voice. "Give me your hand."

I stretch my hand out and the person grabs it; they yank me out of the water and onto the land.

"Are you okay, Leviathan?" the person asks. I nod my head.

"Yes," I say. "Thank you."

The person helps me to my feet; they stare into my eyes.

"Look at me." they say. "You see, it's me."

I can't believe who I'm seeing. Could it be? Could it really be?!

"Revelatianus?" I say. The person nods their head.

"Yes, Leviathan." they say. "It is me. Revelatianus; your master."

"I can't believe it."

"Believe it, son."

I smile and embrace my master; the tears roll down my cheeks.

"Where have you been all my life, Master?" I ask him. "Why haven't you helped me?"

"Leviathan," he says, running his fingers gently through my wet hair. "I've helped you all of your life. You don't have to see me to know that I'm with you. I gave you support after Dalgine mortally wounded you. I sent Colai to heal you after your pyramid accident. Why, I even sent help to console you after you found out who Acanthus of Corinth really is."

I believe my master; he would never abandon me.

"But," I start. "Why wouldn't you travel around? Why wouldn't you meet up with me, like the other Eternal Ones did for their tyrants?"

"I'll explain later." Revelatianus tells me. "I promise." He releases me and walks a few feet ahead. "Follow me, Leviathan."

I walk on the right side of Revelatianus. He leads me to a path; a path that leads to a redwood forest. It's dark, and I can hardly see a thing.

"We need to see." Revelatianus says. He sticks out his right arm and extends his palm; a yellow ball of light forms. "Illuminate."

The ball of light turns white and brightens our surroundings.

"Why are we here, Master?" I ask Revelatianus.

"I need to talk to you." he says. "It's about Imhotep."

"Yes, I know. He wants to kill me."

"He cannot kill you, Leviathan, and he won't; sure, Peteryx seems a bit off-key with you, but it doesn't mean he's stupid; he has a really brilliant mind, and he can find a way to contain you."

"But I will not stay in that situation."

"No. You are *my* tyrant, Leviathan. You will succeed."

We walk further down the path into the redwood forest.

"Leviathan," Revelatianus says.

"Yes, Master?" I reply.

"I have a strong feeling that something bad is going to happen."

"What do you mean?"

"The Eternal Ones are in jeopardy; three of us will be dead soon."

"Revelatianus, you're not making any sense; none of you are going to die."

"Leviathan, we're not the Trio; our lives do not fall into the hands of a Demon who possesses no Hellfire. We, as members of the Eternal Ones, can perish."

As we walk, I think: *Three of the Eternal Ones will die? Which three? Oh god, I hope that Colai and Angeleal live; I hope they all live!!*

"Master," I say. "None of you can die."

"Our times are drawing to an end." Revelatianus says. "And tomorrow, one of us will die."

"One? I thought you said that there would be three dying."

"Yes. One on Saint Patrick's Day, and two the day after."

"Who? Who will die tomorrow? I have to save them!"

Revelatianus will not answer me; I grow impatient and draw my dagger.

"Tell me who will die." I repeat.

Still, Revelatianus will not say one word. I press the tip of my dagger into his back; he seems surprised by this action.

"Tell me." I demand. Revelatianus sighs.

"Did you say goodbye to the Harks?" he asks.

"Azrael and Drakengaard."

"Yes."

"No, Master. They can't die!! They're strong!"

"Being strong doesn't always keep you alive, my boy. You have to think and strategize."

"But they do."

"They've done enough."

Revelatianus is right. Now, I know that the saying *Only The Strong Survive* isn't exactly true. I remove the dagger from his back.

"How will they die, Master?" I ask Revelatianus.

"I know," he says. "But, I cannot tell you; you cannot help them cheat death. Have you ever heard of altering the future . . . killing a butterfly in the past that wasn't meant to die right away, can drastically change the future. Do not kill the butterfly, Leviathan."

"But I have to save them."

"There's nothing you can do. Their time has come; they'll go bravely."

Revelatianus and I approach a tree stump, sitting in the middle of a cleared area.

"Is it true, Master?" I ask. "Is it true that Peteryx trained in the Japanese city of Nagasaki for three-hundred years, just to face me?"

"It is." Revelatianus replies. He sits down on the tree stump. "He really wants to make sure you're taken out quick and clean."

226

"Or slow and painful."

"Perhaps. He may want to rip your heart out and eat it. But you won't let that happen, will you?"

"No, Master."

I stare down at the ground for a while; I don't know what else to say to Revelatianus. I start to think about Azrael and Drakengaard Hark again.

"Master," I say. "Are you sure there's no way I can save Azrael and Draken Hark from dying?"

"No." Revelatianus says. "Do not kill the butterfly, Leviathan."

"But, Master . . . ."

"Don't argue with me, Leviathan."

"Yes, Master." I hang my head. "I won't let that happen." I look up at the moon; it's a full moon. I wonder if this means anything.

"Revelatianus," I say, looking down from the sky. "Does this full moon have any significance?"

"Yes." my master says. "You shall see, Leviathan; it's not just a night for Werewolves." He stands up straight. "Go."

"Go? I don't understand; where do you want me to go?"

I see that Revelatianus is slowly beginning to fade.

"Don't let Imhotep Feathervault live this time." he tells me. "Make sure he is finished; I'm counting on you."

"I'll kill him, Master." I say. "I promise you that."

Revelatianus vanishes, and so does the light; I'm left standing in the pitch black woods. Owls are hooting and the wind is blowing.

I shut my eyes and lean my head back.

"Peteryx is mine." I say. "That's a promise and a guarantee."

A Dim Setup

I open my eyes and see that I am not in the woods anymore; I'm lying in bed, and it's morning.

"Oh," I say, covering my face with my hands. "It was only a dream; I thought it was for real."

I get out of bed and check the clock. 10:20am, okay. I still have my revolver clutched in my hand from last night.

"Peteryx didn't find me last night." I say.

I open the desk drawer and get out my manila envelope that contains the passages I wrote.

"I need to mail this off to Mordecai."

I get dressed quickly.

"In case I meet up with Peteryx, I'll be ready."

I walk out of the room and into the kitchen. I see Powers sitting at the table and reading the newspaper.

"Good morning," I say to him. He shifts uneasily in his seat.

"Oh," he says. "Good morning, Leviathan." he shows me the newspaper. "Take a look at this."

I take a look at the front page.

"Jonathan Note is responsible for the deaths of three Los Angeles men." I read. "Still at large?" I take a look at the picture on the front page. "I remember that one."

Powers points to a sentence in bold print. I read it. It says: **A reward of $100,000 will be granted to the person who gives the Las Vegas Police Department helpful information on the exact whereabouts of the serial killer, Jonathan Note.**

I begin to think: *How did they found out about this?*

"This can't be right." I say to myself as I watch the bold print on the paper become gibberish.

It's a dim setup, Leviathan. I hear my brother's voice say. *The only people who received this newspaper was Powers Bentley and myself; it was delivered to Powers* by an Anubis servant, courtesy of Peteryx, and I had to knock off one of those guys to get a copy. He wants you to be in fear; he's planning his strategies, too. No one in Vegas knows about this.

"One hundred-thousand dollars," Powers says. "In straight American cash, too."

Not thinking about my next actions, I grab Powers' shirt collar and yank him forward, causing him to lean in his breakfast.

"You're not thinking about giving me away, are you?" I ask.

Powers shakes his head no; I release his collar and he sits back down straight.

"Good." I say. "If you tell anyone about who I am, and what I do . . . I will have no choice but to do away with you. Do you understand?"

"Yes, Leviathan." he says in a shaking voice. "I won't tell anyone."

"Good." I grab the carton of orange juice and an empty glass from the table. "Rolfe hasn't shown up yet, has he?" I pour myself a glass of juice.

"No, Leviathan, he hasn't."

I take a sip of orange juice; I would like it better if I mixed it with tequila and grenadine.

"Hmm," I say. "Perhaps he's . . . no. That's not possible."

"What?" Powers asks. "What is it?"

"Do you think Rolfe has told the police about me, and that he's in hiding?"

"No. He told me that he wouldn't turn you in, no matter how threatened he feels by you. Besides, if he went to the police, they would've been here by now."

"Did you know that Rolfe stole my blood twice? He tried it again, yesterday morning."

"What?! Leviathan, Rolfe told me that he didn't take any of your blood."

"Well then, he lied to you."

I walk out of the kitchen and turn back toward Powers.

"I'm going to take a walk." I say.

"Can you stay out of trouble?" he asked me. I nod my head.

"I'm good at that." I reply bluntly.

I drink up my orange juice and toss the glass to Powers; he catches it with surprise. I walk over to the front door.

"I'll be back whenever." I say and shut the door behind me.

A Desperate Attempt

I read the front page of the Las Vegas Sun, that wasn't circulated, to Balcanicus and Spinosus, who are watching large amounts of black blood seep out of an Anubis dog's crushed cranium.

"A reward of one hundred-thousand dollars," I say. "will be granted to the person who gives the Las Vegas Police Department helpful information on the exact whereabouts of the serial killer, Jonathan Note."

"That's botched." Balcanicus says. "It's a trap."

"An ambush, yes." I say, folding up the paper. "Peteryx is going to have to do a little more than print a bogus newspaper to call Leviathan out."

"Does Leviathan know about this?" Spinosus asks, nudging the Anubis servant with his boot.

"Yes, he does. He read it this morning; I let him full well know that it's a scam."

"So, he's ahead of Peteryx."

"When was Leviathan ever behind Peteryx?" Balcanicus asked Spinosus.

"When his soul was cast into that empty Egyptian shell." I say.

My servants nod.

"So," I continue. "Today is Saint Patrick's Day; remember to wear your green."

"We're all tinted a very light green, Acanthus." Balcanicus says.

"Indeed, we are. And, if one is to pinch us, we rip their faces clean off their skulls. Got that?"

"Yes, Master Acanthus." Spinosus agrees.

"Will Leviathan respond to the ad in the paper, Master?" Balcanicus asks me.

"He will." I say. "Eventually. Right now, he's headed to the post office to mail something off, so we'll just see what happens afterward."

"So, we wait?"

"Like always. But before we do . . . get rid of that."

Balcanicus and Spinosus each take a hold of the dead Anubis servant and toss him into some nearby bushes. We then stand on the corner of S. Las Vegas Boulevard and E. Sahara Avenue, basking in our favorite thing . . . the warmth of the sun. What plays out next . . . we'll have to be prepared.

Army Specialist McDaniel

As I run down the sidewalk, I think: *Is Peteryx still at the Luxor? Or maybe he's in a different location, waiting for me to step out.*

"Now," I say. "Where is the post office?"

I search and search, but no post office is located. I then see a young man walking down the sidewalk; he wears a camouflage uniform.

I approach the man, who appears to be a soldier in the U.S. Army.

"Excuse me," I say. "Are you familiar with these areas?"

"Why, yes, I am." he says.

"Could you give me directions to the post office?"

The young soldier looks at me with a hint of questioning on his face.

"Are you new here?" he asks, pacing back and forth with his assault rifle in his hands. I can hear the jingle-jangle of his military dog tags as he does.

"Yes, I am." I say, pacing along with him. "What are you doing?"

"I'm patrolling. There's been some murders around here, and my buddies and I have to keep a lookout for anything suspicious."

"Other soldiers?"

"Yep. Sergeants, specialists—like me, and privates."

"Wow. Anyways, I need help finding the post office; I'm starting to scorch out here."

"You're an albino?"

"It's kind of obvious, kid."

The soldier wipes beads of sweat from his brow.

"The post office is two miles down the street." he says. "It's a huge brick building; you can't miss it. Just keep going straight, okay?"

"Okay." I say. "Thanks for your help, little soldier."

I go to leave, but the soldier calls me.

"Jonathan Note, right?" he asks.

I stand still for a few moments, then I turn toward him.

"Yes." I say, even though I said I wouldn't use that name anymore.

"My name is Matthew McDaniel, active army." he says. "I'm a big fan."

"Oh, well, thanks. I guess I'll be on my way."

Specialist McDaniel waves his weapon toward the direction of the post office; I turn around and take off.

I run down the sidewalk and make the two mile stretch to the post office; I stand in front of the brick building.

"I can't risk going in there." I say.

Or can you? Acanthus's voice asks. I look over and see a palm tree waving in the wind.

I take a look at my manila envelope.

"I'll go in." I say. "Maybe no one will recognize me."

I walk inside the post office; everyone is so busy that they do not notice me. I drop my envelope, addressed to Mordecai Weinstein, into the slot marked *Out of Town*; I hear it drop in a bundle of letters in the mail bin.

"Just hang on for me, Mordecai." I say.

I quickly rush out of the post office before anyone can see me. I retrace my footsteps so that I can know my way back to the Bentleys' house.

I make it back to the spot where I met the young soldier, Specialist Matthew McDaniel. He is still there; he is pacing back and forth.

"Did you find it?" he asked.

"Yeah." I simply said.

Ask him if he took the time to read the front page of the Las Vegas Sun, Leviathan. Acanthus says.

"No." I whisper.

Just do it.

"Um, little soldier," I say to McDaniel. "Did you happen to read the front page of the Las Vegas Sun this morning?"

"Yeah." he says. "It said something about some grave robbers in the Woodlawn Cemetery; police found a weird slime on a lot of the headstones."

"Slime?"

"Yeah; I think they're having it tested to see what it is, but along with that, twenty-five graves were robbed and the bodies were stolen."

So, he didn't read the headlines about how I'm on the run and a reward is set for my whereabouts.

"Really?" I ask.

"Oh, yeah." McDaniel tells me. "The police arrested three Mexican migrants who were hanging around there who looked suspicious."

"Oh, I see."

I highly doubt it was a group of Mexicans who robbed the graves, Leviathan. Acanthus tells me. *What would a bunch of Mexicans want with a hoard of corpses?*

It's kind of obvious what took those bodies; they're known for leaving behind spit, especially after a meal. The slime; I was told once, by Tach Schnep, that it's an ectoplasm that Ghouls produce to lessen the acidity affects of formaldehyde in embalmed corpses.

"Ghouls." I say to myself.

Would Tach Schnep make this up? After all, my dear brother, he is the Ghoul Lord.

"Yes, he is."

"What was that?" McDaniel asks.

"Nothing."

"Oh, okay." The specialist starts to walk around me; he then faces me again. "What can I do to help you get back home?"

"Get back home?"

"Yeah. Where do you live? I'll give you a ride back to your house; my humvee is right over there."

"Okay, then. It *is* a bit hot out here."

Specialist McDaniel and I head over to the humvee; we get in. He puts on his helmet and starts the vehicle up.

Leviathan, I hear my brother's voice. *What the hell do you think you're doing?! Get out of there, now!*

"Levetin, shut up!" I halfway shout and whisper. "So, little soldier," I say to McDaniel as the humvee travels down S. Las Vegas Boulevard. "How old are you?"

"Twenty." he says.

"Where are you from? Do you live here?"

"No. I'm originally from a little town in Arizona called Kingman. I joined the regular Army after I graduated high school. I'm a thirty-one Bravo."

"What's that?"

"Military police; that's why the police department called me on duty over here. I graduated both Basic Training and Advanced Individual Training for Military Police at Fort Leonard Wood, Missouri. I'm now stationed at Fort Irwin, California; San Bernardino County."

"So, you guys have to drive all the way here from San Bernardino?"

"Oh, no. We're all staying, day and night, at an engineer unit in Henderson; that's not far from here. In fact, we'll be there until these murders cease. I think the murders have something to do with the graveyard robberies."

"Oh? You think they're connected?"

"I think they are, yes."

Wrong, my brother tells me. *Two different problems.*

"Okay." I say.

"Can we meet up tonight?" McDaniel asks.

"What for?"

"I wanna see, for myself, what's going on at the Woodlawn Cemetery."

"I don't think that whoever did it will return, and besides . . . . why do you want me to accompany you?"

"Just asking."

"I'll think about it; I'll be in town tonight."

"Where will you be, exactly?"

"You may locate me . . . . around the Luxor."

"Ooh, that big black pyramid. Okay. What time?"

"Nightfall."

"I guess I'll see you then."

Don't Ever Lock Me Out

rmy Specialist Matthew McDaniel drops me off at the Bentley residence. As he drives away in the humvee, I think about that dream I had last night; Revelatianus told me that Azrael and Draken Hark would be the first of the Eternal Ones to die; he also said that one of their deaths will occur on Saint Patrick's Day . . . that's today!!

"Stay where you are." I say. "Stay in the haven."

I know that the Sacred Haven isn't exactly in the safest location; there's a war going on right now, in present-day Iraq, and that's where the haven's located. However, I'm pretty sure that it's in a spot where no one can find it and destroy it.

"Who's going to die today?" I ask myself as I walk toward the house. "Azrael? Draken Hark? And, who's the third one to go? Murabbi? Colai? Angeleal? Revelatianus will be last; that much is true."

I shake the awful thoughts out of my head. "No one's going to die; no one that I love is going to die. Only one person is going to perish, and that's Arch-Peteryx Feathervault."

I walk up to the front door. I turn the knob, thinking that Powers would've left it unlocked, in case Rolfe would return, but it's locked.

I really don't like knocking, so I decide to force my way inside; I back up and charge into the door. With a loud crash, it comes off its hinges and falls onto the living room floor, along with me.

"Whoa," I say, getting up and dusting myself off. I thought that the force I used to knock down the door would've left my outline instead, but no; I think the door wasn't secured properly.

I see Powers, standing in front of me. He drops his cup of coffee in surprise and his mouth is wide open in disbelief.

"What the?!" he says. "What in the world did you do to my door, Leviathan?!"

"Well," I say, picking the door up. "You don't have a doorbell, so I asserted myself." I prop the door back over the entrance. "You can fix it; you'll need a screwdriver and some new bolts; I think the ones in the hinges are all snapped in two."

"*You* should fix it!"

"Excuse me?"

Powers says nothing else, so I simply walk past him.

"I'll just be in my room." I say. "If you need for me to do something, that's where I'll be."

"Please," Powers says. "Fix my front door, Leviathan."

"Did you say something?"

"Yes. Fix my . . . ."

"What?"

"I said fix . . . ."

"Huh?"

"Oh, never mind."

"Okay. Just let this be a reminder: Don't ever lock me out."

"Yes, Leviathan."

"Good. Well, uh . . . that door needs to be fixed."

"Yeah. I think . . . I think I know where my tools are."

I Am Warned

I walk to the bedroom and sit down in the rolling chair. I think I'm going to write some more of my chronicles, so I pick up my fountain pen and grab a few sheets of paper. As I go to write, the telephone rings; I grab it and place it against my ear.

Me: Hello?

Anonymous: Hello, Leviathan.

Me: Who is this?

The person on the other end is breathing hard into the phone; deep, ragged, slow breaths. I know those breaths from many centuries throughout my past; I drop my pen on the desk.

Me: What do you want?

Anonymous: You can't win, Leviathan. You *won't* win.

Me: Peteryx?!

Anonymous: You will die, and so will your precious Eternal Ones. There's nothing that you and your degenerate twin brother can do about it. You hear me, Leviathan?! I'm going to rip your heart out, and you're going to watch me eat it!!

Me: Peteryx, you bastard!!

The person on the other end hangs up. My mind then drifts into thought: *That definitely was Peteryx. Although his voice sounded a bit more raspy and tired, I could never mistake it.*

"Peteryx!!" I shout.

I drop the phone back onto the receiver like it's a disgusting bug. I then pick my pen back up and begin to write quickly.

For The Sake Of The Children

Tieran, Phaize, Rox, Gogough, and I lived in the Khmer kingdom for 71 years; during our stay, in the year 843 A.D., Charlemagne's Frankish Empire finally came to an end.

It was now 885 A.D. We moved to Chartres, a city in France. We began to hear rumors about mainland Europe; it had went under attack by these strange people from the north.

"They're called Norseman." I told the other tyrants. "Better known as Vikings."

"Their name means *Northmen*." Rox said.

"I heard that they sailed from the country of Scandinavia; they want land and riches."

"I heard they also want women."

"Perhaps."

"Well," Tieran said. "I heard that their unexpected attacks and invasions were part of why Charlemagne's Frankish Empire fell."

"You're quite right, Tieran." I said, placing a hand on his shoulder. "You're very smart."

"I credit the oracle bones."

I removed my hand from his shoulder and slightly smiled; I nodded.

Phaize runs his fingers through his spiked brown hair.

"How can we, as tyrants, stop those guys?" he had asked. Tieran, Gogough, and Rox all shrugged.

"It's not our duty to stop them, Phaize." I said to him. "Leave them to the townspeople."

"We cannot!" he shouted. "We have to wipe them out! And, we need blood!"

"The Vikings aren't our issue."

"For God's sake, Leviathan, they're raping women!!"

"How bad can that be?"

"There are children in those villages!!! They *will* murder the children!!!" Phaize took Gogough and Tieran by their hands and knelt down with them. "Pray with me." he began to say a prayer. "From the rage of the Northmen, O Lord, save us!!"

Tieran and Gogough repeated the prayer that Phaize recited. Rox chuckled; I looked at him and shook my head.

"He's afraid, Rox." I told him. "He fears for the lives of the villagers."

"The children." he said.

"It is serious."

"They're just Vikings, Leviathan."

"Yes, they're just Vikings. But, these Vikings crashed the Frankish Empire, and that empire was strong."

Rox stared down at the ground for a bit; he began to scuff his leather sandals in the dirt.

"They're attacking Paris, as of now." he said. "What can *we* do to stop them?"

"As I told Phaize," I said. "It's not our duty."

"Well then, it's the townspeople's duty? The women and children?"

"That's what the men are there for, to protect them."

"Now, you're starting to sound like your brother."

"What are you talking about?"

"Acanthus of Corinth is the Deathbringer; he'd rather watch innocent people die in gruesome ways before wanting to save them."

"That's not one-hundred percent accurate."

"So, what is?"

"I really don't believe that the Trio harms innocents. Acanthus is like me; he will not harm a child. I've never known him to."

I catch myself; Acanthus allowed Arachne to drain Molicles of her blood supply, and did nothing. What if she would've succumbed to the Spider Queen's attack? Then what?

Rox was silent for a moment. He began to walk around me; a trait he had picked up from his master, Azrael Hark. He then faced me.

"First of all," he said. "I want to fight; I need to feed. And second, who died and made you Jesus Christ?"

I didn't say anything, except stare at the Welsh tyrant with a slight smile on my face.

"I think that Leviathan should be the leader." Tieran said. "He's gotten us out of many jams."

"So," Rox said. "Because Leviathan kept a cool head in problems of the past, he's the leader of the Tyranny Squad?"

"Since when are we called the Tyranny Squad?"

"Since India. Did you forget?"

"Kinda."

Rox scoffed.

"Okay." he said. "Leviathan's the leader . . . but we, as tyrants, have to act."

"So . . . ." I said and started to think: *Should we go to Paris and fight the Vikings? Or should we let the people fight them? Do I care enough about the wellbeing of the townspeople?*

"What's your decision?" Phaize asked.

"It's a no-go." I said to him.

"But Leviathan, there are little children that need to be defended!!"

"I want to enjoy my time here in Chartres."

"Now, you're no different from the Deathbringer. You're worse than Peteryx!!"

I said nothing; I slowly began to feel anger build up in my chest.

"What did you say?" I asked.

"Don't be like Peteryx, Leviathan!!" Phaize shouted.

"Yes, Leviathan, please!!" Gogough spoke. "Let's go save the children!!"

"Tyrants, listen." I said. "If they're attacking Paris now, there's a chance that we'll be too late. Do you really want to lay eyes on the dead bodies of the little ones?"

My colleagues said nothing. I did have a point; if there were children already slaughtered over in Paris, I couldn't bear to lay eyes on their beaten, battered, and butchered bodies . . . and neither would the others.

"We shall stay in Chartres." I said. "Agreed?"

"Agreed." the tyrants said in a somber unison.

Blood And Rain

Fifteen years had passed since I decided that we would not travel to Paris to save the helpless children, if there were any left.

Now, being the year 900 A.D., some of the many Norsemen began to set up villages of their own around the mouth of the Seine River, a river that flows from Eastern France northward into the English Channel.

"The Norsemen have a new name." I said.

"Say what?" Rox asked.

"Yes. The Norsemen are now called Normans."

"How's that?" Gogough asked.

"Well, Gogough," Tieran said. "The region that the Vikings . . . uh, Normans, settled in is called . . . uh, um . . . Normandy." He turned toward me. "Right, Leviathan?"

"That's right, Tieran." I said. "You really *are* picking up things quickly, sans oracle bones."

"Oh, Leviathan."

"And," Rox began. "The Normans have adopted the religion of Christianity; they also took up the French language and many of the Frankish customs."

"How do you know this?" Phaize asked him.

"I've been studying their ways for a while." he said. "From the village historians."

"So, you're a Christian now?"

"Hardly."

I become perplexed at Rox's comment on Christianity.

"We don't study the Normans." I said. "And we don't criticize Christianity."

"So?"

I grabbed Rox by his collar and pulled him close to me; our faces were so close that our lips were practically touching.

"We may be tyrants," I said. "We may be damned, but we do nothing to offend Jesus."

"We offend Him just by killing Humans to survive." Rox said. "Now, let me go, Leviathan."

I held onto Rox for a few more moments, and then pushed him to the ground.

"I watched Christ die on the cross." I told him. "Like the day my wife died, it was one of the saddest days of my life. You speak against Christianity, and I'll kill you."

"You wouldn't." Rox said, getting up and dusting himself off.

"Try me, Rothbane."

I felt anger building up inside my chest. I put my hand on the handle of my dagger; I went to unsheathe it, but I thought better of it.

What the hell am I thinking?! I thought. *Am I really going to kill one of my partners?! He didn't do anything wrong; it's me overreacting.*

"I'm sorry, Leviathan." Rox said. "I didn't mean any harm."

I closed my eyes and shook my head.

"It's okay, Rox." I said. "No harm done."

"Can I still study the Normans? For safety's sake?"

"What do you mean?"

"I mean, what if they go back to their old ways . . . raping women and killing children?"

"Yes. That's not a bad idea."

"You were married?" Phaize asked.

"Yes." I told him. "A long time ago."

"My brother was married once. It only got him killed . . . by your brother."

"Yes, I've heard that story one too many times."

We sat down in the grass to enjoy the breeze, but it had ceased. A light rain began to drizzle down on us; it felt great on my sensitive skin; it cooled me off because the sun was being harsh to me.

"This rain feels nice." I said.

"You better believe it." Tieran said. "I love the rain." He opened his mouth, attempting to catch some. "I like the taste of rainwater; I find it to be refreshing."

Phaize and Gogough opened their mouths to try and catch some rain; Rox and I refused to.

"Why won't you have some rainwater, you two?" Tieran asked us.

"I don't like water." Rox said. "It sickens me; my stomach can't take it, and my tongue rejects blandness."

"But you need water to live." Phaize said. "You need water in order to sweat the bad stuff from your body."

"No, thanks."

"How about you, Leviathan?" Tieran asked me. "Rainwater?"

"I'm not thirsty." I said. "Besides, I do drink water on some occasions. A lot of my aqua supply comes from blood."

"Blood." Gogough said.

"Yes." I told him. "Blood gives me great energy and might."

"Yeah," Tieran said. "Fresh blood. I want some."

"Me, too." Rox agreed. "Let's go find some blood right now."

"Did you say blood?" Phaize asked. "Give me some blood; I want the energy, too."

"Tell me about it." Gogough said. "We need our body fuel."

"Yes," Tieran said. "Because we're so hungry, we could die."

I thought about it. To me, blood was a lot more energizing than water, and I imagined that it was the same for the other tyrants.

"I agree." I said. "Let's go hunt for blood, to satisfy our deadly thirst."

"But," Rox said. "Who do we get it from?"

I thought about it; not long, but long enough. I knew who we were going to get our fresh supply from.

"The Normans." I said.

"Really?" Rox asked. "Awesome!!"

Normans On The Menu

We gathered up our swords that we made for combat and we headed for Normandy. There, we planned to enjoy the taste of Norman blood.

We arrived in a little village where a group of those barbaric people were attacking a church.

"I knew they wouldn't stay Christians." Rox said.

"Good prediction." Gogough said

"How many of them are there?" Phaize asked, straining his mint-green eyes to see them.

With my keen sight, I could see how many were there. One . . . two . . . three . . . .

"There's four of them." I said. "And there's five of us."

"So," Rox started. "Who's the odd man out?"

"I'll be it." Tieran said. "I won't have any blood; I can stave off my hunger until later."

"Nonsense, my friend." I said to the Chinese tyrant. "I won't allow that. We'll all get our share of blood. Tyrants, follow me."

I signaled for them to stay behind me. Slowly, we moved closer toward the little church; I turned my head and looked at my colleagues.

"On the count of three." I said. "We attack."

The tyrants nodded. I help up one finger, then two. Once I held up finger three, we attack; we rushed inside the church with our swords drawn, but the four Normans knocked us all back outside.

Before they could harm us, we got out of their way.

"Grab them!!!" I shouted to the tyrants.

With lightning-quick speed and agility, they got behind the four Normans and took them down with ease.

"The best area to drain blood is from their neck." I instructed. "Remove their helmets."

The Normans struggled as the tyrants removed their protective headgear.

"I thought that these guys would be a lot uglier." Rox said; his light-brown eyes glowed bright in the sun. He ran his tongue across his top row of teeth.

"Are you sure these aren't women?" Tieran asked. "They're blonde enough to be."

"I gotta say . . . if these are men, than I'm a woman."

I couldn't believe it. I had to agree with Rox on his comment; those barbarians looked very feminine for the strong warrior type. I actually thought that they would be these hideous, ugly, crooked-toothed monsters, but they weren't. They all had that "Fabio" look; fair hair and blue eyes.

"Blue eyes." I said. "Not a single one of us has them."

"So?" Tieran asked.

"They're not from the regions we're from."

The Asian tyrant chuckled.

"You're really weird." he said.

The Normans were struggling harder than ever; the tyrants needed to drink their blood before they could slip away.

"Make a small gash in their necks." I said. "Make the gash deep enough to cause a flow of blood; cut next to the jugular."

The tyrants pressed the Normans' heads to the ground and held them there; they used their fingernails to slice into their neck to start a blood flow.

"Only one quart shall be consumed." I said. "For now. When they black out, you've consumed a quart; that's when you quit drinking."

They began to drink. Immediately, the Normans began to grow weak.

Rox's Norman blacked out; a quart of his blood was consumed. The whites of the Welsh tyrant's eyes turned red with excitement.

"That's enough, Rothbane." I said. "Don't kill him."

Rox stepped away from the unconscious Norman; his eyes turned back to normal. He licked his teeth and lips in satisfaction.

Just then, Tieran's Norman passed out, so he moved away from him; the same thing happened with Gogough's Norman.

"I'm full." the Irish tyrant announced proudly; blood stained his face.

Suddenly, we received a surprise when Phaize's Norman managed to slip away and began to run.

"Hey!" Phaize shouted, his minty-green eyes flashed red. "Get back here!!!"

"We can't let him get away!!' Tieran shouted.

"I'm not done feeding!!!!"

"Leviathan!!" Tieran called out to me. "What do we do?!"

It didn't take me long to decide.

"Stay there." I said. "I'll catch him."

The escapee didn't get too far before I charged into him like a wild bull. Phaize said that he didn't consume enough blood; I could see it clearly. If the Norman was running, he hadn't had too much blood drawn.

I yanked the Norman's head back and sank my teeth into his neck; I began to drink. A few moments later, he began to shake violently. I realized exactly what that meant; the Norman would die. The very same thing happened to many of my victims in my earlier years.

I saw that Phaize, Tieran, Gogough, and Rox were running over to see what was going on; looks of concern were on their faces.

"What's wrong with him?" Rox asked.

I didn't say anything; I just stared at the Norman, lying on the grass, not moving. He was still breathing, but his breaths were small, shallow, and ragged. I finally spoke.

"Phaize," I said. "Tell me the truth. How much blood did you consume?"

"About a half a pint." the Corinthian tyrant told me. His eyes turned back to their original mint color.

"Are you sure, Pierterch?"

"Yes, Leviathan. I promise."

"I drank about a pint. So, what in the hell happened? He wasn't supposed to fall out like this." I gestured to the Norman. "Only a small amount was consumed by the two of us, and he is near death."

It was very possible that the Norman had lost a large amount of blood from a wound.

"Check for wounds." I ordered.

Tieran, Phaize, Gogough, and Rox began to remove the Norman's armor to inspect for wounds.

"Look," Phaize said, inspecting the Norman closer. "There's a gash on his side; it looks like he's been wounded pretty bad. He had to have lost a lot of blood from this."

I see that the gash in his side was deep; not to mention, it was badly infected. It was, no doubt, the reason why he had hardly no blood running through his veins.

"I have to mercy kill him." I said.

The tyrants watched as I took the Norman's head in my hands; I violently twisted it, hearing the bones in his neck snap; his body went limp and he died almost instantaneous. I turned to Phaize.

"Did you get enough blood for right now?" I asked him.

"Yes." he said, nodding.

"Are you sure?"

"Yes, Leviathan. It'll hold me until later. If I get weak, I'll tell you."

"Okay."

"Did *you* drink enough?"

"Yeah, I think I drank the last few bits, which was about a pint, but I'll be okay for right now."

"Where should we go now?" Tieran asked.

"We can go back to the Asian continent." Gogough suggested.

It wasn't really a bad idea. Europe had been causing us a lot of problems lately. Perhaps the Asian continent would give us a little break?

"We'll travel throughout Asia." I agreed.

"Yeah." Phaize said. "It shouldn't be too harsh right now."

"Where will we settle?" Gogough asked. "We have to have a destination, right?"

"You know," Rox started. "We could travel to Persia; I heard it's nice there, and it's got good fortunes. Think of all the wealthy people I could rob blind?"

"Well," I said. "That's where we'll go then."

Tieran, Phaize, Rox, Gogough, and I left the dead Norman and started to run. Pretty soon, we would be in Persia, or present-day Iran, and Rox would be getting rich off of other people's hard earnings.

Bunny's Jewish Obsession

I stop writing when I hear the phone ringing. I don't pick it up. I think: *What if that's Peteryx again?*

I then discover, on the Caller I.D., that it's coming from the DeFranco residence in Los Angeles; it might be Anticlea calling, wondering when I'm going to come home and get her. No, that's not possible; Mordecai said that she went with the DeFrancos to San Francisco and that they'd be back in about a week.

I pick the phone up and place it against my right ear.

Me: Hello?

Anonymous: Leviathan, it's me . . . Mordecai.

Me: Mordecai? What are you doing out of school? It's nearly noon.

Mordecai: Elsa made me stay home; I was gonna go, but she called me and told me to pick her up at her condo.

Me: What time was that around?

Mordecai: A quarter till eight. I just took her home, and I decided to call you and fill you in.

Me: Mordecai, I have a lot of things to worry about on top of hearing about a German chick's crazy obsessions.

Mordecai: Leviathan, I'm your best friend. Please, listen to me, please?

I sigh. I cannot ignore him now.

Me: Okay, I'm sorry. Let's hear it.

Mordecai: Okay, well, when Elsa called, she told me to have éclairs and cinnamon-hazelnut crème waiting for her. So, I did. When we got back to the house, she got it.

Me: Got what?

Mordecai: Sex, Leviathan.

Me: You got to be specific, Mordi. I can't read thoughts.

Mordecai: Okay, well, she got sex, and then she laid on my bed, without her top on, and ate the éclairs and drank the carton of crème.

Me: Did she make you sit in your underwear again?

Mordecai: Yes. I don't know why she makes me do that, Leviathan. It's not like I'd be wearing a wire.

Me: She wants you to have sex with her, you say?

Mordecai: No kidding. We had sex three times in two hours; three thirty minute sessions with ten minute breaks in between each one.

Me: And she still says you raped her?

Mordecai: Yep. I can't believe it. And what's really weird about all of this is . . . .

Me: Is what?

Mordecai: She says she feels like she's known me all of her life.

Me: Huh?

Mordecai: It's weird for you, too!

Me: Well, what does she say?

Me: Well, after we'd finish, she'd say stuff like how it feels like we're one, and how the sex is perfect. She also said that she loves the way I feel inside of her. She thinks that no one knows me more than she does.

Me: That bitch.

Mordecai: Listen, Leviathan, I finished the section about you and little John. Is the next set coming soon?

Me: Yes, I mailed them off this morning.

Mordecai: Good, because Elsa said that if I don't get them quick enough, she will have her skinhead brothers kill me.

Me: You know she's lying, right?

Mordecai: How do you know she's lying or not, Leviathan?

Me: She says she knows you well, and if her brothers kill you, she won't have you anymore, especially to finish the story. She can't complete the story on her own. Her words are for cooperation.

Mordecai: That's true, Leviathan. You *do* use your brains. I think I'll be okay, then.

Me: Okay, so, while you typed, she laid on your bed . . . topless?

Mordecai: Yes. Come to think of it, she was only in her underwear, like me.

Me: And then, what?

Mordecai: Well, once I got finished with the passages you sent to me about little John, I told Elsa that she needed to stay away for a while.

Me: Didn't work, did it?

Mordecai: No. She refused and said that if she had to do that, she would go to the police about her alleged rape and I would go to jail.

Me: She's trying to scare you, Mordecai. She needs you more than you know; no one's going to finish my chronicles except you.

Mordecai: Yes, I realize that, but her brothers could beat me up.

Me: They may beat you to a pulp. They may even cut you a little, but they won't kill you.

Mordecai: Perhaps so, but it'll be a reminder that I can't play around.

Me: It'll all end, soon.

Mordecai: I hope so. Anyways, I suggested something to her. I said that I could type up a whole new story for her. You know, like a fiction novel.

Me: Okay.

Mordecai: All she would need to do is give me some materials and characters to work with.

Me: And how'd that go?

Mordecai: It went down the toilet; the only story she's obsessed with is yours.

Me: Mine, huh?

Mordecai: Exactly. She knows that you're Leviathan Golgohoth.

Me: And?

Mordecai: She has told me that if she doesn't get your story, she'll expose you to the public.

Me: Who will believe her?

Mordecai: We're in the twenty-first century, Leviathan. People will believe anything nowadays. The belief in Werewolves and Vampires is now relevant.

Me: Also Ghouls and Demons; they all still exist today. Now, tell me, my boy, what do you have to do while you wait for the next passages?

Mordecai: I have to have sex with Elsa.

Me: Will you knock off the Elsa bullshit? To me, she's Bunny.

Mordecai: But her real name's Elsa Behrendt; Elsie, for short. She says she's way too young to be having sex, but she does it anyways.

Me: Way too young? Well, how old is she?

Mordecai: She says she's fourteen, but she looks a bit older than that. Then again, a lot of the Freshmen girls at school look older than what they should be.

Me: Does Bunny go to L.A. High?

Mordecai: No. I never saw her once.

Me: There's a good chance that she doesn't go to school at all. I think she might be a little older than she says she is, just to scare you into thinking it's statutory rape.

Mordecai: Her motives are psycho. I'm so confused, Leviathan.

Me: Confused about what?

Mordecai: The éclairs.

Me: What do you mean?

Mordecai: Well, Elsa . . . I mean, Bunny likes vanilla custard éclairs; I think they're doing something to her.

Me: Excuse me?

Mordecai: Well, like, she eats them, and then she gets all . . . frisky.

Me: Oh really?

Mordecai: Yes.

Me: It must be the custard; it's dairy. And, I suppose that the crème she drinks has a lot to do with it, too.

Mordecai: I suppose. And, you know, her intimacy scares me.

Me: It scares you? How so?

Mordecai: She knows some of the most unusual sex positions, ever. I mean, a fourteen-year-old girl isn't supposed to know about them unless she had her eyes glued into Playboy magazines most of her life.

Me: No kidding?

Mordecai: No kidding; she's a contortionist, Leviathan; she can get her legs behind her head so easily.

Me: Well, that's talent.

Mordecai: And she likes to yell, Leviathan. I wouldn't call it a yell; it's more like a howl of some kind. Candice did it, but she wasn't so loud. I don't want Bunny to disturb the neighbors; there's no sense in that.

Me: I doubt that the Stapletons are going to hear anything; they're approaching eighty and they're nearly deaf.

Mordecai: But still, common courtesy.

Me: I have a hard time believing that the bitch is fourteen.

Mordecai: She showed me her birth certificate at our meeting at The Sports Club/ L.A.

Me: And it says she's fourteen?

Mordecai: Yes.

Me: Did you check for a certified raised seal?

Mordecai: Huh?

Me: Yeah, I don't think she's fourteen; she has to be much older.

Mordecai: Oh god, Leviathan! I want this nightmare to end! I want it all to just . . . end!

Me: The sex, too?

Mordecai: Yes. Especially that.

I don't get it. Mordecai should be lucky that he's even getting to sleep with a woman. With Candice away, he has nothing to worry about.

However, I can't really blame him for being scared; he doesn't like the thought of sleeping with someone who's trying to extort him and threatening to have him thrown in jail or killed. I wouldn't like it, either.

Me: Mordi, about the sex positions. Do you think that . . . .

Mordecai: I'm not going to give my opinion on them, Leviathan.

Me: I'm just trying to see if Tigris and I could . . . .

Mordecai: No, Leviathan! I'm not going to . . . . wait, what?

Me: Never mind; it doesn't matter.

Mordecai: You said Tigris.

Me: I said never mind. So, are you going to be okay for now?

Mordecai: I suppose so.

Me: Good. The next passages should get to you by tomorrow. Make sure you tell your friend that.

Mordecai: She's not my friend, Leviathan. But, I'll tell her.

Me: And listen, don't worry about the sex, okay? Think of it as a little fun until Acanthus and I come back.

Mordecai: Okay, but hurry.

Me: I will. I'll talk to you later, Mordecai.

Final Visit

I hang the phone up and take a look at the clock; it's ten after twelve.

I think about what I want to do right now. I'm so tired of writing, and I don't want to explore Vegas until nighttime. I plan on meeting up with the young soldier tonight; he wants to solve the grave robbing case himself, but I doubt he'll get far on it. I'll just have to tell him that it's Ghouls, and the matter will be settled.

I got it!! I know what I want to do; I want to visit Tigris. I miss her so much; I just have to see her.

I jump up from my chair and grab the volumetric flask with the bromine in it; I pull the cork off and take a huge gulp of it.

"I need you, wife." I say, taking another swig of the disgusting brown fluid. "I need to stay with you."

I put the cork back into the flask and hide it. I then sit down on the bed.

"C'mon, c'mon." I say. "Work!"

Suddenly, I begin to feel horrible spasms in my stomach; it feels like someone is trying to rip my guts out with a heated meat hook. My entire body begins to jerk violently.

"Oh no!" I say, flinching. "I drank too much! I'll be out for . . . oh!"

My eyes roll back and I fall backwards onto the bed; I drift off into darkness and I land on something.

I wake up in a room; I'm sitting on a bed.

"What's this?" I ask myself.

I hear the sound of water; rushing water. It sounds like ocean waves. I walk over to a window and look out of it. I see that I'm correct; it *is* the ocean.

I wonder where I am, I think.

I keep my eyes on the waves crashing onto the sandy shore. I suddenly feel a presence.

"Leviathan," I hear a voice say. I know that it's Tigris; I can recognize her sweet voice so easily. Her voice is one-of-a-kind.

"Hello, Tigris." I say without turning around. She approaches me and puts her hands on my shoulders.

"I'm glad you're here." she tells me, leaning her head against my back. I nod.

"I am, too." I say. I turn around and face my beautiful wife. "I missed you so much."

"I've missed you, too."

We share a kiss and hold each other for a bit.

"It's such a beautiful day." I say. "Isn't it, my sweet?"

"Yes, it is." Tigris says. "The sun's shining, there's a warm breeze. What a perfect day to make love."

"I couldn't agree more."

"My darling. Let's do it, now."

"Yes, my dear."

We begin to kiss. I slowly begin to remove Tigris's light-blue robe; she helps me take my shirt off.

"I thought about when we'd do this again." Tigris tells me.

"I have, as well." I say.

"Let's make it last."

"We will. I promise."

Tigris and I go over to the soft bed; she lies on her back, and I stare into her eyes.

"You know," I say. "We couldn't have picked a better day for this."

We get fully undressed and roll around on the bed.

"I love you, Leviathan." Tigris whispers to me.

"I love you, too." I tell her.

We begin to make love. Not even two minutes pass and Tigris is beginning to moan with excitement; that's how good I am at lovemaking.

The sex positions that I begin to use are making Tigris have multiple orgasms. I think her favorite, so far, is when I had her from behind; she kept telling me to thrust harder, and when I would, she would moan, groan, and grip the bed sheets tightly.

Excuse my method of describing this; I can't help but do it. I'm so very excited.

We finish lovemaking after two straight hours; that's the longest time Tigris and I were ever together.

After I finish filling her up, we cuddle up and pull the sheets over us.

"Leviathan," Tigris said. "We never made love like that before."

"And," I say. "I imagined you enjoyed it."

"Yes. It was the best sex ever; I loved it."

"Two hours."

"We were never together that long." Tigris runs her fingers through my damp hair. "And, I enjoyed every bit of it, especially those wonderful new sex positions."

"I see."

"It was very passionate; where did you learn them?"

"I'm a natural; I know how to excite you."

I stare at the ceiling fan for a few moments. I wonder . . . .

"Is this the present?" I ask Tigris. "Or are we in the past?"

"The present, Leviathan." she says. "Otherwise, we wouldn't be in such a modern beach house, would we?"

I nod. I continue to stare at the ceiling fan; the rotation of the blades is hypnotizing me. I snap out of my trance when I hear Tigris ask me a question.

"Are you in the mood?" she asks.

I know what she's talking about; she wants us to make love again. After two hours of extreme excitement, she wants more . . . and I will give it to her.

"We'll make love again." I say.

We begin to kiss. We gently touch each other, and then it leads to another lovemaking session; it lasted for 30 minutes, but every single second of it was so very precious to me; I know that it was for Tigris as well.

"You know," Tigris says after we finish. "It just gets better and better." She puts her head on my shoulder. "I love your chest hair; it's sexy." She begins to trace her finger around my nipple. "You're so good in bed. How do you do it?"

"It's like I said before," I say. "I'm a natural. And, I intend to make it great when I'm with you."

"I must be special then."

"You're my wife; I love you with all of my heart."

She smiles. I brush my fingers across her cheek.

"You mean everything to me, Tigris." I say, kissing her on her forehead. "You know this."

Tigris kisses me on my cheek.

"I love you, Leviathan." She tells me.

"I love you, too, Tigris." I say.

We kiss. I then turn my head toward the window; I see that the sun is shining.

"Do you want to take a walk with me on the shore?" I ask.

"I'd love to." Tigris tells me. "Let's do it."

I put on a pair of blue jean shorts. I don't wear a shirt; the sun won't burn me here.

Tigris puts on a light-green bikini top and bottom that compliments her soft olive skin; she ties a light peach-colored silk sash around her waist. We then walk outside in the warm sun.

Tigris and I hold hands as we walk, barefooted, in the warm wet sand.

"What shore is this?" I ask Tigris. "Are we somewhere in America?"

"We're in a dream world, my love." she says. "And, as you've figured it out, nothing can go wrong here."

"Does this place have a name?"

"No."

"That's strange. Every place has a name, including Dreamland. Maybe this is Paradise."

"Maybe."

I look over at Tigris.

That light-green bikini top and bottom really does bring out the color of Tigris's skin and eyes, I think. It makes her much more seductive. Not that she's already sexy enough.

I love Tigris's eyes; when we first met, I absolutely fell in love with them. They're a treasure; such sheer beauty radiates through them.

"You know, Leviathan," Tigris says. "This is nice. You and me, taking a walk on a nameless sandy beach; the sun's shining down on us, and the spray of the ocean is refreshing. It can't get any better than this."

"Ain't that the truth." I say. A wave crashes onto the shore and splashes over our feet. "This is the life."

We walk further down the shore. I spot a seashell lying on the sand.

"Look at that." I say. "It's a shell, of some sort."

Tigris bends over and picks it up; she studies it for a moment.

"It's a conch shell." she says. "If you put it to your ear, you can hear the roar of the ocean."

Tigris puts the conch shell to her ear; she smiles and hands it to me. I put it to my ear. I realize that it sounds nothing like the roar of the ocean; not at all.

I take the shell away from my ear. With my powerful vice grip, I crush the shell into tiny fragments and pieces.

"Leviathan," Tigris says. "What's wrong? What did you do that for?"

"It was that sound." I say to her.

I walk away from the shore and sit down next to a huge rock.

SIERRA J. BALL

"What was with the sound, Leviathan?" Tigris asks, walking over to me.
"It's a sound that I never ever want to hear again."

Tigris sits down next to me; she takes my hand in hers.

"Tell me about this." She says, her beautiful evergreen eyes staring into mine.

"It was the exact same sound that I heard for four hundred-twenty years." I say. "When I was trapped inside Arch-Peteryx's shell of a body."

"The sound of the ocean in a shell?"

"It's not the sound of the ocean; it's far worse. It's a cold and empty sound. It was loud and tormenting, on some occasions. It took me some time to get used to it, but I still . . . ." I lean against the large rock. "I don't ever want to hear that sound again."

Tigris doesn't know what to say. She just stares out at the ocean. She finally speaks.

"Peteryx stole your body?" she asks me.

"You know what happened, Tigris." I say. "That sorcerer, Edward Gaudio the First, cast a spell on me; it caused Peteryx and I to switch bodies."

"Yes, I remember now. I thought that Phaize, Tieran, Gogough, or Rox would kill you, but they didn't."

"They knew that it was me inside Peteryx's body."

"And, the whole time you were trapped, I wanted to reach out and help you, but I couldn't; I was long gone and away from you." She leans against me. "I'm sorry, Leviathan."

I put my arms around Tigris and hold her close.

"It wasn't your fault, my dear." I say. "And I'm still alive."

"I feel really bad that I couldn't do anything to rescue you, that's all."

"I said it's not your fault. There really wasn't nothing you could do. Don't feel bad, my dear; I'm alive and well, and back in my regular body."

"I'm still very sorry that it all happened."

I feel tears stinging my eyes, but it's not the usual stinging that one would get from tears; it's a lot worse.

"Peteryx is near me." I say to Tigris. "He's so close to getting his hands on me."

"Or is it the other way?" she asks.

"Huh?"

"You can find him and take him out, Leviathan. I know you can."

"I know. It's just the thought of having to face him again; I may not succeed this time."

"Not another word of that kind of talk, Leviathan Golgohoth. You are the strongest person I know; you will succeed, my love. All you have to do is fight."

"You're a good wife, Tigris. Sometimes, I think you know me more than I know my own self."

I feel the tears roll down my cheeks. One drops onto Tigris's forearm; she gasps and looks at me.

"Leviathan," she says. "You're bleeding."

So, that's why my eyes were stinging worse this time. Tigris reaches her hand out to wipe the tears of blood away, but I stop her.

"Leave them." I say.

"Leviathan," she says. "Please, don't beat yourself up over Imhotep Feathervault; he won't kill you. He'll try to, but he won't accomplish it."

"He won't? I mean . . . of course, he won't. I'm just fearing that I'll inhabit his disgusting hollow body again, with the scratching sensations; the creepy feeling of bugs crawling over me . . . oh, and the roaring in my ears."

"Leviathan, that won't happen again; I won't let it happen."

"How can you do that?"

"I have my ways."

Her quote was one that Acanthus said to me plenty of times before. It makes me wonder if she can influence my brother, the Deathbringer, to do something that will cause Peteryx to fail.

"Here," she says, removing her silk sash. "Let me wipe that away."

Tigris wipes the blood from my cheeks with her sash. She then picks up a sharp piece of shell; she cuts her palm open with it.

"Tigris!" I say. "What are you doing?!"

"You will see." she says.

She wipes the blood from her palm. She then hands me the sash.

"Why are you giving this to me, my love?" I ask her.

"It's for success." she says. "There is something you have to do with it."

"What's that?"

"You have to give this sash to Levetin; with it, the remaining six-hundred Anubis servants will fall within two days."

"Really?"

"Yes, and listen, Leviathan . . . he has to have the sash returned to you before you face Peteryx; If Peteryx knows the Encasement Hex, the sash will prevent him from performing it."

"Okay, Tigris. I'll make sure I have it." I stuff the sash in my pocket.

"And Leviathan, I have to tell you something that you're not going to like."

I see tears come to Tigris eyes.

"What is it?" I ask. "What's wrong?"

"Leviathan," she says. "You cannot see me again."

"What? No! Tigris, honey! I'll come visit you again."

"You can't, Leviathan. This is the last time; if you do it again, you will die."

"Die? How so?"

"You'll float forever, in darkness. You'll never get anywhere and no one will be able to save you . . . and you will never see me again."

"Tigris, I'm already dead. Everything will still be okay." I take her in my arms. "I can still visit you."

"No!" She pulls away from me. "Please, don't! I don't want to lose you again, and this time, it will be permanent."

"Tigris, wife, I will kill Peteryx, and then I will come back to see you."

"No. You must go back to your mansion on the west coast. You must make peace with your brother."

"No, I want to see you."

"You can't!!"

"I will!'

Tigris slaps me across my face; she catches me pretty good. I get very angry about it, but I will not hit her back; I never have put my hands on Tigris in an abusive way, and I never will; I couldn't live with myself if I ever did, and I will definitely put my own damned self out of my misery if I ever hurt her.

"Leviathan," Tigris says. "I'm sorry. I just . . . I . . . ."

"Don't worry." I say, rubbing the sore spot on my left cheek. "It's okay; I understand. I know how serious this must be, and if you believe that I will die if I come back, I'll stay away."

"Leviathan, I have to protect you. And besides, that stuff you're drinking is slowly damaging your insides. Oh my," She presses her hand delicately to my stinging cheek. I don't flinch when it begins to burn. "I left a handprint."

I gently take her hand away from my face.

"Don't worry about it." I say. "It'll go away in a little while." I take her in my arms again. "I'm really upset about not ever seeing you again."

"Leviathan, it's not like that; you'll get to see me again, one day."

"When?"

"It's only until Revelatianus decides when the time is right."

"Revelatianus promised me that I will see him again, but I haven't; I haven't seen him for over five-thousand nine hundred-eighty years. So, tell me this. How can you be so sure that he'll let us see each other again?"

"When Revelatianus says that something will happen, it will come to be. So, I know that we'll get to see each other again; it may take a while, but we will. I promise."

"Did Revelatianus tell you that we'll see each other again? Or, is it something that you just heard him say about me?"

"Revelatianus told me himself; he said it to my face."

"Okay."

I gently rock Tigris in my arms; I kiss her on her temple. She then stares into my eyes.

"I want to tell you something." She says. "It's about . . . our lovemaking." She smiles.

"It's enjoyable, isn't it?" I ask her.

"Of course, it is. I love it; it's better than everything. And, I just love how we got to spend more time together at the beach house; it was absolutely amazing."

"I strongly agree, but I think I was a little bit rough; I'm sorry if I hurt you."

"You didn't hurt me, Leviathan."

"Are you sure? Because that wasn't my intention."

"I know. You didn't hurt me; I enjoyed our time together."

Just then, the huge rock that we're sitting against starts to move; we get startled.

Suddenly, the huge rock sprouts arms, legs, and a tail; a head slowly pops out as well. It starts to walk slowly across the sand.

"A turtle." I say. "Why didn't that thought cross my mind? I noticed that the rock had a weird shape to it, but I would've never guessed . . . ."

"That it was a turtle." Tigris says, finishing my sentence.

I chuckle. I then begin to laugh; Tigris starts laughing, too. We laugh so much that our sides begin to hurt and we come close to tears.

Our laughter turns to silence after a few moments.

"You see, Leviathan," Tigris says. "There is joy in your heart; that's something Peteryx never had, even as a Human."

"All he ever had was pride." I reply. "He's too proud of himself."

"Yes, and that pride is going to get him killed; that's a good thing. You see, in my opinion, joy dominates over pride. The Eternal Ones agree with that as well."

"All six of them?"

"Believe it or not, yes."

I lay down, on my back, in the sand; I stare up at the sea gulls, flying in the sky.

"Leviathan," Tigris says, taking my hand. "I think it's time to say goodbye now."

"What?" I say. "I need to go now?"

I go to sit up, but Tigris stops me. She then climbs on top of me and looks at me.

"Before you go," she says. "Promise me one thing."

"Anything." I say.

"Promise me that you will live. Live, like you did for over six-thousand years."

"I promise." I place my hands on her hips. "To prove my love to you, I promise I will live."

Tigris smiles down at me.

"You promised me you'll live." she says. "Now, that also means that you'll kill Peteryx."

"I will kill Peteryx." I tell her. "I'll rid us of that plague."

"Good."

"With all of my heart, I promise. I'll do away with him quickly."

"Thank you, Leviathan." She places her hands on my chest. "Thank you, so much."

"You're welcome, my sweet."

A smile grows on Tigris's face; I love it. She has the most beautiful smile I have ever laid eyes on.

"I love you." She tells me.

"I love you, too." I say.

Tigris leans down and our lips meet. I slowly sit up and wrap my arms around her; we continue to kiss. I kiss her neck; Tigris leans her head back and begins to moan.

"You're so beautiful." I whisper to her.

I continue to kiss her neck. Tigris brings her head back up. She then removes her bikini top; she hugs me, her large breasts pressing against my chest.

I have Tigris lay down on her back. I lean over her and we lock lips; she puts her arms around my neck. We then roll around on the sand as we kiss.

After a few minutes of hugging and kissing, we part.

"I'm really going to miss you, my love." I say to Tigris.

"I'll miss you, too." Tigris says, putting her bikini top back on. "But it's not like we'll never see each other again; we will be together again, soon."

I embrace Tigris in my arms. I kiss her on her cheek.

"Thanks for the topless thing." I say. "I needed that."

"Sure thing." she says to me.

I feel a sharp pain in my stomach; I lay down onto the sand; Tigris lays down next to me and presses her cheek against mine.

"It's time, Leviathan." she says. "Please, be careful."

"I will, Tigris." I reply.

I see tears roll down her face and drop onto the sand.

"Don't grieve for me now." I say, rolling over on my side and staring into her eyes. "Do it if I don't make it."

"You will make it, Leviathan." Tigris says, putting her right arm around me and hugging me tight. "You promised me. And my sash will protect you from Peteryx's evil intentions."

"Should I form an alliance with . . . ."

"That little soldier? I think it's best that you keep close contact with Levetin instead."

"Why?"

"Levetin is your brother; he will help you, Leviathan, no matter how savage he can be."

"Okay."

I jerk because I get that pain in my gut again; more tears roll Tigris's cheeks. She takes my hands in hers.

"I love you, Leviathan." she says.

"I love you, more." I tell her.

Caught In The Act

I shut my eyes and feel myself sinking; I land on something that's wet and smells like grass. I open my eyes and notice that I am lying on the grass, right outside the Bentley residence.

Why am I not in my bed? Did I jump out of the window?

I realize that I am lying facedown, so I get up; I kneel on my knees while I brush my shirt off. I then rub my sore cheek; it really hurts for a strange reason. Did I really get slapped for real?

I then notice a four-leaf clover; I pick it. I then stand up straight and stare at it.

"Well, well, well," I hear a familiar male's voice say. "A four-leaf clover, on Saint Patrick's Day."

I look over and I see Acanthus standing underneath the tree next to my bedroom window; he walks over to me.

"Leviathan," he says. "I tried waking you up, but you were knocked out. I slapped you in the face, but you didn't even so much as flinch. So, the next thing I decided to do, when your eyelids started fluttering, was toss you out the window." He takes the clover from me. "You smell like you've been in a photo shop."

"So," I say. "Where's your servants?"

"Balcanicus and Spinosus are in Henderson; they have learned of a duo of bomb makers that may be Anubis dogs. What are you up to, besides being a heavy sleeper?"

I think of something; Tigris's sash. She gave me her bloodstained sash in my visit with her.

I reach into my pocket and sure enough, there it is.

"I have to give you something." I say to my brother.

"What is it?" Acanthus asks.

"A sash."

"A sash?"

264

"Yes. It's a sash; it has powers that will help you to wipe out Peteryx's Anubis army. But, I'm going to need it back from you before I face Peteryx."

"Somehow, I believe this. Okay, where is it?"

I hand the bloodstained silk sash to Acanthus; he inspects it.

"Why is there blood on this?" he asks.

"It's Tigris's blood." I tell him. "And mine."

"Okay . . . strange, but alright."

Acanthus folds up the sash and places it in a pouch on his utility belt, next to his bloody pliers.

"I have to go into town." I say. "I'm meeting up with a little soldier; he says that he wants me to accompany him while he tries to figure out what's behind the grave robbing in Woodlawn Cemetery."

"I already told you what it is. It's Ghouls, Leviathan. Ghouls robbed those graves, and if I were you, I wouldn't meet up with that soldier."

"But why? I promised him that I would."

"You didn't promise him shit. You and I are going Anubis hunting . . . together."

"What if I run into Peteryx? I'll need the . . . ."

"I don't think Peteryx is running around in the city; he's closed up. I'll get the sash to you when the time comes." Acanthus seems confused. "Are you sure that the sash contains powers that will eradicate the entire Anubis army?"

"Such a doubting Thomas. I used to be the same way with Tieran's oracle bones."

At the mention of Tieran's name, my brother gets a little uneasy. What is it about the late Chinese tyrant that troubles him?

"Oracle bones." he says. "Oh well, it doesn't matter. Let's head out."

"Good deal." I agree.

As Acanthus and I reach the city, and get onto the Vegas strip, we notice a young red-haired man, who has to be in his early twenties, talking to a young girl, no older than ten or eleven, in an alley.

"That doesn't look good." I say.

"If you study this closely," Acanthus says, "You can sense the fear in that girl's heart; that man's definitely a stranger to her. C'mon."

We approach closer, and we see the man reach out to touch the little girl in an inappropriate area; she screams and tries to run, but she is blocked.

"Hey!!" Acanthus shouts.

The man starts to look for where the shouting came from, giving the little girl enough time to escape.

"Hello?" he says. "Who's there?" I see him approaching us, unaware that we are near. "Who is that?"

"It's just me." I say, walking underneath a streetlight; Acanthus remains in hiding.

"Oh." he says. "You scared me, sir."

"Oh?"

"Yeah. I thought you were a ghost."

"He's no ghost." Acanthus says, surprising me by those words; he always called me a ghost. "He's an albino."

"Uh?" the redhead says. "Who are you?"

"Me? Oh, well, it won't hurt to introduce myself. Most people know me as Acanthus."

"Acanthus; that's a different name." he turns to me. "And, what's your name, sir?"

"You can call me Leviathan." I say.

"Leviathan. I heard that name in one of my favorite video games; Final Fantasy Eight."

I know that game he speaks of, I think. *Too bad he didn't say he saw my name in the Bible.*

"My name's Jared Jenkins." the young man says.

He extends his hand out to me and I shake it. I think: *This is the perfect person to kill and eat.*

Once the young man places his hand in Acanthus's, I sense that things are going to get worse.

"Caught in the act." my brother says.

"Huh?" Jared asks, trying to take his hand out of the Deathbringer's grasp, but fails to. "I don't know what you're talking about."

"So, you didn't just try to attack a young girl in that alley there?"

"No, sir. We were just talking."

"I saw you try to touch her!!"

"Uh, hey . . . I see you're not wearing green today; don't you know it's Saint Patrick's Day?"

"My eyes are green. But let's not worry about that; let's talk about you."

"Me?"

"Yes, you . . . you, who was about to rape a child."

"No!!" he jerks away from Acanthus. "It's not true!!" He goes to run, but bumps into me. "I didn't try to rape her!! We were just talking!!"

"Not good enough!" I shout. "And, how can I let you go when I have my chance to feed?"

Jared turns to Acanthus.

"What does he mean, to feed?" he asked him.

"You cannot deny Leviathan fresh blood." Acanthus tells him. "When you don't deserve to carry it around anymore."

"Look," Jared says. "I swear to you . . . it wasn't what it looked like!!"

"So," Acanthus replies. "All those other young girls that you raped in alleys in the past; you were just talking to them?!"

"I never meant any harm!!"

Acanthus and I chuckle. This man won't get too far away from us; we do not harm children, and child molesters don't deserve to live.

"Still." I say. "It's not good enough."

Demise Of A Death Dealer

I grasp Jared's wrists while Acanthus removes a long spike from his belt compartments; I've seen him use it before way back when. It's used to pierce the eyeballs and tongue.

"What are you gonna do with that?!" Jared asks in horror.

"Simple," Acanthus says. "I'll do whatever I have to do to make you stop raping children. Don't blink."

"No!!"

Jared struggles with me as Acanthus holds Jared's right eye open with his fingers. Just as my twin is about to drive that metal spike through his eye and pierce his brain, a screech is heard in the distance; a screech of terror.

"That doesn't sound too good." I say.

"You're right." Acanthus agrees. He looks Jared straight in the eye. "You forget this, and you never harm another child again . . . or we'll find you."

"Yes, sir." Jared says.

I turn the redheaded rapist loose. Before he can get far, I see Acanthus produce a gun from a pocket of the jacket he's wearing; he aims it at Jared and pulls the trigger. The bullet hits him in the back; he falls to the pavement and doesn't move.

"Levetin," I say.

"A change of heart, Leviathan." he tells me. "Come, we have to see what that screaming was."

Acanthus and I take off running; we run toward the shrieks until we reach the area right outside the Woodlawn Cemetery.

"Was there another grave robbing?" I ask.

I see a crowd standing out by the gates of the cemetery; they seem to be crowded around something.

"Watch out," I say, pushing myself toward the crowd. "Coming through."

I make it into the cleared area; I see what the crowd was looking at, and it shocks me to the highest limit.

"Darken Hark!!" I shout. "Oh god!! What happened?!"

Draken Hark is lying on the pavement in a pool of his own blood; his throat had been slit. However, he's still alive and clutching at the wound.

"Draken Hark." I say, placing his head in my lap; I am careful not to make him move his hands from around his neck. "Who did this?"

"A . . ." he tries to speak. "A . . . a monster."

"A monster?"

"Yes." he looks up at me; his green eyes slowly becoming faint. "Leviathan . . . it was . . . it was . . ."

"Who? Who was it? Was it Peteryx?"

"No. Not . . . Peteryx . . . not Peteryx . . . at all."

Who, other than Peteryx, would've done something this horrible to Draken Hark?

"You saw who did this." I say to him. "What did they look like?"

"The face . . . of evil." Draken Hark whispers; blood gushes out of his mouth. "Those eyes . . . those evil . . . black . . . eyes." He clings a hold to my shirt. "Listen . . . to me . . . Leviathan. He did it for you. He did it . . . for you."

"Did what for me? Who did this?!"

Although my eyes are blurry from tears, I can see my brother walk up; he has no sympathy, whatsoever, on his face.

"Please," Draken Hark whispers. He tries to hold his hand out to Acanthus; the motionless look still remains on my twin's face. "No. No . . . fear."

Draken Hark gasps; more blood gushes from his mouth. His hand falls to his side and he stops breathing. He has died; his eyes still open, staring out at Acanthus.

"I love you, Draken Hark." I say, hugging the Eternal One's lifeless body. "I'll get the bastard that did this to you."

I look up at Acanthus; I see the moon's light flash in his dark-green eyes.

"Close his eyes." he says.

"Levetin," I say. "Who could've done this?"

"No time to grieve. Close his eyes; he needs to sleep peacefully."

I gently pass my hand over Draken Hark's face, closing his eyes. I then leave him there, on the pavement and slip past the crowd, entering the cemetery lawn.

"Leviathan!" Acanthus calls out to me.

The Zombie

A light rain begins to fall as I rush through the moonlit cemetery, looking for a place to hide. I see the different areas where the graves had been robbed; slime covers the headstones and yellow police tape surrounds the deep holes.

I spot a large mausoleum and duck behind it; I can't let anyone be around me or try talking to me.

"Leviathan," I hear a voice say; I feel something grasp my upper right arm.

"Levetin," I say. "How did you . . . ."

"Why didn't you wait for me?"

"Don't you see, Levetin?! I had to get away from that!! Someone killed Draken Hark!! They're still out there!!!"

"And we will find them, but you have to come with me; we have shit to do."

"I can't."

"You must. Now, c'mon."

Acanthus forces me to step out from behind the mausoleum. As we make our way toward the gates of Woodlawn Cemetery, we see some guy clinging to a helpless woman; they're standing in a pool of blood.

"Hey!!" I shout. "You!!"

"Let her go!" Acanthus demands.

The guy releases the woman; she crumples to the ground and doesn't move. She is, no doubt, dead.

"Turn around, now!" I demand.

Slowly, the man turns and faces us. I cannot believe what I am seeing; I know that man.

"No way." Acanthus says. "A zombie?"

This is, indeed, a zombie that my brother and I are looking at; a zombie that I once knew as a live Human being. His red hair is disheveled and matted with a dark fluid; I say it's dried-up blood. His eyes, which used to be dark-brown, are now light-blue and glazed over; the whites of them are bloodshot. His peach-colored skin is now bluish and pale. His clothing is torn and saturated in blood. He groans in a somber tone as he walks slowly toward us.

"Rolfe," I say. "What happened to you?!"

"He's a zombie, Leviathan." Acanthus tells me.

"Was it Dante?"

"It couldn't have been Dante . . . or perhaps . . . ."

The zombie walks a little closer toward us; it appears that he is headed toward me.

"This isn't Dante's work." Acanthus says.

"How do you know?" I ask as I begin to back away.

"This man was alive when he was zombified; Dante's victims are usually dead when they are drained of their youth. It's usually because I killed them first."

"How can you tell that he was alive?"

"No wrinkling of the skin. Plus, the smell of the decay isn't as overpowering."

"I see."

"Zombies all have a taste for blood, however, the ones who were alive when they were changed have a more insatiable thirst than the dead ones; it seems as if they . . . want their life back, and flesh and blood is the answer."

Rolfe approaches me. He reaches out to me and his cold, clammy hands wrap around my neck. He begins to lick my neck; such an awful feeling that's somewhat pleasurable. His slimy tongue brushes across my cheek.

"Leviathan," Acanthus says. "What the?"

Rolfe nuzzles his face into the left side of my neck; he begins to bite into my skin; I feel a suction feeling and I know that he has found blood.

After he drinks some of my blood from the left jugular, he looks into my eyes. He breathes into my face; the smell of decay hits me. Then, a dark, black fluid drips from his mouth; it's so vile and disgusting that it makes me want to vomit.

Rolfe moves to the right side of my neck; he bites into it and sucks more blood. Wow, he steals my blood when I'm unconscious in bed, and now, after death, he's still filching it.

I am shocked when Rolfe presses his cracked and bloody lips against mine; once he starts nibbling at my lower lip, I see Acanthus walk over to us; he pulls Rolfe away from me and grabs his head. With a violent twist, he breaks his neck.

His head makes a complete three-sixty spin; the bones make such loud snapping sounds that I get weak in the knees.

Acanthus shoves Rolfe forward and he heavily plops, face down, onto the wet grass.

"My brother is not on the menu." he says.

The Luxor

A canthus and I stare down at the dead zombie that was once Rolfe Bentley; the rain stops falling and there's a cool breeze flowing through the graveyard. I wipe the slime from my mouth.

"If you weren't going to kill him," my brother starts. "I was."

"Who could've done this to Rolfe?" I ask.

"Peteryx, no doubt."

"Peteryx knows how to make zombies?"

"The scarabs drain blood, I'm sure. C'mon, we have to leave here."

We head to the entrance of Woodlawn Cemetery. Once we exit the gates, more trouble awaits us.

"THERE!!!" someone shouts. We look over and see a squadron of cops not even fifty feet away from us.

"Gotta run!!" Acanthus and I both say.

I take off running down N. Las Vegas Boulevard, heading toward the Vegas Strip; Acanthus heads the opposite way I go.

"STOP THEM!!!" one of the cops shouts. "SHOOT THEM!!!"

Shots are fired, but none of them hit me; I doubt that Acanthus was hit.

Leviathan, Acanthus voice says. *They're not the cops.*

"Huh?" I ask.

They're not the cops; they're Anubis servants; do everything in your power to stop them in their tracks.

"Levetin, what if . . . ."

They're after me as well; I have that sash you gave me. If what you say is true, and it has powers to take these fools out, then I have nothing to fear.

"What do I do? Where do I go?"

The Luxor.

As I race down the road, the cops, or rather Anubis servants, chase me in their squad cars. I have no clue where I'm going. Acanthus mentioned the Luxor Hotel and Casino Resort.

As I approach the Vegas Strip, I see it; the big black pyramid. I see that its spotlight shines brightly in the distance, signifying where its location is.

Good luck, Brother.

"Stop, Leviathan!!" shouts one of the guys on a megaphone.

As I approach the Luxor, I get a blast from the past; I need to climb it to get away.

"Here goes nothing." I say to myself.

With my great speed and stability, I race up the pyramid. Unlike King Khufu's pyramid in Egypt, which was made from bricks, this pyramid is made from slick glass, but I manage to stick without sliding down.

I know what I am going to do; I'm going to run to the top, and slide down to the other side! That's the perfect escape method.

It's also the perfect way to get killed. Acanthus says. *They will wait for you to come down, on the other end.*

The Anubis squad starts to fire more rounds at me, but their target seems more like the Luxor instead of me; the bullets ricochet off the black glass.

"You missed!!" I shout back at them.

I finally manage to reach the top of the pyramid; I cling onto the huge spotlight at the tip of the giant 3-D triangle.

"Get down from there, now, Leviathan!!" the guy with the megaphone shouts.

I look down and see the Anubis dogs surrounding each side of the Luxor; five men total. Acanthus was right; if I slide down, I will slide right into their waiting hands.

"You can't stay up there forever, tyrant!!" another servant shouts.

I am temped to let go because the giant light is playing war with my eyes. I look down and see people staring up at me through the glass.

I see a very familiar face staring up at me; one I have seen many times throughout my past; I even had the opportunity to be that person.

"Leviathan?" I hear them ask in disbelief.

"Peteryx!" I shout.

I hear the sounds of a helicopter's blades whirring nearby; I begin to feel a strong gust of wind and realize that a chopper is flying rather close to the Luxor; it shines a light on me.

There's one thing I decide to do: Take it out.

I get out my revolver; I plan to shoot out that light.

"Okay," I say as I cock the hammer of the gun back and take aim at the chopper. "One, two . . . three!"

I fire three rounds at the chopper; one penetrates through the fuel tank.

The aircraft starts to sway and a fire ignites where the fuel runs out; it starts to fly away. It goes farther and gets lower.

About a hundred feet away, the chopper crashes into the sand and explodes; the vibration is so strong that it shakes the Luxor's foundation, causing me to let go of the spotlight.

I slide quickly and cleanly down the giant black pyramid. It feels as though I'm sliding on ice; nothing like King Khufu's pyramid, which was an incredibly bumpy ride.

I'm getting closer to the ground; some of the Anubis dogs are waiting for me to reach the bottom.

"Here he comes!" one shouts. "Get ready!"

I make it to the bottom, rolling past them. As I travel, I twist my right ankle up real good; getting away from them may now be a challenge.

Anubis Star, Burning Bright

I stop rolling and lie on my back; the Anubis servants crowd around me and aim their guns at me.

"Well, well, well." one of them says. "If it isn't Leviathan Golgohoth. Oh, we've been looking all over for you."

"You haven't really been searching too well." I say.

"A little birdie told us that you have an accomplice, and he's taking us all out while you search for our master."

"Indeed, that *is* how it's playing out. Aren't you scared?"

"Who would help *you*, Leviathan Golgohoth?"

"My twin brother."

"You don't have a brother!" Another servant shouts.

"Oh, but I do." I sit up. "Apparently, Peteryx has never communicated with any of you; he just snatched you up and made slaves out of you. He doesn't care about your needs and your knowledge; he only cares about getting revenge."

The Anubis servants say nothing. The leader grabs me and makes me stand; my ankle really hurts, so I stagger.

"Wounded." he says. "Just the way we like it."

"It's just a sprained ankle." I say. "It'll heal."

One of the guys fires at my feet; I stagger back.

"On your knees, Golgohoth." he demands.

I do what he says; I struggle to get on my knees.

"Hands behind your head!" another shouts.

I smile and place my hands behind my head.

"Now, tell us." the leader says, aiming his gun to my head. "You tell us who's killing the Anubis army off."

"I thought Peteryx told you." I say.

"Tell us!!"

I chuckle. Can this get anymore comical?

"I told you," I say. "It's my twin brother."

"You have no brother." the Anubis group leader says.

"Yes, he does." says a familiar voice in the background. "*I'm* his brother."

The group turns to see Acanthus standing in the distance. He has the light-peach bloodstained silk sash in his right hand.

"No." the leader says. "It can't be . . . ."

"The Deathbringer." another says.

"In the flesh," Acanthus says. "Or so, I think."

Instantly, large vines emerge from the sand; they grab each of the five Anubis servants.

"HELP!!" one shouts.

The vines drag each servant to a designated spot: One stands off to the very back, there's two in front of him, that includes the leader; one on the far right, and another to the far left. The remaining two are to the front; one on the inner right, and the other on the inner left.

"Why are they . . . ." I say as I struggle to get to my feet.

"Let us go!!" the leader shouts at Acanthus. "Let us go, now!!! You'll be sorry!!"

"First off," Acanthus says, smiling. "I don't do requests. And second, I don't take threats too seriously."

Suddenly, the Anubis guy, who is on the inner left, gets a surprise; his clothing begins to smoke.

"What the?" he asks.

Before he can wonder any more, he bursts into flames.

"NOOOOO!!!!!!" he shouts in pain. The others begin to fear for their lives.

"Oh god!!!!" the one to the very back screams as a trail of fire heads right toward his way.

Once he's ignited and screaming, the trail of fire heads to the guy on the inner right.

"What are you doing?!!!" he shouts. "STOP!!!" he ignites.

The trail heads adjacent, to the guy on the far left. He struggles to get out of the vines, but he cannot; my brother's vines are overpowering.

The fire ignites the helpless Anubis servant; only one is left . . . the leader; the trail of fire leads straight to him.

Before the flames hit him, I see, what I believe, is a roaring Demon at the beginning of the trail; it gnashes its teeth as the trail travels.

The leader lets out a yell, and the flames claim him.

The five Anubis servants' screams fill the air with pain and agony; I begin to smell their burning flesh.

About a minute later, they all collapse to the ground, in the order they were ignited; their bodies are charred and smoking . . . the smell of their scorched flesh is worse now.

Acanthus cannot believe what he has done; he takes a look at the sash questioningly.

"Are you sure you didn't get this thing from Death himself?" he asks.

"I got it from Tigris." I say, limping over to see the damage that has been done. I see that the trail of flames left black travel marks.

"Why were they burned like they were?" I ask. "One by one?"

"I didn't demand it that way." Acanthus says. "It played out that way."

I watch as he kneels down and draws, in the sand, the path that the flames took; I see that he has drawn a star.

"That's it." I say. "The trail burned them, in the order of their evilness . . . and it left the shape of a star."

"I suppose that's it." Acanthus says.

"Strange, but effective. Now, I have to go back to the Bentleys' house. I have to rest this foot."

"And you have to keep those bite marks from getting infected."

Acanthus takes some weird leaves from a compartment on his belt; he places them in his mouth and chews them up. He then takes them out of his mouth and places them onto both sides of my neck; it stings really bad.

"Ah!" I shout. "What is that, Stinging Nettle?"

"It's called Immuno-Bitter." he says, placing small pieces of cloth over my wounds. "It draws deadly viruses out of one's bloodstream. You could call it the cure for AIDS, if you want. Don't tell anyone about it, okay? I don't need Humans raiding my lair; with Goliath the Juggernaut and the rest of my acanthus servants guarding the place, the bodies will start piling up. Can you feel this working?"

"Yes, thanks. Well, I have to get home. I guess I'll see you around."

I start to walk towards the Vegas Strip.

"Don't move." my brother says, heading over to me; he has me drape my arm over his shoulders and helps me to stand. "I'll hail you a cab; you don't need to be walking on that foot."

As we walk to the Vegas Strip, I think: *Where's that little soldier I was supposed to meet up with? I wonder what he's doing.*

"What a night." I say.

My brother agrees.

Hailing A Cab . . . Acanthus Style

Once we make it to the Vegas Strip, we stand over by the street; it seems as though a crowd of people are headed over toward the Luxor.

"I saw Peteryx." I say.

"You did?" Acanthus asks.

"Yes; he was at the very top floor, and he was looking up at me."

"So, he knows now that you shot the chopper down."

"How did you know that I shot the chopper down?"

"I arrived right when you reached the top of the pyramid. I took a detour back to the strip. I knew you'd survive the Anubis attacks, but I couldn't risk it."

"Oh, I see." I think of something. "Hey."

"Yes?"

"Who's watching Poppy while you're here? You don't just leave her along for this long, do you?"

"Syriacus is watching her."

"Syriacus?"

"An acanthus servant, just like Balcanicus and Spinosus. He was born Oniwaka Luchesse, and he was only fifteen when he became a member of my team about a hundred years ago, but he has served me well." Acanthus looks to the right and then to the left. "You should've seen the look on his face when he learned that he would be one of my top men; both shocked and happy." He points. "There's a cab."

"Oh good," I say. "But I can't pay for cab service; I don't have any . . . ."

"Any money? Don't worry about that; I got it."

I wave my hand to flag the taxi down.

"Taxi!" I call out, but it drives right past us. "Hey!!"

"Hold up!" Acanthus says. He holds out his right arm and hand. Instantly, the taxi stops right in the street.

Acanthus positions his hand in a *come here* motion. The taxi begins to back up; its tires are screeching loudly as it does. Acrid smoke emits from the tires; the smell of burnt rubber fills the air.

After the cab is about five feet away from us, Acanthus brings his hand down. We then walk over to the cab.

"How'd you do that?" I ask.

"Never mind." Acanthus says. He knocks on the driver's side window and motions for him to roll it down; the cabbie rolls it down.

"Thanks for stopping, huh?" Acanthus says.

"Uh . . . yeah." the driver calmly says. "Anytime."

Acanthus opens the back door and helps me get in.

"You're going to go home and get some rest." he says. "I'll be finishing up the job out here.

"Levetin," I say. "You'll be out here all night."

"Don't worry about that. Now, do as you're told."

"Sure, sure."

Acanthus shuts the back door. He heads over to the driver and hands him some money.

"Take him to the Bentley residence." he says to the driver. "Two-seventeen Desert Palm Drive. North Las Vegas. Keep the change."

"Sir," the cabby says. "This is a hundred dollars."

"Too much? Too little?"

"I can't take all of this money."

"I said keep the change; my brother's destination is top priority, and if you don't get him to where he needs to be, I'll find you. Got it?"

"Yes, sir."

"How did you know the address, Levetin?" I ask.

"I pay attention to streets." he tells me. "Goodnight, Brother."

That Poor Ugly Hungry Little Thing

I watch as the cab takes off, down the Vegas Strip, with Leviathan in the backseat. I then turn around and see that a crowd has formed around me.

"What?" I ask and shrug. "Show's over. But, what happens here stays here."

The crowd gasps as I walk past; I decide to go back to the Woodlawn Cemetery to try and make a connection with Dante Haven, the Vindicator and one of my colleagues.

I can't help but wonder why Leviathan wanted to meet up with that soldier to study robbed graves. I mean . . . it was Ghouls that robbed them; they marked their territory with their slime, the slime that keeps them from getting formaldehyde poisoning.

After a good distance of traveling, I make it to the cemetery. I head over to the area where Leviathan and I were, and I see something: It appears that someone, or something, is making a snack out of the Bentley zombie's corpse.

"Who are you?" I call out. The thing looks over at me; he abandons the dead body and takes refuge behind the nearest headstone.

"Away with you, Human." says a raspy voice.

"I saw what you were doing with that body."

"Yes, for I am a Ghoul. Now, away with your filth, Human!!"

This Ghoul has to be kidding me! He really thinks that I am a Human. Perhaps his sense of smell isn't as good as it used to be.

"My filth?" I ask. "Do I smell like a Human to you?"

I see the Ghoul's head slowly peek out from behind the headstone.

"If you're no Human," it says. "Then . . . what are you?"

"Don't you recognize me?" I ask. I advance to be recognized; the Ghoul sighs and appears again.

"Acanthaceae." he says, addressing me by my modern name; the name that describes me as the father of all the acanthus species. "I didn't know it was you; I thought you were in Corinth."

"Just because I'm Acanthus of Corinth doesn't mean that I have to stay in Corinth." I let him know. "So, are you going to tell me a little bit about what you were just doing?"

"I was hungry, so I decided to dig up a grave and eat, but I saw a Human nearby . . . and I ran away."

"A Human?"

"Yes. He had an assault rifle with him, and it looked like he was studying our ectoplasm that we left behind on the graves."

No doubt, this Ghoul spotted the young soldier that Leviathan was supposed to meet up with.

"I retreated," the Ghoul continues. "And, I didn't get too far away before I smelled that wonderful mouthwatering smell of rotting flesh; it was very strong, so I followed my nose, and I found that body . . . and I was so very hungry." he sniffles. "I'm Getty, by the way." He holds out his bloody and gnarled hand to me.

"Okay . . . Getty." I say, lightly tapping the top of his hand. "So, I approach you, and . . . ."

"I thought that you were the Human I spotted surveying the robbed graves, so I hid. But now that I see it's you, Acanthaceae, I have nothing to worry about, really."

"Were you, by any chance, scolded for eating pieces off of that body?"

"Huh? No. Why?"

"Well, it was walking around before it ended up still."

"You mean . . . it was a zombie, and you're wondering if it was one of Dante's?"

"Yeah, but I don't think it was one of Dante's; he'd let it be known."

"Oh, so . . . do you think I can finish eating it? I am still very hungry."

I smile and nod softly.

"Help yourself," I say. "You poor ugly, hungry little thing."

Getty chuckles dryly and excitedly. He hurries back over to the Bentley corpse and rips at its flesh; he stuffs it hungrily into his mouth.

I remove a dead twig from underneath my hair, and think: *Well, no reason to contact Dante; I have to get the job done with the Anubis dogs.*

I leave Getty the Ghoul to finish off the carcass, and I rush out of Woodlawn Cemetery to start searching for the remaining servants loyal to Arch-Peteryx Feathervault.

Back Home

The cab drops me off at the Bentley residence. I thank the cabbie and hobble my way up to the house. I climb through my window; I close it and lock it.

"Peteryx saw me." I say to myself.

I must tell Powers that Rolfe is dead; he isn't coming back home. What will he think of that? If anything, there will be some definite denial.

"I'll be okay." I reassure myself. "Levetin's out there; I have my twin brother's help."

I strip naked; I toss the clothes into the trash. I have to discard the evidence that shows I have been up to no good.

I throw on a pair of fresh clothes; a white T-shirt and a pair of dark-blue pajama bottoms. I then jump into bed; I have my dagger on me for extra protection.

"In case I get an unwanted intruder," I say. "I'll stab them right through the heart."

I pull the sheets over my chin; I breath a sigh.

"Goodbye, Drakengaard Hark." I say. "Be safe, wherever you may be."

I turn my head and look over at the clock; it's ten till eleven. It doesn't seem like it would be that time; that mess with the Anubis servants and running up the Luxor seemed like it just went by in a jiffy.

I start to think about that little soldier, Matthew McDaniel. He was really wanting me to go with him to study the robbed graves. Is it possible that he and I would've seen Rolfe the Zombie? Perhaps I'll see him somewhere else, but . . . the thing was . . . both Tigris and Levetin said it was a bad idea to hang around him. What do they know that I don't?

I think about Mordecai's issues and hope that he is doing okay. That crazy German bitch is ruining his life, and possibly his relationship, but I told him that help is coming soon; I told him to hang on, and all he has to do is cooperate.

My mind switches over to Jessica. Where is she? What is she doing? I haven't heard from her since I confessed to killing her brother and her boyfriend. Levetin has told me that she is about eight weeks pregnant; nine weeks now, if it's true that she is. Also, Mordecai told me that she's hanging around with a guy called Anson Vickers, who was a cousin to Caleb Hershee. But, isn't he supposed to be seeing that nice girl who works at the Hark Rock Café in Los Angeles . . . Megan Cosgrove . . . who is a cousin to Candice, Mordecai's girlfriend?

It's all one big web of drama, and a crock of shit. I hear Acanthus's voice say to me. *And you don't need to get yourself entangled in that right now. Get some rest, will you?*

Deciding that my brother is right, I close my eyes and fall asleep.

You Are What Again?!

I wake up. Today is Thursday; March 18th, 2004.

My head aches; it's probably because of all that trouble that happened last night with me, my brother, and the Anubis servants.

I get out of bed and see that my ankle is all healed up. I then go to the bathroom; I take a shower. I wash my hair and scrub thoroughly.

I rinse off and get out. I then go back into the bedroom and dress; I pull on a long-sleeved black shirt and a pair of khakis.

"I wonder if the police told Powers about Rolfe yet." I say.

I don't think the police will be locating a body anytime soon, Leviathan. Acanthus tells me.

"No body?" I ask.

It was consumed . . . by a Corpse Grinder.

"A Ghoul ate him?"

What else would "consumed by a Corpse Grinder" mean?

I decide that *I* will have to be the one to tell Powers about Rolfe.

I go to the kitchen, but he isn't there. I then walk to the living room; he's sitting on the couch, watching TV, and drinking coffee.

"Powers?" I say. He doesn't answer me; his eyes are glued to the TV screen.

"Powers?" I repeat. "I went out last night; I was chased."

Powers still doesn't say one word to me; I decide to just break the news to him.

"Rolfe's dead." I say.

Powers slowly turns his head and looks in my direction.

"Dead?" he asks in disbelief; his coffee cup trembling in his hand. "I . . . I don't understand."

"He was turned into a zombie."

"Dante Haven?"

"I was told that Dante may not have done it; according to his condition, Rolfe was still alive when he was zombified."

284

"I don't follow you."

"My brother told me that it may have been the work of scarabs."

"Scarabs . . . Imhotep Feathervault."

Powers takes out a bottle of pills; he pops a few into his mouth and takes a sip of coffee.

"You know of Peteryx," I say. "Just as well as you know of me."

"Yes." Powers says. "He's the Egyptian tyrant from Thebes. I saw your painting of the giant octopus. That's what killed Rolfe?"

"Uh, no. The octopus symbolized the wrath of Peteryx. He's a man, just like me."

Powers nods. He then takes two more pills and sips more coffee.

"Are you thinking about overdosing?" I ask. "I don't want to have to call nine-one-one."

Powers has tears in his eyes.

"Leviathan," he says. "I'm not trying to OD. There's a confession that I need to make."

"You're not suicidal?"

"No. Nothing like that. It's about me and Rolfe."

"Okay?"

"Well, you see . . . Rolfe wasn't my cousin."

"Really?"

I could've guessed that; I saw them the other night, acting like a married couple.

"He was actually . . . ." Powers hesitates. "Oh, this is too embarrassing to say to someone like you."

"It's okay. You can tell me; I'll keep it a secret."

Powers rubs his hands together nervously.

"Rolfe," he says. "He and I . . . were a couple."

"Huh?!" I ask, not feeling any surprises. "Are you kidding?"

"No. I'm dead serious. Rolfe and I got married in San Francisco two months ago, and we decided to live here, in Las Vegas."

"What about your brother, Ronny?"

"Ronny, my twenty-five-year-old brother. Oh yes. Well, I used to live here with him, and I introduced him to Rolfe, who was then Rolfe Caraway, about two years ago, but I didn't introduce him as a lover. Well, when Rolfe and I got a lot closer, about a couple of months later, I came out to Ronny and told him that I was gay. He flipped out and left; he never came back to get his stuff, nor did he ever call me."

"And, how long has he been gone?"

"Nearly two years."

"So, how old are you and Rolfe?"

"Rolfe was eighteen; I'm twenty-three."

My stomach churns; just listening to this makes me more sick than smelling burning flesh. Yes, it's a little hard to accept that Powers and Rolfe were husbands, and not cousins, but I could've guessed it; after seeing what I saw, it was so obvious that they were gay. But . . . Powers seemed so . . . straight.

"Leviathan," Powers says. "Is this a surprise to find out that I am gay?"

"Not really." I say. "I kind of knew for a while now."

"How?"

"I saw you and Rolfe together the other night."

"Leviathan . . . I asked you if you saw anything."

"I know, but I felt too weird to come out to you about it. Anyways, who cares if you're gay; it's not a problem to me. Homosexuality was a big thing amongst many men in the ancient past."

Powers nods his head slightly. He then takes another sip of coffee.

"There is something else that I need to come clean to you with." he says. "It's about my health."

"Okay," I say.

"You see, Leviathan. I am HIV positive."

"Isn't that . . . ."

"Oh, no. It doesn't mean I have AIDS; it's the virus that can cause AIDS. Rolfe had full-blown AIDS though."

"Oh?"

"Yeah, I gave him the HIV virus, and he didn't take care of it, like I do. And, it turned into the Acquired Immunodeficiency Syndrome."

"I see."

"Rolfe didn't want to die at such a young age; he was seventeen when he got AIDS. He wanted to find a cure that would make him live forever."

"That explains him stealing my blood."

"Yes. He told me why he wanted to take it, but I said that it wasn't a good idea. However, as a scientist, I did find out about this rare little marvel in medicine called Immuno-Bitter; it's said that it can cure all kinds of ailments."

My brother placed Immuno-Bitter on my bite wounds last night; he had to have known that Rolfe was infected with AIDS. Also, he told me not to tell anyone about it, or there would be a pile-up of Human bodies at the Lair of Acanthus.

"It doesn't exist." I say.

"Huh?" Powers asks. "I read about it online, in an excerpt on the Lair of Acanthus."

"Lies; there is no cure for AIDS. Besides, the measurements of my blood, and how it's introduced to one's body, plays a big role in cures and immortality."

"Like how?"

"It takes about twenty cc's to cure diseases; ten ounces to become immortal. How much did he collect?"

"About a pint."

"Drinking a pint of my blood, all at once, would've just killed him."

"I see." Powers is silent for a moment. "Your blood is a cure."

"Yes." I say.

"Can you cure me?"

"Yes."

"Will you?"

"No."

Powers is taken aback. He can't seem to understand why I won't use my blood to get rid of his ailment.

"You knew that Rolfe was stealing my blood." I say. "And yet, you denied it to me, left and right."

"Leviathan," Powers says. "I'm sorry. I'll do anything to get better."

"Search for that mythical Immuno-Bitter, but watch out for Goliath the Juggernaut and the acanthus boys."

"I'll pay you for some of your blood."

"Sorry, Powers. I don't do requests."

"It's not a request."

"It's a bribe."

"No."

"Then what is it? You're talking about paying me for something that I refuse to give away. What would you call that?"

"It's . . . nothing. I understand where you're coming from."

"Good. Now, I'm going to head back to my bedroom. I need to write some stuff to send to my best friend in Los Angeles."

"Okay, Leviathan."

You Will Not Intervene

I leave Powers to watch TV and guzzle coffee. I go back to my room and sit down at the desk. I run my fingers through my damp hair.

"Okay," I say. "Powers and Rolfe were gay; they were married in San Francisco. I knew something about the other night seemed different. Also, the lisp in Rolfe's voice and when I first saw them holding hands."

Just then, I hear the phone ring. I see that it's the DeFrancos' residence calling. Mordecai should be in school; why is he calling me at eight in the morning? I pick up the phone.

Me: Hello?

Anonymous: Leviathan, it's Mordecai.

Me: I had a feeling it would be you calling. What are you doing at home again?

Mordecai: I'm sorry, Leviathan. I know I'm supposed to be in school right now, but . . . it's Elsa.

Me: Is she there now?

Mordecai: Yes. She called me this morning, around six, and told me to go pick her up.

Me: Why?

Mordecai: I guess she wanted to know if the next set of papers are arriving soon.

Me: You should get them by today.

Mordecai: Okay, well, when we got back to the foster home, it was around seven; she wanted us to screw again.

Me: And you guys did?

Mordecai: Yes, unfortunately. For an hour.

Me: So, you guys must've just finished.

Mordecai: Yes, and she's taking a shower; I'm not supposed to be making any phone calls.

Me: Well, this is *your* house; you have every right to.

Mordecai: Yes. I'm stressed, and I needed to talk to you.

Me: Well, I had an interesting night; wound up sliding down the Luxor.

Mordecai: What?!

Me: Yeah. Oh, and Rolfe Bentley's dead.

Mordecai: How'd that happen?

Me: He was turned into a zombie; I don't think it was Dante Haven that did it, either.

Mordecai: My goodness, Leviathan.

Me: Oh, and Draken Hark's dead, too.

Mordecai: Draken Hark?! Leviathan, how did he . . . .

Me: Something with great black eyes killed him.

Mordecai: Was it Peteryx?

Me: He said that it wasn't Peteryx. And, on top of it all, Peteryx's eyes are yellow; you saw that.

Mordecai: Yes, I remember now. He had the eyes of a cat, or a wild bird, or something. Well, I am sorry about Draken Hark. I hope that . . . .

I hear a door open and someone talking.

"What are you doing?!" they ask. "Give me the phone!!"

Me: Mordecai? Mordecai!! What's going on?!

Anonymous: Hello? Hello? Who is this?

It's a female's voice; it sounds German. No doubt that it's Bunny; she must be done with her shower.

Me: Who is this?

Bunny: I asked first, asshole!!

Me: You must be Bunny.

Bunny: Call me Elsie.

Me: I'll call you what I want . . . Bunny. I believe you know who this is.

Bunny: Ah, yes. Tyrant Leviathan Golgohoth; Mordecai has told me so much about you.

Me: He wouldn't reveal me to anyone.

Bunny: No; he referred to you as Jonathan Note, but his words gave me a clue to do some extensive research; the manuscript mentions all kinds of things in the past, and I knew that Jonathan Note was an albino as well. It's very obvious that Jonathan Note is Leviathan Golgohoth . . . you.

Me: Very clever, you are, Miss Behrendt. Did you gain your intelligence from school?

Bunny: Perhaps, and you sound so very interesting from the stories I've read on you. It's so amazing how the legendary Deathbringer turned out to be your long lost twin brother.

Me: You leave that in the past.

Bunny: Well, it's in the present now. I feel like I know the two of you so well.

Me: Trust me, honey . . . you don't want to know us.

Bunny: Is that a threat, Leviathan?

Me: You bet your life, it is.

Bunny: Well, no matter. I'm still going to get your story, and you will not intervene . . . or I will kill Mordecai.

Me: If you harm one hair on his head, I'll tear you to pieces. And then, I'll kill your father and your brothers. Do they still beat your ass on a regular basis?

Bunny: How do you know about my father and my brothers?

Me: Don't worry about that, sweetie. So, tell me about yourself. What do you do for fun?

Bunny: Lots of things.

Me: Mordecai told me that you're fourteen.

Bunny: Yes, that's right.

Me: Well, I have a hard time believing that.

Bunny: I'm just mature for my age, that's all.

Me: So, you have a condo?

Bunny: Yes.

Me: Is it just for you?

Bunny: Yes. Why?

Me: Where do you get the money to pay for it?

Bunny: What?

Me: I see now. You pay for it with Daddy's money; I'm sure you have to take plenty of abuse for it.

Bunny: My father and brothers live in Torrance.

Me: He doesn't wire you the money?

Bunny: No. It's money that I make myself?

Me: How? A babysitting job? Condos are a little pricey in California, and you're a little too young to be making enough money to pay for one.

Bunny: My father sends it to me.

Me: You just said that your father doesn't wire you money.

Bunny: Wiring and sending are two different things.

Me: No, honey. I have bank accounts; I'm very aware as to what wiring money to someone or something is. It's the same thing as sending it, only it's a lot quicker and safer. Tell me the truth. Where do you really get the money to pay for that condo?

Bunny: I have a great body.

Me: When it's not covered in bruises, I take it.

Bunny: Shut up!! I have no problems in any areas; my body is my moneymaker.

Me: What are you, a slut?

Bunny: No. I'm a working girl.

Me: You're sleeping around with men you don't know. It's called prostitution; that's illegal. Oh, and it's also statutory rape.

Bunny: So? I always do what I want.

Me: And that's why you're screwing my best friend?

Bunny: Yes; he's excellent in bed. The sex is great. I know him too well.

I feel my blood boiling; my anger rises and my temperature flares up, but I stay calm.

Me: Well, I hope that you two are using protection; I think Mordecai needs it a little more than you do.

Bunny: I don't need protection to have a good time.

Me: You bitch. You cold-hearted bitch.

Bunny: I can read your mind, Leviathan, and I know what you're thinking: *Poor little Jewish boy. Who will save him now? Surely, it can't be me.*

Me: I didn't say it would me. Perhaps Acanthus will do it? He knows all about what you're doing. It would be his pleasure to hang you upside down from a tree and flay you alive . . . but not before removing your fingers and teeth.

Bunny: I'd like to see him try.

She underestimates me greatly, Leviathan. I hear Acanthus's voice. *Whether it's me, or you, or someone else, that bitch's fate is sealed.*

Me: Just watch your back.

Bunny: Oh, I'm so scared. Anyways, when are those papers you wrote going to arrive?

Me: Sometime today, I imagine.

Bunny: Okay, great. Well, I gotta go now. Me and Mordecai are gonna celebrate.

Me: Oh?

Bunny: Yes. To celebrate, we're gonna make love. Good luck on your next set of papers.

Me: Yeah. Let me talk to Mordecai again.

Mordecai: No can do, Leviathan. Mordecai needs to take the time to get hard, if you follow me.

Me: Yeah, I do.

Bunny: Don't disturb us, okay?

Me: Fine, I won't!

Bunny: Thanks. Later, asshole.

In anger, I slam the phone onto the receiver and shout a swear word.

"That evil little swine!!" I shout. "I'm really beginning to hate her more than ever. When I get back to L.A., she's going to bite it."

I pick up my pen and grab some paper; I start to write the next chapter in my chronicles.

Meeting Master Shang-Kai Zhao

I t's the year 1042 A.D. Tieran had begged me to take him and the other tyrants to China after leaving Persia. So, I did.

Being wealthy from having filched from rich sheiks for many years, we were able to settle in a prominent part of a Chinese city called Hangzhou (pronounced *Hang Joe*) during the Song Dynasty.

"Tyrants," Tieran said. "I heard of a great teacher, who used to be a soldier, who lives here; he stays in a dojo here in Hangzhou. Do you want to go and visit him?"

"Sure, Tieran." I said. "Why not?"

"Well," Rox said. "Maybe he can teach us how to fight properly, so that we can take Peteryx out."

"Like we can't fight already?" Phaize asked.

"We just need more style."

"Yeah," Gogough agreed. "It sounds like a great idea."

"Let's go visit him, Leviathan." Phaize said to me. I nodded my head.

"Let's go." I said.

Tieran decided to lead the way. We got lost a couple of times and had to ask for directions.

An elderly Chinese man gave us a piece of parchment with the exact location of the warrior's dojo. He also handed Tieran a compass.

"Give me that." I said.

Tieran handed me the compass, and with my help, we finally located the dojo; it was in the mountain ranges.

When we arrived, we saw a young-looking Chinese man, standing still and staring at us. He had on a green robe with unique blue-green designs on it. He had long black hair that was tied back into a neat bun and decorated with a dark-turquoise ribbon and two ornamental hair sticks made of ivory. He looked a little like Tieran, but there was some differences.

"Hello," he said to us. "Welcome to my dojo; my name is Shang-Kai Zhao." (pronounced Shang Ky Joe).

"Greetings, Shang-Kai Zhao." I said. "May we call you Master Shang?"

"You may."

"Do you still train people for combat?"

"Yes, I do."

"Well then, you should train me."

"Silence. I shall train you, Leviathan Golgohoth."

"How? How do you know that I'm . . . ."

"I said silence; speak unless you're spoken to." He turns to Tieran. "Ah, Tian Fang-Xia; the last living member of the legendary Xia Dynasty."

"Yes." Tieran said.

"And, who are your friends?"

"They're tyrants, like Leviathan and me." he gestured to Rox. "This is Rox Rothbane." He looked over at Phaize. "And, this is Phaize Pierterch." He then glanced over at Gogough. "This here is Gogough Celdeklause."

"Very pleased to meet you all." Master Shang said. He took a bow. "And, where is the sixth tyrant?"

"Uh . . . we don't claim Arch-Peteryx Feathervault." I said.

"I see. Follow me."

We were taken inside Shang-Kai Zhao's dojo. We loved how it was decorated; very ornamental. It had a great oriental touch to it, and it smelled great, too . . . . like fragrant tea.

Shang-Kai Zhao turned and faced us.

"I sense something." he told us. "I sense . . . that all of you can put up a fight, but only two of you have been successful in victories; Leviathan Golgohoth and the . . . uh . . . tyrant with the piercings." Master Shang spoke of Rox. "You two are very strong, yes."

"How did you know about our victories?" Rox asked.

"Hearsay, but I will train only one of you."

"What do we have to do, Master Shang?" Tieran asked.

Shang-Kai Zhao walked over to an ivory chest and opened it; he pulled out a roll of papers. He handed it to Tieran.

"Read that." he advised.

Tieran unrolled the papers. He gasped.

"Hey, wow!" he exclaimed. "This is the Diamond Sutra. This is the first book ever written!"

"The Diamond Sutra?" Phaize asked him.

"Yes. It's a Buddhist religious text that was printed here in eight sixty-eight anno Domini, during the Tang Dynasty."

Tieran began to read the Diamond Sutra to Phaize and Gogough; Master Shang turned his attention to me and Rox.

"You two," he said. "You will both try to take me down, with ease. You, uh . . . ."

"Rox Rothbane, Master Shang." Rox said.

"Yes . . . Rex,"

"Rox."

"Silence. You will go first; show me your combat skills."

Rox got ready. The skills test began. Rox tried so hard to weaken Master Shang and take him down with his combat skills, but he was failing . . . and the teacher wasn't impressed.

"You fight dirty." he said.

The tyrant, with his superhuman skills, charged toward the Human . . . but was taken down with effortless ease.

"Oh dear," Master Shang said. "You are strong, but not strong enough." He helped Rox to his feet. "Please, join the rest of your companions and listen to the reading of the Diamond Sutra."

"But," Rox protested. "I wanna train to fight; I wanna sharpen my skills as a warrior. And my name is Rox, not Rex!"

Master Shang shook his head; he pointed to the other tyrants again.

"Do as I say." he demanded. "Now."

"This is trash!!" Rox yelled. "It's always about Leviathan, isn't it?"

Rox walked over to the other tyrants and took a seat next to Tieran. Master Shang stared at Rox.

"No need to express thoughts of envy." he told the Welsh tyrant. "Leviathan Golgohoth is a strong tyrant."

"Again?" Rox said. "Who died and made him king?"

"Silence!"

Rox scoffed in frustration; he turned his attention back to the reading of the Diamond Sutra.

"Hate flows through him like a raging river." Master Shang said.

"You'll have to excuse Rox." I said. "He's a bit ill-tempered sometimes."

"I have heard about your entrapment of Imhotep Feathervault, in the pit of scarabs."

"Yes."

"I heard that he has escaped, and I want to train you to extinguish him for good."

"Uh, don't you want me to try and take you down with ease?"

"Nonsense. I know that if I gave you that challenge, you'd succeed." he bowed. "Do you accept this training?"

"Yes. I will accept it greatly, Master Shang. On one condition."

"What's that?"

"I feel like I need to show you that I'm worthy."

"No need to show me your skills; I know that you possess them."

I stood there for a moment. I then threw a surprise punch that caught Master Shang full in the face; he dropped to his knees and clutched his nose. Blood spurted out from between his fingers.

"Now," I said. "I'm more than ready for your training. What do you say?"

Shang-Kai Zhao looked up at me. He then took his hands away from his face, which was spattered with bright-red blood; he pulled a handkerchief from his pocket and wiped it away. He then stood and tossed the handkerchief off to the side.

He took a bow. He then walked over to a wardrobe closet and got out a gray training uniform; he handed it to me.

"You really *do* have a true warrior's skills." he told me. "Put these on and we'll go outside of the dojo to train."

"Yes, Master Shang." I said.

I went to a dressing area and put the uniform on. I then walked toward the entrance of the dojo. I turned to Phaize, Tieran, Gogough, and Rox.

"Master Shang said that I'm the chosen one to defeat Peteryx." I said to them. "He thinks that I am a true warrior."

"Well," Rox said. "I think you *are* the one who should kill Peteryx; I won't do it."

"Yeah," Gogough said. "Peteryx seems like he's only after you anyway."

"I wonder what Master Shang will teach you." Phaize said.

"Something he'll already know." Tieran said.

"I don't know." I replied. "I'm not too familiar with Oriental fighting techniques. But, if I learn something great, I'll teach it all to you."

"Sounds good, Leviathan." Gogough said to me.

"Hey," Phaize said. "Do you think that a normal Human's training methods can help you defeat another tyrant?"

"Well," I said. "My method, as a tyrant, hasn't succeeded yet. We'll just have to see how this plays out."

I opened the double doors of the dojo.

"Good luck, Leviathan." Rox said. Phaize, Tieran, and Gogough nodded.

"Thanks, tyrants." I said to them.

The Master's Tasks

I walked out of the dojo and closed the doors behind me. There, Shang-Kai Zhao waited for me.

"Now, Golgohoth-San," he called me. "Are you ready for the first task?"

"Task?" I asked him.

"Yes. Your first task is to break this thick board in half, with your fist."

Stretched out across two stacks of cinder blocks was a board that looked to be at least 6-8 inches thick; I just stared at it and said nothing.

"Can you break it?" Master Shang asked me.

I nodded; I drew my right fist back and took a shot; I split the wood, barely. I gashed my hand wide open.

"Try again, Golgohoth-San." Master Shang said. "And, use the same fist."

"What?" I asked.

"Use the same fist. You must battle through the pain; it's the only way you can destroy your enemies." Master Shang approached me. "Think, tyrant. If your enemy was standing only inches in front of you, would you stand there and have a staring contest with him, or would you put your fist through his face?"

At first, I thought that Shang-Kai Zhao was crazy, but then I understood what he was saying; pain is a part of training to fight, and I must not cower at the sight of the enemy.

I drew my injured fist back again and took another shot. I took another, and another, and another . . . until the wood was broken completely in half.

"Very good, Golgohoth-San." Master Shang praised me. "You've passed the first task."

I bowed and tried to pull the splinters out of my sore hand.

"Leave them there, tyrant." he said. "Pain is good; pain is a part of combat." He put his hands together. "Are you ready for the second task?"

"Yes, Master." I said.

"Okay. Your second task is to break the cinder blocks with your fist."

My eyes widened. I took a look at my injured hand, which was starting to bruise up; Master Shang chuckled.

"Do it with your good hand, tyrant." he said.

The second task was quite easy; I pounded those cinder blocks to rubble. What I didn't understand was . . . how did I manage to break up those concrete bricks so easily, but I had a hard time breaking through the wood? I couldn't figure it out.

Master Shang clapped his hands together.

"Excellent." he replied. "You've passed the second task. Are you ready for the third and final task?"

"I am." I told him.

"Very well. Your third task is to face me, in hand-to-hand combat."

"Really?"

"No questions asked, Golgohoth-San. And this time, no surprises; just straight-forward fighting."

I got ready to fight, but Shang just stood still and stared at me. I took a swing at him, but he dodged it.

I tried to land a kick, but it was no good.

How did I manage to strike him in the dojo, I thought. *But, I can't hit him outside of it. Maybe it's because of all the open space he's got.*

I found that my skills were very warrior-like, but Master Shang seemed to be avoiding them.

"C'mon, Golgohoth-San." he said. "You must pass the third task, so that you can learn more."

Learn more, I thought.

I needed to do everything to pass the third task. In frustration, I took a look up into the sky, and to my surprise, Master Shang looked up; I took advantage of that.

Just as he was lowering his head, I charged into him. He spun me around, and as he did, I grabbed his arm; I managed to get behind him and twist it back.

As he was slipping free, I hit him in the back of the head with my elbow, causing his hair to come loose and fall over his face.

I released Master Shang, who then fell to the ground.

"Ow," he said.

"Ow?" I asked.

"What was that, Golgohoth-San?"

"My takedown. Did I pass?"

Shang stood up straight; he took a bow.

"Yes," he said. "You've passed the third task. You fought well."

"Splendid; it was simple. Am I supposed to use the three tasks to take down Peteryx?"

"No."

"Then what did I just do all of that for?"

"To show me that you are strong; Now, I need to show you what I do to take down my enemies. Come; we shall practice."

The Master's Method

aster Shang took me back inside the dojo; Tieran, Phaize, Gogough, and Rox all looked happy to see me.

"Okay, Golgohoth-San," Master Shang said, grabbing one of the practice dummies. "As a former soldier, I served proudly in Japan; I have leaned many ways to kill the enemy. The General said that chopping off heads was the quickest way to extinguish those who hold evil intentions against you."

"I've ripped plenty of hearts out, in my days." I said. "That kills."

"Indeed, but not in an instant."

"Huh?"

"When you ripped your victims' hearts out, did they spend a few seconds looking at you gripping it? Did they glance at the large hole in their chest?"

Yes, they did. Someone who would die instantly wouldn't have done that.

"I suppose." I said.

"Then you're wrong." Master Shang said. "Though ripping hearts out is a fatal way to die, it's not the quickest way to go. Of all the ways there are to die, decapitation will kill you in the blink of an eye."

"Did the Deathbringer tell you this?"

"What?"

"Nothing. Well . . . death by decapitation. One doesn't feel anything?"

"Supposedly. But, how can you really be sure, Golgohoth-San, unless you've experienced it?"

I thought about what Phaize had told me once; he said that Acanthus of Corinth had been decapitated in Rome, but since the Immortal Trio cannot die, due to Thanatos not having an internal Hellfire, he lived . . . his body picked his head up and put it back on his shoulders.

I never asked my brother about it because I always believed it to be a myth.

"I don't know, Master Shang." I said. "I don't know if I've heard of anyone who has lived through a decapitation."

"His brother did!" Phaize shouted from a distance.

"Is it inhumane?" I called back to Phaize.

"If it kills you in the blink of an eye," he started. "No."

"Then I don't need to learn this."

"Golgohoth-San," Master Shang said. "If you truly want to destroy your enemy, you must do it . . . ."

"As inhumanely as possible." I said. "For I am a tyrant."

"Think, Golgohoth-San. What other way are you going to make your enemies not come after you? To do it permanently, you must remove the head, therefore destroying the brain."

"Yes, Leviathan," I heard Rox say. "Remember the philosophy of losing a head."

After careful considerations, I decided that it didn't matter how I would kill Arch-Peteryx Feathervault; however I would do it, I wanted to make sure that he'd never get up again. But perhaps, decapitation would be the answer?

"Teach me." I said to Master Shang.

Shang-Kai Zhao took me to a cleared area of the dojo; he then grabbed a sword from the wall and handed it to me. He then grabbed one for himself.

"When performing the perfect decapitation," He said. "One must position their weapon in the perfect angle, in order to slice through the neck cleanly."

Master Shang gripped his sword tightly. He then drew it back and brought it forward, horizontally and with extreme force; the blade sliced through the dummy's neck, sending its head flying off its shoulders; it rolled over into a corner.

"Whoa." I said. "That's all?"

"You must know the right position to place your weapon, Golgohoth-San." Master Shang told me. "There's more to decapitating than meets the eye." He goes and gets another test dummy, for me to work with. "Remember . . . your enemy is weak; you can cut off his head when he's standing straight or halfway straight. It's good that you don't let him know you're going to decapitate him . . . not just yet; give him a clue . . . then take him out."

"So be it."

As a superhuman, I have lightning-quick reflexes and speed; something that Shang-Kai Zhao didn't have. Before the teacher knew what happened, I took that attack dummy's head off, with one quick horizontal stroke of my sword; it rolled over by the other tyrants.

Tieran gasped and picked the head up.

Master Shang stared at the headless dummy as if he saw a ghost; he looked over at me.

"I . . . ." he stammered. "I . . . I saw you do it, Golgohoth-San, but . . . you were so quick. I believe you already know a lot about the art of decapitation."

"Not much." I said. "However, I am a killer, and fatal strikes come naturally."

"I saw the whole thing." Rox said.

"Me, too." Tieran said, dropping the attack dummy's head onto the floor. "I saw it; a tyrant's eyes are powerful enough to follow another tyrant's speed."

"That's right." Gogough said. "A normal Human's eyes could never do that."

Master Shang walked over to inspect the headless dummy. He then went and got three more; he mounted them on wooden posts.

"Try it again." he told me.

"Why are there three dummies now?" I asked.

"Cut them all off, at the same time."

I believed, at the time, that he wasn't trying to teach me anything; he wanted to see if my fighting skills compared to his. Was he finally being outmatched? You bet.

I focused on the trio of dummies and thought to myself: *After taking off three heads, will I have to remove five at a time?*

I drew my sword back. I then brought it forward, with great speed, and force and took all three of the heads right off!!

My companions all jumped up and cheered.

"Way to go, Leviathan!!" Tieran said. "That was better than when I tore that Roman soldier to pieces during the Fall of Rome!!"

"Yeah," I said. "Just as good."

"That was so wicked cool!!" Rox said. "I got chills."

"Well," I said. "Thanks, Rox."

"Oh, I was talking to Tieran, but you did good, too, Leviathan."

I scoffed.

As the tyrants continued on, Master Shang couldn't believe what he had saw; he shook his head.

"You have done extremely well, Golgohoth-San." he said to me. "Superb fighting skills."

"Congratulations to me." I said.

"Indeed." Shang-Kai Zhao took a bow. "Death by decapitation never fails."

"Unless you're Acanthus of Corinth." Phaize said to us.

We looked over at the Corinthian tyrant and nodded.

"If you feel like you need to weaken your enemy first," Master Shang said. "That is, if he is strong, then do so."

"Master Shang," I said. "I have tried to weaken Peteryx with my strongest attacks ever, but they just don't seem to faze him."

"Did you say *Phaize?*" Phaize asked us.

"No, Phaize." I told him.

Shang-Kai Zhao smiled. He took another bow.

"That's enough practice." he said. "Come, all of you; my servants have dinner waiting."

Dinner With Shang-Kai Zhao

We were taken to the dining area of Shang-Kai Zhao's dojo; sitting there, waiting for us to devour, was Chinese food.

I ate it before, back during the beginning of the Zhou Dynasty; there was fresh fish and fruit, stir-fry, egg rolls, chow mein noodles, rice, and green tea for us to drink.

"Oh wow!!" Tieran said. "Chinese food!! You even have chopsticks!!"

"That's right, Tian-San." Shang-Kai Zhao said. "Help yourself to as much as you like."

We all sat down and began to eat and be merry.

"Master Shang," Tieran said. "We're in the Song Dynasty, are we not?"

"Yes." the teacher said. "We are, indeed, in the Song Dynasty."

"What's happening?"

"Well, Tian-San, this dynasty is an age of high culture."

"Do you create things?"

"Lots of people here in Hangzhou create things."

"What kind of things?" Phaize asked.

"Well, Phaize-San," Master Shang started. "It's mainly printing, poetry, and calligraphy; the movable types were developed so that we can print books and documents. Also, paper money has been developed, since there's paper. Someone also invented a little direction device; it's called a compass."

I had a compass. It was intended for Tieran to use, but since he got us lost on the way here, I decided to use it myself.

"You know," Master Shang said. "A compass can fall into the wrong hands."

I took that statement into consideration; if a compass *did* fall into the hands of an evil person, they could locate someone they've been looking for and kill them. However, if they had no knowledge of where that person was, the compass would be useless.

"We have a compass." Tieran said. "We're evil."

"Oh," Shang-Kai Zhao said. "You fellows aren't evil."

"Yes, we are." Rox replied. "We're tyrants."

"But," the teacher said. "It was a name you were given, beings that you're immortals."

"We *are* savage." I said, taking the compass from around my neck. "We survive on blood and carnage." I handed the compass to Tieran; even though he'd probably never know how to use it. "However, it's better that we possess a compass instead of Arch-Peteryx Feathervault."

"Indeed," Master Shang said. "When you and your colleagues leave here, he will not come."

"Are you sure?" Gogough asked.

"Yes. He'll sense your powers somewhere else."

"But he'll smell our scent here." I said. I drank my green tea and got up. "Thanks for the chow; I think it's time for us to start traveling again. Maybe we'll locate Peteryx before he can find us."

"Maybe you will."

I took a bow. I then left the dining area and went to the dressing room to get my traveling clothes; I put them back on and went back to the dining area.

I saw Tieran grab a handful of the egg rolls from the tiny table.

"For the road." he said.

"Anything to stay full." Rox said. "There's plenty of food out there."

"But none like this."

I smiled. I then bowed to Shang-Kai Zhao again.

"Thank you, Master Shang." I said. "Thank you for the training and the hospitality."

"You're quite welcome, Leviathan Golgohoth." Master Shang said. "And good luck." He took a bow.

"The Diamond Sutra was great, Master Shang." Tieran said, and took a bow; Phaize, Gogough, and Rox all bowed as well.

"Good luck to all of you, tyrants." Master Shang told us. "And be strong."

We nodded and left the dojo. As we traveled through the mountains, I thought all about the art of decapitation; I'll need a sword for it, so I decided to get one, wherever I could find one; I'm sure there were plenty of them in China.

Little Time Left

I stop writing; I straighten my papers out and put them in one of the manila envelopes and seal it. I then look over at the clock to see that it's ten till eleven.

What will I do now? I'm a bit tired of writing. All that's left for me, really, is to find Peteryx.

I think about something: *Tigris told me not to visit her with the bromine again, or I'd kill myself.*

I get the flask of bromine out; I look at it and sigh. I want to drink it so badly; I want to see Tigris again, but I cannot. Not even a tyrant's insides are built for chemicals like this; something's too strong for everyone.

I take the flask with me to the bathroom; I remove the cork and pour the rest of the contents down the toilet.

"I love you, Tigris." I say as I flush the toilet. "I'll see you again, someday."

I walk back to my room. I then go over to the bookshelf and grabbed the book *Beowulf*; I sit down and begin to read it.

As I read, I think to myself: *If Arch-Peteryx Feathervault hates me so much, how come he never tried to be more aggressive in attempting to kill me? He allowed me to live so long, and met up with me ever so often, saying that it was going to be the last time we'd meet . . . but I continued on. It definitely had to be his fear for the Trio, and my connection to them. On top of this, what is Tigris and Acanthus keeping from me about that soldier, Matthew McDaniel? He seemed really nice and pleasant.*

I will not let anything bad happen to me; I'm the strongest tyrant that has ever lived. Peteryx will not kill me, or even come close to doing it. And that soldier . . . I suppose I'll find out more about him in the near future.

I finish reading *Beowulf* and I feel my eyes getting weary, so I sit the book down and lay back on the bed.

"Tomorrow will have to be the day." I say. "The day that I have to confront Peteryx."

I close my eyes and fall asleep.

Financial Crisis: Starring Mordecai

I wake up when I hear the phone ringing; it startles me and I fall out of bed. I had my dagger with me, and it came close to slicing through me.

I scramble to my feet and pick up the phone.

Me: Hello?

Anonymous: Leviathan, it's Mordecai.

Me: I know. Why are you calling?

Mordecai: I just received your passages.

Me: Oh? What time is it?

Mordecai: It's almost noon.

Me: Noon?

Mordecai: Yeah, noon. Is it noon over there in Vegas?

I take a look at the clock. It's about five minutes till. Close enough.

Me: Yeah, it's right about noon over here; I took about an hour long nap. So, what's the report on our German beeotch?

Mordecai: Nothing good; she's starting to charge me for sleeping with her.

Me: She's making you pay her?

Mordecai: Yes, Leviathan. The sex is expensive, and I think she's lost her mind.

Me: That's nothing new. So . . . what are we looking at here? A couple hundred bucks?

Mordecai: No. Over here, that's dirt poor prices; you know that.

Me: Where are you getting the money to pay for it?

Mordecai: I haven't paid her yet; I told her I don't work and that I don't have my own bank account. I'm not going through the trouble of finding Marilyn and Ned's checkbook.

Me: And, I suppose they took it with them to San Francisco.

Mordecai: Too right; they don't travel with much cash.

Me: So, you're making out I.O.Us?

Mordecai: Yes.

Me: What's the deal?

Mordecai: Well, Leviathan, I don't have a job.

Me: I'm sure there's an opening at Abdullah's Palms, beings Cindy Hershee got canned.

Mordecai: She got fired?

Me: Yeah, and I'm sure you're old enough to work there. Go talk to Abdullah; tell him I sent you.

Mordecai: Uh . . . Leviathan. I'm Jewish; Abdullah is Saudi Arabian.

Me: That says nothing. Hosni Kharoufa is Jordanian.

Mordecai: The guy that sold me the condoms? He's Jordanian?

Me: Yeah. Hosni is also the assistant manager at Abdullah's Palms.

Mordecai: Oh, well . . . I'll see.

Me: Tell me what Bunny's wanting from you, on top of the money and the story.

Mordecai: On top of the money and the story, she wants those damn vanilla custard éclairs and that disgusting hazelnut crème.

Me: Does she know you got the passages?

Mordecai: No; I haven't called her yet.

Me: Aren't you supposed to call her when you get them?

Mordecai: I'm not calling that bitch before I call you!

Me: There's an easy way to end it all, Mordi. Go grab a hammer and hide it under the pillow.

Mordecai: No, it isn't that easy, Leviathan; I don't have a wicked heart like you or Acanthus do . . . no offense.

Me: It's a compliment; no offense taken.

Mordecai: I know you'll be back soon; I'll leave her to you.

Me: But you have to take action, you know. Besides, what has Bunny charged you so far?

Mordecai: She's up to three-thousand dollars.

Me: Three grand? For sex that you claim isn't that good?

Mordecai: She's crazy!!

Me: Where is she now?

Mordecai: She's at her condo.

Me: You need to call her about the passages.

Mordecai: NO!!

Me: Mordecai, listen to me. Keep her near you, as much as possible; make sure she's not up to anymore funny stuff that'll put you into more jeopardy.

Mordecai: I want her away from me as much as possible. Leviathan, I'm sleeping with a psycho.

Me: I slept with a psycho once; I believe I told you this though.

Mordecai: And I typed it up.

Me: Can you think of at least one thing that you like about Bunny?

Mordecai: She is gorgeous. Oh, and she smells really good, too; like peaches and cream.

Me: Good; think of the positives.

Mordecai: Have you found Peteryx?

Yes, I saw him at the Luxor last night; he watched me shoot down that chopper . . . which I do believe, now, that Anubis servants were flying it.

Me: Yes, I found him.

Mordecai: Are you ready to take him on?

Me: More than ready, and that's how you have to be with Bunny.

Mordecai: I can't do it; her father and her two brothers will kill me.

Me: Did she ever talk to you about her brothers?

Mordecai: Yeah. She said that they're twins; their names are Stefan and Ulrich. They're both twenty-two. Apparently, they served some prison time in San Quentin for reasons unbeknownst to me.

Me: They'll be taken care of.

I open a drawer to the desk; I see a note written on papyrus paper, addressed to me.

Mordecai: Leviathan?

Me: Yes?

Mordecai: Are you still there?

Me: I have to go for right now. You be safe, okay?

Mordecai: Leviathan? Leviathan!!

Today's The Day

I hang the phone up. I then pick up the papyrus paper and watch as the words written on it become meaningful, yet dangerous.

LEVIATHAN GOLGOHOTH,

YOU THINK YOU CAN KILL ME? YOU THINK YOU'LL BE VICTORIOUS IN THIS ORDEAL? WELL, I AM A CHANGED MAN, AND I WILL SUCCEED IN MAKING HISTORY OUT OF YOU . . . . FOR GOOD!! I HAVE SOMETHING THAT I THINK YOU MIGHT WANT TO CONSIDER. FIND ME NOW, OR THERE WILL BE THE DEVIL TO PAY.

—ARCH-PETERYX ◎◎

I study the Matisse style letters on the papyrus paper. My eyes then catch something near the canvas painting of Octopus Peteryx; the light from the sun is shining off it.

"What is that?" I ask myself.

I walk over to the shining thing and pick it up; I can't believe my eyes.

"A sword." I say. "This looks just like the one Shang-Kai Zhao let me use to learn the art of decapitation back during the Song Dynasty." I examine it and I notice something; the initials (S-K J) on the blade, near the hilt. "S. K. J.—Shang-Kai Zhao." I smile. "This is *his* sword!"

And, I hear Acanthus say. *I got most of the job done; you're nearly clear for the final fight; only three Anubis servants left. This time, make sure he doesn't get back up.*

"Today's the day." I say to myself. I stare at Shang-Kai Zhao's sword. "Today, I must face Arch-Peteryx Feathervault."

I'm heading to Henderson; there's only three of those dogs left, and Balcanicus and Spinosus spotted two. See you there, Brother.

There's no questioning what Acanthus has said. Peteryx, I believe, is no longer in Las Vegas.

To Henderson With Intent

I grab my revolver out of the desk drawer; I walk out of the bedroom and into the living room; I see Powers cleaning a gun. Where did he get that?

"I have to go." I say.

"I'm going with you." Powers says.

"You cannot; it's too dangerous."

Powers stands up from the chair he was sitting in.

"I think that Peteryx had something to do with Rolfe dying." he says. "I'm going to help you kill the son of a bitch."

"The fight between me and Peteryx is personal." I say. "You cannot get involved."

"I have to avenge Rolfe."

I sigh. Nothing I say to Powers will change his mind; I have no choice but to bring him with me. I was really wishing that the little soldier, Specialist Matthew McDaniel, would accompany me; he has artillery power. But, where is he? Could *he* possibly be the thing Peteryx mentioned, in his letter, that he has . . . and that I might want to consider it? Also, Acanthus said that he would see me in Henderson; I have a feeling that I know where I need to be.

"I don't suppose you know about a Guard armory in Henderson, do you?" I ask.

"I know my way around Henderson." Powers tells me. He loads his gun with a six round magazine. "I'll take you there. We're going to kill that bastard, once and for all."

"And then I can go back to Los Angeles."

"And I can rest, knowing that Rolfe was avenged; do you think one shot between the eyes will do it?"

Shang-Kai Zhao said that destroying the brain will finish one's enemy off for good, but I do believe that Peteryx's reflexes are a lot faster than ever before, so no; one bullet won't work.

"Maybe." I say.

SIERRA J. BALL

I want to tell Powers, so badly, that he'll never survive facing Peteryx. I mean, really. Edward Bentley is a Human being; Arch-Peteryx Feathervault is a tyrant, just like me. He'd never hold up.

"Are you ready?" Powers asks.

"Let's go." I say.

Powers and I exit the house and get into his car; we take off down the little suburban road and head to Henderson.

"How long have you and Peteryx feuded?" Powers asks as we head down a desert highway.

"Too long." I say. "I pushed him into a pit of scarabs shortly after the Great Pyramids of Giza were constructed."

"Really?! That long ago?"

"I thought I had killed him, but he returned shortly after the Ascension of Jesus and vowed to get revenge on me."

"Has he ever come close to killing you?"

"A couple of times, but let's not mention it, okay?"

We ride in silence; I see, out of my peripheral vision, that Powers is studying his gun; I have a feeling he can't wait to use it.

Plans Of The Last Anubis Servants

After about a half hour of driving, we arrive to a military-based building; it's an armory called the 1225th Engineer Company.

"This is it." I say.

"This must be where Peteryx is hiding now." Powers says.

"We have to be quiet, okay?"

"Okay."

"Do not let him hear us, under any circumstances."

Powers and I sneak quietly toward the armory; we can hear movement inside.

"What's going on in there?" Powers whispers.

"I don't know." I say. "Let's listen."

We begin to listen; there is more than one person in the building.

"Who's talking in there?" I ask myself. I listen to the conversation through an open window.

"This is almost done." someone says. "All that's needed is the C-4 carbon and the ignition wires, which I will install now."

Whoever's in there is making a bomb; I'm very familiar with what C-4 carbon is.

"They're constructing a bomb." I whisper to Powers.

"A bomb?!" he whispers in disbelief. "We better be careful."

We continue to listen to the conversation.

"Master Peteryx isn't happy with us." says another person.

"But we won't fail him." the first person says. "Acanthus of Corinth won't go near a bomb, will he?"

"He might. After all, I think that one of his powers is that he cannot die."

"It's a myth."

"But, sir . . . we're the last two of three; all the others failed Peteryx by falling to Acanthus. How did we manage to make it?"

"He hasn't located us yet . . . but, when he does, he won't kill us."

"What makes you think he thinks differently of us, from the other Anubis servants?"

"Fire power."

"And what about our third guy?"

"Same thing; fire power."

I move in closer to try and get a look at the Anubis servants. At the same time, I can't help but believe that Acanthus will be here, and he can help me in the battle with Peteryx; we can join forces, as brothers, and stop this evil fiend . . . once and for all.

But first off: Where is Peteryx?? It was to my understanding that he would be here, in Henderson, at this Guard armory; I do not sense his presence, and the servants are speaking of him in the third person point of view.

I listen as the conversation continues.

"Now," the first guy says. "All I need to do is set the time on this thing, and we're all set."

"What time are you going to set it for an explosion?" the second guy asks.

"Well, it's one-fifteen right now. So, I'll set it to go off at two-thirty; that should give us some time to do what we need."

"But sir, why such little time?"

"Because Leviathan is here."

They know that I'm here. But how? Is it possible that they have the power to sense a tyrant's presence?

"It's time, Powers." I say.

"Yes." he says.

Bad Timing: On Leviathan's End

We get our weapons ready; we run inside the armory. What I see next is confusing: With the two Anubis guys are two hostages; I realize that it is Murabbi and Azrael; they seemed a bit perplexed. I also see that they are bound in rope.

"Well, well." One servant says. "Look who decided to show up; it's Tyrant Leviathan Golgohoth. How charming."

"Who are you?" I ask as I stare into their bearded faces and red eagle-like eyes.

"We're the last two of the three remaining Anubis servants." he says. I see that he has, in his right hand, a suitcase; no doubt, it's the bomb they made.

"Where's the third one?" I ask.

"No need to wonder. You won't find out who he is before we kill you."

Leviathan, I hear Acanthus's voice say. He's the soldier! That last little bastard, the one who escaped the Monte Carlo massacre and ratted us out to Peteryx, is in disguise an a U.S Army soldier! I told you not to trust him!!

I know now. The little soldier, Matthew McDaniel, is the third Anubis servant. No wonder both Tigris and Acanthus said not to associate with him!! But . . . he never showed any hints of evil; his eyes were not revealing anything, and I was unaware.

"Where's Peteryx?!" Powers shouts.

"And," the other guy asks. "What are you, a Human, going to do? Are you going to shoot at us? One bullet could trigger that suitcase to do something drastic."

"Let my friends go!" I demand and cock the hammer of my revolver back. "Or I will shoot it."

"Careful, Leviathan." the guy with the suitcase says. "You do want to live long enough to see Peteryx once more, do you not?"

"I'll shoot you in the head; I'm an expert shooter."

"Unless you want to trip the detonator with the vibrations of a loud sound, do not pull the trigger."

I decide better on it; I think I will decide to live a little longer, to confront Peteryx, wherever he is. I lower the gun to the ground.

As I do, a horrible thought comes to my head: Revelatianus told me that one of the Eternal Ones would die on Saint Patrick's Day, and two on the day after. Draken Hark died yesterday, and . . . Murabbi and Azrael are down here, bound in ropes, and two Anubis guys have, in their possession, a suitcase bomb.

Oh, god!! The bomb is due to blow up within the next hour, and Murabbi and Azrael are ready to die!!

I raise my weapon again.

"Think about it, Leviathan," the suitcase guy says.

"No, I won't!" I shout. "You think I won't blow you away!?"

"The bomb is only a device for negotiation."

"Negotiation?"

"Yes. It's set to go off in an hour, but Peteryx will be here in way less time than that."

"Where is he?"

"Not far."

I look over at Powers; the gun in his hands is trembling.

"You're afraid," Azrael says.

"Be strong." Murabbi tells him.

Instantly, Powers stops shaking and focuses on the Anubis servants and the suitcase.

"I'd put the firearms down," the suitcase servant says. "On the floor."

"If you let my friends go," I say. "I'll put down the gun and go with you to meet Peteryx."

"What is this?" the other guy asks.

"Negotiation." I say. "Your friend says the bomb is a negotiation device; I'm willing to negotiate."

"No, Leviathan." Murabbi says.

"Shut up!!" the suitcase guy shouts. He focuses on me again. "You, Leviathan and friend, put the guns down, and we'll let your friends go."

"You put the bomb down first." I say.

"I'll detonate it first. Now, guns down, and your friends go . . . and then, you come with us."

I nod. I tap Powers' shoulder to accompany me; we both put down our firearms.

"Very good." the suitcase servant says. "Now, Jamal, go untie the Eternal Ones."

Jamal, the other servant, grabs a knife from the table; he cuts Murabbi and Azrael free. I can't believe we're actually negotiating all of this.

"Okay, Leviathan," the suitcase guy says. "Now, we take you to Peteryx. Are you sure you're ready to die?"

"I'll see." I tell him.

As Jamal and the suitcase-toting servant walk over to me and Powers, we see that Murabbi and Azrael haven't moved from their spots.

"Murabbi?" I say. "Azrael? You're free; you can go back to the haven."

"No, Leviathan." Azrael says.

"It's not over." Murabbi says.

"Oh, but it is." Jamal says. "Leviathan is ours, and Peteryx will be pleased."

"So," the suitcase guy says. "What makes you think that . . . ."

Before he can get the rest of the sentence out, we hear the unmistakable beeping sound of a bomb that's ready to detonate!!

Jamal and the suitcase guy look at each other, open-mouthed. Suitcase Guy then looks at his watch; he looks up again.

"WE'RE IN PACIFIC TIME!!!!!!" he shouts to the top of his lungs.

"NNNOOOOOOOOOOOOOOO!" Jamal screams.

I see Murabbi and Azrael run opposite ways from each other and brace themselves against pieces of large armory equipment.

Before Powers and I can high tail it out of the armory, a huge massive explosion occurs; I feel myself fly backwards, out of the armory. I'm way in the air; at least twenty feet.

I land on my back, in the sand, and the wind gets knocked out of me. I hear screaming and shouting in the distance.

Shortly after the screaming stops, I hear gunshots being fired; no doubt, it's the guns Powers and I placed on the floor. The bullets make a whirring ricochet sound as they bounce off metal.

I struggle to catch my breath, but it doesn't work; I stare at the flaming Guard armory for a moment.

I try to get up, but I am too damn weak. My vision blurs and then I black out.

Bad Timing: On Acanthus's End

Balcanicus, Spinosus, and I walk through the warm rough sand in Henderson, Nevada. I shield my eyes from the glare of the sun, seeing if I can spot any signs of a large building.

"Are you sure this is the way to the engineer armory, Acanthus?" Spinosus asks.

"I'm leading the way," I say. "I know where I'm going; I sense a strong presence of evil; not too strong . . . but strong enough."

"Is it Leviathan?"

"No. It's the Anubis servants; we're close to where we need to be."

"Wish we had binoculars." Balcanicus announces and chuckles a bit. I turn toward him.

"No need." I say. "We're close enough."

We walk a little further through the desert sands. I begin to see, in the distance, a building; it's surrounded by a wire fence. I can see that there are large vehicles parked in a large motor pool of sorts.

"Is that it?" Spinosus says.

"It is." I say. "I can smell those dogs from over here . . . there's two of them."

"Isn't there supposed to be three?"

"Yes. That soldier that Leviathan wanted to follow around is one, but he isn't there. And now, Leviathan knows about his true self."

"Is Peteryx there?" Balcanicus asks.

"No." I say. "And, I think that the soldier may be with him. Come."

We hurry toward the armory. As we get about a hundred yards away, I hear a faint beeping sound. I then hear someone shouting something frantic, and then it's followed by a scream of terror.

"Leviathan," I say and start running; my servants follow me in pace.

Just as we are about to approach the fence, the entire armory explodes with massive fire and force; the power of it shakes the ground.

"NOOOOOOOOOOOOOOOOO!!!!!" I shout as I shield my face from the extreme blast of heat. "LEVIATHAN!!!!"

"MASTER ACANTHUS, NO!" Balcanicus shouts and grabs my arm. I try to pull away; I have to find Leviathan.

My hopes for finding my brother are cut short when we hear screaming behind us; Balcanicus and I see that Spinosus is flailing around; he is on fire!!!

"NO!!" we both shout. We head over to our colleague.

"Drop!" I shout as I pull off my black coat. Just as Spinosus falls to the sand, I throw the coat over him, attempting to snuff out the fire.

Once it's put out, we see that Spinosus is still alive, but he's good and burnt; his eyebrows are singed and his hair is all gone, leaving him bald.

A few seconds later, we hear gunshots firing.

"Duck!!" Balcanicus says, dropping over the burnt Spinosus.

I can't stay down; I have to get over there. I rush toward the fence, and I hear the ricocheting of the bullets.

Suddenly, I feel it; the pain of an object smacking me in the head. One of the fired bullets catches me dead in my temple and exits out the other side; I stand, surprised by the blow, for a few seconds.

I feel my legs go limp, and I fall backwards onto the sand.

"MASTER!!!!" I hear Balcanicus shout. He rushes over to my aid. I stare up at him as my vision fades to black. My breathing lessens and my hearing becomes more diminished.

"Master!!" I hear Balcanicus shout from what it would sound like in a cave; low and hollow.

I begin to sink, and then I fade to nothing.

Peteryx Must Be Stopped, NOW!!

I feel something stroking my hair; I want to open my eyes, but I can't. If I can open my eyes, will I still be able to see?

Where will I be? Will I be in Heaven? Hell, perhaps? Will I still be out in Henderson? Perhaps I'll be with Tigris again? Oh please, let it be that!!

"It'll be alright, Leviathan." a voice says to me. "I'm right here; I won't leave you."

The voice is a female's, and I know I've heard it before. I begin to talk, but I keep my eyes shut.

"Where am I?" I ask. "Am I alive?"

"You're alive, Leviathan." the woman's voice says. "You're back at the Bentley residence in Las Vegas; you'll be able to sit up." I feel myself being pulled up and embraced. "You're fully recovered from your injuries. Can you open your eyes for me?"

"I believe so."

I open my eyes and see that a beautiful woman is staring at me; she has long orange hair and bright-green eyes. She also has a light complexion and rosy-pink cheeks.

"Colai," I say.

"Yes, Leviathan," she says. "It's me."

"How? How did I survive that? What . . . what happened? They set it for . . . ."

"There's a logical explanation to what happened, Leviathan; it was bad timing."

"Bad timing?"

"Even the Anubis servants were surprised."

"Murabbi . . . Azrael . . . are they . . . ."

"They're dead, Leviathan." Colai dashes a tear away. "And so is Edward Bentley. There was a police report; only Bentley's body was discovered among the carnage."

"No Anubis servants?"

"The two servants, Jamal and Malik, were disintegrated when the bomb exploded; Murabbi and Azrael's remains were spared and cast into the earth by the Master. Also, there's something else."

"What could it possibly be?"

"Levetin witnessed what happened from a distance."

"Levetin?"

"He ran to see if he could find you amongst the trouble, but . . . but he . . . ."

"He what?"

"He took a stray bullet to the head."

"NO!!" I jump up from my bed. "IS HE OKAY?!"

"He's still alive, Leviathan. Calm down. He got up about an hour after being shot and discovered that he's the size and age he was when he was first killed."

"So, Acanthus of Corinth is walking around as twelve-year-old Levetin Golgohoth?"

"Yes. For right now."

"I need to see this."

"He's been in this position before, but you've never seen it. You'll have to hurry; if he consumes fresh Human blood, he'll become the towering and intimidating Acanthus again."

My brother was shot in the head. It had to have been one of the bullets from the shooting I heard from the burning armory.

"How's Angeleal?" I ask.

"She's grieving over Murabbi and the Hark brothers' passing, but she will continue on."

"Where is she?"

"In the haven; she's praying at the shrine."

"I see. What time is it?"

"It's a little after four-thirty; March nineteenth."

"March nineteenth?! You mean I . . . ."

"You slept for more than a day; Peteryx is still out there."

"Peteryx must be stopped, now!!"

"Yes, and you must go to him."

"Is he still in Henderson?"

"No. He's back here in Vegas."

"I have to find him, now!"

I get up from the bed. I then grab my dagger and the revolver; I also retrieve the mysterious sword of Shang-Kai Zhao.

"Today's the day that I succeed." I say. "Peteryx cannot get away with his ways."

"Be careful, Leviathan." Colai says, getting up. She runs her fingers through her long orange hair. "Imhotep Feathervault is a lot closer than you think."

"He's afraid; he won't find me."

Colai says nothing. She then looks out the bedroom window; she turns her gaze back to me.

"Stay strong." she says and disappears.

I scoff. I then rush out of my room and to the front door. Once I open it, I get a surprise; there is someone standing in the doorway.

Before I can confront this person, they raise their arm over their head; they grip what appears to be a crowbar in their hand.

They bring their hand down with such extreme force; I am smacked in the head with the metal weapon. I feel vibrations rattle my brain and I lose function in my limbs; I fall to the floor and black out.

The Last Anubis Dog

I wake up and discover that I am in some sort of old building; the paint is peeling off the walls and broken furniture scatters the floor.

"Where am I?" I ask. I feel a painful throbbing in my head; I touch a sore spot and discover a knot there.

"What happened?" I ask myself.

I look around and see that there are stairs that lead to an upstairs area. I decide to see what's what.

I rush up the stairs; my right foot hits a spot of dry rot and breaks through.

"Shit," I mutter as I pull my foot out.

I make it to the upstairs area; I look around for any moving.

"Hello?" I call out. "Peteryx?! Are you here?!" I draw my new sword. "Show yourself, Peteryx!! I'm ready!!"

"He's not here." says a voice I've heard once before. I feel something poke me in the back of my neck; beyond the scent of mold and mildew, I can smell a strong scent of gunpowder. "Hello, Leviathan. Remember me?"

I hear the jingling of thin metal; it's the same sound I heard when that Army specialist walked. It's the sound of military dog tags clinking together.

"McDaniel?!" I ask.

"That's right." the Specialist says. "You should've followed me to the cemetery."

"For what? You should know that it was Ghouls that robbed those graves."

"Indeed, it was, but my intent was to lead you to that zombie."

"Rolfe Bentley? Oh, don't worry; I saw what became of him."

"And he would've killed you, if that stupid plant thing wouldn't have stepped in!!"

"I doubt that, seriously. Oh, and word to the wise . . . that stupid plant thing has a name."

"Acanthus of Corinth; that joke!!"

"Well, that joke just happens to be Levetin Golgohoth."

"Who?"

"Levetin Golgohoth; my twin brother."

I feel the muzzle of McDaniel's assault rifle poke me harder.

"Acanthus of Corinth is your twin brother?!" he asks. "You look nothing alike!! You're a liar!! I ought to shoot you for wagging your tongue!!"

"Then shoot me. Get rid of me; do what Peteryx could never do."

I can smell the fear radiating off of this guy in the form of sweat; I feel the muzzle of the weapon trembling against my skin. He will not shoot me; he is to spare me for Peteryx's sick pleasure.

"What are you waiting for?" I ask. "Squeeze the trigger and shoot me."

Just as McDaniel plans to take matters into his own hands, another person enters the room; I sense a more evil presence.

"Very good, Mattie." a male's voice says. "You've done well."

I know who's speaking. I know that low, mellow voice; the Egyptian accent with a hint of evil in it. It belongs to none other than the Egyptian tyrant from Thebes—Imhotep Feathervault, better known as Arch-Peteryx.

I turn around and face my worst enemy.

"YOU!!" I shout.

Peteryx smiles; that shit-eating grin that always made my blood boil.

"Leviathan Golgohoth, Master Peteryx." McDaniel says.

"Splendid, Mattie." he says. "Now, take a break."

I watch as Peteryx whacks Specialist McDaniel over the head with a crowbar; the soldier falls to the dirty floor, unconscious.

"It was you!!" I shout. "*You* hit me in the head at the Bentley residence!!"

"Why would it have been Mattie?" Peteryx asks. "He carries a firearm." He casts the crowbar off to the side. "Now," He draws his sword. "It's you and me; I shall reign supreme . . . as the strongest tyrant that has ever walked the earth."

Tyrant Vs. Tyrant

I see the little soldier begin to move; he's a bit groggy from the blow to the head. Before McDaniel can do anything else, Peteryx extends his right arm and hand. Instantly, the young Specialist freezes; his mouth opens and a huge cloud of yellowish-orange smoke pours out. After it's all out, McDaniel turns gray and doesn't move. He lies on the floor with a blank expression—eyes and mouth wide open.

"What the hell did you just do?" I ask Peteryx.

"I call that one the Medusa." Peteryx tells me. "I learned it in Corinth. It turns those that I wish harm on into stone. The spell cannot be broken unless I'm destroyed."

"And how many victims have fallen to this . . . spell?"

"Enough. And you're next, tyrant."

"Oh really?"

"Yes, because you know how much I hate you." Peteryx comes closer. "I warned you once, when I turned that Bentley guy into a zombie; you didn't listen. So, I recruited two Saudis into my Anubis army; they wanted a chance at getting rid of someone—like you, for instance. And they even got the Eternal Ones, Murabbi and Azrael. Oh, I am so excited! But not that much. It should've been *you* that died in that explosion."

"It was messed up."

"Ha ha!! Indeed, it was."

"No, I mean the bomb they made; it was messed up. It was faulty; it blew up at the wrong time."

Peteryx smiles.

"Ah, yes." he says. "That."

"What happened?" I ask.

"It doesn't matter. Point is, Azrael and Murabbi are dead, and it's Revelatianus's fault."

"It is not!! He's a wise Eternal One!!"

"Then why did he let Murabbi and Azrael die?"

"He didn't!! You have no proof that he did!!"

"You're right, Leviathan, I don't. But who says *you* do? Oh, by the way, Mattie hated his way of life; he said his bitch of a mother made him sign up for the military."

"Why?"

"He said she told him that it would straighten him out; apparently, he was a rebellious boy over in Kingman. So, he volunteered to help me out. He gladly accepted my offer to find you, so that I can destroy you."

I don't say anything about McDaniel, but I know about Revelatianus visiting me in my dream and telling me about the deaths of the Eternal Ones. If I told Peteryx about that, he'd take me for a psycho. Oh well—he already does.

"You know, Leviathan," Peteryx says. "I thought that the Anubis bombers would've surely taken you out in that explosion, but I guess not."

"I'm not that easy to kill." I say.

"So, you're not, huh? Well," I can see his skin crawling; the scarabs are becoming riled up. "I think I can fix that."

"Where's my brother?"

"Oh, the other freak? I'm not his keeper. All I know is that he got shot in the head, and now he's nowhere to be found. What a pity. He won't even take time out to help you."

I say nothing. I begin to think: *Where is he? He said he'd return Tigris's silk sash to me for when I'd meet up with Peteryx. Here we are, but where's Levetin? And where's the sash?*

"How do you know that Levetin was shot?" I ask.

"Well," Peteryx says. "I gotta tell you, I saw the whole thing from a distance; I saw the plant freaks, you, the Bentley faggot, and the two Eternal Ones. I saw everyone and everything . . . . and there's nothing you can do now."

I smile. I then pull my revolver out from my belt loop; I aim it at Peteryx.

"A firearm won't kill me, Leviathan." He says, laughing. "I have no vital organs, so a bullet won't kill me!!!"

"Perhaps not," I say. "But you still have your brain." I cock the hammer of the revolver. "The brain is a vital organ; one shot, right between the eyes."

"A swing and a miss, Leviathan. A swing and a miss."

I shoot Peteryx in the head, right between the eyes; his head whips back from the force of the bullet.

I am surprised that he is still standing; he hasn't fallen to the floor.

"What the?" I ask myself.

Peteryx brings his head forward. He then cocks it to the side and chuckles.

"What did I just get finished telling you, Leviathan?" he asks. Peteryx takes a deep breath, and the entrance and exit wounds heal completely, leaving no trace of him being shot. "You just—don't—listen." He spits the spent brass bullet out onto the floor. "I have no vital organs . . . my brain is just an accessory."

I begin to fire more rounds at him. As a skilled swordsman, Peteryx knows his way with swords; he uses his sword to knock the flying bullets away; they ricochet off the walls. I make sure I'm careful that they don't hit me.

"Will you ever learn, tyrant?!" Peteryx shouts.

I cast the revolver off to the side and draw my dagger; I take swings at Peteryx, but as he dodges, he catches me in my arms with his sword, drawing blood.

Seeing that I need to be equal in this feud, I draw my sword.

"I'm going to teach you a lesson," I say. "One that you needed to learn since I first dealt with you!!"

We begin to sword fight furiously. Our swords clash loudly and a lot of angry swear words are exchanged. As I try to wound Peteryx, he is slashing my shirt. Pretty soon, it'll be my skin.

"Is *that* the best you've got?!" I shout.

"*You* should have something better!!" Peteryx says. "After all, you claim that you're the strongest and most talented tyrant that has ever lived."

A scarab crawls out of Peteryx's skin. I believe that he's trying to distract me with it, so that he can cut me down and get an easy win; he can't fool me.

I stomp on the scarab and Peteryx gasps as if he's in pain.

"Your vital organs," I begin. "must be the scarabs."

More of the large black beetles begin to crawl out from under Peteryx's skin. The Egyptian tyrant continues to flinch in pain while I step on these nasty little creatures. Suddenly, I feel a very sharp pain in my abdomen; I look down and I see that I have been stabbed with Peteryx's sword.

"Now," he says. "You will still be able to fight, but I wouldn't want you to do that; you could do more damage. Let me help you."

Peteryx pushes his sword deeper into my stomach; it begins to throb when the blunt tip presses against my spine; I can feel my legs going numb.

I gasp and let out a painful groan.

"What's wrong, Leviathan?" Peteryx asks. "Does it hurt? C'mon now, I thought you were a sword man."

I don't answer him. Just then, blood begins to gush out of my mouth.

"You know," Peteryx says, smiling. "My scarabs are very attracted to blood—and so am I."

I can hear a screeching noise. The scarabs begin to pop out of his skin.

"No!!" he shouts. The scarabs retreat. "Now," Peteryx pulls his sword out of my stomach. "I need to talk to you before I kill you."

Trapped

Peteryx pulls me over to a chair and sits me down in it.

"Don't move." He says.

He ties my hands to the handles of the chair with thick ropes. He then begins to rotate his head around in circles.

"What—are you doing?" I ask him.

"I need to treat one of my little buddies to some fun." He says. He stops rotating his head. He then reaches into his mouth and pulls out a scarab. "Oh yeah. This one needs a little excitement. Ah, it's a fat one, too."

The scarab that Peteryx is holding on to is one of the hugest ones I've ever seen.

"Peteryx," I say. "What are you . . . ."

"Open wide, Leviathan." he says.

The Egyptian tyrant grasps my lower jaw with his free hand and forces my mouth open; he jams the huge black beetle into my mouth and holds it shut so that I cannot spit it out. I can feel the scarab crawling around on my tongue. It then makes its way down my throat.

"Splendid." Peteryx says, letting go of my mouth. "Soon, it will eat your heart away, and I won't have to."

"You're insane, Peteryx!!" I shout. "You won't get away with what you're . . . ."

My chest begins to hurt; it feels like the exact pain I felt when I was cast into Peteryx's body. It feels as if my muscles are being sliced with a knife. One thing's not there, and that's the hollow sound—like that conch shell.

"Feeling good yet, Leviathan?" Peteryx asks.

I look into his scarred face; I smile.

"When's the fun going to start?" I ask.

Peteryx's face remains blank; he's not impressed.

"Can you answer me one thing?" I ask as I feel the scarab's legs tickling my trachea.

"Fire away, Leviathan." Peteryx says.

I exhale, tasting a sour sensation in my mouth.

"Why did you create a group of Anubis dogs," I say. "And all of them were so unintelligent?"

"They weren't unintelligent." the Egyptian tyrant tells me. "They were just overtaken by the Deathbringer and his lap dogs; do you think they were expecting that?"

"It all depends. Would you allow them to kill me before you could get your hands on me?"

Peteryx seems a bit uneasy. What if his servants did take me out before he could get his justice? Would he have killed them all?

I look down at Peteryx's right hand and see that he is sporting a golden ring with ancient Egyptian symbols on it.

"Is that . . . ." I start. "The Ring of Ra?"

"Indeed, it is." Peteryx tells me. "In my country, it was worn by pharaohs, queens, and other great people; they attributed their power and dominance to the ring, which in turn gave them good luck." he holds his hand up to show off his piece of jewelry. "Like your pendant, it is my keepsake."

"Did Draken Hark give it to you?"

"Mercy, no. I stole this out of a tomb in the Valley of the Kings. I think this may have belonged to Ramses the Third. Had to break off his little finger just to get to it." He chuckles. "And, Leviathan, I know you still must be wondering why that bomb Malik constructed blew up early."

"Yes. He set it to blow up in one hour and fifteen minutes after it was constructed."

"It was just bad timing."

Colai had said something about bad timing, but she didn't explained what happened.

"Jamal and Malik spent some time at a military camp in Alaska." Peteryx continues to talk. "They managed to smuggle C-4 off the base and they made their way to Nevada. At that Guard unit in Henderson, they made a bomb; they were going to use it to negotiate you into going with them to surrender yourself to me."

"I see."

"It was their plan to set the bomb off in a little over an hour; Malik, no doubt, went by the time he had on his watch. Ah, the plot thickens." He chuckles. "You see, Leviathan, Alaska has a different time zone than Nevada does; it's one hour ahead. Dumb-ass Malik set the bomb to go off at two-thirty p.m., and his watch was still set to Alaska's time, one-fifteen. It only took a few seconds for the timer to set properly, to the current time; meaning the bomb was set to blow in only fifteen minutes, not an hour and fifteen minutes. So, to make a long story short, when you all heard the bomb's timer go off, it was already two-thirty p.m., Pacific time."

I get it; the bomb wasn't faulty . . . it was just bad timing; Colai said it. What idiots those bombers were. When something is to be done correctly, and professionally, it's all about the timing.

"Tell me, Leviathan," Peteryx says, walking around me. "Why did you do it?"

"Do what?" I ask.

Peteryx walks back in front of me and stares at me. He then whacks me across my face.

"You know exactly what I'm talking about!!" he shouts, ripping my shirt down the front. "Why did you ruin me?! Why did you shove me into that dreaded scarab pit?!! Why did you steal my baby?! That was my son!!"

"You deserved it." I say. "I couldn't have done a more horrible thing to another person because no one is as ugly and disgusting as you are!!"

Peteryx chuckles at my comment. He then picks up my dagger from off the floor. He examines it.

"Well," he says. "You've had this dagger for many years. It has been good to you; made enough mayhem and cut enough skin." I watch as Peteryx attaches my dagger to his belt strap. "I'll just be taking it as a souvenir."

"It's mine!!" I shout.

I go to move forward, but my arms are secured to the chair, and my chest begins to burn again; I am forced to sit back, to ease the pain.

"Stay." Peteryx says. "Good; I placed my scarab into your body to control you." Peteryx grabs my right wrist. "Did Draken Hark like you better than me?"

I realize that Draken Hark never hated me. He had confided in me on the night he died.

"He might've." I say.

"You know who killed him." Peteryx says to me.

"No."

"Lies!!"

"NO!! I don't know who killed him!!"

"It wasn't me. It had to be someone that was against the Eternal Ones; I am a tyrant. Why would I be against the Eternal Ones if I was created by one?"

Peteryx has a point; no matter how evil and disgusting this tyrant is, he'd never attempt to kill one of the Eternal Ones.

As Peteryx slips his sword back into its sheath, I feel a presence next to me.

"Leviathan," it says. I look over to the right and see my brother; he takes the form of Acanthus of Corinth, not twelve-year-old Levetin Golgohoth, and is sitting next to me, on the floor, by my chair. "Peteryx cannot see me or hear me, but you can."

"How?" I whisper.

"I'm not really here; I'm just in your imagination. We can communicate through our minds; you picked this up. Remember when you drank the water with the leaf in it at Archipelago Bar?"

"Yes? But, why are you here?"

"Who are you talking to?" Peteryx asks, looking over to his left, my right. I look up at him and smile.

"What?" he asks. "Why are you smiling?! Do I amuse you?! Do I make you hot? Does your length grow when you look at me?"

"He likes men, Leviathan." Acanthus tells me. "It got him in trouble with me and my colleagues once."

"Do you like men, Peteryx?" I ask, continuing to smile.

Peteryx draws my dagger from his belt; he brings it down and slashes my right wrist with it; blood gushes out like a geyser.

"Shut up, you filth!!" he shouts. In anger, Peteryx grabs my left wrist and cuts deeply into it with my dagger; more blood gushes out of me. "You don't get to ask me stupid questions!!!"

"How would I know if they're stupid or not?"

"Every time I cut you, you've messed up."

"Then I shall remain silent and be thought of as a fool."

"Yes. A very *trapped* fool."

Peteryx's Heartless Deed

eteryx shakes his head. He then looks down and sees my sword. He places my dagger back around his belt, bends over and picks it up; he starts to inspect it and laughs.

"It seems as though he's made a discovery." Acanthus tells me and pats my knee.

"I know this sword." He says. "This is Shang-Kai Zhao's old samurai sword he got from Japan. How did *you* get it?"

I don't tell him. I sit in the chair and stare down at my wrists, which are bleeding freely; the blood drips onto the floor and creates little red pools. I look over and see that my brother's dark-green eyes haven't turned coal-black from the scent of it.

"Levetin," I whisper. "I thought that when you smell blood, you . . . ."

"I'm not really here, Leviathan." he says. "I'm only in your mind. The real me would be on the floor, licking it up."

I look up and stare into Peteryx's eyes.

"How do you know Shang-Kai Zhao?" I ask.

An evil sneer crosses Peteryx's face. He pokes me in my chest with his index finger.

"I went to Hangzhou in one thousand forty-two anno Domini," he tells me. "A few weeks after you and your dimwit friends left." He runs his fingers across the blade of the sword. "I traveled to Shang-Kai Zhao's dojo to receive some training and information on your whereabouts; he told me that I wasn't worth it, then he told me that I'm not even worth the dirt on his floor, and he wanted me to clean it up."

"Did you do it?"

"Why would I? I take orders from no one!"

My slashed wrists are beginning to sting and I feel extremely weak from the blood loss.

"Stay calm, Leviathan." Acanthus says to me. "No panicking, no rapid blood loss, no victory for Peteryx."

"Master Shang was right about that." I say to Peteryx. "You're *not* worth the dirt on his floor. You're not even worth anything on the face of this earth. You're not worth the crud on an outhouse toilet seat."

Peteryx squints his eyes, and suddenly, I feel something burning in my chest. It must be the scarab; he's commanding it to do his bidding and shut me up.

"Bite your tongue, tyrant." Peteryx demands. "Don't say anything that I don't like, or I'll mop the floor with you." He inspects the weapon a bit more. "Ah, yes. There are his genuine calligraphy-style initials. So, anyway—although I genuinely don't take orders, I offered to scrub Shang-Kai Zhao's floor, on one condition: If he'd train me. Shang-Kai Zhao agreed—so, I scrubbed his floor. After I got finished, and the floor was squeaky clean, I was eager to learn some of his fighting skills, but he changed his mind about training me. *Thank you. Now my floor is spotless.* Is what he had said. He pissed me off, badly."

"Well," I say. "You shouldn't have offered to clean his floor; you knew you'd get burned."

Peteryx's yellow eyes flash angrily in the sun's glare; my chest begins to hurt again.

"That scarab is just itching to eat your heart." he says. "Now, bite your tongue!!"

I decide to stay silent and listen to what he has to say; I already know that this is not going to remain idle chit-chat.

"No one can help you now," Peteryx says, grasping my chin with his thumb and forefinger; he tilts my head up to look at him. "I thought big brother would be by your side, yes?" he smiles. "His only concern were my servants; it isn't about you; it's about the numbers, Leviathan. The number of kills." He releases my chin. I feel more blood gushing out of my wrists and my chest feels tight. "Okay, so I wasn't happy about Shang-Kai Zhao not wanting to train me, and I was a little perturbed about cleaning his floor for nothing. Perhaps he saw something he didn't like about me."

"I can think of a few things." Acanthus says, chuckling. I smile.

"This is not hilarious." Peteryx snaps at me.

"I was laughing with you, Imhotep." I say.

Peteryx gets a look of disgust on his scarred face.

"I wasn't laughing." he says. "And don't call me Imhotep."

"Why do you hate your original name so much?"

"I was my father's namesake. He was a traitor to Egypt; he abandoned me, my mother, and my two younger brothers. But, you know what people say—like father, like son. I abandoned them and became the tyrant you know today. Then I went back home and killed them."

"You know, I felt like my father favored my twin brother over me. But at least our two house servants appreciated me, while they were around."

"Do you really have to wonder why your father would favor Acanthus over you?"

"His name's Levetin."

"It's Acanthus now."

I see, in my peripheral vision that Acanthus is a bit fidgety; perhaps being called Levetin isn't what he wants. I, however, always addressed him by his birth name; he has told me to stop, but I will not.

"Don't worry about my past." Peteryx says to me. "It's not important. So—after Shang-Kai Zhao told me that I was not going to be trained under him, he told me to leave and never come back."

"And you left?" I ask. "Just like that?"

Acanthus snaps his finger.

"I left the dojo," Peteryx replies. "But I didn't leave Hangzhou; I went down to the waters of the Chang Jiang and caught a fish."

"You went fishing?" I ask.

"Yes." Peteryx says. "I went fishing."

"It holds a significance into what comes next." Acanthus says to me.

"I caught this brown oriental fish." Peteryx replies. "No one in China would eat them, and I knew exactly why."

"Was it a harmful type of fish?" I ask.

"Oh, tell me about it." Peteryx says to me. "The most poisonous type of fish in China. Your little mind cannot begin to fathom just how poisonous that fish really was, yes? Its toxins were considered to be undetectable, and they still are today, somewhere in China. They mimicked what the puffer fish's tetrodotoxin poison does."

"It zombifies." Acanthus says. "Minus the walking and attacking."

"What?!" I ask.

"So," Peteryx goes on. "I went back to the dojo with the fish and extracted its poisons. I confronted Shang-Kai Zhao again and asked him if he and I could have just one training session. He said no, and he told me to go away, again. And he said that if I didn't stay gone, he would kill me himself. So, I left, but I didn't leave for good. I sneaked into the dining area and put the poisons in his sweet and sour chicken."

"None of his servants saw what happened," my brother says. "Yet they were all in the dining area, not the cooking area."

"No one saw anything?" I ask my brother.

"Nope." Peteryx says, thinking that I was talking to him. "It was all too easy. Well, I slipped out and ran around the front, where Shang-Kai Zhao was, and I asked him if I could have chow with him, and then he'd never see me again."

"Did he refuse the offer?"

"No. He said that it was a deal; I could have a meal with him, and then I had to leave for good. So, he took me to the dining area, where his servants brought us the delicacies, and the spiked sweet-and-sour chicken; needless to say, I didn't touch it. Even if I did, it wouldn't harm me; no vital organs, you know."

"That bastard." Acanthus says.

"So," Peteryx goes on. "So, as we are dining, I told him that I would be on my way, for good, once I got done eating. I saw him nod. I then watched him as he ate the poisoned chicken."

Peteryx laughs. I hang my head; I watch the blood running out of my wounds and onto the floor.

"Leviathan," Acanthus whispers. "Don't you do that!" He slaps my leg. "Don't you do it!!"

I start to feel that pain in my chest again. Peteryx stops laughing.

"Hey!" he shouts, picking my head up. "Stay awake! I haven't finished the story!" He slaps my cheeks. "You can't pass out on me and not hear the rest of the story!!"

"I thought that you wanted me to die." I whisper, feeling very lightheaded.

"Yes, but not yet." Acanthus says, grasping my shirttail. "Listen to the rest of his story, then you can kill him."

"Yes. I *do* want you dead," Peteryx tells me. "But not right now; you have to hear what I did, yes? So, Shang-Kai Zhao began to twitch a few minutes after eating his sweet and sour chicken that I poisoned; I stood up and watched. He then knew, right away, that I had did something to it; it was right after I asked him how it tasted. He swore at me; he called me a fool—he called me a Demon! I said, '*No! I'm Peteryx!!*' And then—he fell over. He didn't die though; he just appeared to be dead. He was alive, but in a zombie-like state. I then called his servants and told them that he must've had a heart attack or something."

"You son of a bitch." I growl at him.

"Anyways, I knew that the amount of toxins I put in his chicken would keep him in that state for about twelve hours or so. So, I helped one of his servants construct a coffin made from thick wood; I had to make sure he couldn't get out. I then went out back and dug a twelve foot hole; couldn't let them hear his screams when he'd come to, yes? Well, before nailing the coffin shut, the servants made sure Shang-Kai Zhao was buried with some of his most prized possessions; one of them included this sword, right here." Peteryx holds up Shang-Kai Zhao's old samurai sword; the light from the sun reflects off of it. "I told one of the servants that he had given that sword to me, at dinner, but they refused to believe it; he said that Shang-Kai Zhao would never hand this sword down to anyone, and that it was his dying wish to be buried with it . . . . so, I let them bury him with it; I'd fetch it later, once he would be dead."

"Peteryx, you scum."

"So, the service was held for the fighting teacher; I decided to stay around the dojo for the rest of the day, and all night." He chuckles. "Once night fell, I began to hear screaming and cries for help; I knew that the servants couldn't hear it . . . . they were only Human, and their ears could never pick up cries coming from a thick wooden box buried twelve feet in the ground."

"Peteryx . . . ."

"Well, after a while, the cries stopped, and I went to sleep in his magnificent dojo. The next morning, while the servants slept in their quarters, I sent my scarabs to make a little snack out of them."

"Delicious death." Acanthus whispers to me; I feel my chest burning again.

"You killed—Shang-Kai Zhao." I say. "And His servants!! What did they do to deserve this?!"

"First off," Peteryx says, placing the blade of the sword against my neck, in the manner that's used for decapitation. "He didn't train me!!! And, my scarabs were hungry."

"You good-for-nothing piece of shit!!" I spit blood in his face. "Fuck you!!"

Peteryx catches me in the face again, with one strong swing of his hand. I'm lucky it wasn't the sword that caught me.

"I'd be real careful how you talk to me, Leviathan!" he shouts. He grabs my hair and pulls my head back. "Unless you want my story to be cut short, you better seal your lips." He releases my hair and steps back. "I went back to Shang-Kai Zhao's grave and dug the coffin up. I unsealed it to find that he had been trying to claw his way out; his once dainty fingers were now worn down to the bone. Luckily, his sword was still there."

"Why wouldn't it be?" I ask.

"Because I had a hunch that it would be gone."

"Really?"

"Shut it!! Well, I left Hangzhou and settled in a small community in what is today Tibet; I planned to train myself there, and get ready to take you and your little friends out, yes? So, when I went to get my new possession and use it for practice, it was gone."

"Gone?"

"Yes; gone. I decided that someone had stolen it, but I saw a note on my table. It read: *We're watching you*. At the bottom right corner, there was a symbol, etched in blood; it looked almost like . . . . a trinity knot. I wasn't sure where it originated, but I knew that it had something to do with the number three."

Acanthus chuckles. I know now that it was him, along with Arachne and Dante, that left the note; the symbol that Peteryx saw was the triquetra:

That symbol was originated somewhere in Europe, where the Immortal Trio is based, and was used by the group to show where they had been; all three of them bear a tattoo of the triquetra on their bodies: Arachne's is present right above her left breast; Acanthus's is on his back, between his shoulder blades, near the two long vertical scars; and Dante's is on the right side of his neck.

"Seriously," I say. "You had no clue who took the sword?"

"Oh, I know who it was." Peteryx says. "I just couldn't care. Now, it's here with me!! It's all mine!!!"

"You freak!!" Acanthus shouts. Too bad Peteryx can't see or hear him.

"It's *mine*!" I say and spit some blood out by his feet. "Be a man and accept that!"

I feel that awful pain in my chest again; Peteryx smiles. He then stares at my chest. He smiles and shakes his head.

"And you call *yourself* a man?" He asks, grabbing my bound and bleeding wrists. "Just because you have a hairy chest doesn't mean you're a man. I think that's stupid!"

"What the hell's wrong with this guy?" Acanthus asks me.

I don't say anything. I just stare blankly into Peteryx's big, golden-colored eyes. He releases my wrists and begins to do that Egyptian walk that everyone and their mother knows. He then stops and licks the blood, my blood, from his hands.

"The Egyptians don't walk like that!!" Peteryx shouts. "At least not the ones from today. You know, Leviathan—over the years, these stupid, foolish American people have turned the Egyptian heritage into garbage!! Pure idiocy!! And you agree with it! I can guaran-damn-tee it!!"

"Seriously," Acanthus says. "Why didn't my colleagues and I just kill him when we had the chance?"

"Because you left him for me." I whisper to my brother.

"What did you say?" Peteryx asks. "Left who to you? Me?" Peteryx takes my sword and holds it to my throat. "I don't think so. It is *me* who has *you* bound and helpless. Now, you'll die, just like the rest of your little friends!"

"Consider it an honor."

I glance over at Acanthus. It looks as if he's tying an invisible rope or cloth around my right leg; I feel something tighten around it, but I do not see what it is.

"Just wanted to return that to you." he says. "Use it wisely."

He disappears.

Levetin, I think helplessly. *Don't leave me.*

The Wicked Heart Bears No Head

Peteryx's yellow eyes shine in the sun as he's ready to kill me.

"I've tried, for so many years, to get rid of you the right way." Peteryx tells me. "And now, you're right here! There's no Immortal Trio here to mess it up this time!! It's time to die!"

I stare into Peteryx's eyes.

"Are you going to slit my throat?" I ask.

"Oh yes." He says. "And I'm going to drink your supernatural blood and become the strongest tyrant that has ever walked this earth. Then, I'm going to kill the Immortal Trio, for making my life so miserable in the past!!"

"Good luck with that."

Peteryx seems a bit confused by my well-wishing; he should know that it's not possible to kill the Immortal Trio unless Thanatos of the Waters is destroyed.

"Peteryx," I say.

"Leviathan?" he says.

"Would you mind if I stare at you as you're killing me?"

"Whatever you want, Leviathan. Look at me all you want. It won't make me feel guilty." He smiles. "Say goodbye."

I can feel my own sword slicing into my skin. I feel blood running down my neck. I also see that there are beads of sweat forming on Peteryx's forehead. He must be a bit nervous.

I then realize what Acanthus said before he disappeared: *Just wanted to return that to you. Use it wisely.*

The invisible object that he tied around my leg is Tigris's silk sash!! My love told me that I'd need it when I'd face Peteryx, and now it's in my possession. I must act now.

I focus on Peteryx's eyes. Just then, he starts to blink. He starts moaning and drops the sword. He brings his hands up to his eyes.

"AHHH!!!" he shouts in pain. "My eyes! My eyes! They're burning!!" He begins to rub them. "Make it stop!! Leviathan, help me!!!"

I manage to slip my wrists out of the ropes; I then succeed in gaining Shang-Kai Zhao's sword in my possession again.

"Leviathan?!" he shouts.

I could kill him now, but I choose to mess with him a bit.

"Peteryx," I say.

Peteryx begins to look around, but he can't seem to find me. He starts to swing blindly for me.

"I'm blind! What did you do to me, you filthy scum bastard?!"

"Relax. It's only the side effects of my magic."

"Magic?!" Peteryx draws his sword. "What magic? You have no magic! You couldn't even find a solution to break Gaudio's encasement charm!"

"If I don't possess any magic, then who was it who blinded you?"

"Ha!!" Peteryx swings his sword at me, but misses. "I may be blind, Leviathan, but I can still hear you—and I sure as hell can still smell you!"

"Why don't you send forth your precious scarabs? I'm sure *they'll* find me, if you can't."

"No! Shut up!! SHUT UP!!! This is between you and me!!" He swings his sword again; it comes close, but contacts with nothing. "When I find you, tyrant—I'm gonna slice and dice you into a million little pieces!!"

Peteryx swings his sword at me; I back away. He rushes toward me and stumbles over the chair I had been sitting in; it breaks and one of the legs sticks into his stomach. He yells in pain.

"Peteryx," I say. "Imhotep—I'm in here, you dog!"

I go into this empty room. It's dark, damp, and smells like mold and mushrooms; it's the same smell that radiated off of Acanthus after he executed Sturgeon Grahn, the Fungus King, in 1356 A.D.; seven years after Phaize died.

"Where are you, tyrant?!" Peteryx shouts out. "And what gives you the right to call me that?!"

He's still swinging his sword, hoping that he gets a lucky shot. His left hand is gripping the chair leg that is wedged deep into his stomach. I see that his eyes are leaking a thick black fluid.

"Imhotep Feathervault." I say calmly. "I thought you wanted to kill me. Don't be shy; I'm over here."

"Don't call me that!!" Peteryx shouts. He swings his sword again; it comes close to connecting with me. "You don't ever get to call me that!!"

"Imhotep?"

"That's it!! When I find you, I'm gonna kill you!! I swear it on my life!!!"

"Walk straight ahead, genius, and you'll find me."

Peteryx slowly walks forward and enters the old dirty room. He removes his grip from the chair leg and rubs the fluid from his eyes.

"If you hold still," I say. "I'll help you pull that obstruction free."

"If you come near me," Peteryx says. "I will kill you. I will gouge your eyes out!! I will rip your heart out, and I will eat it!"

He begins to hiss like a cat as he senses my approach.

"I can give you your sight back." I tell him. "Just hold still for one moment."

"I know you!! You'll kill me!" Peteryx takes another swing with his sword. "You'll do me wrong if I stand still!"

Peteryx suddenly begins to cough; he drops his sword and begins to tug at the chair leg. I walk over to him. He doesn't seem to notice.

"Once I pull this thing out," he says. "You're dead! You hear me, Leviathan?! Dead!! Mark my words!!"

"You know," I say. "You're perfectly vulnerable to any of my attacks; you're not armed with a weapon."

"I have a dagger!!" He pulls my dagger from his belt. "I'm well armed!!"

He has my dagger; I forgot. It is mine, and I must have it back.

I touch Peteryx's shoulder. He quickly jerks away from me and hisses angrily; that pain returns once again. I back away and clutch my chest.

As I struggle to breathe, I see that Peteryx is looking around, as if his sight is being adjusted.

"Hey," Peteryx says. "I can see again. You really must *be* magic, Leviathan."

This isn't good. I think. I must do something quick, while Peteryx is still disoriented.

I notice that there's a trickle of blood running down Peteryx's chin. That means something; he still has his cardiovascular system—a bloodstream—and that means his heart is still there. The scarabs must've spared his heart, in order for him to live and pump Draken Hark's blood. After all those years, it's still there, and I didn't even know it!!

I face him and smile. I plan to kill him now so that I can go home, back to Los Angeles.

"Philosophy." I say.

Peteryx coughs and a fountain of blood gushes out.

"Philosophy what?" he asks.

"Have wicked heat . . . ."

"What??" He stands up straight and squints his eyes.

"Lose wicked head."

"Huh??"

With one powerful stroke of Master Shang's sword, I cut off Peteryx's head. While it's still in the air, I kick it and it flies out of a window, breaking the glass.

Peteryx's body is still moving; blood violently gushes out the top of his neck. The scarabs begin to pour out of the many scratches on his skin. The body's arms begin to flail haphazardly, feeling around frantically for its missing head. It starts running all around the room and then it comes to a halt. Peteryx's decapitated body drops to its knees and then falls forward; it gives a few final jerks, then it remains still.

"I thought it was supposed to kill him in the blink of an eye." I say.

The scarabs begin to crawl out of the broken window, so I walk over to see where they are headed. I see Peteryx's head; it has fallen seven stories down and landed in one of the sandpits below. There's a look of surprise on its face. The scarabs take the head and bury it in the sand, along with themselves.

Standing next to the sandpit is a young boy, no older than twelve; he looks up at me, and I see that he has dark-brown hair that kicks out every which way, and his eyes are dark-green.

The boy smiles and waves.

"Bravo, Brother." he says. "Bravo!!"

The boy is my brother, Acanthus of Corinth; he is still in the form of twelve-year-old Levetin Golgohoth.

"I did it." I say, turning back toward Peteryx's headless body. "I perfected the art of decapitation. And a special thanks goes out to you, Tigris. Without your sash, I wouldn't have slipped away from Peteryx so easily. I love you, wife."

Suddenly, I drop to the floor and try to catch my breath. I cough and out pops the scarab that Peteryx forced me to swallow, along with a bit of my own blood. It crawls a few feet and then, it turns into ash.

Peteryx's blood is all over the place, and it is still running out the top of his neck. I drink what's on the floor and what flows from his body. I start to feel a strong surge of power course through my veins. I feel much more stronger and a whole lot more stealthy. It's like I'm impervious to all damage and danger. Also, my wounds are completely healed. And I feel no more pain; I've become a new tyrant.

After consuming Peteryx's blood, the dead tyrant's headless body turns into a pile of ash.

"And therefore," I say. "Your body meets the same fate as Molicles's."

I reach out and retrieve my dagger and the Ring of Ra from the ashes.

"I really *am* the strongest tyrant to have ever lived." I say, getting up. "No one can stop me now."

Putting The Last Dog Down?

I look down at Specialist McDaniel; I see that he has turned back to his normal self, no longer made of stone. He begins to move around, but he doesn't wake up. I walk over to him and stare down at him; a smile automatically grows on my face.

"The enemy is defeated." I tell him.

"Really?" he asks. His eyes pop open and he looks up at me. "What happened to him?"

"He lost his head."

"What?"

"He lost his head . . . ." I bend down next to him. "And now, it is your turn."

"What?"

"I think you heard me loud and clear." I produce my dagger. "Anubis servant."

"What are you talking about?!"

"You are the last of Peteryx's Anubis dogs, and you need to be euthanized."

"No! Don't kill me!" he sits up. "I didn't mean to turn you over to Peteryx!!"

"Peteryx claimed that you willfully volunteered to become an Anubis servant. You escaped the shootout at Monte Carlo and ratted Acanthus and his servants out to Peteryx. And, you gratefully accepted his offer to get rid of me. You need to be put down."

"Leviathan!! He was lying to you! I was cursed! You have to believe me! He was capable of mind control! Please don't kill me—please!"

I stare the young specialist down. I then take his weapon away from him.

"I suppose I have no reason to kill you, Specialist." I say. "After all, your mind was being controlled."

"Oh, thank you, Leviathan." McDaniel says. "Thank you!!"

"But, you are an Anubis servant."

"Huh?"

"You're not Human. Don't move." I walk over to where I tossed my revolver. "And besides," I pick the firearm up and check for rounds; one left; perfect. "Even though they were reported, Acanthus of Corinth and his servants wiped the rest of your kind out." I spin the chamber of the revolver. "You have to tag along."

"No, please! You can't do this!!! I don't wanna die!!!"

"And now, you regret having been born." I chuckle, sticking the barrel into his mouth. "Happy trails."

I squeeze the trigger of the revolver, but it clicks; no bullet has been fired. I squeeze the trigger again, and again, and again. Nothing.

I swore I saw one last round in the chamber; is it jammed? Has the revolver been through enough and broke??

I hear McDaniel chuckling; apparently, he has gotten off lucky. However, I know that I *did* see one round left in the revolver's chamber.

As McDaniel begins to laugh, the revolver's barrel still in his mouth, I begin to smell gunpowder; the round is ready to be fired.

I smile. I watch as McDaniel stops laughing; the smirk on his face turns into a look of shock.

I pull the trigger; the round is fired. It exits the back of his head, leaving a nice blood spatter print on the old wooden floor.

I watch as the little soldier's eyes slowly close in death.

"Good deal." I say. "The deed is done." I smile. "Feeding time."

After I drain the specialist, I leave the building. I see that his Humvee is parked outside, across the street from the ramshackle building.

"Time to go home." I say to myself.

I cross the street and arrive at the vehicle. I climb in the back and find a first aid kit; I use alcohol swabs to clean the blood off of me.

As I clean myself up, I start to think about my time here in Vegas. It was okay, while it lasted, and now it's over. Acanthus killed the Anubis army, and I killed Peteryx; we're both still alive.

I have to admit, it was pretty easy to take Peteryx out. I guess that the three-hundred year period of training in Nagasaki, Japan really didn't pay off for him; I guess it got to his head and he didn't focus on getting rid of me. To be truthful, I didn't train that much, and I killed him. I suspect that he was weakened before meeting up with me; perhaps the extinguished Anubis dogs took atoll on him mentally and emotionally? Peteryx was so hell-bent on killing me, and he failed.

"All set." I say as I toss the bloody alcohol swabs off to the side. "Now, I need to go back to Los Angeles and rescue Mordecai from his chat room buddy."

I get into the front of the humvee; the key is still in the ignition.

"I don't know how to drive one of these." I say. "But I'll learn."

I start the vehicle up and begin to drive.

I drive past the Bentley residence. I see that the house had been burned; it most likely happened after I was knocked out and taken to the abandoned building.

I smile; I begin to daydream. What will I do, once I'm back in L.A.? First, I'll kill Bunny and rescue Mordecai. Then, I'll go back to my mansion and live in as much peace as I can, all while having to deal with Acanthus. I'm sure he'll be going back to living next to me.

I'm finally going home. I mentally thank all of the people that helped me in this. Basically, that would be the Eternal Ones, Shang-Kai Zhao, and especially Tigris and Acanthus. Without their help, where would I be right now? Because of them, I killed Arch-Peteryx Feathervault, and I'm still alive.

"Thank you." I say.

You're welcome, Brother. I hear Acanthus's voice say to me.

Going Back To L.A.

B alcanicus, Spinosus, and I stand by the old building; we watched Leviathan leave in the Humvee, and now it's our turn to head back to Los Angeles.

I still take the form of my former self; the twelve-year-old boy that used to be me. As soon as I can require some Human blood, I'll become Acanthus the Deathbringer again.

Spinosus is still a burned and bald acanthus servant; he sniffles as he rubs the blackened, flaking skin on his arms.

"I'm so ugly." he says. "I want my foliage back."

"You'll get your foliage back." I say. "I have some Unholy water in the greenhouse; I'll pass you a vial when we make it back." I look over at Balcanicus; there's nothing wrong with him, at all. "How are you the only one who made it out of that explosion okay, Tarsus?"

"I'm good like that." he tells me.

"I see." I walk behind him. "Now, we're going back to L.A.; give me a piggyback ride."

"Huh?"

"I said give me a piggyback ride. Now."

Balcanicus bends over and I climb onto his back; he stands back up and locks his arms underneath my legs. I throw my arms around his neck.

"Don't choke me, Acanthus, sir." he says.

"I'm not." I tell him. "Now, let's go."

"We're walking all the way back to Los Angeles?" Spinosus asks.

"No, we're taking the next bus." I say. "Yes, we're walking. Now, let's go. Leviathan's going to need me to monitor him for a little while longer."

Balcanicus, Spinosus, and I head down Highway 15, back to Los Angeles. When I get back, some people are going to have to answer to me. No one breaks my brother's heart and gets away with it. I swear it on my torturous ways.

To Be Continued . . . .

Tyrant Leviathan's story will conclude in
The Chronicles of a Tyrant III: Destiny.